This is the story of a clockwork man.

Across every world and throughout all flavors of reality, tales are told of artificial girls and mechanical boys whose dream is someday to become a living thing. This is not that kind of story.

This clockwork man was alive, and he dreamed of becoming mechanical.

He turned away from flesh and stink, from birth and blood and mess; he sought even to replace limbs and trunk and head with shining metal. He made of his mind a glittering construct of gears and ratchets, of springs and weights and balances of impossible precision, and he engineered his heart into an assemblage of levers and pulleys, of fulcra, ramps, and gleaming screws.

Flesh is corruption. Metal is incapable of sin.

This is the tragedy of how the clockwork man's fondest dream began to come true.

MAGIC
The Gathering®

Walk the Blind Eternities . . .

Discover the planeswalkers in their travels across
the endless planes of the Multiverse.

AGENTS OF ARTIFICE
ARI MARMELL

Jace Beleren, a powerful sorcerer and planeswalker whose rare telepathic
ability opens doors that many would prefer remain closed, is at a crossroads:
the decisions he makes now will forever affect his path.

THE PURIFYING FIRE
LAURA RESNICK

The young and impulsive Chandra Nalaar—planeswalker, pyromancer—
begins her crash course in the art of boom. When her volatile nature draws
the attention of megalomaniacal forces, she will have to learn to control
her power before they can control her.

ALARA UNBROKEN
DOUG BEYER

The fierce leonine planeswalker Ajani Goldmane unwittingly uncovers
the nefarious agency behind the splintered planes of Alara and their
realignment. Meanwhile, fellow planeswalker Elspeth Tirel struggles to
preserve the nobility of the first plane she has ever wanted to call homeland.
And the dragon shaman Sarkhan Vol finds the embodiment
of power he has always sought.

ZENDIKAR: IN THE TEETH
OF AKOUM
ROBERT B. WINTERMUTE

Nissa Revane, a planeswalker and proud elf warrior, is witness to what the
Eldrazi can do when she stumbles into the vanguard of their monstrous brood.
What she doesn't know is that they are merely pale reflection of the titans
that spawned them. But the ancient vampire planeswalker Sorin Markov knows
all to well the power of the ancient Eldrazi titans. He was among the
original jailers of the ancient scourge and he has returned to Zendikar
to make sure they do not escape.

MAGIC
The Gathering

A PLANESWALKER NOVEL

TEST OF METAL
matthew stover

Test of Metal

©2010 Wizards of the Coast LLC

All characters in this book are fictitious. Any resemblance to actual persons, living or dead, is purely coincidental.

This book is protected under the copyright laws of the United States of America. Any reproduction or unauthorized use of the material or artwork contained herein is prohibited without the express written permission of Wizards of the Coast LLC.

Published by Wizards of the Coast LLC

MAGIC: THE GATHERING, PLANESWALKER, WIZARDS OF THE COAST, and their respective logos are trademarks of Wizards of the Coast LLC in the U.S.A. and other countries.

Printed in the U.S.A.

Cover art by Michael Komarck

First Printing: October 2010

9 8 7 6 5 4 3 2 1

ISBN: 978-0-7869-5532-9
ISBN: 978-0-7869-5805-4 (e-book)
620-25487000-001-EN

U.S., CANADA,	EUROPEAN HEADQUARTERS
ASIA, PACIFIC, & LATIN AMERICA	Hasbro UK Ltd
Wizards of the Coast LLC	Caswell Way
P.O. Box 707	Newport, Gwent NP9 0YH
Renton, WA 98057-0707	GREAT BRITAIN
+1-800-324-6496	Save this address for your records.

Visit our web site at www.wizards.com

*The author respectfully dedicates this story
to everyone who is almost as smart
as they think they are.*

TEST OF METAL

THE METAL ISLAND
TRUTH AND DARE

At the farthest reach of a world that is ocean, there is one small island, and this island is made of metal.

The metal has the appearance of age-tarnished silver, or perhaps of burnished pewter, though it can be made more resilient than tool steel and harder than diamond. This metal is not armor, nor paving, nor is it built into structures for shelter. This metal is instead the grass, and the trees, their leaves and their fruit. It is the moss that clings to boulders and the algae in the tide pools, as though some eccentric god had, on a whim, decreed that every material thing on this island be transformed to metal in a single instant. This metal shines in the sun, sings in the winds, and gleams on moonless nights as though gathering starlight against the dawn.

The only living thing on the Metal Island was one lone man, naked on the metal beach, resting on doubled knees, his head lowered as though in meditation or prayer.

The island's metal does not occur in nature, in any form on any world, from the highest heavens to the deepest hells. This metal is called *etherium*, and it is arguably the most valuable substance in the Multiverse. Etherium is magic.

Not magical. Many things are magical. In the jigsaw world of Alara, a horse can't piss without splashing something magical. Most magical things are powered by *mana*; nearly any kind of magical operation is simply a directed use of mana. Etherium is not magical. It is not a device powered by, or used to direct, mana.

Etherium *is* magic.

The energies bound into etherium transcend mana as lightning transcends a lightning bug. Etherium is an expression of reality itself. Its power is the power of existence. It can be worked with, transformed, shaped into useful structures, but its power cannot be exhausted, and its substance cannot be unmade.

All of the etherium in existence, on any plane or flavor of reality, had been created by one crazed being—known even to his admirers as Crucius the Mad—in an insane attempt to heal the wounds of broken worlds. One day Crucius had a moment of clarity, and in that moment of clarity he understood what he had done . . .

And he vanished. Forever.

The island is, all in one place, more etherium than can be found in the entire aggregate of elsewhere. It is wealth enough to buy a medium-size universe. This made it all the more remarkable that the man who kneeled naked on the Metal Island's shore seemed to have no interest in anything outside his head.

He simply kneeled, thinking.

He was not thinking about the unimaginable wealth that lay before him. He was not even thinking about the power of existence that can be wielded by the metal's master. He was contemplating a riddle.

This was not the riddle of the island, why one lone speck of dry land should appear in a world that was ocean. This was not the riddle of the island's etherium, of whence it had come and why it has been worked into all the shapes of life. No: it was an actual riddle. A classical riddle, posed in a classical manner by a classical riddler.

This riddle lies between the etherium talons of the Metal Sphinx.

The Metal Sphinx reclines upon the etherium sand shore, its face toward the rising sun, its shadow stretched for miles upon the sea. Its open-worked form is a structure of graceful curves and elegant arches that somehow suggest bone and blood and flesh in the different colors of light gathered and reflected by its endless array of polished surfaces. It is vast beyond even the considerable magnitude of actual sphinxes, those winged leviathans of the mountains of Esper. The Metal Sphinx is larger than a house, larger than a warship, larger than a castle; a whole conundrum of young sphinxes might play aerial tag through its curves and angles without any risk of soiling its slightest span by the brush of a wing tip.

The Metal Sphinx rests upon a plinth, also of etherium, that is as tall as a tree and as broad as a good-size farm. The eastern face of this plinth carries a legend, carved deeply into the metal in letters that form themselves into the alphabet most familiar to the reader, and into words that can be understood as though composed in any given reader's milk tongue. This legend reads:

I AM THE STONE THAT COMES NOT FROM THE SEA
I AM THE BLOOD BUT THE BLOOD IS NOT ME
I AM THE KEY TO THE DOOR WITH NO LOCKS
I AM THE MAINSPRING THAT WINDS BROKEN CLOCKS
I AM YOUR TEARS ON THE CHAINS OF THE RACK
I AM YOUR GIFT AND YOU CAN'T GIVE ME BACK

The naked man had been kneeling there on the shore for a very, very long time—so long that had he been an ordinary man, he would have starved to death, his flesh rotted and bones bleached by the sun long ago. This man was not ordinary. He was prepared to remain there in silent contemplation until the stars themselves burned out.

He spent this time in a state of extraordinarily focused concentration, applying all his considerable resources of mind to this riddle. Sphinxes are uniquely dangerous creatures—even metal ones—and undertaking to unlock their riddles is notoriously perilous.

Guessing the answer wouldn't help, even if he guessed correctly. He had to *know* the answer, which is an altogether trickier proposition. His knowing had to be more than words; words without comprehension are as empty as the whistle of wind through dead trees. He had to *understand* the answer. He had to breathe it in and breathe it out; he had to eat it and drink it and make it as much a part of him as his hand, or his eyes, or his heart.

And when he had kneeled there on the sandy shore of the Metal Island long enough to do all these things, the answer was obvious. He lifted his head, squinting up at the blank etherium eyes of the Metal Sphinx. "Is that it?" he said. "It's that simple? Really?"

The statue did not seem disposed to reply.

The man sighed. There was one way to know for sure.

He brought his right hand up before his face, turned it this way and that, waggled his fingers, examining its every curve, crease, and follicle, until he had all of these details fixed firmly in his mind. He had learned, from long experience, that people who say, "I know 'something' like the back of my hand," are often correct only because they don't actually know the backs of their hands—or their fronts, for that matter—in any meaningful way.

"All right, then," he said at length, speaking aloud with the unselfconsciousness of a man who has become comfortable with solitude. Though he was accustomed to expressing himself (even *to* himself) in a way that emphasized his impressive vocabulary, in this case, what he expressed was as simple as what he was about to do was complex. "It will suck to be wrong."

With his left hand, he picked through the tangles of his graying hair until he located a tiny shard of sharp crystal, shaped like a needle the length of the last joint of his thumb. This crystal needle was warmer than could be explained by the man's body heat, or by the rays of the sun, and even in the brilliant noon, the needle displayed a faint rosy glow.

He made a fist of his right hand until the veins on its back stood out, then shoved the crystal needle lengthwise into one of those veins until it lay wholly under his skin. The blaze of sudden pain, far more intense than a mere pinprick, he had anticipated, and so he was not dismayed even when his hand burst into flame.

While his flesh blackened and charred, he gathered his concentration in a particular way, then extended his arm as though reaching with his burning hand for something invisible in the air before him. As if dipping through the surface boundary of reflective water, his fingers began to disappear, wiping themselves from existence, followed by his burning hand—for there was indeed a surface there through which he reached, though it was not water.

It was the surface of the universe.

The end of the wrist, from which his hand had now disappeared, did not display bone and vein and muscle; instead, it presented a mirrorlike surface of polished metal, which appeared to have roughly the luster of burnished pewter.

The man said, "So far so good," then closed his eyes to focus every scrap of his attention on what his hand was doing on the far side of reality. He could still feel it as though it were on the beach with him, because it wasn't actually in another universe, but between universes, in the æther soup of unrealized possibility that he, and those like him, named the Blind Eternities.

What his hand did there took considerable time, as such things were measured on the world that was ocean. When at last he decided his experiment was complete, he focused his mind again as he had on insertion, then pulled his hand back into the universe he shared with the Metal Island.

His hand was grievously burned, flesh blackened and peeling, and the skin on the back of his hand, where he had inserted the crystal needle, was gone altogether, exposing a charred mass of bone and tendon. He nodded to himself; this was one of the possible outcomes he had anticipated. For this outcome, he had planned a further experiment.

He took another needle from his hair and drove it into his burned flesh where the first had been. He focused his attention very much as he had when his hand had been outside the universe . . . and charred muscle began to heal, and fresh pink skin crept back over it. The last place to close was the back of his hand, where the skin had been altogether missing. Here, just before pink skin covered it altogether, there could be seen—just along one metacarpal and a fractional length of vein—a tiny glint of metal, like burnished pewter . . . or, of course, etherium, for that was what it was.

He lifted his gaze once more to meet the blank etherium stare of the Metal Sphinx. "Thank you."

The Metal Sphinx did not reply.

He took a deep breath and settled back into a comfortable position. "And for the rest," he said to himself, "patience. When using unfamiliar bait, one can only cast it into the ocean and wait to see what bites."

No great amount of patience was needed; presently, his anticipation was rewarded with the sound of the universe screaming in pain.

This is a sound that ordinary ears cannot hear—it's more akin to a ragged, rending silence deeper than that of airless space—but the man knew this sound well, and he did not even lift his head as vast talons sliced into the world-ocean from the outside, ripping a hole in reality, pulling the shreds apart, slicing the universe in a gruesome parody of birth. Shortly, the rip in reality was torn wide enough that a scaled shoulder appeared, bringing with it a vast leathery wing, and finally a dragon the size of a house forced itself into the world.

The dragon held a human in its jaws, wedged in the corner of its mouth as a rich man might hold a fine cigar. All that could be seen of this unfortunate individual was the lower half of his naked body, which was how the man who knelt on the shore could tell—with the help of excellent vision—that this man was in fact a man.

The dragon's eyes shone with a yellow flame that cast a pale dandelion glow on the white sand. Actual flames licked out from its eyeballs, sending greasy pale smoke twisting upward between its horns. Smoke of a different sort leaked from the dragon's nostrils. Someone familiar with dragons would have noted that this one seemed angry—to say it burned with fury would be literally accurate.

This dragon pounced like an enormous cat. One taloned forelimb slammed the man on the shore onto his back, pinning him to the ground, then began, ever so slowly, to crush the life from him.

"Bolas." The man did not show the slightest discomfort. "Took your time, didn't you?"

"Oh, very funny. Took my *time*." The dragon's voice was compounded of thunder and landslide. Even spoken out of the side of its mouth, each word might have been crushed from a granite mountain. "You have a refined sense of humor, for a dead man."

"I'm surprised you even realized it was a joke."

"This is what I think of *comedy*." In its free hand, the dragon took the man's legs, which kicked weakly at the corner of its jaw, and bit the man in half. His scream of agony was brief, and mostly muffled, being inside the dragon's mouth. The dragon broke off the corpse's lower half as though it were a celery stick as he chewed on the rest. A black tongue flicked up, around, and across the dragon's mouth, gathering the sprays of blood that had splattered its scales.

The dragon, whose name was Nicol Bolas, was not known for his sense of humor.

The man pinned under the dragon's other hand did not look impressed. "That wouldn't happen to have been Jace Beleren, would it?"

"B'l'rn?" The dragon made a face and spit the mangled remnant of torso into the sea. "Ychh. Raw free-range human. Tastes like goat balls." The dragon made another face and spit again. "No, sorry to disappoint, Tezzeret—that wasn't Jace. He would taste like, oh, spring lamb, I imagine. That . . . inedible *crap* . . . was that clockworker of yours."

"Renn?" The man, who was called Tezzeret, broadened his smile. "The last time I saw him, he was nothing more than a head and etherium. Even his heart. No lungs at all, nor any of the other bits. Getting himself a whole new body must have been a substantial undertaking, even for him."

"He didn't," the dragon said. "I did. The rebuild was his fee for telling me where you went."

"Ah." Tezzeret nodded. "The contract didn't specify *how* you'd rebuild him."

"Why would I waste all that etherium on someone who isn't me?"

"A question he should have considered before making the deal."

"He was a little agitated at the time. Emotional. It wouldn't be an overstatement to say he was foaming at the mouth with uncontrollable rage." The dragon cocked his head an inch or two. "You have that effect on people."

"Do I? Well, well. At any rate, thank you."

"What?"

Tezzeret gave as much of a shrug as would fit between the dragon's talons. "I said *thank you*. It's an expression civil people sometimes use. It means I'm grateful for your help."

"I *know* what it—" The dragon's jaw clamped shut, and the weight on Tezzeret's chest suddenly doubled. "Is this really the time to be *mocking* me?"

"I hadn't decided whether or not I should kill him; you have thoughtfully removed one horn of my potential moral dilemma. Not to mention that finding him at all might have been a challenge. I appreciate the favor. I'd say I owe you one, but under the circum*waurggh*"—his voice thinned as the weight on his chest suddenly doubled—"it might be . . . *guhh* . . . redundant. . . ." His voice faded to a gurgle as the dragon leaned on his chest hard enough to spring a couple of his ribs.

"Banter," said Nicol Bolas, "gets on my nerves."

The drool that spooled down from his jaws toward Tezzeret's head was tinged strawberry with blood, smelled like offal, and had the consistency of half-melted gelatin. "Have you been here all along? Is this your hiding place?"

Tezzeret shook his head. "Wasn't . . . hiding," he wheezed. "Was waiting . . . for you."

"Flatterer." The dragon increased the weight on the man's chest. "You were given a task."

Tezzeret only rolled his head, nodding toward the Metal Sphinx.

"Please," Bolas rumbled. "You think you can buy me off with mere *treasure*?"

Tezzeret only blinked mutely up at the dragon, who presently realized the man's face was turning black. "Oh, fine." He eased up on the pressure until Tezzeret could breathe.

"It's not . . . treasure . . ." Tezzeret coughed. "It's just how this place is. And how it will always be. More or less. Ever hear the expression 'You can't take it with you'?"

"Really?" Bolas lifted his head, frowning at the etherium gigafortune all around. If Tezzeret could have taken even an armload or two of etherium back across the Blind Eternities to Esper, Bolas would hardly have found him naked on this beach.

He probably wouldn't have found Tezzeret at all.

"So . . ." Bolas again bent his neck to bring his jaws within biting distance of Tezzeret's face. "You know where he is."

"I know everywhere he isn't."

"Close enough. Tell me."

"That's a long story, even for you."

"What, is he dead?"

Tezzeret cocked his head as though this question had only now occurred to him. "It would be most accurate to say that he's not yet alive."

"Oh, I *love* when you do that. I do. Really. Tell me another." Dragon drool began to puddle near Tezzeret's ears, and the dragon's voice went deep as a mine shaft and twice as dark. "I can take the secret from your mind."

"There is no secret."

"I can peel your brain like an onion."

"What do you know about onions, carnivore?"

"A fair point," Bolas conceded. "How about instead, I peel your brain like the skull of an obnoxious artificer who has about a minute to live?"

"Is this multiple choice? None of the above."

"You haven't heard all the choices."

Tezzeret smiled. "With you, it's always none of the above."

"You think you can play sphinx with me, you filthy little scut?" Those yellow eyes darkened toward red. "You don't have the power. You don't have a *millionth* of the power."

"Power's irrelevant," Tezzeret said apologetically. "And I'm not playing sphinx, nor any other game; why would I? You're too stupid to understand the rules."

"*Stupid?*" Bolas snatched Tezzeret into the air, shaking him like a doll. "Will I be stupid while I skin you and gut you and roast you alive? Will I still be stupid after the last of your bones digests in my third stomach?"

"Yes. You will. You," said Tezzeret, wheezing a bit from the shaking, "are not what you eat."

The dragon made a sound as if boulders might be grinding together in his crop. "I was master of the Blind Eternities when your pathetic species didn't yet know how to make *fire*. I have not survived twenty-five thousand years by being stupid."

"That's true," Tezzeret allowed. "You survived in spite of being stupid."

"What do you gain by insulting me?" The dragon seemed honestly puzzled. "Are you so tired of living?"

"That's exactly what I'm talking about," Tezzeret said. "Telling you that you're stupid is not an insult. It's an explanation."

He spoke very slowly, and very clearly, as though speaking to a dim-witted child. "It's not your fault, Bolas.

You can't help it. You are probably the most powerful being in the Multiverse—"

"Probably?" the dragon sneered. "Another insult."

"And that's why. That right there. Power makes you stupid, Bolas. Power makes everyone stupid. You don't have to be smart when you can be strong. When was the last time you had to, say, outwit someone? Why bother, when you can destroy them—destroy anyone—with a shrug?"

"Which you should keep in mind."

"That's the difference between us. I *have* to be smart; my intellect is my only useful weapon. That man you just killed—Silas Renn? He had the power to squash me like a bug. He used to do exactly that, regularly, back when we both studied with the Seekers of Carmot. He was ten times the mage I'll ever be . . . yet what's left of his corpse is drifting with the tides in a universe he could never have imagined. And I . . . ?" Tezzeret smiled. "I am about to teach the most powerful being in the Multiverse a lesson in weakness."

"We'll see who teaches whom." He opened his claws to hold Tezzeret cupped in his palm. One wickedly hooked talon, as long as Tezzeret was tall and sharp as a stiletto, traced a complex design in the air around the human's form. Where the talon passed, lines of actinic white fire ignited, becoming a spherical lattice around Tezzeret, anchoring his wrists and ankles and stretching them to full extension—and then a bit more.

Nicol Bolas hummed to himself as he wove the restraints. "Comfortable? No? Good."

Gap-spark blue energy crackled between the dragon's horns like lightning leaping from mountain to mountain. "This, by the way, is going to hurt. A lot."

"Everything . . . hurts. . . ." His body locked outstretched within the globe of white, Tezzeret could only barely force the words past his clenched teeth. "Whenever you're . . . ready . . ."

"You can spare yourself this pain."

"No . . . I can't. . . ."

"Share your secrets willingly, and I'll leave your mind intact."

"The only secret . . . is that there *is no secret*. . . ."

"Have it your way. You were warned."

The gap spark between Bolas's horns intensified, gathering itself until it became a seething blue-tinged sun, too bright to look at. This blue sun grew horns of its own, two writhing jets of energy, one from above and the other from below. These jets spidered out, paused for a heartbeat or two in the air between the dragon and the man, then lanced through the Web of Restraint and stabbed into Tezzeret's head.

Bolas grimaced, fanning the air with one wing as he peeled Tezzeret's mind. Burning hair was one odor he'd never enjoyed—and burning bone wasn't much better. He sighed for a moment, thinking of Jace Beleren. If he'd still had a tether on that grubby little mind ripper, he could have farmed out this business. He decided that when this was over, he would take himself off to, oh, say, Esper's Glass Dunes for a good sand bath—something nice and abrasive, to really scour this stink off his scales.

The dragon's memory siphon was very reliable and very thorough. As long as the spell was active, Bolas could replay Tezzeret's memories, as vivid as a nightmare. It was very much like being Tezzeret as he endured the original experiences.

"Really, the things I put myself through . . ." Nicol Bolas said with a melancholy sigh. On the other hand, it would give him one more reason to punish Tezzeret. Not that he needed another reason.

Or any reason at all.

"Let's see what's inside this head of yours, shall we?" he murmured to himself. "Right from the moment I woke you up . . ."

The memories began to flow, slowly at first, then with increasing speed and force: the sensation of being rudely awakened, naked and alone, in the crystal cavern . . . then Tezzeret's fuzzy, almost incoherent thoughts, before the artificer had even opened his eyes. . . .

TEZZERET
A MAN OF PARTS

Being alive meant I was in trouble.

I remembered dying. Your own murder is not something that slips your mind.

That vicious little gutter-monkey Jace Beleren had reached inside my skull with the invisible fingers of his mind and scrambled my brain into . . . what? An omelet didn't seem right—too orderly. Too *intentional*. A chopped salad? Not meaty enough. My brain felt like something sliced, or scooped, fried in bacon grease . . . yes.

Head cheese.

But having a brainpan filled with head cheese would leave me incapable of iterating concepts such as *brainpan* and *head cheese*, and likely lacking the mental resources to recall my death and formulate a metaphor to describe it. This recursive self-realization developed slowly, because having a functioning brain, which I did, didn't mean it was functioning very well, which it wasn't.

I passed some indeterminate interval speculating that perhaps I was not in fact alive, but that my corpse had been reanimated by some ambitious mage—perhaps that tasty little necromancer Jace Beleren had been so fond of . . . Vess. Something Vess. Lolita? Lilith? Something like that.

I also, for thoroughness' sake, considered the possibility that my undead essence had been conjured by an embattled wizard on some nearby plane, either to win a duel or to

TEZZERET
A MAN OF PARTS

prepare for his next one. But despite my diminished intellectual capacity, I knew that either of these possibilities was unlikely to result in a seemingly interminable span with nothing to do but chew my mental cud.

Further: I was mostly sure that being dead wouldn't hurt this much.

I seemed to be lying on a pile of jagged rocks. Apparently, I had been lying on these jagged rocks for some significant amount of time—long enough for every single edge and point to work as deeply into my flesh as was possible short of drawing blood. I lay there experiencing the discomfort without attempting to ease it; I was not yet ready to move.

As an artificer by inclination as well as vocation, I have always known that anything worth doing is best accomplished in a deliberate, structured, and meticulous fashion. Feelings and dreams are useless, and imagination is worse. Reality doesn't care how you think it *ought* to be, or what you fantasize it *might* be. Effective action is achieved only by the intelligent application of what *is*.

An unsentimental perspective on the 'what is' of my current situation offered no good news. To have healed and reconstructed my brain, after Beleren puréed it, was itself a feat of impressive power; to have done so after (or in the process of) *raising me from the dead* expanded the power requirement from impressive to astonishing. This premise led to a grim two-horned conclusion. I'd been returned to life and placed here by a being of astonishing capability who was either unconcerned with my personal welfare, or actively my enemy.

There was no third possibility. I don't have friends.

Worse: my right arm hurt.

It ached as though it might be nothing more than simple flesh over simple bone. This was overwhelmingly wrong.

So powerfully wrong that when I opened my eyes, I looked only to my left.

Not because I was kidding myself; I did not waste mental energy fantasizing that my good right arm—my precious arm, the only feature of my existence in which I can truly take pride—might be intact. Instead, my refusal to look at it arose from a similarly unsentimental understanding of my own psychology. There is a difference between knowing the abstract and seeing the specific.

There was a difference between knowing my mother was dead, and finding her battered corpse trampled and crushed into the muck of a Lower Vectis by-lane.

By looking only to my left, I kept the comprehension of my maiming safely abstract.

My prison appeared to be a natural cavern cloaked in a dull, bloody gloom, as though the light came from hot iron. The jagged rock on which I lay, the floor, the walls, and the ceiling were all some sort of crystalline mineral I did not recognize, darker than ruby quartz, shading toward carnelian—and the light in the cavern was apparently the product of a crimson glow from the deeper deposits of this crystal. From somewhere nearby came the liquid patter of what I hoped might be water.

There was neither sight nor smell of anything to eat, nor of any bedding, clothing, or fabric of any kind with which I might cover myself. The strongest odor in the cavern was of unwashed human armpit, likely my own. I found no indication of anything that might be fashioned into tools, only ever-deeper deposits of glowing red crystal.

This did not mean I was helpless. Fastening my mind upon the gray waves that crash against the cliffs below Vectis, I began to pull mana. At the very least I might fashion temporary covering for my body and protection for my feet, both of which would be useful while exploring the further extents of the cavern.

I discovered, however, that my effort to gather mana resulted only in a barely perceptible brightening of one large crystal in my immediate line of vision. This was not in itself dismaying, as I had not expected to succeed. A number of constructs and magics can deny mana to even the most powerful mage—I've designed several myself—but the attempt had to be made.

Everything at which I've ever succeeded has been accomplished by exacting attention to detail; a full commitment to exhaustive investigation. To have left a possibility unexplored would be like, well . . .

Like cutting off my own hand.

And so then, finally, I had to look.

My reaction was largely what I had anticipated it might be: a rush of rage and denial so intense I could only lie there and scream, followed by a flood of nauseous horror so overpowering that I vomited blood-laced saliva and green bile, and then passed out cold.

✻ ✻ ✻ ✻ ✻

I began constructing my right arm when I was roughly nine years of age. Though my arm's completion would require more than a decade, and I would continue to refine it for some years after, the process of acquisition, design, and construction actually began when I finally found myself clever enough to steal from my father, which was, approximately, age nine.

My age has always been approximate.

My birth had been no occasion to celebrate, and so neither were my birthdays; my parents never bothered to share with me the date, if they even remembered. I calculated my approximate age by my size and development relative to the other Tidehollow cave brats.

My parents were scrappers. Scrappers sift the garbage, runoff, and sewage of the city of Vectis, hoping that with careful and patient work they might gather bits of copper, silver, gold, or even the occasional sliver of mislaid etherium. Scrapping is, in Vectis, a less honorable profession than is begging, and it is ranked far, far below whoring. This I understood despite my age; my mother had once been a whore, as she often bitterly reminded my father whenever money ran short, or when the hearth fire sputtered, or the sun rose, or the moon set. When the winds blew, or when they fell silent.

Before her health and looks failed and she was forced to stoop so low as to share a hovel with my father, she would not even have spit on a scrapper in the street; to do so would have meant acknowledging the scrapper's miserable existence.

I was seven years old when she was killed.

Approximately.

The news of her death arrived in the company of taunting and jeering from the ragged pack of cave brats with whom I commonly associated—children in Tidehollow being not only unsentimental, but largely incapable of understanding the concept of empathy, much less exhibiting any. One of their fathers, who had been begging on the same street in Lower Vectis as had my mother, had seen the incident. By his report, she had pressed too close to a passing guildsmaster's carriage while supplicating alms. The blow of a whip from the carriage driver had knocked her down, and she had fallen under the wheels. The merchant lord had rolled on without so much as pausing to determine what he had crushed.

φ

My father's face at first had flushed, and angry color rose toward his eyes—but after only an instant all color drained away. I never saw it return. He became expressionless as a statue, and when he spoke to me, his voice had no more life or emotion than the sound of gravel rolling off a slate roof.

"Boy. Come folla. We has to git yer mother."

He always called me *boy*. I am uncertain whether he and my mother had given me a name. Tezzeret is how I was called among the cave brats; a *tezzeret* is, in Tidehollow cant, the word for any small, improvised or homemade weapon kept concealed on one's body—knives made from beach glass wrapped in packing twine; slings and garrotes woven of one's own hair, a carriage spring bent to protect the knuckles of one's fist. The cave brats had dubbed me Tezzeret after I had used one to butt shank an older boy who had pushed me down into a muck puddle.

My father gathered three or four potato sacks, told me to bring the sheets off his bed, and we went to get my mother.

My father and I did not speak on the long trudge upslope from Tidehollow to Lower Vectis. We didn't speak while we threaded through the murky lanes and alleys. The sum total of our conversation took place beside my mother's broken corpse, just before we dug her body out of the greasy muck in the middle of the lane.

"Even this," my father had said softly, in a bitterly sullen murmur as though reminding himself how angry he should be. "Even this, theyz tooken from me."

When I asked whom he meant, he sullenly nodded upslope. "Bankers 'n' merchants. Guildsfolk. Them as lives up the city."

I could not imagine why anyone rich enough to live upslope would want anything of ours, and I said so.

"Futter *want*. They don' has to *want* for them to *take*. Take is what they do. Take is their whole life. Us downslopers myz well be butt rags. One swipe 'crost some arsehole and down the shitter."

When I told him I felt this wasn't right, he cuffed me on the side of the head hard enough to send me staggering. "Right, nothin'," he said. "Ain' right I whap ye on the ear, but I do. Cuz I can. Cuz ye ain' big enow to stop me."

I didn't care about the smack; his heart hadn't been in it, and so I'd barely noticed. I cared only for discovering who might be big enough to stop them. When I asked, my father only shook his head.

"Nobody," he said. "They owns the whole world, boy."

Even at seven, my political instincts were already developing; I pointed out that somebody had to be in charge, or nothing would ever get done.

"Dunno 'bout bein' in charge. Only folks as scares guildsfolk 'ud be mages. When them mages talk, best believe them guildsbuggers chew their tongues 'cept for *yessir*."

"Mages?" I'm fairly certain that this was the first time in my life I'd heard that word. It's certainly the first I remember. "What's mages?"

"Sumpin as ye need not know, boy. You'll never see one."

This was the longest conversation my father and I ever had.

So this was my lesson: The strong—the wealthy, the powerful, the influential—take. The weak are taken from. The strong do to the weak whatever the weak can't stop them from doing. The strong could run my mother down in the street without even *thinking* about it.

This did not strike me as injustice. I'm from Tidehollow; I didn't know what *injustice* meant until years later, when I came across the word in the course of my self-education. The concepts of justice and injustice struck me at that time as inherently suspect, and nothing in my life has since moved me to alter that opinion. To complain of injustice seems as useful as complaining that the sun shines or that the winds blow.

No: the casual destruction of my mother's life struck me instead as a reason to make *myself* strong. She was taken from me because I could not stop them from taking her. I understood that if I remained as I was—a scrapper's boy in Tidehollow—anything in my life could be taken from me . . . and everything that could be taken *would* be taken.

The most reasonable solution, to my young mind, was to make of myself a stronger man. But even if I did, I could be robbed by folk stronger still. How could I stop them?

The answer seemed obvious. The experience that had earned me my nickname left me with an enduring appreciation for the power of precisely applied violence. By the second or third time some other people's mothers were found dead in the street—the mothers of, say, individuals who had attempted to *take* from me—I was confident that the warning would be generally understood.

The power to revenge injury a thousandfold was my fondest boyhood dream. No one would dare take what is mine. Ever.

And the word my father taught me that evening, the word meaning "the strongest," was *mage*.

I undertook my own investigation into the nature of mages, and how one achieves that title. To ask anyone in Tidehollow would have been futile; I would have gotten more useful answers from my reflection in a mud puddle.

Over the course of some weeks, my investigation took me on surreptitious scouting expeditions into Upper Vectis. There, I discovered for the first time what the slivers and oddments of pale metal that my father gathered were actually used for. I came to understand why a week's food could be purchased with an amount of etherium that might barely equal the weight of my fingernail parings.

I learned that an individual's wealth could be calculated to a nicety by observing how much etherium that individual exhibited in jewelry, articles of clothing, slaves, and vehicles. The wealthiest had etherium magically melded to their flesh, and mages—whether human or vedalken or even the great sphinxes of the distant islands—shared one distinguishing feature: a limb, or a body part or several, wholly replaced by a structure of etherium, enchanted to duplicate (and often exceed) the function of the part it replaced.

I also learned I could work as a scrapper for my entire life and never save enough to buy so much as an etherium nose ring.

I was very taken with the esthetics of the etherium enhancements, as well. The indestructible metal for structure and magic for muscles and nerves, clean lines and curves, and elegant purity of operation made them irresistible. Having spent some hours on that street in Lower Vectis, gathering up the filthy shreds of meat and bone that had been my mother, I was—I am—entirely too familiar with the muck restrained by human skin.

I know the color of raw human liver. I know the texture of ripped-open human lung. I saw gobbets of my mother's brain, and the undigested remnants of a breakfast we had shared in a stew of blood and bile within her torn stomach. And I knew even then that the organs I helped my father scoop back into my mother's abdominal cavity were no different than what lurked in my own guts, and that the foul stench of corruption lived inside me, too. To this day, I see and smell them again, fully as vivid as they were to my seven-year-old self, in the nightmares that overtake me when I must sleep.

Someone more interested in human psychology than I am might find something ironic in this; I do not think in such literary terms. I am what I am. The key to successful artificing has nothing to do with *why*; *what* is the relevant issue. Combined with a properly structured *how*, one can unlock the universe.

Relevant facts change as circumstances develop, but still . . .

I've known what I am since the night my mother died. I knew what I intended to make of myself, and how to achieve it.

The next day, I entered the family business at my father's side. I undertook to learn every detail of how one finds and gathers cast-off shreds of etherium. The activity is surprisingly technical, requiring considerable expertise, as the value of the metal makes it very much sought after. One must learn to search where others won't and learn to retrieve where others can't.

I very shortly discovered that I surpassed my father in this work, though he'd been a scrapper since he was my age. For a time, I arrogantly assumed it was due to some innate superiority of intellect or character; there were untapped caches of a gram or less of etherium in any number of places, and I assumed my success in finding them—where my father could not—meant I was smarter than he was. I discovered I was wrong when my father decided he no longer needed to work at all, beyond assessing what I had found, calculating a price, and trekking upslope to Vectis to sell it.

He knew as well as I did that I was a better scrapper than he was, and—unlike my ignorant self—he knew why. I chance to have a talent that the vedalken call *rhabdomancy*. In plain terms, when I have a sample of a particular material, I have a sort of intuition that leads me to wherever I can find more. As rhabdomants go, I was not—nor am I now—especially gifted. My talent enabled me to find etherium because it's an intense substance, one that casts a vivid shadow upon reality.

One might say that it's loud.

If gold, for example, were to be counted equivalent to the sound of a man snapping his fingers across the street, etherium would be the sound of an angry sphinx hammering upon a gong larger than a rich man's house.

My skill had nothing to do with superiority. It was simply an artifact of heredity, like my height or the color of my eyes—or, for that matter, my intellect.

Where I did find myself superior was in the diligence I was willing to exercise in the pursuit of my goal. My father watched me every second; he had learned all too well to read my face—over which I, not yet nine, had little control. If he even suspected I might have located a piece and had not told him, I would endure a memorable beating and would spend the next night, or several, chained to the main ceiling post in the room that served us as both kitchen and bedroom. I never gave over trying, and eventually I hit upon a workable tactic.

Working as a scrapper kept the skin of my hands and feet in a state of continual disrepair. My work involved wading through sewage-drenched cesspools and piles of rotting garbage, pulling out any item that might have come in contact with any etherium—even a smudge of the metal was valuable in its own right. I had no shoes or boots, and my hands were always scratched and torn, and usually infected. Every so often, I would discover slivers of etherium, almost like splinters of glass. The smallest—rarely more than a tenth of a gram—I could conceal by sticking them under the skin of my hands or my feet. Later, after my father was safely snoring in his drug-addled stupor, I could cut these splinters from my flesh and hide them away again.

At that age, I was already an experienced contingency planner. I had secreted four cover stashes in our hovel, each more difficult to uncover than the last. These were used when my father actually caught me stealing—which I took pains that he did, every few months; it made him confident in his vigilance and enabled me to steal all the more. On these occasions, after the customary beating, he would force me to "reveal" the location of my treasure. After absorbing enough physical abuse to make it believable, I would tearfully direct him to the next cover stash.

What my father never caught on to was that my real stash was on—in—my own body. The rank tangles of my hair helped conceal the forty-five grams of etherium splinters I had shoved under my scalp; another thirty grams was in my upper groin, at the tops of and between my thighs. By the time I was ready to leave Tidehollow forever, my permanently grimy flesh concealed two hundred grams of etherium—a princely sum, which, with judicious trading up the sloping streets of Lower Vectis, was enough to purchase clothing, bathing, and adequate food, as well as what I desired most in the world: an apprenticeship in an artificer's workshop. There I began to learn the ways that metal, glass, and stone can be worked, manipulated, and bent to the tasks my will might require of them.

To this day there are slivers and tiny fragments of etherium lodged in a number of variously private places upon my body. To remove these fragments would be laborious and time-consuming—and, after all, they are my last remaining link to my father, to my childhood, and to the harsh realities of life in Tidehollow.

Keeping them is a symptom of an unfortunate sentimentality. I admit to being sentimental, though perhaps less so than most. Because I acknowledge this, I am able to compensate for the influence this flaw might have on my judgment. I don't conceal this particular trait—it's more useful on display, as it often leads others to misread my intentions and to underestimate my capabilities.

I left Tidehollow without saying good-bye. I did look back, but only to ensure that my father was not in pursuit. I was, approximately, eleven years old.

My apprenticeship to the artificer was to span the standard term of seven years; after three, when I had determined to my satisfaction that I had learned all my master could teach, I departed his service in the late hours of a moonless night. Fear of my father's vengeance had driven me to enter my apprenticeship under an assumed name, which meant that deciding on a new name was no burden and carried no risk of exposure, even by vedalken truthsayers or suspicious sphinxes. Since I had been given none of my own, whatever word I might choose to call myself in any given moment *is* my real name.

I have known since a very young age that I am not like other people, be they human, vedalken, viashino, or elf. I have sometimes wondered if the root of that difference might lie in my concept of self, which seems distinctly at variance with the concept others have of themselves. Ask a man who he is, and he will tell you his name. Ask me who I am . . . and if I wish to give an honest answer, it will come only after a certain amount of detailed self-reflection. I am not a name, and no word truly names me. Who I am is a fluid concept.

It can make social encounters awkward.

I immediately went in search of a new situation—a particular position for which a great deal of wealth would be required. The position I sought was far removed from the humble workshop I had fled; it was beyond the means of all but scions of the wealthiest families of Vectis. Being largely insolvent save for my few remaining grams of etherium, I undertook to supplement my personal financial resources with some judicious prospecting.

There is a particular type of individual—again, species is irrelevant—who is constitutionally incapable of trusting others. (Some say I am one such, but they are mistaken. Unfortunately. The expanding roster of catastrophic betrayals inflicted upon me speaks all too clearly of my trusting nature.)

In Vectis, the inability to trust can lead to some unfortunate behavior; for example, distrusting the reliability of counting houses ends with concealing one's wealth on one's person, or on one's property. When one seeks to conceal wealth, it's often done by converting said wealth into the most valuable material available, thus lowering the volume and sturdiness required of the hiding place. In Vectis—on the whole of Esper—the most valuable material is etherium, so a rhabdomant might find it in unlikely places.

Buried in someone's garden, for example.

It was possible to find caches so old that the people who had stashed them away had either forgotten them or had perished without leaving a record of their locations. These were ideal, as one was far less likely to encounter outraged misers who might be armed with any given variety of lethal weapon. Bandits—and worse, rippers—were an issue, especially beyond the city limits, but my time at the artificer's shop had provided me with the materials for, and the means of, constructing several varieties of lethal weapons of my own. More than one overly optimistic ripper ended up decomposing in the sluice pools of Tidehollow.

It amused me to think of my father investing hours or days in the painstaking dissection of these rotting carcasses, especially because by the time I was through with them, none of these corpses had so much as a microgram of etherium among them.

My unfortunate sentimentality is balanced, I believe, against an elegantly precise capacity for maintaining a grudge.

When I had accumulated five pounds of etherium, I was finally ready to begin my new life. Two pounds was the fee for a year's study in the Right Ancient Order of Mystic Constructionist Masters—the Mechanists' Guild.

A mechanist is as far beyond an artificer as a dragon is beyond a goose. At the artificer's workshop, I had learned how ordinary metal, glass, and stone can be shaped to useful ends. In the Mechanists' Guild, a student is taught the working of magical materials—and how magic can be used to work one's materials—as well as how devices, machinery, and automata can be imbued with mana, to give them wholly extraordinary capabilities. After one achieves elevation to journeyman of the Guild, one begins to learn the working of etherium. Then, eventually, as a master, one undertakes the construction of etherium devices—devices with, literally, life of their own.

Mana is, functionally, only power. That is, energy—the capacity to accomplish work. A device of etherium does not require mana to operate; etherium is, itself, a *source* of mana—and, as I learned in my tenure at the Guild, it is a conduit that channels power from outside the universe.

In the service of the artificer, I had been taught that energy and matter are fundamentally one and the same, regardless of the form of either, and that energy can be neither created nor destroyed. The only change we can force is to alter its form. Even mana is a finite resource. Etherium, on the other hand . . .

Well, etherium itself is a finite resource—but the power it channels is not.

The Mechanists' Guild teaches that etherium is the stuff of reality itself, and that by working etherium, one can touch directly the mind of god. It is, however, exceedingly bad manners to inquire "Which god?" They prefer to keep the nature of their purported deity carefully abstract. He sometimes is said to reside in etherium, sometimes in ourselves; sometimes he is said to actually *be* etherium itself . . . and sometimes etherium is said to be a channel for his grace.

The being who supposedly introduced etherium to Esper—who was reputed to have personally created, in fact, all the etherium that exists—is known there as Crucius the Mad Sphinx. Crucius is a figure of some renown and of considerable dispute. He is considered by the Mechanists to be not a sphinx at all, for example, but rather an incarnation of the will of their abstract god. This peculiar conviction was certainly sparked by the vast list of the Mad Sphinx's gnomic utterances about "atonement with the æther," and by his dramatic disappearance some decades past.

Matters certainly aren't helped by the fact that no one actually *saw* Crucius, with the possible exception of the Hegemon of Esper; he's a figure one learns of only by repute, and tales grow in the telling. This bizarre cult of the Vanished Mad Sphinx is maintained and evangelized to this day by a vast and increasingly influential rabble of insufferable fanatics who name themselves the Ethersworn.

These demented pebbleheads decided—based on no actual evidence whatsoever—that the key to the "redemption" of the entire plane of Esper is to infuse *every living creature* with etherium. They have never been able to explicitly define what it is Esper needs to be redeemed *from*; again, pointing this out to them is excruciatingly bad manners. Given that the supply of etherium is finite and already fully exploited—its supposed creator may have been mad, but it seemed he was not mad enough to scatter deposits of etherium underground or at the bottom of the Sea of Unknowing—the activities of these simpletons have actually accomplished nothing other than driving the price of etherium to preposterous heights.

The normal progress through the Mechanists' Guild from student to master is seventeen years; seven years as a student—essentially an apprentice, save that one must pay for the privilege—and ten years as a journeyman.

I was a master in five.

My rapid ascension was due, in part, to the same obsessive diligence that enabled me to escape my father and the slums of my birth, but it was also due to my experience as both scrapper and artificer. Sons and daughters of the rich cannot comprehend the actual value of an object. Nothing real is useless to a scrapper, and the limits of available finance and material are, to an artificer, absolute. If you can't afford steel gears, you make your own, of whatever happens to be available in your shop—or if you are possessed of a mind like mine, you design your device to work without gears at all.

The pampered children of privilege who were my schoolmates had no concept of the tension between waste and elegance. Assigned to design and build a particular style of chronometer, for example, my supposed peers amassed truly baffling arrays of springs and chains, wires, gears, pendulums, ratchets, precious woods, and baroquely filigreed decorative elements. Many of their designs encompassed several hundred parts; the most efficiently elegant of their designs had no less than seventy-three.

Mine had nine.

On nearly every assignment, I completed my work far ahead of my fellows. To amuse myself while waiting for them to finish, I would gather their debris and cast-off materials from the shop's dustbin and use them to create oddments—children's toys, tiny automata, the sorts of fanciful devices that have no actual purpose other than to delight by their design and action—which I then sold in the Lower Vectis Grand Bazaar, for what eventually became a tidy sum, to help finance my education.

It was not long until my schoolmates lost the habit of throwing away anything at all; they would, however, *sell* their leftover materials and discarded parts to me for pocket change, and so for a time I ran a thriving little trade. This lasted until our supervising master noted that every dustbin was as clean after our shop hours as it had been before them. The explanation—that they were selling their scraps to me, and I was peddling devices I made from them—earned me a visit from the three Governing Masters.

The masters looked over my impeccably organized work space—I had built a variety of storage devices to keep my materials clean, separate, and easy to locate at need—and one of them asked me why my bench was stuffed with trash.

"What trash?" said I. He indicated my multitudinous cabinets and arrays of drawers, which were stocked with everything from crumpled scraps of gold foil to tailings of badly tanned sluice serpent hide.

"With apologies for daring to disagree with my betters, Masters," I said, "none of these contain trash; their contents are simply materials I have not yet found a use for."

They elevated me to journeyman on the spot.

The position of journeyman was the only reason I'd come to the Guild in the first place. I did not plan to spend my life flattering the vanity of the wealthy and powerful by providing them with self-powered trinkets and enhanced body parts. I was there to learn to work etherium, and nothing else.

I was ready to build my right arm.

I had known what I was to build—I had dreamed it a decade before, and spent every intervening day of my life refining its design until I knew it would make of me the man I had decided to be. My right arm was why I taught myself the art of scrapping for etherium, why I had trained myself to steal from my father, why I'd apprenticed as an artificer, and why I had become a sneak thief and a killer of bandits and rippers. My right arm was the reason I had devoted my life to the study of all conceivable elements of design and construction.

When my father had been in one of his occasional expansive moods—merely intoxicated by the drugs he craved, rather than unconscious and prostrate—he liked to say that there were only two things in all creation he knew would never fail him: death and his right arm. Fool that he was.

His right arm was *nothing*. Flesh and bone. As corrupt and rotten as his filthy heart.

My right arm is none of these things.

There are some who have spoken of my arm, and claimed it to be psychological compensation for my lowly birth. Others have called it the badge of my self-creation. Still others have named it a symbol of power, a fetish, a talisman against self-doubt. All these people have one defining trait in common.

They're idiots.

The circumstances of my birth are irrelevant. I have no need for a "badge" of any kind; I *am* the proof of my self-creation. And my arm is not, nor has it ever been, a symbol of power, nor of anything else. It's not a symbol.

It *is* power.

Most "etherium enhancements" barely warrant the name. Etherium in its unworked state is a soft metal and almost infinitely ductile. Even the richest mages use baser metals that are stronger, and a great deal easier to come by, such as titanium or cobalt. They build their enhancements of these, merely threading the structure through with infinitesimal strands of etherium—only enough to power the enchantments that enable the prosthesis to mimic the function of the part it replaces.

I delved deeply into the mysteries of mana quenching and ætheric tempering, and I invented some variations of my own. No one can do with etherium what I can. In my hands, the metal's soft and ductile structure can be crystallized until it is harder than diamond but as durable as tool steel. In my hands, etherium needs no mana-sapping enchantments to power its magical muscles. It is instead a *source* of power, and one that can never be exhausted. Temporarily depleted, yes, by extraordinary expenditures—but not for long.

I went days at a time without sleep, learning to use mana to keep myself alert and focused, for my nights were passed risking my life against bandits and my freedom against thief-takers to search out new and ever-larger caches of etherium.

I learned to make my new arm do not only all the work of my old one, but everything else my imagination could devise. Though I am no more gifted a mage than I am a rhabdomant, I again found ways to exploit my minimal talents to accomplish maximal results. When my arm was completed, it comprised more than ten pounds of solid etherium from shoulder to fingertip. Merely having that amount of the metal bound to my will allowed me to channel as much mana as a gifted mage—and more, as my arm constantly renewed its power, drawing upon what I now know is the substance of the Blind Eternities itself.

One black midnight, I alone, without witness, assistant, or aid, performed the ritual that severed my arm of useless flesh and permanently attached the arm that would make a scruffy, ill-fed scrapper's boy into a man to be reckoned with. A man with the power to revenge injury a thousandfold.

A mage.

When morning came and the Masters saw what I had achieved, they elected to elevate me to Mastery and immediately began preparations for the weeklong ceremony. I thanked them, and walked out from the Guild Hall that same morning, never to return. This time, I did not look back.

I had what I'd wanted from them. *Master* is just a name. Names are nothing.

Power is everything.

I had not been out of the Mechanists' Guild a week before I was approached by the Seekers of Carmot.

It seemed the Seekers had been aware of me for some considerable time, as early as the first year of my apprenticeship to the artificer. I later learned that several of the rippers I had killed had been aspiring Seekers. The Anointed Fellows of the Seekers of Carmot had been most impressed, as these aspirants had been possessed of talent for magery in proportion to their avarice ... yet they had fallen before a Tidehollow boy whose talent was limited to a knack with gadgets.

When that knack had produced an arm of tempered etherium, the Seekers decided I might be useful, and so allowed me to study at their Academy.

The Seekers of Carmot styled themselves a noble order, committed to the service of all Esper. The *carmot* from which they'd taken their name was an arcane substance necessary to the production of etherium, some sort of catalyst that allowed the Anointed Fellows to create etherium by infusing æther into sangrite.

They *created* etherium.

Supposedly.

And they would teach me the secret.

Supposedly.

And they were committed to giving etherium away until it became as common as dirt.

Supposedly.

The Seekers of Carmot had been the last thing I'd ever believed in.

When I discovered the truth, I demonstrated to them that my talent wasn't so much a knack with gadgets as it was a knack for using gadgets to kill people.

In the end, I had come to appreciate my father's lesson. Only two things would never fail me: death and my right arm.

My arm was everything I had. It was everything I would ever have.

When I awoke in that red crystal cave to find attached to my right shoulder an arm of mere flesh, already corrupt and rotting, that was exactly what had been taken from me.

Everything.

❋ ❋ ❋ ❋ ❋

When I regained consciousness, I undertook to examine my new appendage. It appeared, in every functional sense, identical to the one I had severed some years before. Missing were only an array of minor scars across my knuckles and into the palm of my hand—souvenirs of

MATTHEW STOVER

ᏟᎮ

a particularly tricky midnight etherium retrieval—and a much larger scar along my biceps, a knife wound. This scar, while I had still used my flesh arm, had been a useful reminder to never assume I had killed the last bandit.

So: the limb very likely had been regenerated. Another extravagance of power—and an astonishingly potent personal affront. There is literally nothing else that could be done to me that would hurt as much, as deeply, and on so many levels.

Without my real arm, the one I had created, I was nothing more than a Tidehollow scrapper. I had been made into my father.

Except with a better vocabulary.

I tallied up the facts of my situation, relevant to whose prisoner I was most likely to be: life, sanity, nudity, maiming, and the bitterest psychic wound I could even imagine.

Framed in those terms, the conclusion was obvious.

"Bolas." I said it aloud, but not loudly. I knew I didn't have to. "I know you're here."

As a demon is said to be conjured by the sound of its name, after only a single heartbeat he materialized out of the rose-tinged gloom, all sixty-some-odd feet of twenty-five-thousand-year-old dragon.

"You always were clever," he said, and casually backhanded me with one wall-size fist so hard that I flew across the cavern, slammed into a jagged wall, and sank to the floor, stunned into immobility.

"Hello, Tezzeret," said Nicol Bolas. "Welcome to the rest of your life."

TEZZERET
THE DRAGON'S JEST

The hand I brought to my mouth came back bloody. Hot oil trickled down the back of my head: scalp wound. No concern there: my great mass of thick hair would both absorb blood and trigger coagulation. If any bones were broken, they didn't yet hurt, though I anticipated that once the shock wore off, I would be in considerable pain.

Bolas paced toward me across the cavern, smiling, which on a dragon indicates neither amusement nor friendliness. It's a display of how many large and pretty teeth he has, and how sharp they are. "Tezzeret, Tezzeret," he murmured, insufferably pleased with himself. "Tezzie—may I call you Tezzie?"

"Can I stop you?"

Almost too fast to be seen, his foreleg lashed out, and he seized me in his talons. "The list of what you can't stop me from doing is, I'm pretty sure, infinite."

To demonstrate the truth of this, he tossed me sharply upward, as a child might a ball. I bounced off the ceiling, got a mouthful of fresh blood when my teeth clacked together and ripped open my cheek, and then tumbled helplessly back into his grasp.

It occurred to me that Bolas might possibly have done all this simply for the pleasure of killing me personally.

"I admit and confess that you are larger than I am," I said, a bit thickly due to the blood and ragged scraps of the inside of my cheek. "You are stronger than I am. You can snuff my life with a thought. Can we skip the rest of your Intimidate the Naked Prisoner game and jump straight to what you want from me?"

His talons closed around me so tightly that black splotches bloomed in my vision. "But I *like* this game," he said. "What I like best about it is that it's not over until I get bored. By then you'll be free ..." He smiled again. "Or lunch."

He let up on the pressure, as I'd known he would; if he aspired to mutilate an unconscious body, he had no need to use mine. "How long have you been here?"

"Before just now?"

This answer meant either that he thought me stupid, or that he was playing stupid.

Stupider.

I decided to explain. "You didn't arrive by teleport—no air displacement. Nor did you shift in from the Blind Eternities—even you can't planeswalk swiftly or accurately enough to make that sophomorically dramatic entrance. Finally, I could smell you."

"Smell me?" One scaly brow ridge took on a deeper arch. "Really?"

"At first, I thought it was my armpits. I have two words for you, old worm." I held up a finger. "Dental." I folded that finger and lifted the next. "Floss."

I fully expected him to crush me until I passed out; or, alternatively, that he would start bouncing me off the walls again. Instead, he did what I was least expecting: he chuckled and set me down. He then lowered himself into what might have been, for a dragon, a comfortable position, looking for all the Multiverse as though he'd just stopped by for a friendly chat.

Bouncing off walls seemed to be a more attractive option.

I waited for him to speak. He seemed content to simply recline on the crystal floor, wrap his tail around his neck, and chuckle. A dragon's chuckle is very like rubbing two bricks together. Against your teeth. I didn't wait very long; if I wished to play patience games, I would have chosen an opponent younger than, for example, human civilization. "You need me for something."

"*Need* you? Don't insult me. It amuses me to employ you in a particular task. If you fail?" Bolas rather absently began to clean out his nose with the tip of his tail. "That will amuse me, too. If you succeed, you may be rewarded . . . with other tasks."

"What's in it for me?"

"The opportunity," Bolas said, "to obey me by choice."

"I've had better offers."

"It's not an offer," the dragon said. "It's a description of reality. Do you understand the difference?"

"Let's not start on what we do and do not understand," I said. "What *specifically* do you want of me?"

"Not yet. There is one feature of our new working relationship that I've really been looking forward to showing you."

"Are we back to Intimidate the Naked Prisoner already?"

"Oh, yes. Yes, we are, but with a new rule. As much as I enjoy bashing you into the rocks, the scent of your blood is making me peckish. And I can't be wasting my life showing up to slap you around every time you need it. I'd hardly have time for anything else. So I've brought a friend for you."

"I don't have friends."

"You do now," he assured me, in a cheerfully evil tone, like a demonic used-carriage salesman. "But don't worry, he won't hurt your reputation. And he doesn't have a reputation to worry about. I call him Mr. Chuckles."

"I'm bored already."

"I can fix that," the dragon said. "Though I suppose you're right—Mr. Chuckles *is* an undignified name. Let's call him Jest, shall we? And make him a doctor. Doctor Jest. Do you like it? Doesn't matter." This seemed to tickle the dragon in some private way, as though it referenced a joke only he knew. "Doctor Jest, be polite. Introduce yourself to Tezzeret."

This introduction took the form of a shattering blast of agony so overwhelming that I instantly collapsed. It felt like being hit by lightning while I was roasted alive in wasp venom. Over and over and over. I spasmed into convulsions, which did me the favor of banging my head into the floor hard enough to knock me unconscious.

Briefly.

"I know you're awake, Tezzie. Sit up."

My hand found yet another scalp wound. "Do I have to?"

"Unless you'd rather get the invitation from Doctor Jest."

"All right. All right, don't," I said, my voice husky. I had probably been screaming. I didn't remember. "Doctor Jest?"

"You don't think he's funny? I just about laughed my tail off."

"What is it?"

"He."

"He. Whatever. What is he?"

"You don't need to know," Bolas said. "All you need to know about your new best friend is that he has only two purposes in life. The first, as you've discovered, is to cause you pain. Unsupportable agony, in fact."

"Anytime I do something you don't like."

"Almost. I don't ask Doctor Jest to read my mind. So he has some leeway; he'll hurt you anytime he thinks you *might* be doing something I won't like—or that you might be about to. Get it?"

"So that 'obey me by choice' business was a joke."

"You never did appreciate my sense of humor."

"I get it," I said. "You don't have to show me again."

"The other thing Doctor Jest lives for is to make sure you don't do anything foolish, like try to run away from me. At your first inkling of attempting to planeswalk without my *express* permission, he will put you right back here. And I think you understand that here is a place you can't get out of on your own. Still with me?"

"I told you: I get it." I held up my right arm of meat. "Whatever it is you want me to do, I'll do it better if I'm not crippled. If this task is something you prefer I succeed at, give me back my arm."

"Well . . ." The dragon shrugged. "Can't really help you. Sorry. Best I can do is cut off the new one."

"Give me my real arm and I'll do it myself. I have before. Is watching me suffer your petty revenge more important than this task you *raised me from the dead* for?"

"Raised you from the dead? Don't flatter yourself. I undid some of Beleren's damage to your brain, that's all."

"Ah." At the time, that was all I could think to say.

"It's kind of complicated. You were dead enough for me; I'm not a philosopher. He just didn't bother to finish the job on your body. Probably thought you're not worth the trouble."

Not worth the trouble. "I'll have to thank him. Personally."

"If you find him, I wouldn't mind thanking him a bit myself. He'd make a better agent than you ever will."

"And my arm?"

"It was gone when I found you," he said. "Probably a lovely parting gift from Jace. Lying in some swamp on

Kamigawa, I'd guess—if he'd tried to take it with him, I'd have known. I did arrange for the new one. Don't you like it?"

"I'm not that attached to it."

The dragon gave me a cough's worth of courtesy laugh. "So ... wait, Tezzie. Really? You thought I raised you from the dead? You thought I took off your arm? Really?"

"I was reasoning from available evidence." And, I realized, my conclusion was accurate even though both of my premises were flawed; a curious phenomenon, and one that might bear further investigation.

Bolas shook his head pityingly. "I know you have an irrationally high opinion of yourself, but seriously, Tezzeret, get a clue. You're not *remotely* that important."

"Important enough for you to arrange all this."

"Tezzie, it's not about you. Really. You're here because I have spent a *very* long time setting up an exceedingly elaborate prank, and you're the only person I know who'll really appreciate it. You're audience. Nothing more. Well—let's say, you're an *educated* audience."

"I can hardly wait."

"You'll be impressed."

"There's always a first time."

"Satisfaction guaranteed or double your money back. Do you remember," Bolas said, mock coy, "when we first met?"

"Sure I remember. You wore red. The demons wore black." Even the threat of agony wasn't enough to make Bolas interesting. "Ah, the romance of Grixis when the corpse fungus blooms ..."

Bolas started scraping those bricks together again. "The question's relevant, Tezzie. We met not long after you murdered the Hieresiarch of the Seekers of Carmot."

My jaw locked; playtime was over. "I *murdered* no one."

"You ripped a sick old man's head off his shoulders and left it on the desk in his study," Bolas said. "What should I call it? Self-defense?"

"Call it a better death than he deserved," I said through my teeth. "Amalex Pannet was just another bandit."

"A bandit? That wheezy old fart? What did he ever steal from you?"

"Three years of service." Even now, well beyond a decade on, the wound was raw. "Three years of devotion. Three years I spent doing their scut work. Enduring their petty humiliations. Three years studying their useless pretend wisdom to show them I was worthy of learning their made-up fraud of a mystery. Three years of belief in their horseshit."

"You sound like you're angry all over again."

"Not again," I said. "Still."

"After all these years? Whatever happened to forgive and forget?"

"I don't forget, and I don't trade in forgiveness; I give none and I don't expect to get any. There are consequences," I said as evenly as I could manage, "for abusing my good nature."

Bolas snorted. "What good nature?"

I sought to replicate his too-many-teeth smile. "The *good* may be rhetorical. The consequences aren't."

"Oh, Tezzie, I'm *flattered*," Bolas said, splaying one taloned foot against his chest like a blushing debutante. "A threat? Just for me? You shouldn't have."

"It's not a threat, Bolas. It's a reminder." I could play his redefinition game, too—better than he could.

He pretended to find something interesting on the ceiling. "And what was your original disagreement with the Seekers of Carmot? You killed what, four of them?

A respectable body count, especially against an order of mages. Why so angry?"

"Don't pretend you don't know." My jaw ached with strain. "The Seekers were *your* damned hand puppets in the first place! You *invented* the whole festering *Order*!"

"Humor me." The dragon turned his eyes on me, and the fake insouciance evaporated, leaving only bleak malice. "I'm about to spring the punch line, Tezzie. This little prank that I've been setting up for years. Decades. Play along."

This did not sound like a friendly request.

"All right," I said. I managed a deep breath, and another, and got a better grip on my temper. "All right. I joined the Seekers of Carmot for only one reason: to learn the secret of etherium creation. I had considerable hope invested in them and their secret. I had spent more than ten years, with great effort and at considerable personal risk, to amass the etherium for my right arm."

I held up my meat arm and wriggled its fingers. 'My erstwhile right arm,' I corrected myself. The Seekers said they could create etherium. They had supposedly uncovered the secret during intensive study of the legacy of this imaginary Mad Sphinx of theirs, something to do with a mythological mineral called sangrite that can be infused with æther by using another mythological substance called *carmot*. Presto change-o, new etherium. If they'd been telling the truth, it would have revolutionized life on Esper."

"If," Bolas said, getting those bricks scraping again. "Go on."

"Only the Fellowship—the Fellows of the Arcane Council, the most advanced and holy adepts of the entire Order—were allowed to read and care for the book they called the Codex Etherium, where they had recorded everything they'd learned about Crucius, about his life and wisdom, his disappearance, his techniques of working etherium . . . and the secrets of carmot and sangrite. With the ancient sphinxian wisdom in the Codex, the Fellowship—alone among all the mages of Esper—could create etherium. So I joined them. I studied with them, trained with them, took their orders—I even mucked out their damned toilets—for *three years*. Because I believed. I did. I thought we were going to transform Esper into paradise. I even told—"

I bit down hard enough to draw fresh blood from my injured cheek. There was no reason to tell Bolas about my last visit to my father's hovel in Tidehollow—about how I had been practically babbling with enthusiasm, and what my father had said. . . .

Bolas didn't need to know.

"So?" the dragon said, his upper lip peeling back. "Tell me about this paradise, Tezzie."

I shrugged with a great deal more nonchalance than I felt. "There's nothing to tell. It was all lies. As you know. Every scrap and every shred. Lies."

The curve of his upper lip twisted toward a definite sneer. "Are you sure?"

"I was *there*, Bolas. I broke into the Sanctum. I read the Codex—no. I *opened* the Codex. There was nothing to read. *Nothing*. The whole rectum-blistering book was *blank*."

Bolas unwrapped his tail from his neck and stood, folding his wings and looking so happy that I knew whatever came next would be bad.

"So, Tezzie, nice story," he said. "Entertaining, and enlightening! You deserve a special surprise, and here it is—the task you will perform for me. You're going to find Crucius."

"Oh, is *that* all?" I could not restrain a snort. "Brilliant. Is that your genius punch line? Where should I start looking? Up your ass?"

MATTHEW STOVER

He laughed. "That's what I like best about you, Tezzie. Repartee, gold-plated vocabulary, culture and education and refinement ... Scratch that cultured Esper mage with one fingernail, and all you find underneath is just another filthy scrapper's spawnling. . . . What did they call you? Cave brats? You can take the boy out of Tidehollow, but ..."

"Who I am—what I was—has never been a secret. I have nothing to be ashamed of. Nothing."

"But you are anyway." Bolas had his too-many-teeth smile going again. "Now: Crucius."

"Haven't you been paying attention? He's not real—that whole Mad Sphinx business is just more of the Seekers' lies."

"How sure are you?"

"As sure as I—" The dragon's hideously smug grin stopped me in mid-reply. "I don't ... I mean, what are you saying?"

"There. See? *That's* the punch line."

I could only stare in dumb incomprehension.

"You don't get it? Joke's on you, cave brat. Crucius is real. He is a sphinx, and he did create etherium. He's a Planeswalker, just like us. Come on, Tezzie—did you really think *everything* the Seekers taught was a lie?"

"I ..." I couldn't think of anything intelligent to say. "I suppose I did."

"Now, *that's* comedy—but wait, there's more!" The dragon shrugged open his wings and spread them as if to say, *Look around, dumbass.* "Where do you think we are?"

"What do you mean?"

"This." He reached over, and with a casual yank he broke loose a chunk of the rose-glowing crystal bigger than my two doubled fists. He tossed it to me.

The chunk of crystal was heavy, far denser than it looked ... and in its depths, I could see little flaws, like tiny cracks spidering through the rock . . . and it was from these flaws that the glow came. . . .

A sort of existential horror began to squeeze my throat. "I don't understand. . . ." I looked up at Bolas. "I don't . . . What *is* this stuff?"

"Blood."

I blinked. "Blood?"

"Petrified dragon blood," Bolas said with a sort of savage satisfaction, as if he really had spent fifteen years putting together a prank just for me, and he was enjoying the payoff more than he'd ever dared hope. "This particular blood belonged to . . . Well, you don't need to know, do you? There was a serious dragon-war thing going on here some few years back, as you can probably guess."

"Jund," I said. "We're on *Jund.* . . ."

"These days, we say we're *in* Jund."

"What?"

"You'll find out. The important thing, here, is that dragon blood spilled in battle is different from what you'd get if, oh, you were somehow foolish enough to actually cut *me*, for example. It's a stress hormone thing, as well as all manner of esoteric metabolites left over from powering our various magical abilities. And here in Jund—in the high mountains, in fact, probably something relating to some unique quality of mana here—dragon blood leaves this interesting residue. That you are holding in your hand. Right now."

I could feel some of what made this crystal interesting—mana leaked from it, giving it the warmth and the light, but it was also *absorbing* mana from some unknown source. . . . It was *gaining* power, not losing it . . .

I couldn't raise my voice above a whisper. "What in the hells is it?"

"You're the Giant Brain, aren't you? So proud of your self-education. So tell me: what's the etymology of the word *sangrite*?"

"It's vedalken for *bloodstone*," I said reflexively.... Then, when I heard the words that had come from my lips, I found I could no longer breathe.

"You must be *joking* ..." I managed.

"Oh, I certainly am. But I'm not lying. It's all true. Those lies that you murdered all these people over? All *true*. Every single one. That's what makes it funny."

I had to sit down. "All ... *true* ... ?"

"Except for the part about them actually having the stuff. Other than that ... ? Yes. All true. Every rectum-blistering word. How's *that* for a prank?"

I could only stare.

Nicol Bolas, twenty-five-thousand-year-old dragon, Planeswalker, sometime god, destroyer of worlds, winked at me like a demented carnival barker. "How do you like me now?"

Before I could answer, he produced a globe of milky glass and cast it at my feet. It exploded with a binding flash ... and when I could see again, I was in Tidehollow.

TEZZERET
EXCHANGING UNPLEASANTRIES

I knew it was Tidehollow. I cannot mistake my birthplace for anywhere else in the Multiverse; the cavern slums below Vectis have a unique odor, compounded of mildew, rotten fish, feces, poverty, and despair. The air feels as if it's been breathed already—as if the distinctive odor is actually the product of someone's breath.

Everyone's breath.

I stood exactly as I had in the crystal cave: two flesh arms, one large chunk of sangrite, and no clothing at all.

And it was raining.

There was no wind—there almost never was—and the permanent drizzle of condensate that is Tidehollow's rain felt icy and tasted of mold. Thank Bolas for small favors; he'd put me in deep shadow on one of the twisty beast paths that serve for streets down here. He could just as easily have dropped me in the Grand Bazaar at noon. Or the Hegemon's bedchamber. I took my reasonably surreptitious arrival as a sign that Bolas, so far, actually wanted me to pursue his preposterous mission.

Probably.

Dragons as a species tend to be of uncertain temper, and Bolas in particular is uniquely opaque. Guessing his intention in any given sphere is a hazardous undertaking. Even his practical jokes can blossom into deadly serious schemes, and what appear to be substantive projects can, as I had just learned, turn out to be elaborate pranks.

Though, I reminded myself, the fact that Bolas *claimed* the Seekers of Carmot had been a prank didn't mean anything. With Bolas, nothing is ever wholly one thing or another.

He was playing some deeper game. He *always* plays some deeper game.

I suppose I am not entirely different. It struck me then, for example, that I should pay a visit to the Seekers, as I was in town anyway—which could be read as a flaw of sentiment, and perhaps it was. But that's not all it was.

First: clothing.

It should have been a small matter to summon mana sufficient for an illusion of clothing. In previous days, when I'd had my arm, I routinely wore illusory clothing of such sophistication that it was, for all intents and purposes, real. It was solid to the touch and interacted normally with sun, wind, and weather. I could carry small items in my pockets, hang pouches from my belt, and I could fine-tune it to provide warmth in cold climates, keep me cool in warm climes, or even function as armor against physical attack.

But that had been when I'd had my arm.

Now to gather the mana alone was time-consuming and difficult, despite my proximity to the deep mana wells of the Sea of Unknowing. Binding myself to them to replenish my reserves actually fatigued me instead of reviving me. Clearly, my newly reduced capacity would take some getting used to. The chill drizzle intensified, as it often did through the evening, and I was already shivering.

Not far away, however, a line of seastone topped with sharp slate served someone as a fence ... and it seemed this someone had been overly optimistic about the weather here, as several large tunics and one pair of breeches had been hung over the fence to dry.

The actual caverns of Tidehollow—about three-quarters of the slum's total extent—afford considerable protection from the weather on the Sea of Unknowing, but in exchange one must live in a state of perpetual gloom and permanent damp. The exhalations of each cavern's inhabitants inevitably condense on the stone, forming much of the drizzle that falls through every night. The owner of these articles had either forgotten them, or simply did not care enough to take them in from the rain. In either case, I had more need of them than did their owner.

But I could not make my hand close upon them.

I stood at that fence for an indeterminable interval; it seemed a very long time. I needed clothing, and here this was, laid out before me like an offering to honor my homecoming. There was not one reason in the Multiverse I should stand naked in the rain while in front of me lay perfectly appropriate clothing that had been forgotten or discarded here. Or abandoned. One might argue that I'd be doing these people a favor by helping them dispose of what they clearly considered to be trash.

It wasn't as though I haven't done worse. I've done much, much worse. Without hesitation. Many times. In my roster of criminal activity, this oh-so-petty theft would not merit even a glancing reference.

But still I could not make myself do it.

There at the improvised fence in the dark Tidehollow drizzle, I kept hearing my father's voice. "They don' has to *want* for them to take. Take is what they do. Take is their whole life."

To take these pitifully ragged, nearly valueless scraps of clothing would somehow break a vow I didn't remember

MATTHEW STOVER

swearing—a vow I'd made with all my heart. An oath sworn to my seven-year-old self.

Yes: I am sentimental, and sentiment is a flaw, and despite knowing full well how irrational it was, I found myself up against a wall of unexpected principle. I have never hesitated to steal from the wealthy, from the powerful, from beings who might crush me with a thought. Even my thefts from my own father happened only while he had absolute power over my life and my death. To pit my skill and wit against the greats of the worlds, with my life as the stake, is what gives my existence meaning.

To take from people who already have nothing is too vile, even for me.

I am not known for honesty, nor for fidelity. I don't think I've ever made a promise I haven't broken. Except, apparently, this one.

It seems that filthy little scrapper's brat is the only person I've ever met whom I am unwilling to betray.

I may very well have stood there all night but for a woman's voice, a harsh whisper in the darkness, that came from the dimly lamp-lit window of the stone hovel on the other side of the fence. "Hsst! Chammie! Theyz sumpin over th' fence! Chammie, look!"

An infant began to bawl, and a large shadow filled the tiny window. "Hoy!" The shout was a man's, hoarse and sudden and Tidehollow swampy. "Git out from there, sluice sucker! Garn! Fore I git out to shoo yer!"

For an instant I lingered, snared by memory. There had been a boy named Chammie among my gang of cave brats. . . . Small, ginger hair, a cast in one eye, he'd fight anyone, anytime, any odds. . . .

The shadow vanished from the window and reappeared rounding from the far side of the hovel, a pickaxe held high in both hands. "Garn! Git, you! Less yer after a taste a this!"

I faded back into the shadows, away from the fence. "Your clothes," I said softly, astonishing myself. "Your clothes are getting wet."

The shadow stopped, suddenly uncertain. "I come 'crost th' wall, I come back with yer blood on my axe," he said, trying for a gruff warning but sounding as though he spoke more to bolster his own nerve than to shake mine.

And had he crossed that wall . . .

He would have found himself facing a creature beyond his darkest imagining. All his strength, his raw courage that brought him out into the dark to put himself and his weapon between his family and the unknowable dangers of night in Tidehollow, all his fierceness, all his love, all his skill . . . In the end, these would only be the *why* of his death.

And *why* is nothing at all.

"You'll never see me again," I said. "Take in your clothes."

"Garn," he said, gathering the tunics and the pants with one hand while the other still held the pick high, and his eye never wavered from my dark silhouette. "Git yerself gone."

Having mana sufficient for a minor seeming, I wrapped shadows about myself and watched. I found myself, inexplicably, wanting desperately to talk to him—to ask if he'd been the Chammie I had known, to ask if he remembered the boy he and his friends had called Tezzeret . . . but Chammie is a name not uncommon in Tidehollow. Could this be the man who'd grown from the boy I'd known? The odds were ridiculously slim. I couldn't even see if he had the ginger hair.

And if it was he, and if he did remember me . . . what then?

Would I tell him of my life, of what it's like to be an artificer and a mage? A confidence trickster, a racketeer, and a slayer of bandits? Should I tell him of Nicol Bolas and how I had stolen the Infinite Consortium from the most powerful being in creation? Would I boast of walking worlds he could not imagine? And if I did, would he even understand, let alone believe me?

Would I want him to?

In the end, I had been only a shape in the darkness. He cast a last glance toward where he'd seen me fade away, then shook his head and went into his hovel with his clothing, there to be with his woman and their child.

I gathered my cloak of shadows around myself and went my way alone.

As I always have.

✳ ✳ ✳ ✳ ✳

Considering how much effort was required merely to drape myself in shadow, I decided I shouldn't depend on magic for dress and shelter. Fortunately, mana is only one variety of power; there are others, one of which I could put my hands on with only a little effort.

I keep stashes of local currency or items of value on every plane I've ever walked; every single city in which the Infinite Consortium does business has funds on deposit that only I can retrieve. These were placed against the eventuality that someone—say, for example, Jace Beleren—should pull the same trick as I had, and take the Infinite Consortium from me as I had taken it from Bolas. Admittedly, I had failed to credit Beleren with either the power or the ruthlessness to kill me outright. Short of that, there was always a chance I might be stranded somewhere, in the sort of trouble that can only be cured with cash.

Money is a fungible resource. Virtually the only thing of value that can't be purchased is mana itself . . . though with funds sufficient to interest particular sorts of mages and sorcerers, even mana can be bought. Since I had never anticipated returning to Tidehollow itself, my nearest stash was a considerable distance upslope, built into the rear wall of a small brewery in the mazy backways of Lower Vectis—and it was considerably more valuable than mere money.

I moved though the slums like a brinewraith, slipping from shadow to shadow, working my tortuous way up out of the caverns, avoiding crowds, brightly lit lanes, and heavily trafficked streets. At one point I was less than a fifteen-minute walk from my old neighborhood, where for all I knew my father might still live. I did not succumb to a passing urge to drop in.

I'm not *that* sentimental.

The brewery stood two stories taller than the surrounding buildings, which were primarily warehouses and handcraft workshops. At this hour only scattered windows showed lamplight, but here, above the caverns, the night was clear and the moon provided light enough for me to find my way. A wall of stone twice my height and topped with razorglass closed off the brewery's midden, and theoretically prevented rats and other local vermin from feasting upon the rotting remnants of the malted grain and dead yeast dumped here to drain.

The smell alone was a powerful deterrent to potential interlopers. Also, being who I am, the stash was concealed not only from mortal eyes, but from every magical sense I could replicate. The most powerful rhabdomant on Esper might lean against this wall for however long he might fancy and never get the faintest glimmer of what lay inside.

I paused only long enough to reach inside the wall with the fingers of my mind; to trip a hidden catch, where none but a mage could use it. A section of the wall above the plinth turned sideways just long enough for me to slip through. Wading through the chest-deep trub, the slimy high-protein residuum of the wort, was an unattractive but necessary step; here in the midden, the trub was allowed to drain much of its water through gratings into the sewers, after which it was scooped out and pressed into the yeast cakes that are the only protein source most Tidehollow folk can afford.

At the buttress, I spent a bit more of my available mana to press the trub away from the stone; to give myself room to work, and also to clear a spot to set down the chunk of sangrite Bolas had given me. I didn't know what dropping the sangrite into the trub might do, and I had no desire to find out.

There was no sign of any kind that a treasure might lie within the wall. This particular treasure had, in fact, been built into the wall at its first construction, when the brewery was expanded some seven or eight years ago— the brewery being a local venture financed and partly owned by the Infinite Consortium. Having built my career on etherium salvaged from inadequately concealed caches, I had made quite certain that this could not be found by anyone who did not already know it was there.

I pressed the flat of my left hand against the block I knew to be hollow, and cast my mind within it, allowing the device within to slowly define itself within my consciousness. Once it had, I tapped the device itself for the power necessary to recover it; being cast of pure etherium, it was a generous source. Though at clockworking I am not even competent, much less great, I know a trick or two; creating a localized hypertemporal field in an inanimate object is no large feat. Only seconds later, the stone collapsed to powder.

But as I reached for the device, my hand burst into flame—of a sort. I saw a flare of scarlet fire, and I felt my flesh char and peel back from the bone . . . but my instinctive recoil drew back my hand, uninjured. Not even smoking. And I had seen the flare and the flames only from my left eye.

The source of the pain was obvious. "Doctor Jest," I murmured grimly. "Interesting. It seems you're hooked into my optic nerves in addition to my touch/pain network."

"WOW. YOU *ARE* A GIANT BRAIN, AREN'T YOU?"

I clapped the hand now to my left ear. The roar had been so overpowering that had it been actual sound, I should have been bleeding from a ruptured eardrum. That I was not, and that I had heard the titanic roar only with my left ear, made its source obvious.

"You can talk."

"SO CAN YOU."

Flinching, I could not help pressing my hand more tightly to my ear . . . though of course it could do no good at all. Bolas must have given this "Doctor Jest" access to my entire sensory system; the incredible roar had to be the result of direct neural stimulation, in very much the same fashion as had the pain. "Um, can you speak a bit more softly?"

"How's this?" This time the voice was only that of a large man standing too close and shouting.

I took a moment to catch my breath and settle the trip-hammer race of my heart. "That's . . . tolerable. Even softer would be better. Um, hello."

"We've already met."

"I recall," I said grimly. "How should I call you?"

"Anything but late for breakfast."

My hand went from my ear to my forehead. "You did *not* just say that. Please. You didn't."

"My friends call me Doc. You can call me Doctor Jest."

I had to sit down. "Let's go about this in something like an organized fashion, can we? So. You are conscious; are you a living creature, as opposed to a device?"

"Yes. Nineteen. And I'm smaller than a bread box. Whatever in the hells a bread box is. That one's free."

"Are you a naturally occurring creature? That is, you are not a homunculus, golem, nor other form of constructed life?"

"Yes. Eighteen. Wait—no, I'm not. Still eighteen. But . . . aw, crap. Truth is, I don't know. I'm still kinda new at this consciousness business."

"Really?"

"Sure. Why would I lie?"

Say rather, I thought, why would you tell the truth? "Why do I hear you only with my left ear?"

"Shrug. I might screw something up."

"Did you just say *shrug*?"

"How am I supposed to gesture? Smoke signals?"

"All right," I said. My head was pounding, and it wasn't because of Doctor Jest. Well, it was, but not in the usual fashion, so . . . "All right, wait. Let me think."

"I won't hold my breath."

"What?"

"Because I *can't*, dumbass."

"Look, can you . . . Can you please just be *quiet* for a moment? Not very long, I promise. Please."

"Aww, you don't like me anymore. . . ."

"Please," I said. What else could I do? To beg was my sole remaining option short of bashing my head into the stone until I lost consciousness and drowned in the trub.

Though that option became more attractive with every passing second.

After a few moments of careful questioning, during which I was tempted to kill myself only three times, my—our—situation began to come clear.

Doctor Jest was a fully conscious individual, who inhabited—or had some sort of magical bond with—my sensory

TEST OF METAL

nerves. He had exceptional control over them, though it seemed their activity remained largely electrochemical, as it is by nature—he spoke only through my left auditory nerves because misuse might cause nerve damage and deafness, and he was, as he'd said, still exploring the parameters of his power.

Beyond that, he knew—or believed, which amounted to the same thing, under the circumstances—that the binding that joined us could be unbound only by Bolas himself. His fate was linked with mine, since Bolas would have no reason to do either of us any favors until we finished his job. And any others that the dragon might think up in the meantime. Our fates were inextricably linked; whatever happened to me would happen to him as well.

I also discovered, to my considerable relief, that he could not read my thoughts. I was able to keep private my suspicion that Doctor Jest had no separate existence at all, being nothing more than a phenomenon of the alteration of my nervous system accomplished by Bolas in the process of repairing what Jace had done to my brain. I wouldn't put it past the dragon, for example, to have built Doctor Jest into this meat arm he had inflicted on me.

We also determined why gathering sufficient power for any major effect seemed so difficult. Yes: ripping away my right arm had left me magically crippled—but that wasn't the whole story. It seemed that while Doctor Jest had some not-inconsiderable powers at his command, he did not draw mana directly, but instead existed as a vampirelike mana parasite, living off my own reduced reserve.

"Another gift from Bolas," I muttered.

"Yeah, I hate that scaly monkey dunker," said Doctor Jest. "You know what he needs? A good hard boot to the nads. Do him a universe of good."

"I don't think he *has* nads," I replied glumly.

"Can we try anyway?"

"You're not thrilled to be working for him."

"Is anyone? Is there a worse boss in the Multiverse?"

"If we ever find one, don't tell Bolas," I muttered. "He'd never resist proving us wrong."

"So, how're we gonna get him?"

"Excuse me?"

"Come on," Doctor Jest said. "You're not the type to take this kind of rumpthumpin' lying down."

"You've been conscious less than three hours, and you're already an authority on my type?"

"You're planning something," he insisted. "You gotta be planning *something*."

"And if I am," I said, "why would I tell you?"

"Aw, c'mon, Tezzie! I'm on your side! We're in this together, shoulder to shoulder—ah, you know what I mean. Man to—well, to whatever I am."

"Don't call me Tezzie."

"No wonder you got no friends."

"I'm not interested in your friendship."

"Aw, c'mon . . . I'll let you call me Doc," he offered.

Painfully aware—and I do mean *painfully* aware—that while no power at my command could cause Doctor Jest the slightest discomfort, he could make of my existence an endless carnival of suffering, I decided to compromise. "Tezz," I said reluctantly. "You can call me Tezz."

"All right! And we're buds, right? For real. I'm your best friend?"

I sighed. "You're my only friend, Doc."

"That's sad. Really. Man, do you have a crummy life or what?"

"If I do," I said through my teeth, "you're not making it any better."

"Aww. That hurts, Tezz. Really."

I decided to change the subject. Any discussion of *hurt* with Doc would potentially be cataclysmically one-sided. So I picked myself up—hmp, I suppose I picked *us* up to my feet—and stepped closer to the hollow stone that contained my device. "Doc?"

"Yeah, bud? Er, chum, you think? Best pal?"

"Doc, why did you stop me?"

"Huh?"

"When I reached for the device, you made me feel like my hand was on fire. Why?"

"*Why?* What am I, an idiot?"

With considerable exercise of self-discipline, I resisted offering an answer. "Why don't you want me to pick it up?"

"Because whatever happens to you, happens to me," he said slowly, overenunciating as though explaining the obvious to a small, not especially bright, child. "Can't you see that whole friggin' thing is just one big trap?"

"Of course *I* can," I said. "I built it."

Being a mechanist, when I went to hide a substantial amount of etherium, I had seen no reason to stash it as bullion or bars . . . and I have always had a knack for small, intricate automata. I had fashioned the entire stash into a trap—and a rather nifty one, if I do say so myself.

This trap would fishhook the hand of anyone other than me at first touch, and insinuate a network of hair-thin etherium wires transdermally, to hijack the thief's nervous system and magically override the voluntary motor nerves, inflicting permanent paralysis. This would leave the thief alive, awake, and aware, but unable to do anything save, oh, for example, die of thirst. Or drown in a particularly large dumping of trub. Or meet some other unpleasantly lingering death.

No: the pertinent fact here was not that it was a trap, but that Doc could *see* it was a trap. My nifty little device no more resembled a trap than it did a clod of dung. Even an exceedingly skilled mechanist would have needed hours, if not days, to detect the hazard I had built into it—and would most likely have fallen victim to it in the process.

This meant that Doc had access to some portion of my memory, or that he could perceive things on a level that I could not. Or both. Any of these eventualities was interesting, and all were potentially significant. "How did you know?"

"Well, it's *obvious*. Isn't it?"

"Not to anyone but you."

"Huh. No kidding?"

"Doc," I said with uncharacteristic sincerity, "you have unplumbed depths of talent."

"You're welcome. That was a compliment, right? Right?"

I didn't answer. My attention had been captured by a potential feature of the trap that had never struck me before. After all, if the device could hijack its victim's motor nerves, it might do all manner of interesting things. It suddenly became obvious how I could tune it to hijack someone's whole form and function—to make of its victim an unwilling telemin, acting wholly in my control—or as directed by the device, because I now saw also how I might imbue it with a consciousness of its own . . . to make it into, for example, a mechanical Doctor Jest. It was obvious. It wouldn't even be difficult.

Curious that I'd never seen it before.

Perhaps among all the changes inflicted upon my form and function by Jace and Bolas, some few might have to be counted as positive. It was a sobering thought. Did I actually have something to *thank* Bolas for?

Or worse, to thank Jace Beleren for?

Distracted by this unpleasant possibility, I somewhat absently deactivated my device, only to discover there had been something I must have missed; I felt a tiny whisper of a mana release that had not been part of my design.

"What was *that*?" Doc said. "Did you see that? Was that supposed to happen?"

"No."

"Is it a problem?"

"Yes."

Above us on the wall, the stone began to burn.

"A bad kind of problem?"

"Potentially fatal."

I had underestimated Jace again. Only now did it occur to me that anything I had known—*anything*—he could have taken from my mind when he attacked me. Including the location of my local etherium stash.

The burning stone sputtered and flared, white-hot now, so intense I had to shield my face with my useless right arm. The stone began to melt, dripping like hot wax, and where these droplets struck, what they struck ignited with unnatural intensity.

"We should be running away, right?" Doc said. "Why aren't we running?"

"Fire is not Jace's strength," I said. "He's a mind ripper."

"That's good news, right?"

"No."

Where the stone burned away, the hole in the wall didn't open onto the brewery. Through the hole I could see black clouds on fire, burning above a volcanic cone that spilled white-hot lava.

I was about to find out just how worried Jace had been about my possible return.

First through the fire gate came a glossy, jet-black lobsterish pincer bigger than I am, which latched on to the unburned stone, followed by another that did the same. . . . Where they touched, the stone went red and soft, and from the joints of the pincers glared flesh that burned white as the sun. Because these claws did not belong to any variety of lobster, and I no longer needed to see the rows of compound eyes that were to follow, I intended to actively avoid seeing the upcurving jointed metasoma with a white-hot barb the size of a greatsword.

I am not, as a rule, given to either profanity or vulgarity, but when confronted at close range by hippopotamus-size scorpions whose very flesh is white-hot rock, I might be forgiven for indulging in both.

"Holy *shit* . . ."

Apparently Jace had been very worried indeed. Worried enough to have signed up at least one very, very serious pyromancer.

"That's bad, isn't it? I can tell it's bad. What are we going to do?"

"We? Nothing. You're going to shut up," I said, "and I am going to run like hell."

TEZZERET
THE HOME FIRES, BURNING

Being about to die did not strike me as sufficient reason to abandon either of my treasures. So it was that I undertook to flee with my etherium trap in one hand and my hunk of sangrite in the other. Even without having replenished my mana reserve, I can do surprising things with etherium by using its innate energy to power its action. Reasoning that the least flammable thing in the entire neighborhood was the neck-deep trub in the midden where I stood, I decided to put as much of it as I possibly could between myself and the magma scorpion.

I took a deep breath and went in headfirst. As I clawed my way blindly downward, my fingers found the grating of the sewer drain—a grillwork of chrome steel, set in cement. Encouraged not only by Doc yammering in my ear—"What are you doing? Are you crazy? It's right up *there*! Why aren't you running?"—but also by the sudden impact of something large and heavy landing on the surface of the trub above me, I engaged the etherium device with my mind.

Chrome steel is hard, but even the hardest metal can be overcome by the proper application of force. Working by feel, I brought out from the etherium an assemblage of gears, ratchets, and levers. Jamming levers through the holes in the grating, I then turned the device's innate

MATTHEW STOVER

mana wholly to working those gears and ratchets and levers to pry apart the bars of the grating as swiftly as possible . . . because the trub was becoming unpleasantly warm, and I could hear, through the slimy mass itself, a series of minor detonations, which I took to be the steam blasts generated as the scorpion struck blindly downward with its tail barb—a stinger made out of white-hot rock. Again and again and again.

I managed to avoid picturing what that stinger would do to my flesh.

With a squeal that came only dully to my ears, the bars gave way. Well-lubricated by the rotting, yeasty mass around me, I managed to slide through headfirst, and tumbled ten or twelve feet until I hit the sewage stream, which was only a few inches deep. It did nothing to improve the stench.

Entirely the opposite, in fact.

I pulled myself up from the muck and took a quick look around. Witchlight globes were strung every few dozen yards, enabling me to see a lot of straight tunnel to either side, and very little else.

"Hey, not bad," Doc said brightly. "*Now* we run."

"Not yet."

"Yes yet," he said, and punctuated his reply with a sensation that felt as I imagine it might if someone were to rip off my testicles. Slowly.

The pain dropped me to my knees. "If I pass out, we both die."

The scorpion's blazing stinger jabbed downward through the drain, unleashing a burst of steam and greasy smoke. "And dying is different from what's about to happen exactly how?"

"You have to trust me."

"Trust *you*? Never kid a kidder, chum."

And somehow when he said it, *chum* sounded less like the word for pal than it did the word for the rotting fish guts one uses to attract sharks. "This is my hometown. I know every inch of it. That knowledge is the only chance we have."

The pain vanished. "So what are we waiting for?"

The stinger struck again and again, and the sewer began to fill with smoke. I extended a hand—my right, from reflex, even though I couldn't help flinching when it entered my field of view—and down through the drain and out of the smoke came my device, sprinting along on spider legs. I had it leap up and wrap itself around my arm, and then I passed the chunk of sangrite over to it. From there it was a simple matter of encasing the sangrite in etherium, and arranging the whole thing to make a sort of yoke, or a harness, holding the sangrite at my back and leaving my hands free.

This took barely a second, but in that time the cement around the drain burned away, and the top curve of the sewer collapsed, dropping a very large, very hot arthropod into the sewage, which did nothing at all to improve its temper; nor did the instant blast of superheated steam that very nearly blew it back up to street level. Catching itself at the rim, it started toward me along the ceiling, leaving a trail of burning footprints.

This was when two more of the creatures clambered down through the hole and clattered along after the first.

"Three?" I said. "Really?"

I could just imagine Jace whipping up this little trick with his pyromancer, whistling cheerfully as they worked, thinking *You know, one indestructible monster just isn't enough. Better double the order.*

And one to grow on.

"Um, hey there, Native Son?" Doc chirped in my ear. "Are we running yet?"

"Yes," I told him. "Yes, we are."

And we did.

✳ ✳ ✳ ✳ ✳

Pelting along the sewer tunnel as fast as my legs could carry me, I very soon discovered a piece of compelling evidence in favor of Bolas's story that I had not, in fact, been raised from the dead: I found myself gasping and stumbling with fatigue in under a minute—very like how I might if I'd spent a span of time getting no exercise more strenuous than breathing. I was forced to funnel mana into my legs, which burned my limited reserve even faster.

And behind me clattered the magma scorpions. They were gaining.

"How much do you know about these things?" Doc hissed in my ear.

"Not . . . a lot." I took a sharp turn into a side tunnel that sloped more sharply downward. Running downhill was vastly easier, and I picked up speed. "They're not . . . local."

"Really? There's something you *don't* know everything about? Stop a second—I gotta mark my calendar." Doc, having no need to breathe, kept up a running commentary that made thinking even more difficult than being chased by indestructible monsters.

"Magma scorpions," I said between gasps of breath. "Shells . . . unbreakable. And *hot* . . . set afire . . . anything they touch. The barb . . . venom . . . magma . . . temperature of a planetary core . . ."

"Oh, awesome. So if they don't grab us and burn us to death, we get spiked with planetary core gunk in the back? That'll leave a mark."

"No," I wheezed. "Steam burst . . . blow me to pieces. Nothing left . . . to mark."

"*That's* comforting. Um, hey, it sounds like they're gaining. Are they gaining?"

The growing heat on my backside told me all I needed to know. "Want me to . . . stop and *look*?"

"Never mind."

It seemed, however, that our impending mutual demise was not enough to make him be quiet. "They're still coming. They're still *gaining*. Don't they get tired? I mean, they're really just giant bugs, right?"

I did not have the breath to explain to Doc that while ordinary bugs—arthropods in general—are cold-blooded, and thus tire quickly when they overheat, magma scorpions are exactly the opposite; the heat generated by exertion makes them *stronger*. They tire only when they stop, which they weren't going to do until I was on the well-done side of dead. Not to mention that they are an apex predator in their ecosystem, fearless, that their brains are larger than mine, and that they are, generally speaking, as intelligent as a medium-size dragon. And nearly as tough; there are only six ways to kill them, of which five would remain out of reach for too long to be useful.

"Um, hey," Doc said. "They sound different."

"What?" I was too busy running to waste time listening.

"Still gaining—but down a third." Doc, it seemed, could use my nervous system more precisely than I could. File the data.

I stifled a curse that I didn't have breath for anyway. "That means . . . there're only two . . . there."

"That's *good* news, right?"

"They're not . . . *bugs*," I rasped. "The other . . . gone ahead to *cut us off* . . ."

"Oh. That's bad."

I declined to comment on his penchant for stating the obvious, because to do so would make me guilty of exactly that.

"So what do we do?"

"I'm open . . . to *suggestions.* . . ."

"Ohhh, sure, *now* he wants my advice. Yeah, let's ask the guy who's been alive for, like, three *hours* to come up with a plan. Great idea!"

Two hundred yards ahead, the roof of the sewer burst into flame, burning so hot and fast that molten gobbets of burning cement cascaded into the sewer, blasting a wall of superheated steam toward us.

"Can't you *fight* them?"

"I can," I panted grimly. "Just not today."

"So what's the plan?"

"Same . . . as before. You . . . shut up and I . . . run."

If there are guardian spirits of fortune somewhere in creation, they must have been smiling upon me then; just ahead was a dump valve.

When hurricanes blow in across the Sea of Unknowing, the huge surge in rainfall can overfill the standard sluice pits around Tidehollow in less than an hour. The sewers are designed with dump valves that can be triggered from the city service center above to divert some of the billions of gallons of water and sewage that otherwise might drown the slums altogether. This was not from any concern for the residents, but only to avoid poisoning the fisheries that are Vectis's main source of protein.

"What? You're *stopping*? Why are you stopping?"

"Shut *up*."

I reached up to the gearing of the valve control and sent a shining thread of etherium up along my arm and gave it half a second to spread through the mechanism. I yield to none in my skill with devices; what another being can design, I can subvert, which I proved by causing an earsplitting screech of half-rusted metal as the valve into the dump shaft ground itself open. The etherium was warm to the touch as it trailed back up my arm, almost as though pleased with a job well done.

"Great work!" But when I looked down, Doc discovered why it was called a dump shaft as opposed to, say, a dump tunnel—it is, in fact, vertical. "Um . . . really? Isn't that kinda *steep*?"

"Yes," I said, and dived headfirst into darkness.

Doc's reply, "Yeee*aaaAAAHHHH*!" screeched in my ear as we hurtled downward, free-falling for some seconds. This was enough time for me to recover a bit of my breath, which would become vital, according to my best estimate, in a minute or so. Give or take ten seconds.

"Hey . . ." he said uncertainly when he finally gave up screaming. "There aren't any witchlight globes in here, right?"

"Yes."

"Then where is that light coming from?" He was referring to the rosy glow that now began to catch highlights on the shaft walls.

I said, "Where do you think?"

"Oh, come *on*! Really?"

"Yes."

"I'm starting to see why nobody likes you."

"Not now," I said, tucking my knees while I reached out and brushed the shaft wall with my fingertips, just enough to flip myself feet-downward. "This is going to hurt."

"See, that's *exactly* what I'm—"

This was as much as he managed to get out before we hit the slant at the bottom of the vertical shaft. I was wrong about it hurting; the impact was a shattering blast that whited out my vision for a second or two. It would hurt later. After I came out of shock.

If I lived that long.

The slant was wet and covered with thick oilmoss, which meant that we slid along it not much more slowly than we had fallen. I had plenty of time to peer backward and see the following magma scorpion hit the slant—and set the oil moss instantly ablaze.

Flames licked down toward us even faster than we could slide "What, *fire*?" Doc said. "You knew it was gonna catch fire?"

"No." I chalked it up to the exigencies of planning a clever escape while running for one's life. "Take it as a lesson to shut up when I need to think."

"It's not much of a lesson if learning it *kills* me!"

"We're not dead yet," I said. "Chum."

At which point we burst down from the shaft through a cavern ceiling to the terminal chute of the spillway, whose semi-radical angle was shallow enough to send us skipping across the surface of the semicoagulated goo of the collection pool instead of burying us in it.

"Hey, not bad," Doc said as our spinning slowed. "Maybe you are a Giant Brain after all."

"I believe the appropriate phrase is, under the circumstances," I said, "you ain't seen nothin' yet."

I turned so that I could start sculling us toward the shore, just as several tons of burning magma scorpion hurtled out of the terminal chute. Straight for us.

"This was your *plan*?"

"Yes."

"You are *completely*—"

The rest of his assessment was lost as the magma scorpion splashed down into the collection pool; instead of skipping across the surface as we had, the magma

scorpion detonated with the titanic BOOM of a catastrophic volcanic event. White-hot stone went everywhere,
and entire segments of scorpion armor flew shrieking like
a lobster in the pot through the dank Tidehollow gloom. A
huge swelling shock wave picked us up and hurled us onto
the bank. I scuttled back from the muck, which had now
caught fire with an odor very much like one would expect
from well-fermented burning sewage.

"Did *you* do that?" Doc sounded awed. "Sweet mother
of petrified dingleberries . . . ! How did you *do* that?"

"That steam-burst effect," I said with what I felt was,
under the circumstances, entirely justified satisfaction,
"works both ways."

"Wow. I mean, *wow*. Good plan!"

"Thank you." I jogged away from the collection pool
even as people from the surrounding hovels began to
stream out to see what the noise had been.

"Where we going now?"

"Tide caves."

"Tide caves?"

"They lead to open sea."

"You're saying—"

"I'm not saying. Here, watch." I stopped and looked
back. In the uplight from the burning collection pool,
I could clearly see one magma scorpion scuttling sideways across the cavern wall below the dump shaft. Even
as I looked, the other one came out and went the other
direction.

"I believe what they're going for is called, excuse the
expression," I said, "a pincers maneuver."

"Ah, I, ah. . ." Doc stammered. "Um, all right. We can
run now."

"Thank you." But when I started to run, the battering
I'd taken these past few minutes finally announced its

presence. Vigorously. Though it didn't hurt nearly as much as a shot from Doctor Jest, it was enough to slash my foot speed to a limping stumble. "Can you do anything about the pain?"

"Without doing permanent damage? Only this," he said, and my whole back from neck to heels burst into flame. Metaphorically, but nonetheless vividly.

This cleared up my running problem admirably. Not that I was in any way grateful for Doc's assistance.

"The human pain system," he said conversationally, "is an interesting place. Ever notice that when you break your toe, you forget all about your headache?"

I did not reply, as I needed all my breath for screaming.

"Huh, wait—how's this?" Instead of being on fire, I felt as though a colony of soldier ants had taken up residence inside my spine and was currently exploring its new territory. Thousands of ants marching along under my skin, along my veins, burrowing into my muscles, crawling around the inside of my ears. . . .

"Tolerable," I said through clenched teeth. At least it didn't hurt.

"Itching uses the same nerves as touch/pain—that's why scratching works, did you know that?"

"Yes, I did," I said. "And thank you so much for mentioning *scratching*."

But at least we were mobile, which was fortunate, given that the magma scorpions had already rounded the collection pool and were nearing flat ground behind us. I ran with not only every ounce of my own energy, but with all the mana I had left. There was no point saving it for later until I found some indication that I would have anything resembling a "later."

The curious residents of the neighborhood gave back as I ran toward them. It seemed no one was interested in stopping, or even getting significantly in the way of, a large naked running man covered in fermented shit.

"Aren't you gonna warn people?"

"Of what?"

"Uh, giant, killer rock-bug monsters that set everything on fire?"

"I believe," I said, "the situation is self-explanatory."

This was amply demonstrated as people around us began to not press away from us so much as run after us, presumably on the assumption that having survived one of the beasts, I might actually know where I was going. This was a development of which I thoroughly approved, as a large mob of people at my back might slow the magma scorpions enough to let me reach a sculler skiff before they could overtake me—which was why I was astonished and no little amount dismayed to find myself stopping and turning back to the swelling crowd that followed.

"They're after *me*!" I shouted with all of my considerable natural lung power. Amplification would have expended mana that I could not spare. "Stay out of their way and they will not harm you! They're after *me*!"

They must have gotten the message, as they scattered in all directions, leaving me with a very clear view—vividly illuminated by the great swathes of fire that roared up from everything they touched—of the two remaining monsters coming after me faster than ever.

I turned and, excuse the expression, streaked away.

"Oh, sure, when *I* want to warn people, the *situation* is *self-explanatory*—"

"Shut up."

There was very little I could do to evade them here in Tidehollow, besides which they were almost certainly tracking the etherium that had triggered their summoning—etherium I had no intention of abandoning.

MATTHEW STOVER

φ

76

Ever. My best remaining idea was to run tiny hair-thin wires out of the etherium on my back, and stab them into my hamstrings and buttocks, using the etherium's innate energy to add strength to my failing muscles and send us along at a very brisk clip.

"This is good. This is *fast*," Doc said. "How come we didn't do this before?"

"Because you never stayed quiet long enough for me to think of it."

"Awww..."

"If you shut up now, I might be able to gimmick a way to fly."

"Seriously? Because that'd be *really*—"

"Shut up."

He actually did, for a brief interval, during which I did not endeavor to think up a way to fly; I was too busy trying to think of a way to kill him.

All too shortly, I ran out of ground. A lightning detour during a second or two that I was out of their line of sight sent me skidding down a steep and slippery path that ended in a salt-caked bank of an utterly, utterly still pool. Only a few yards beyond the shore, the pool and the cavern overhead faded off into dank and impenetrable night. The bank around me was featureless save for the sculler's cleat of worn-smooth moonstone, glowing with a soft pearlescent light that did nothing to hold back the gloom.

"Awesome!" Doc said. "Now all we have to do is swim—"

"No." I clapped a hand to the back of my head, and as I had expected, the exertions of the chase had reopened the scalp wound with which Bolas had so considerately supplied me. I took the handful of my blood and smeared it into the slightly concave summoning dish on the top of the sculler's cleat, hoping that the admixture of sewage wouldn't interfere with the cleat's magic.

Then there was nothing to do but wait.

"We're not swimming? I can *make* you—"

"Do you know what sluice serpents are?"

"Are they as bad as magma scorpions?"

"Not remotely. But they are entirely bad enough to kill me."

"You mean us."

"There are also three distinct species of kraken that use these tide caves as their spawning ground. Kraken are viviparous, and the young are born hungry."

"Uh. Yeah. I get it. We can wait."

The clatter of armored feet announced the approach of the magma scorpions even before the tunnel showed the light of the fires they left in their wake. I waded out into the tide pool as deep as I dared, salt water doing such unkind things to my varied array of cuts and scrapes that for a moment, the sting overwhelmed the itching.

The magma scorpions moved toward me from the tunnel mouth with gratifying caution. One stayed on the bank, scuttling back and forth to cut off escape in that direction, while the other went to the cavern wall and began to climb.

"Where's *he* going?"

"She."

"You can tell? How can you tell?"

I glanced up to the erosion-pitted limestone of the cavern's ceiling. "That's where she's going."

"What's she think she's gonna do from up there?"

"Fall on us."

"Um . . ."

"Summoned creatures usually accomplish their bound task or die in the attempt. Or—like this one—both."

MATTHEW STOVER

"Uh . . . can you *un*bind them? Send them home?"

"Not today." To avoid more whining, I offered a scrap of hope. "But this kind of trigger-based summoning has a fixed amount of mana attached to it. Without a mage to maintain their presence, they'll return to their own plane when the fixed mana is exhausted."

"Which will be when?"

"No matter what everyone says about me," I said, "I don't actually know *everything*."

"Oh, ha ha. Ha. So what's the plan?"

"You need me to say it again?" A sudden stabbing crick in my neck forced my head back and turned my face toward the ceiling, where the magma scorpion was picking its way in our direction. "Stop that."

The crick only intensified. "I want to see."

"I need my eyes for something else right now."

"More important than dying?"

"How about *instead* of dying?"

"Fine." The pain vanished. "I'm in."

"Thanks so much." I turned away from the bank and, as I had hoped, caught sight of a silent, spectral shape approaching through the gloom, gaining solidity as it came. Having a great deal less to fear from scullers than most, I have availed myself of their services in the past. Familiarity, however, did nothing to put me at ease as the creature poled its skiff toward us out of the darkness.

The skiff had witchlight globes hanging from both its upcurved prow and similar stern, but while these lights were easily seen, they did not actually illuminate the shroud of shadows within the craft. The sculler itself was visible only as a thin drape of hooded cloak in the darkness. Its sleeves draped along skeletally thin arms fleshed with corpse-pale skin as it leaned on its pole to drive the skiff forward.

"Uh, did I miss something?" Doc said dubiously. "Did we get killed already and just now woke up in Grixis?"

I extended an arm, and the sculler bent his course toward me. Lacking leisure for haggling, I wasted no time in clambering aboard.

The shadowy cloak turned the infinite black of its hood toward me, and one clawlike hand held the skiff pole vertical, motionless in the water. I extended my right hand for the creature's inspection, but the sculler did not react.

"What's going on? Why isn't it moving?"

"They don't start until they're paid." I touched my left eye. "We're negotiating the price."

"This is negotiating?"

I touched my temple with a single finger. "They don't speak. No one knows if they understand language, or even hear. They don't make noise of any sort. A habit you should cultivate."

The sculler did not move.

Two fingers, and still no response.

A glance back to check on the magma scorpion's progress gave no reassuring news; even though the monster was picking its way with great caution, we had perhaps a minute.

I put four fingers against my temple.

"What do these buggers charge?"

"Something of value."

"Erm."

"Something of value to me. Or I would have offered *you* already." I laid my whole hand against my temple.

"What's with the fingers?"

"I'm offering memories."

"Memories?"

"Five of them. There are some experiences I cherish," I said. Few enough, but some. "It doesn't appear to be interested. Nor in my eye, and it doesn't want my right arm."

MATTHEW STOVER

"Neither do you."

"Which is the problem." Another glance back, and the magma scorpion twitched its metasoma at me, squeezing a handful of its burning venom from its barb. With a jerk of its tail, it flicked the white-hot glob of magma in my direction.

The venom fell a few yards short. The steam burst it created rocked the skiff.

"How about some of that etherium?" Doc was starting to sound desperate.

"I'll die first," I said.

"I can *make* you—"

"You can make me pass out. Then we both die. Good plan."

The magma scorpion hurled another glob of venom, which blew apart when it hit the surface of the water and managed to splatter enough of itself up onto the bulwark to start a small fire on the far side. And, apparently understanding that we were not going to be escaping back into Tidehollow, the other magma scorpion had taken to the cavern wall as well, and was working its way toward us rather more swiftly than had its companion.

"Wait—how about the *sangrite*? You've been hauling that chunk of petrified blood from the hells to Grandma's and back again—it *has* to be important to you!"

I reached behind my neck and had the etherium deliver the sangrite to my hand, which was as close to admitting he'd had a good idea as I intended ever to come.

As its dull rose glow warmed my hand, the sculler—for the first time in my experience—showed interest in an item before it was even offered. It released its pole and took a step toward me, leaning forward to get a better look. The sculler extended one long-fingered, skeletal hand, as though the creature wished to feel the warmth of the sangrite with its own withered flesh.

This gave me considerable confidence in my bargaining position.

The etherium of my trap device had never been tempered or treated for hardness; it would be useless to try and form it into a blade capable of cutting the crystal. However, the near-infinite ductility of the metal offered an option. One of the hair-thin wires that had been feeding strength to my legs detached itself and quested over the surface of the crystal until it found one of the glowing flaws. There, I had it insinuate itself into the crystal, forcing more and more metal into the flaw until the sangrite cracked, calving a sharp-pointed shard roughly the size and shape of my forefinger.

The sculler's hand struck like a snake, snatching the shard from the air. It shook its other hand free of its cloak and cupped the crystal with both, bringing it up before the shadow gape of its hood as though entreating the blessing of a holy relic.

A magma bomb now came from the other monster, and this one managed to strike full on the stern, setting the entire rear of the skiff on fire. The sculler didn't seem to notice; it stood enraptured by the sangrite. I stood, grabbed the sculler's forgotten pole, and shoved us away from the shore.

"What's with the boatman?"

"I don't know."

"Come again?"

"I don't *know*," I snarled, leaning into the pole to gain velocity. "We have bigger problems."

The magma scorpions seemed to be unwilling to let us simply float away, even though the aft quarter of the skiff was now burning merrily. They cast aside caution and began scampering after us at a profoundly dismaying speed.

Leaning upon the pole for all I was worth, I managed to get us out through the cavern's mouth into the echoing reach of the Hollows before the scorpions could catch up—but the Hollows are no place to sail blind. The numberless caves and caverns extend for tens or even hundreds of miles; some are navigable, some are dead ends, and some present in various hazards, from razor-sharp slashcoral to periodic sinkholes and tide spouts.

"Do you have any idea where we're going?"

"Away from the monsters."

"Well, *that's* reassuring. I meant, do you know your way around down here?"

"No." My breath was going short again, but at least I didn't have to run anymore. "Nobody does."

"Oh, great. What about a map?"

"If there were *maps*," I wheezed, "no one would need *scullers.*"

As if triggered by this exchange, the sculler standing at my back suddenly screamed.

The earsplitting shriek it unleashed was like nothing I'd ever heard: a horrible ragged ululation that rose and fell by no pattern I could discern. I discovered that even despite Doctor Jest's phantom soldier ants, I could distinctly feel every hair on my body attempt to stand on end at once. I was possibly the first living creature in the history of Esper to hear a sculler's voice . . . and that voice was eerie as a banshee's wail and horrible as the death scream of a berserk dragon.

"Uh, yow," Doc said. "And probably yikes. Plan B?"

Through the rising flames of the stern, I could see the magma scorpions scuttling up toward the gloom-shrouded ceiling. Without the sculler to take us to the open sea, we could only hope to keep ahead of the monsters until the summoning expired. This, given my physical exhaustion and mana-depleted condition, would be more difficult than it sounded—and it sounded impossible. Not to mention the further complication of the skiff being on fire.

On top of all this, the skiff-pole lost contact with the tide pool's bottom suddenly enough that I very nearly pitched over the side; without knowledge of the caverns' submarine topography, I had blundered into water too deep for the pole. And there weren't any oars.

We were adrift.

With a long, slow sigh, I sat down, unshipped the pole, and laid it across my knees.

"What are you *doing*?"

I was too exhausted to play any more banter games. "Getting ready to die."

Before either of us could pursue this line of conversation, the sculler suddenly spread its hands, raising them wide to the ceiling as though imploring a benison from some dark god. The ragged edge left its shriek, making it sound less like a scream and more like some kind of call....

The sculler clapped its hands together with great force, driving the crystal of sangrite *through* both of its palms, nailing its hands together in an attitude of prayer. Some sort of milky ichor ran from the wounds, and while I was still processing the idea of being not only the first human to hear a sculler's voice, but also the first to see a sculler's blood, the creature's hands burst into flame.

They burned at first like a torch, but soon brightened, and the color of the flame became yellow as a watch fire, and very shortly the light they gave off was white as the inside of a blast furnace, along with a palpable heat. By this time, the creature's arms were on fire to the elbows, and its call had begun to modulate, taking on a definite tone and a sort of rhythm, and seemed to be gathering harmonic overtones in the echoes from the cavern walls. . . .

The sculler wasn't screaming. It was *singing*.

And the echoes and harmonic overtones were no artifact of the tide caves—they were the answering voices of dozens of scullers, hundreds, who came poling their silent skiffs out from the dark-shrouded caves around us, forming an eldritch chorus of voices never raised before.

The flames now spread across the sculler's chest and up and down its cloak . . . and then like a scrap of burning paper, the sculler lifted into the air.

It rose like the sun, and cast out the cavern's permanent gloom.

Even in the face of imminent death I could not restrain my awe. I found myself quite overcome with an inexplicable sense of *sanctity*, a distinct intuition that what we were witnessing here was something holy, beyond what mortals are meant to see—a sensation with which I was, to the surprise of no one who has ever known me, largely unfamiliar.

But now, here, I found myself flooded with awe . . . and gratitude.

Perhaps this is one more way in which I am not like other men: to be granted a glimpse of some deeper truth—a hint of mysteries beyond the mundane puzzles of day and night and health and work—meant more to me than my own life. Though perhaps other folk are not so different after all. Perhaps such a sight would mean fully as much to anyone who might ever be granted the gift of seeing it . . . but they've never lifted their eyes.

I know that there are no true gods; that gods worshiped here and there throughout the Multiverse are imaginary—or worse, creatures like Bolas. That knowledge was bitter to me then as never before. When granted such an astonishing blessing, when feeling gratitude so profound that words stumble, too lame to evoke it . . .

There was no one for me to thank.

The magma scorpions themselves had paused in their pursuit, as though uncertain of the portent of this unexpected flare. They clung to the cavern ceiling, watching. Now engulfed in flame, the sculler continued to rise, higher and higher, while its fellows gathered around the burning skiff where I sat transfixed.

The song's interlocking harmonics rose toward a climax, and suddenly, shockingly, stopped. Even the echoes. I caught my breath.

The only sound was the lick of flames from my skiff's stern.

And just as I was about to observe that the proceedings appeared to be about over, the burning sculler exploded in midair.

A far more spectacular detonation than that of the magma scorpion, this had the look of a military explosive, or the burst of a fireball cast by a mage of the power of Nicol Bolas himself. It filled the entire upper reaches of the cavern's ceiling with a blast of fire that scraped both magma scorpions off the rock and dropped them flat on their backs in the tide pool, adding their own explosive blasts into a roar that blew away my hearing.

This may explain the silence from Doc as well.

It was fortunate that I had sat in the skiff, as the huge swell of shock wave would certainly have cast me into the water—but even that, it may be, would not have presented the sort of hazard it might otherwise have.

It appeared the scullers had decided to look after me.

One of them nearby reached toward my skiff with one empty hand, which it then clenched as though plucking an invisible fruit. The fire at the stern was extinguished instantly, without so much as an ember remaining. Two other scullers maneuvered their skiffs in tandem, just off the forward bow to either side, and leaned into their poles in their usual slow, silent rhythm. Either the deep spot I had found was much smaller than I'd thought, or they had motive powers beyond the leverage of the poles, for they had no difficulty making headway, and though no rope or visible energy bound my craft to theirs, I found my skiff following along as though theirs were mountain geese and mine an obedient gosling.

I was tempted to make an observation to Doc about being out of danger for the moment, but decided against it on the off chance that Doc's uncharacteristic silence was not, in fact, due to temporary deafness. There was much to think about, and very little time to ponder.

I knew all too well that this moment of safety would not last. Jace would know his trap had been triggered. And he knew of my sentimental flaw, which made it all too obvious where his next trap would be set.

And if I didn't get there fast, my father would be dead before I could spring it.

THE METAL ISLAND
THE FIRE THIS TIME

O n the shore of the Metal Island, under the blank etherium stare of the Metal Sphinx, the small blue sun between Nicol Bolas's horns flickered once, then winked out. The jet-chains of energy that had linked the blue sun to Tezzeret's head vanished as well.

"Don't stop now…" The human, still hanging within the crackling white Web of Restraint, seemed to be breathing with some difficulty. "You were just getting… to the *good* part…."

"Quiet." Bolas enforced his command with a gesture that sewed Tezzeret's lips shut with white fire.

The dragon lifted his head, and his immense forked tongue flickered out, stirring air into his even more immense nasal cavity, though what had captured his attention was not a scent. It was a peculiar imminence— a gathering of potential that was escalating toward the actual—and the sensation it produced was not one for which there are words in ordinary languages, because to feel this sensation required senses far from ordinary.

"We're about to have company," the dragon said in a tone suggesting that unexpected guests were not necessarily unwelcome, as long as they brought food—or, alternatively, were food. "Some friend of yours? Oh, right, I forgot the friends thing. A lackey, then. Reinforcements? Who is our Special Mystery Guest?"

Immobilized within the web of white energy, Tezzeret could do nothing but breathe and blink. So he did both for several seconds, until Bolas hissed in exasperation and gestured again.

The white fire vanished. Gasping in sudden relief, Tezzeret collapsed on the etherium plinth between the forepaws of the Metal Sphinx. "You do that . . . a lot," he wheezed. "Act before you think . . . then have to undo what you've done. Embarrassing, isn't it? Must make you feel rather . . . ah, hmmm. What's the word I'm looking for? Starts with *st* and rhymes with *oopid*?"

Smoke trickled up from the fire in the dragon's eyes. "Who is this incoming Planeswalker of yours?"

"How can you tell a Planeswalker is coming?"

"He starts breathing hard," Bolas said absently. "It wasn't a riddle? Never mind. I'll let you make any necessary introductions."

The dragon wrapped himself in his wings and with a shrug wiped himself from existence. Even his footprints disappeared from the etherium sand.

With considerable protesting of his abused joints and muscles, Tezzeret slowly organized himself into a seated posture on the eastern edge of the plinth, letting his feet dangle above the riddle's first line.

Not far up the metal beach, air rippled with heat shimmer. This effect intensified until a thermocline refraction of the images of etherium and ocean spun into a shining swirl of metal and sea. Out from this swirl stepped a woman.

Apparently human, she was large enough that one might be forgiven for speculating that a giant or two had contributed to her bloodline. She was nearly a head taller than Tezzeret—who could be fairly characterized as a tall man—and though Tezzeret was muscled like a boxer, the woman's shoulders were half again the width of his.

Her hair was gray, and cropped close to her skull in an "I'm too damned busy to waste time doing my hair" style. She was dressed in a similarly utilitarian fashion, heavy drakeskin boots, with tunic, pants, and jacket of tightly woven fibers of stonewort, a Bantian mountain herb widely recognized for its fire-resistant properties. The reason for her peculiar ensemble was prominently announced by the flames that licked from both of her hands, and the swirl of fire dancing across her head and shoulders.

Due to an array of carefully maintained pyromantic magics, she herself was virtually fireproof; she wore stonewort and drakeskin because she had simply gotten tired of having to replace her outfit every time she got in a fight—which was, as announced by sundry scars on her face, neck, and head that she did not bother to conceal, an all-too-common occurrence.

A more curious feature of her equipment appeared to be a sort of harness, constructed of thin metal cable strongly resembling etherium. As the woman strode forward from the mirror-swirl of reality, she dragged into the world a young man who appeared to be unconscious, tethered to her by the same cable that made up her harness. As soon as he was fully on the beach, she shucked her harness and undid the one around the young man's chest. Exchanging her personal flame for a more general fire shield some ten feet in diameter, she threw him over her shoulder as if he were no more than a broken mannequin.

She moved along the metal beach with the alert caution of a warrior in enemy territory. Her expression had the blank intentness that signifies complete concentration on surroundings and movements, and none at all on doubts, fears, or anything that might go on inside her instead of outside; she moved as though she'd decided not to worry about what to do until after she discovered to whom she'd have to do it.

So it was that when Tezzeret spoke, she jerked and her sizzling globe of fire shield crackled outward around her, bright enough to hurt the eyes, even though all he said was, "Baltrice. Over here."

The blazing shell around her dimmed, but it did not fade away. "Tezzeret?"

He waved to her, and she moved cautiously along the beach until she could see him. When she could, she stopped and straightened up, frowning. "You're naked."

Tezzeret nodded. "And you're not."

Baltrice's frown dissolved, and she shrugged. "Better than the other way around, I guess."

Tezzeret privately agreed with her, though he was too wary of her temper to say so. "Thank you for coming—and for bringing Beleren."

"It's as good a time as any to find out if your word's good." She set the unconscious young man down on the etherium sand. "Hey—*hey*! You're not wearing the damn *ring*!"

She shook her fist at him; on her smallest finger was a plain band of etherium, and in her eyes were flames. "Where is it, you bastard—where?"

He spread his hands, inviting her to inspect again his nakedness. "As you might notice, a number of my personal possessions did not accompany me on this journey. And you hardly need the ring when you have me, yes?"

"Well . . ." She looked down, sighing, then gave him an apologetic shrug. "I guess."

"That etherium tether," he said, "is an interesting workaround. Is that yours?"

She shrugged. "It lets me activate his Spark, kinda like secondhand. He's out because—well, you'd be the one to know. Awake through a planeswalk? Your gadget would probably kill him."

"It was designed to. My compliments on your solution."

"Ahh, you know. Wasn't my idea. Him, though, he's good at figuring stuff out."

"I remember. How is my father?"

Baltrice made a face. "Next time I see him, I'll give him your love," she said. "What in the hells is this place?"

He took a long, pensive look around. "It's a mausoleum," he said at length, "for the fondest dreams of Esper."

"Oh, for the love of—" Baltrice shook her head, and the fire around her brightened. "Look, can we not start that crap this one time? Please?"

"Crap?" he said mildly.

"Where you talk in metaphors and literary references and junk to show me how smart you are. Just cut it the hell out, can you?"

He considered this with a slight frown. "I'm not sure I can."

"So okay, do we do the thing now? I mean, this was the deal, right? I did my bit. Now you do yours. You've put Jace through enough already."

"Oh, *Jace*, is it now?"

She flushed. "There's been some hard types sniffing around—could be working for the dragon themselves—"

"Nicol Bolas's interest in Jace is not homicidal."

"Yeah, okay, but even so—"

"I am more curious about *your* interest in Jace," he said. "You like him."

"Sure I like him." Her flush deepened. "He pays me."

"Does he? Still?"

"Better than you ever did."

MATTHEW STOVER

"I had thought Jace's personal finances might be currently ... shall we say, a bit stressed ... ?"

She made a chopping motion with her hand that spilled fire on the beach at her feet. "He looks after his people."

"Or is it that he pays you in coin that can't be measured in weights of gold?" He peered into her eyes with a focused intent not unlike hers had been on arrival. "Does he give you reason to believe that he, ah, likes you back?"

Her flush now became a full-on blush—one that was accompanied by the kindling of dangerous fires in her eyes. "We get along," she said evenly. "We're friends. That's all."

"Ah. Friends. Has he ever told you what happened to his friend—his *best* friend—Kallist Rhoka?"

"That skull banger he jobbed with, back in the day? What about him?"

"Ask Jace. It's an entertaining story. Jace Beleren trades in friendship as I trade in money. The difference between doing business with him and doing business with me is that money buys things you *want*."

"That's a long way from the only difference." The flames in her eyes licked outward, threatening to ignite the air between them.

He held up a hand. "I'm not trying to antagonize you, Baltrice. If to remove my device from his brain is what you truly wish from me, I am willing—for your sake, not for his."

"What do I care about *why*?"

"A fair point," he conceded. "But I do hope you'll keep in mind that the last time Jace Beleren had me at a disadvantage, he *killed* me. Murdered me, in fact, with malice aforethought."

The fires around her dimmed a little. "You're afraid of him."

"I have reason to be."

"I won't let him hurt you, all right?"

"I'm flattered that you think I might trust you."

"I mean, sure, you and me, we've had our differences—"

"A mild phrase for betrayal, torture, and several attempted homicides."

"Still, you know, we worked together pretty good for a while, back before . . ." She shook her head again. "And then on this sphinx hunt of yours. I even chased off your little black-haired, zombie-sucking slut bag for you."

"And I am grateful for it," he said. "How is the . . . ah, zombie-sucking slut bag?"

"Better at hiding than you are." She let the fires she'd been holding flicker out. "Tezzeret, I'm not here for a fight, okay? Just get your gadget out of Jace's brain and we'll be on our way."

Tezzeret sighed. "There are two major flaws with your plan—and that's if we overlook your presumption that I have told you the truth about myself and my intentions; specifically, that I am not only willing to remove the item in question, but that the item can actually *be* removed without killing Beleren."

Flames around her hands brightened. "If Jace dies, so do you."

"I believe you," he said. "Here are the flaws in your plan. First, as you can see, here I have no facilities nor equipment nor tools, all of which might be required to make such an operation successful."

"Then we *take* him to your damned—"

"Second," Tezzeret said, raising a hand to interrupt, "is your presumption that either of us is going anywhere."

The fire shield flared around Baltrice and Beleren until the etherium sand began to fuse at her feet. "I'd like to see somebody try to stop me."

"Your wish is about to be granted."

"You're ready, aren't you," she said. It wasn't a question. "You're ready for any move I can make. Fight, walk away, cooperate, whatever. You're ready."

"It's not impossible to surprise me," he said. "It's only difficult."

"You planned all this," she said accusingly. "You had it all worked out in advance."

"I allowed for a range of possibilities. Something resembling this situation was among them," he said. "I certainly didn't plan for it to be here; *here* is a place that at the time, I did not believe existed. And I did not plan on being naked. Fortunately, there is one thing about you that I can always count on, Baltrice."

"Yeah?"

"I can count on you to be Baltrice."

"What's *that* supposed to mean?"

"Do you remember how I tried to teach you contingency planning? How to analyze a situation in all its possibilities and permutations, and how to be sure you're prepared against the ones you won't like?"

"Never cared much for lessons." The pyromancer shrugged. "If I can't blow it up or burn it down, I pretty much don't give a damn."

"I know." He smiled a bit, a fond sort of smile, slightly sad, like that of a father watching his most difficult child leave home. "Do you remember my slogan—my watch-word—about being thorough, careful, and distrusting anything that might blur your perception? 'It's never a question of whether you're paranoid . . .'"

" 'It's a question of whether you're paranoid enough,' " she finished for him. "Yeah, sure, what of it?"

He sighed. "All you know are the words."

Instantly the fire shield around her roared back to full power, and both of her hands ignited with the intensity of the sun. She could barely be seen within the sphere of raging fire. "I don't much like the sound of that."

He had to lift an arm to shade his face. "You're a great pyromancer, Baltrice. You really are. You're not only incredibly powerful, you are almost unbelievably fast. Better in a straight-up fight than anybody I've ever seen. Except . . ."

"Yeah?" Fire swept outward from her like a phoenix spreading its wings. "Except what?"

"Except fire magic won't help you much against an elder dragon."

"What?"

A massively taloned hand the size of a horse flashed into existence and clenched around Baltrice so tightly that it instantly extinguished her fire shield. As the rest of him returned to visibility, Nicol Bolas lifted Baltrice bodily into the air.

He said, "Let me explain."

She snarled a string of obscenities while she summoned a flare of power around her right hand that would have done credit to a medium-sized star. Cords bulging in her neck, she ripped her arm free of his casual grip and aimed it at Bolas's face.

"Really?" he said. "Well, since you've gone to all this trouble . . ."

He leaned down until the corner of his mouth was only a few feet from her outstretched hand, and he winked at her. "All right. How's this?"

"You tell me," she said, and a blast of incandescent flame roared from her fingertips and caught the dragon squarely in his right eye. The raging fire ripped across the dragon's cornea. It almost made him blink.

Almost.

"Oh, you *are* adorable," he said with an indulgent chuckle. "Hush now. Settle down before I smoke you like a cigar."

Before she could even begin to regather her power, Bolas cocooned her in a Web of Restraint, sealing her lips as well as her limbs and magics. This web was more than double the size of the one he'd used on Tezzeret, which may have been a gesture of respect for her power, but probably wasn't.

Many traits can be truthfully ascribed to Nicol Bolas, but respect is not among them.

He balanced her on one extended talon, regarding her with the dispassionate interest he might have given to an exotic insect. "I should thank you," he said. "Until you got here, I had only Tezzeret's memories to amuse me. Yours might be more entertaining. In fact, they'd have to be."

He tilted his face back toward the artificer. "A couple hours of your life and I'm ready to strangle myself in my own vomit. How do you stand it?"

The artificer, still sitting with feet dangling over the edge of the plinth, appeared to give the question serious consideration. After a second or two, he shrugged. "I'm not sure," he said. "Probably because, unlike you, I don't have a choice."

"About much of anything," Bolas said. "You must be getting used to it."

The artificer's only reply was a blank stare. Nicol Bolas snorted, and without even a gesture, he buried Tezzeret in a fresh Web of Restraint. "I'll be back with you in a minute or two. You won't have time to feel neglected. I promise."

The dragon returned his full attention to the pyromancer in his hand, and the searing blue star rekindled between his horns. "I should probably tell you this won't hurt. But why lie?"

Scintillant blue energy lanced from the star and poured into Baltrice's forehead—and didn't burn her at all, likely due to her enchanted fireproofing, so there wasn't even any stink; yet another way in which she was more agreeable than Tezzeret. "I think you and I are going to be friends," he said. "Very good friends. Good friends don't keep secrets, hm? So . . . let's see what you were up to, the night I turned Tezzeret loose."

Baltrice's memories began to unspool into his mind.

BALTRICE
THIS OLD MAN

The whole place stank.

No wonder Tezzeret never talked about where he was from. This Tidehollow of his smelled like dead fish and ass. And not in a good way.

His dad's house—what he was using for a house—was mostly just a heap of mud bricks and broken rock with some fish oil lamps, a little oil stove, and a pallet of something that smelled like dried seaweed for a bed. One of the local talents—Pisser? Nutless? And who gives a crap anyway?— one of them had the old man shackled to a pillar, and was massaging the geezer's kidneys with the toe of his boot. The other local talent came at me like he was about to take my arm and pull me aside, which I put a stop to by igniting that arm to the elbow.

I don't mind the *aside* part, but no skull banger puts hands on me. Until I tell him to.

He read his future in my flames and backed off. Probably didn't realize he was sweating like a cross-dress whore in navy nick. "I dunno, Baltrice. He swears he ain't seen him. Swears. Ain't seen the kid in ten, twelve years."

"Tezzeret's no kid."

"I'm startin' to believe the old bastard. I really kinda am."

"You're not paid to believe. Work him till you hear me say stop."

"I dunno, really, I mean, he'd of told us, Baltrice—"

I had had more already of back talk from the local talent than I was prepared to swallow. I stepped next to him. Filthy little squit barely came up to my armpit. "You're getting awful free with my name, Pimple."

"I'm Posner—"

"You want to argue your name before you get mine straight?

"Uh, *your*—?"

"*My* name, Pimple," I said, leaning over him enough to give him a good look at the underside of my chin, "is *ma'am*. You get that? Say it, bitch."

"Uh . . . ma'am."

"You and the rest of your bitches keep it straight, and nobody goes home with a fatal sunburn. Right?"

"Uh . . . yeah, okay, sure."

I stared at him, waiting.

"Ma'am," he said. His tongue located some of that sweat on his upper lip. "Okay sure, *ma'am*. About the old guy—"

"Keep on him."

"What if he really don't know nothing?"

"I'm not paying you to get answers. I'm paying you to inflict casual damage."

"I don't get it."

"Well, *there's* a twist I wasn't expecting."

Meanwhile, Nozzle had given over the boot-leather kidney massage. He'd found a pair of pliers somewhere and was now applying a clumsy Wojek manicure. I stepped over and undertook my own boot-leather massage to Nozzle's left butt cheek while the geezer still had some fingernails left.

Nozzle's opinion on the subject—which he delivered sprawled on the dirt floor—started with "What the," included a "you" or three, and indelicately named some of my delicate parts before going on to suggestions that might have made me blush if I hadn't done everything on his list at least twice, not to mention a couple already this morning.

I looked at Pimple. "Why am I about to deep-fry your partner?"

Pimple blanched. "I—I dunno...."

I cocked my head at him, and his whole face lit up as somebody in the vast whistling darkness of his empty head finally managed to strike a match. "*Ma'am!*" he almost shouted. "I don't know, *ma'am!*"

I looked at Nozzle. "So. What was it you said should have improbable varieties of sex with unlikely parts of my anatomy?"

"Uh, I . . . uh, I forget. Uh, *ma'am.*"

I pointed at a bench against the far wall. "Sit."

Nozzle decided the better part of valor was to glue his butt to the bench.

I took a minute to look over what was left of the old man's left hand fingertips. There wasn't much. I'd have to get more local money from Jace and buy the poor old bastard some healing, since my own particular talents run mostly in the opposite direction. "Who told you it was a good idea to start with the pliers?"

Nozzle went paler. "I just thought—"

"You thought. Really. As in *thinking*. Wow." I shook my head. "Listen, chucklebrain, you know who Tezzeret is, right?"

"Uh, well, sure I do. Uh, ma'am."

"So you understand what your future is gonna look like if he slips our noose here?"

"Uh . . . what?"

I tried to say it slow enough that even these two could understand. "You two ass-clowns are, right now, the guys who *maimed* Tezzeret's *father* . . . unless, maybe, the old man goes into shock. And dies. Then you'll be the guys who *tortured* Tezzeret's father to *death*. With me now?"

Both skull bangers' eyes went round as soup plates.

"One of your bitches outside must have some kind of bandages and first-aid crap, in case one of you nancies stubs a toe or something. Go get it, then come back in here and fix his goddamn hand."

Nozzle jumped up like he'd been shot from a bow and bolted for the door.

I beckoned Pimple over. "Forget about answers, all right? When I say work him, you work him. If I want him maimed, I'll say maim him. If I want him dead, what do you think I'll do?"

"Uh . . . you'll say *kill him*?"

"No, dumbass. I'll kill all three of you and pretend I was never here."

Idiots. But you can't do everything yourself. If you could, all these brain-dead bastards would've starved a long time ago.

Nozzle got back with the first-aid stuff. The geezer was bleeding from eight or ten places, not just his hands and mouth but an ear and his crotch, so it took a little time there to get the shackles off, and get him cleaned up, bandaged, and straightened out at the table. I had Nozzle bring him a cup of water, but he didn't seem too interested in drinking until I pulled my flask, at which point he lit up and his mouth started twisting like a hooker's hammock. I let him take a swallow that made his eyes cross. Cross more. Tezzeret told me once that alcohol's a luxury item on Esper—not enough surplus fermentable starches. It looked to me like an opening.

"You like that?" I said, weighing the flask in my hand. "Want some more?"

"Garn," he said sullenly, which I took to be the local term for "Quit pulling my leg" or "Get the hell out of town" or something. "Garnen git. I sezafore whuddize godda say."

I should've bought a damn phrase book; I'd freeze my naked ass to a glacier before I'd ask Pimple and Nozzle to translate, so I went with my best guess. "I'm not even asking, geeze. Want another hit, help yourself."

He squinted sidelong at the flask. "Etz pizen."

"Well, sure." I took a whack myself, just to be neighborly. "If it weren't poison, it wouldn't be any fun."

Given enough time, even this wetbrain geezer could calculate that if I wanted him hurt or dead, I didn't need to booze him up to do it. "Arright," he said, taking the flask from my hand. "I thanks ye."

"You're welcome. Go ahead and kill it if you want. Because I think I believe you."

Pimple snorted and opened his mouth to object. I shut him up with a look.

"It's a shame, though," I said. "If you had been able to give us Tezzeret, we'd be long gone by now. Since you can't, I guess we're staying."

I got up and headed for the door. "Pimple. Don't let him get bored."

"Yes, ma'am."

"And you," I said to Nozzle, "if I see those pliers in your hands, I'll start using them *on* your hands. Got it?"

He nodded vigorously. "Ma'am."

Time to check in with the boss. I left them to their work and went outside.

Outside? Yeah, tell me another. *Outside* is where you can see sky. Not here. Nothing to see here except rock, seawater, and poor stupid bastards without enough brains to know their lives suck.

103

Being poor sucks. I *know* it sucks. I don't need to be reminded.

Especially since being poor could still happen to me, if we didn't smoke Tezzeret in a tenth of a damn hurry. Who would have guessed that stuck-up fancy-pants sonofabitch would turn out to be so damn hard to kill?

Jace should have let me handle the bastard in the first place. Get it done proper.

Still, though, I might have trouble against three em-scorps myself. Some, anyway. Wish I could have been here to see the look on his face when they were chasing him bare-ass naked right through the middle of his hometown.

I did a so-so job of being inconspicuous while I walked the perimeter. Too good a job, and not even Tezzeret would know I was there; too bad a job and he'd know I was showing myself on purpose. But I walked the walk nice and slow, all the way around, and nobody took a shot at me. Even though I'm a plus-size target.

Not that I was really expecting anybody to try me. Hanging myself out there was mostly just for fun. Gave me something to do while I waited.

There's lots of things I'm good at. Waiting's not one of them.

Say what you want about the Conflux and this Planes War going on all over Alara; one thing it's good for is turning out bucketloads of combat-trained mages. I had eight of them in camouflaged blinds in a double-diamond setup, where at least two had eyeballs on every approach, and each of the eight was in sight of at least two of his mates. And I had another six of the local skull bangers primed and ready to tangle with anything on two legs, because you never know when you might need somebody to do something stupid. Like put a sword to Tezzeret. My skull-banger reserve was lying flat on the highest point in the neighborhood, which happened to be the top of the geezer's hovel.

In this toilet, that probably makes him some kind of nobility.

I had four of Jace's summoning stones out there, too, loaded with all kinds of Jumbo Economy Nasties that Tezzeret would never know were there until way too late. In any given five seconds, I could put critters on the ground that'd make those em-scorps look cuddly as kittens. I had the place tagged and bagged eight ways from Gruulsday, signed and sealed and stamped and shipped, but I was starting to get the feeling that somehow I wasn't going to deliver. Something had already gone wrong.

It wasn't just a hunch. I'd had time enough to get everything together, and enough time left over to get bored. It just didn't scan.

Tezzeret's a methodical sonofabitch, but there's not one slow bone in his body. The Tezzeret I knew would've hit me like a thunderbolt while I was still trying to separate spellers from choppers. Even coming back from the sort-of dead without that frappin' arm of his wouldn't change him *that* much.

So either something fatal had gone wrong for him—which meant we'd be waiting till the wrong side of forever—or else he got here, grabbed the skinny with both hands and then bailed like the Giant Brain bastard he is. Either way, it wasn't good news.

We'd missed him. Somehow.

I pulled my Jacequin out of my breast pocket and stood it up on a fold of rock. After straightening its clothing, I had to adjust the legs to keep the damned thing upright, which it mostly refused to do.

I *told* Jace this was a bad idea. I never played with dolls when I was a girl, and I'm too damned old to start now.

If Tezzeret was watching me, I knew he was laughing his ass off. I could feel my ears burning—which for me can be literal—and I had to clench my jaw to keep myself from looking around to see if any of the local talent was smirking, because if they were, my ears wouldn't be the only things burning.

Pretty soon, though, I found the mana channel to activate it, and the Jacequin's shimmery blue aura lit the thing up vividly in the cavern gloom. The doll shook itself, took a couple steps to find its balance, then turned its painted face up toward mine. *"Do you have him?"*

That little squeaky voice usually tickled the crap out of me, but right now my giggles were frozen out by stone cold dread. "I don't think he's coming. Any luck topside?"

The doll shook its head. *"I've got reliable eyes all over the Seekers, the Ethersworn, and the Mechanists' Guild. We must be missing something."*

"Maybe it was never him."

"Had to be," the doll insisted. *"Nobody else could have even found his trap, let alone triggered the em-scorps by disarming it."*

"Maybe he's got a flunky, right? Somebody he can just send, instead of coming himself. Told the guy where it was, and how to disarm it."

"I don't buy it."

"All reports have the guy running from the em-scorps as having two arms. Both flesh. On this plane, they notice that kind of crap."

"Try to imagine Tezzeret trusting someone enough to tell him where he keeps his spare etherium."

Couldn't argue with that. "Unless he tipped to the gaff," I said. "He could have sent somebody expendable just to trigger the trap, right? Somebody he didn't like anyway. To make us *think* it was him. So we'd waste our time laying the ambush here, instead of reinforcing defenses on Ravnica. He's probably back there right now, killing everybody we ever met."

The doll lifted a wooden hand to its painted eyes, like Jace was getting a headache. Tezzeret can do that to you. *"Ideas?"*

"I think he's got all the edge there is to go around," I said. "The thing about Tezzeret is that you can't outthink him. It's useless to try and guess what he might do, because he can figure what you think he'll do based on what you know about him . . . and then he'll do something else."

"Then what's our play?"

"I don't much like the idea of looking over my shoulder for the rest of my life, but if this kind of stunt was going to work, it would've worked by now. We might get lucky. We probably won't."

"What about his father?"

"Tough old hunk of gristle, that geezer. I've had a couple of my skull bangers work him a couple hours now, and the old bastard hasn't even told them his name." I shrugged. "If a beat down on his dad won't draw him, I can't guess what would. I been around the perimeter four times. If he was gonna take a shot . . .'"

"There's only one more thing he'd be waiting for."

"Jace, don't. Don't even think about it. You do *not* want to tangle with Tezzeret when he's ready for you."

"If the two of us together can't handle him, we might as well just—"

"Might as well and likely will," I said, even though I could tell he wasn't listening.

"And if the old man does know anything, I can get it. With you in a sec."

The blue shimmer faded, and the Jacequin was just a doll again.

I went over to the door of the hovel. "Blade up. Both of you. If Tezzeret has a move to make, it's gonna be basically now."

They drew the thick, squarish hacking swords the local talent favored, and pretended to be smart enough to be on guard. The old man just sat there staring at the ceiling, completely pie-eyed, the flask lying forgotten on its side in front of him.

There came a soft *whumpf* like distant artillery, and the ghost of a breeze stirred the hair on the back of my neck. I turned around. "Hey, boss."

"Don't call me boss," he said, but just on reflex. Jace figures that if nobody in the organization actually knows he's in charge, nobody will show up to take him out like he took out Tezzeret. It seemed to be working. So far.

"You're getting faster with that teleport."

"Practice makes perfect," he said. "Never know when you might need to make a hasty exit." He leaned sideways to peer around me, which for a guy his size is a considerable lean. "That's Tezzeret's old man? He looks drunk. He *is* drunk."

"Hey, nothing much gets by you, huh?"

He flashed me that quick and easy grin of his. "Well, if it does, I've got you for a backstop, right?"

I gave him a sidelong squint. "Is that a fat joke?"

"Nah, I'm a fat joke," he deadpanned. "That was a tall joke."

"Next time use a ladder. And somebody else's sense of humor. And you're not fat. Just soft enough to be cuddly."

So we had our little chuckle there before Jace got down to business. He's like that. It's one of the things that make him a good boss—he wants his people to be happy. Tezzeret only wanted us to be obedient. Though I guess maybe Jace's mind powers could be part of the deal; it'd have to be hard for a telepath to spend all his time around people who think he's an asswipe. But even if that's true, it's not the whole story.

The big picture is that Jace Beleren really is a damn fine human being. The Multiverse'd be a better place if there were more people like him in it, and I'll never forget it.

That last dustup, against that little rot-sucking slag Liliana Vess, had left me in bad shape. There wasn't much I could do except moan and crawl. When I finally managed to drag myself into the Blind Eternities, I made for Ravnica. Not for any reason. I don't remember being able to even think about it. Just blind instinct, like any other wounded animal. All I wanted was to die at home.

But Jace found me.

He had plenty reason to hate me. Hells, if our situations had been reversed, I would've healed him up just so I could torture him to death. Even if he decided not to hate me, he didn't have any reason to help. He could have left me there to die in the sewers. Instead he picked me up and put me back together. Took care of me while I tried to get past the nightmares of all those shades and spirits Vess had plastered me with. And as soon as I was strong enough to work, he offered me a job.

If I spend the rest of my life paying him back, I'll never even the score. Every breath I draw, I owe to him. If there is such a thing as a good man in this toilet of existence, it's Jace Beleren.

He frowned a little as he turned himself around and reached out with his mind, checking off each of my local talents in turn. "Double diamond, huh?"

I shrugged. "Classics never go out of style."

He glanced up toward the hovel's rooftop. "Good spot for the spare mercs, too. They'll never stop him, but at least we'll hear him killing them."

ᏋᎮ

"This isn't the first time I've set up an ambush."

"So: his dad, eight mercs—two inside, six topside— eight mages, and you. And me." His frown deepened. "There's nobody else here."

"We booted the locals. A handy way to ring the neighborhood bells, y'know? News would have been all over the ghetto hours ago."

He nodded. "Good idea, but it's not working. He's nowhere around here. If he's even watching, it has to be through some kind of remote device—scrying pool, magic mirror, something. I don't think he can hide from me, but if he can, he's not taking his shot. Even with me out here in plain sight."

I shrugged. "Maybe he forgave you."

He snorted. "And *I'm* the one who needs to borrow a sense of humor?" He shook his head. "Y'know, when I killed him—"

"You didn't kill him enough."

He waved a hand. "Whatever. Look, I got into his brain. I found every scrap of memory and personality and power and everything else that made him the man he was, and I ripped it out of him and threw it away. *Tried* to throw it away. I thought I could purge all that stuff. Just bundle it up and let it dribble out my ears or whatever. But it's not that simple. There's a reason I haven't done a mind kill since."

He paused there, staring off into the caverns, and I thought he was waiting for me to reply somehow, but I couldn't think of anything to say except, "Must be hard."

"You have no idea," he muttered. "It's still there. *He's* still there. In my head. I can wall him off, and stuff him down into like my deepest mental subbasement. But I can't get rid of him. I don't know if I ever will. I mean, that's how I knew the codes and stuff to take over the Ravnica cell, right? It's how I knew that if somehow he wasn't dead,

MATTHEW STOVER

he'd be coming back here to replace that arm of his. I'm not guessing. I *know*."

He turned to me, and for just half a second—something about his eyes, some cold-ass clinical distance, like I was some kind of exotic bug he was deciding whether to squish—he looked like him. Like Tezzeret. "He hates his father. *Hates* him."

"Hey, I can relate," I said. "If my old man was on fire, I wouldn't pee on him to put him out."

"It's not like that. It's worse than that. It's like ... It's like his father is a nail that went all the way through his foot. It's infected and scraping the bone, and every step hurts so bad, he's always trying not to scream."

I found myself frowning. "Then how come the big ambush here? Why the beat down? If he hates the old bastard so much, what makes you think—"

"Because he's never pulled the nail," Jace said darkly. "Because it's *his*."

I thought of the few times I'd seen Tezzeret really lose it. Not just get angry, because angry was how he got up every morning, but out of control. Wild. Breaking stuff. Slaughtering people. "Yeah," I said slowly. "Yeah. Anything that's his, you better just put it down and walk away fast enough that he never sees your hand on it."

"That's how I know I'm not wrong. I *know* Tezzeret is here. Somewhere. Because I *know* he'd expect me—us—to go after his father. And I know he'll never let me get away with it."

"Like I said, Jace," I told him. "Sure, you know him. He's in your head, whatever. You know why he's not behaving the way you expect him to? It's because *he knows you know*."

Jace looked grim. "I get it."

"Do you? You also got to wonder if whoever put him back together has made some, you know, adjustments."

"What, that nezumi shaman on Kamigawa?"

"I bet it wasn't the nezumi—after what he and I did there, I'm surprised they didn't roast him over a slow fire and *eat* the sonofabitch—but it's not like he would have just gotten better on his own, either. So somebody wanted him back, and had the power to do it for him, yeah? I'm just saying. He might not really be the same guy. We don't know who did it, or why, or what they might want him to do. Until we do, we're just grape-shotting the smoke and hoping to draw blood."

Jace looked like he was really seeing me for the first time. "Tezzeret never mentioned how smart you are."

I had to laugh. "When you work for Tezzeret, thinking just gets you in trouble."

"I remember." He gave me that grin again. "It's lucky you found a better job."

"Something like it," I said, smiling back. "Boss."

He was already squinting through the hovel's door. "There's something weird about the old man."

"Yeah?" A little chill settled into my guts. Anything weird is something bad.

"His mind is . . . hmp. I don't know. It's like there's not quite *enough* of him there."

"He's been a rustweed addict since forever, I think. There wouldn't be much of him left, you know?"

"Yeah, but . . ." Jace said, tilting his head like he was trying to listen for something that human ears can't really hear. "I don't know. I can't quite bring it into focus . . . doesn't help that he's drunk off his ass. . . ."

"Hey, sorry. Next time write me a memo, huh?"

"Forget about it," he said. "It's just . . . I mean, Tezzeret's not the kind of guy to do magic just for the hell of it."

"Magic?" A cold shiver flickered up my spine. I do *not* like to be cold. "I didn't sense any magic."

"You're not a telepath," he said absently, squinting now through a frown deep enough it should have shown bone. "It's like . . . there's something in there, in his mind, that I can't quite see."

That was all I needed to know. I ignited my fire shield and felt in my pockets for Jace's summoning stones. "You know what? I'm not having fun anymore."

"Be ready," he said, low, as he moved cautiously through the doorway, layering shield upon shield around himself until he looked like a man-shaped patch of blue fog.

"*Screw* ready—don't you get it? He got here *first*. It's time to burn this toilet down to bedrock and run like hell." I came up as close behind Jace as I could without knocking shields. "Pimple. Nozzle. Change of plan. Kill the old bastard. Now."

"No, *wait*—" Jace started.

"Screw *wait* too." He had enough shields in place to walk through whatever it'd take to kill everybody else in there. I cranked up myself a Sunball bigger than my butt, which meant it'd make a credible solar flare, but I had to shove Jace out of the way to get the damned thing in through the door. Before I could get Jace clear, the old man dived under the table and rolled out the other side, and the stupid festering skull bangers didn't even have time to figure out where he'd gone.

The old man rolled up to one knee and snapped his arms wide like he was throwing plates in opposite directions, and in his hands were two little metal toy handbows, comically kid size, neither one as big as the hand that held it, way too small to do any actual damage, which made it altogether sonofabitching *astonishing* when he fired them both with a couple of high-pitched *thocks* like squirrel coughs and two little red quarrels not even half the size of a pencil shot out, one into Pimple's chest right through his armor and the other into Nozzle's sword arm, and with a noise like *fwaptch* Nozzle's arm blew off above the elbow and skittered across the floor along with his sword and Pimple just plain exploded.

Pimple's head bounced off the ceiling and his right arm went one way and his left went the other, his legs sprayed blood as they flopped onto the floor and his breastplate hit Jace so hard it knocked him back into me like he'd been pimp-slapped by a really, really pissed-off ogre.

While I was trying to get my balance back and at the same time clear Jace out of the way so I could show this bastard what a *real* explosion looked like, the old man dropped one of the handbows, ripped one of the trestle legs off the table with his bare hands and slung it like a spear at Jace's chest.

Having just seen something impossible jump out of this bastard's handbows, I was not prepared to trust Jace's shields to repel anything at all, so even though the table leg was just a hunk of wood and not even sharp I flicked my Sunball away because it was *not* something I wanted near Jace if his shields went down, while with my other hand I reached out and flash-fried that hunk of wood so fast there wasn't even ash, just a puff of white smoke.

What didn't fry, though, was a little metal gizmo that had been *inside* the table leg and which flipped right through my best fire like it wasn't even there. It hit Jace in the chest and sprouted little jointed legs and knives and drills, and it grabbed on to him and started digging through his shields like they were made of grape jam, and right about the time I realized it was made of the same stuff as Tezzeret's metal arm and that I didn't have a goddamn clue how to stop it without killing Jace myself, Jace started to scream.

He screamed like a man watching his children die.

He was bucking and writhing in what kind of pain I couldn't imagine. I had to do something, but his shields were shredding like smoke, and I realized if I didn't move back I was about to set him on fire.

That pretty much left me only one thing to do. If I couldn't save him, I could at least for damned sure stop his killer from outliving him.

I reached toward the sky, and when my hand came back down it was full of sun.

I wound up to throw, but the geezer was just standing there, covered with Pimple's blood, and his shaky hands were about as shaky as the rock I was standing on, and he was taller now, and younger, and he had a two-handed grip on one of those little handbows which was aimed at my left eye.

"Tell your hirelings outside that they're fired. Then power down, come inside," he said, "and I'll tell you how to save Jace's life."

Even if I could have forgotten his face, I'd never mistake that voice. "You bastard—you murderous sonofabitching pile of rotten ratshit scumchucking slugbucket—" I ran out of words because I was too mad to breathe.

"Hello, Baltrice," Tezzeret said. "I've missed you, too."

THE METAL ISLAND
THE GAME, WAITING

The blue star between the dragon's horns winked out, and Baltrice sagged in her Web of Restraint. Nicol Bolas aimed a toothy grin at Tezzeret, who hung nearby in a web of his own. "You know, these little tricks of yours are actually cute, when you're pulling them on somebody else."

Tezzeret managed what was, for a human, a reasonably good approximation of the dragon's grin. "You ain't seen nothin' yet."

"Really? And what exactly are you intending to show me?"

"Good question." He coughed a couple of dry laughs. "I'm sure by the time you get around to digging into my brain again, I'll have forgotten."

"And people wonder why I like you so much." The dragon chuckled. He turned back to Baltrice. "And *you*—what an adorable little creature you are. Like a fire-breathing puppy."

"Screw you, scaly," she ground out around a clenched jaw, as though she hung on to consciousness by only her teeth. "Your turn'll come."

The dragon sighed. "If only I could live a year for every time someone's said *that* to me. Oh, wait, I have," he said.

"Keep laughing, gatorface," she panted, sagging again. "Just you . . . wait. . . ."

"Do I have a choice?" He reached down with one talon and touched her lightly on the forehead. She slumped into unconsciousness. "Dull. I can stand almost any kind except *dull*. She just doesn't have your gift of conversation, Tezzie."

"She'd take that as a compliment."

"Hmp. Might be one, too. So—from nothing more than professional interest—after you did the illusion to look like your father, you, what, partitioned your consciousness? And how exactly did you convince Doctor Jest to let you sit around and be tortured for a few hours?"

"What's *really* interesting," Tezzeret said, "is how you're *asking* me. Instead of going back to digging around in my head."

"You say that as though slogging through that septic tank you call a mind might be somehow less than revolting."

"It's your game, Bolas. If you're not having a good time, take your balls and screw off."

"Clever as usual. Which is less than very." Bolas went over to where Jace Beleren lay, also within a Web of Restraint despite not yet having regained consciousness. "What's this device of yours that Baltrice is so anxious about?"

"You're asking again."

"Humor me."

"Let's just say it's a mechanical Doctor Jest."

The hump of scaled muscle that served Bolas for an eyebrow arched. "You've finally managed to surprise me."

"And it's still early." Tezzeret squinted up at the dragon, who now was sneaking a glance along the beach in the opposite direction from which Baltrice and Beleren had come. "Expecting someone?"

For a silent span of a second or two, it seemed the dragon would decline to answer, but at length he said, "Apparently not," and Tezzeret detected in the dragon's voice a faint undertone of puzzlement, perhaps even dismay.

Bolas gave an irritated snort that blew twin smoke rings uncoiling down at the immobile man. "This device of yours, the, ah—" the dragon began, as if he'd lost the thread of the conversation.

Tezzeret smiled. "You're still asking."

The dragon's distraction curdled into hostility.

"Bugger asking." He glared down at Beleren's unconscious form, his eyes slitted in a fashion suggesting that his entire reservoir of malicious playfulness had suddenly evaporated. Gap sparks of lightning leaped from horn to horn, swirling about one another to condense into the blue sun. "I'll find out for myself."

"Now, *that's* interesting," Tezzeret said. "Back to the memory siphon—because whoever you thought was coming didn't show up."

"Shut up."

"How is it you know they're not just a couple of minutes late?"

"Tezzeret." Nicol Bolas swung his vast head close enough that Tezzeret could clearly see Silas Renn's shredded flesh, still dangling from tendons caught between the dragon's teeth. "Keep pushing me," he growled. "Go on. Keep it up."

Keeping up the snappy patter became a great deal more difficult when he could smell Renn's guts on the dragon's breath. "You've gotten very cranky all of a sudden. What went wrong?"

The dragon angled his face so that his huge yellow eye, larger than Tezzeret's whole head, was only inches from the artificer's nose. "In no more than minutes, I can make you beg me to kill you," he said in a low and deadly growl. "And a thousand years from now, if I'm in a good mood, I might let you speak long enough to beg me again."

Tezzeret stared into his own reflection in the vertical slit of midnight in the center of that great yellow eye. "I was only keeping up my end of the conversation."

"Don't." The dragon had already turned back to Beleren. "If I want a conversation with someone worth the breath, I'll talk to myself."

He cupped one foreclaw around the unconscious telepath, and the blindingly white energy of the Web of Restraint detached itself from the Metal Sphinx, binding instead to the dragon's talons. Bolas lifted Beleren to his face as though the man were a glass of fine wine, and the dragon wished to luxuriate in his aroma. "Oh, Jace, Jace, Jace," he hummed, softly enough that Tezzeret could barely make out the words. "If you only knew, child, how long I have been waiting for this moment. I hope you appreciate the honor. I expect that your first encounter with our newly minted artificer was at *least* as entertaining as Baltrice's."

As the twisting energy lash of Bolas's memory siphon attached itself to Jace Beleren's forehead and the mind ripper's memories began to flow into the dragon's mind, an attentive observer might have noticed a slight, almost infinitesimal, deepening of the wrinkles at the corners of Tezzeret's eyes and mouth, as though the artificer might be trying, and failing, to keep a straight face.

The dragon was, however, too busy with Jace's awakening in Tidehollow.

JACE BELEREN
FRIENDS LIKE THESE

I woke up coughing. My throat felt like I'd been trying to dry swallow barbed wire. Probably screaming when I passed out. I couldn't remember. The taste of vomit made my stomach heave, but all that came from my mouth was half-clotted blood.

The strong hands cradling me I would have known anywhere. That helped pull me together. As long as Baltrice was with me, whatever this was couldn't be too bad.

Could it?

"Jace, listen to me," she was saying, low and urgent.

I tried to nod, but moving my head made me retch again. "Sorry . . ." My voice sounded blurry and cracked. Notes played on a broken woodwind. "Sorry . . . I'm sorry, Baltrice, I . . . don't know what happened. . . ."

"Jace, you're in trouble."

"Oh . . ." I said, "oh . . . crap . . ."

Even semiconscious, I didn't miss that she said *you're*, not *we're*.

"How . . . bad?"

"Don't do any magic, Jace. You hear me? No matter what happens. Don't do *anything*."

"What . . . ? What? Why not?"

"Because," said a voice I hear in nightmares, "that will make a bad situation even worse."

And I turned my head, and there he was, just standing, standing and smiling and it was instinct, or training, or practice, that snapped my shields into existence and whichever it was didn't matter at all because before my shields could even fully form, a blast of agony whited out the world.

This time, I remember screaming.

I didn't quite pass out, even though it felt like a lightning bolt had exploded inside my head. It had me convulsing in Baltrice's arms, and I thrashed for a lifetime or two until I finally let go of the magic. When my vision cleared, he was still standing there. He wasn't even watching, though I could feel his attention attached to me, the sort of link I can back-chain almost without effort and get into his mind—

This time rats were chewing through my skull. From the inside.

Within a second or two the pain shredded my concentration; even the most basic telepathy was shut behind a door locked with agony. All I could do was lie there across Baltrice's knees. Lie there and look at Tezzeret and wait to die.

Tezzeret didn't look happy. Or angry or triumphant or really anything at all. He wasn't even paying that much attention to me. Instead, he seemed to be cutting some bandages off his fingertips with a small curved knife. The whole place was drenched with bucketsful of blood. Some random-looking body parts lay here and there, and one live mercenary sat propped into a corner, ashen and shaking, clutching at a tourniquet that closed off the stump of his arm.

All the different ways my nightmares had shown me this moment never looked anything like this. I guess as prophets go, I'm a pretty good telepath.

"Baltrice, are you hurt? Because if you are—"

She gave her head one tight shake. "Wasn't much of a fight, boss. Didn't get a nick."

"You need to go," I told her. "Get the hell out while you still can."

"Not a chance. We go together or we stay right here. Both of us."

That damned *spell*—of *course* she wouldn't leave me. She couldn't. And it was my fault.

Canceling the spell wouldn't take five seconds; then at least she'd have a choice. Maybe even a chance. I reached out with my mind—and collapsed again under the surge of agony. All I could do was let out a shuddering moan.

I had no idea how to get Baltrice out of this alive.

There had to be a way. Had to. I couldn't let her die just because she liked me too much to be sensible.

Especially considering *why* she liked me so much.

The moan had finally gotten Tezzeret's attention, but only for a second. He gave me a level stare for maybe a heartbeat, then went back to work on his hand. When he spoke, he sounded distracted. Affectless.

Like a machine.

"Beleren. I have never verified how much pain a human nervous system can endure without permanent damage. Nor do I know whether a person can be killed by pain alone—if you can 'hurt to death,' as it were. If you try something as extreme as planeswalking, we likely will find out."

"What . . . What did you do to me?"

This earned me another look. It was as cold as his voice. "I let you live."

"Am I supposed to thank you?"

"*Boss*," Baltrice hissed. "For the love of *crap*, don't antagonize him!"

"What you are supposed to do, Beleren," he said as he removed the last of the bandages, "is what you're told."

He held the hand up to inspect the damage. He had some kind of wire twisted so tightly around his wrist that it was cutting into his flesh. Two of the fingers on that hand were missing their last joint, and all had only ragged bloody splotches where his fingernails should have been. His only reaction was a tiny compression of the lips, as though he were mildly irritated.

"It was you," I said. "It was you all along."

"No," he said. "The body was mine, within the illusion, but the mind you felt was my father's. Inspired by the trick you pulled with Rhoka, in fact—you can be surprisingly resourceful. It was the closest I could come to a prudent course. My estimate of your ability is comprehensive. And apparently accurate."

"Have I told you lately that you scare the crap out of me?"

"I should." This earned me another look—and there was a hint of softening to his features, as though he might actually smile. A friendly smile, instead of the predatory grimace I always used to see. "That's a compliment," he said. "My estimate of your intellect is similarly comprehensive."

He stepped over a body part or two on his way to the shocky mercenary in the corner. The mercenary looked up at Tezzeret with eyes like moons on a clear night. "Don't . . . come on, don't . . ." the mercenary managed to say. "I can . . . I can *help* you, right?"

"Right." Tezzeret leaned down and took the mercenary's remaining hand as though to pull the man to his feet. When instead he produced the small hooked knife he'd used to cut away the bandages, the mercenary started to scream.

He didn't stop screaming until Tezzeret had severed the man's hand at the wrist. It wasn't a gentle kind of thing. Or fast; the guy stopped screaming because he was bleeding out. When Tezzeret finally dropped the arm, its fountain of blood had already slowed to a trickle. He held the dying man's hand upright on the palm of his own injured hand as he unlooped the wire around his wrist.

As the wire came free, blood spurted from his two severed fingers—and just as swiftly, the blood stopped, and the last joints of the dying man's fingers turned black and rotted away. The fingernails disintegrated, and shortly Tezzeret tossed the dead hand onto the body of its dead owner.

"Necromancy," he said, holding up his hand again, which was now only bloody. His fingertips were back, all his nails were in place, and now he did smile, just a bit. "A useful trick I picked up from an unlucky bandit, when I was just a teenager."

With Baltrice's help, I eventually managed to sit up. "Tezzeret . . ." I began, then shook my head. There had to be something I could say. Some way to convince him to let her go. "I have these dreams, sometimes. Ever since I . . . uh, you know, since our fight. Nightmares, I guess. Where you were still alive. Coming after me."

The smile wiped itself from existence. "Likewise. Except in mine, I catch you."

"And then I'd wake up and tell myself I was being stupid, because I knew you were dead. You *were* dead. I felt you die. But I could never make myself believe it."

"The avenging revenant." He nodded. "Your conscience always did have a way of manifesting itself at . . . inconvenient times."

And this would be one of them, I thought. "You know that Baltrice was fighting for you, all the way to the end, right?"

She made a face sour as old vinegar. "Do we really have to bring all that up again?"

"She went toe to toe with Liliana Vess. What Liliana did to her—well, never mind. She suffered a lot for being loyal to you, that's all."

"And?"

"I just hope you won't make her suffer for being loyal to me."

The crow's-feet at the corners of his eyes deepened a bit. "She won't be the one who suffers."

"I guessed that part already," I told him. "I don't expect to get out of this alive. I thought—I *knew*—that if I ever saw you again, you were gonna snuff me like a candle."

"I considered it," he said. "It would have been an inelegant solution."

"What?"

"And . . . well, not to grind too fine an edge on it, but it seemed rather foolish for me, *alive*, to kill you in revenge for my murder."

"That wasn't your attitude at the time."

"I recall. I also recall that I was, at the time, *hmmm*, a bit emotional. If my eyes had been knives, I would have yanked them both out of my face to throw them at you."

"Yeah," I said. "I was there."

"Perhaps returning from the dead has altered my perspective. All I know is how I feel now, and what I think now—which is at some considerable remove from what I felt and thought then."

"So—what, you're *forgiving* me?"

"I do not forgive," he said with a level stare. "But a blood vendetta between us is of no use to anyone but our enemies."

"We have enemies?" I said. "We as in *you and me*? Really?"

"Dead, you would be nothing more than an excuse for Baltrice to kill me."

"*That* decision isn't made yet," she growled.

"You see?" He opened a hand toward her, as a conjuror might invite his audience to observe a nifty trick. "You're an excellent hostage, a fact that has saved my life already tonight. As for you, Baltrice, well . . . you have your own reasons to hate me, and I'm sorry for that. I can only plead exigent circumstances, and ask that you accept my apology."

She blinked up at him, her face slack in surprise—which was pretty much how I felt, too. "Are you yanking my chain?"

"I am not the man who cut you with the mana knife, Baltrice. I am not the man who ordered you into that last battle. Whether I am a better man, or a worse one, is not yet determined. Meanwhile, I am truly sorry for what I—the man I was then—did to you."

Color was rising in Baltrice's cheeks—never a good thing. "You think that gets you off the hook?"

"I don't expect it to," he said. "I wish only to express my regret. What to do with that knowledge is a decision you'll have to face on your own."

"I got a decision *you* can face in the seat of my *pants*."

Tezzeret stepped over another body part or three to squat down in front of me, close enough that if I'd had a dagger I could have stabbed him. His face still displayed nothing beyond that eerie calm. "Please believe me when I tell you that I do not desire your death. I have done this to you because I have been saddled with a fiendishly difficult task, and I can't risk any interference. Especially from you. You need to understand your situation, Jace—may I call you Jace?"

"I guess not killing me lets you call me whatever you want."

MATTHEW STOVER

"Thank you. You have some idea already of the gross parameters of what I've done. To make sure you don't inadvertently take your own life, I must share with you some of the subtleties that underlie your condition."

"As long as it doesn't involve any more demonstrations," I said. "Tell, don't show, all right?"

"See this?" He held out the coil of wire that he'd used to tourniquet his hand. "This is a metal called etherium."

"It's what that arm of yours was made of, right?"

"Very similar. It is also what the device is made of, the one that is currently inhabiting your central nervous system. The salient feature of etherium is that it doesn't wholly exist in this universe. Or in any. In ways that can't be precisely explained in words, etherium simultaneously exists in the Blind Eternities; it is an alloy of æther itself. Etherium, in a very real sense, has a, oh, I suppose you'd say, an inanimate version of a Planeswalker's Spark. Understanding this is essential for your survival. Are you following me so far?"

"I guess . . ."

"I know that you will try to remove my device, or deactivate it. You will fail, and the attempt may kill you."

Well, of course he'd *say* so. Didn't make it true. "Go on."

"First, the device cannot be drained of power, or choked off from its source of mana; etherium, by virtue of its special nature, is a *source* of mana. Or it channels mana from the Blind Eternities, or carries with it the energy that is reality. As I said, words are imprecise.

"You have experienced already the sort of pain that attempting magical operations can cause. You need to understand that even worse effects will be created by someone using magic *on* you. You also need to know that analgesic treatment, up to and including magically deactivating your brain's pain center, will only hasten your death.

It would be a death you wouldn't want me to even describe. Trust that it will be torment that transcends description.

"The special nature of etherium also means that it cannot—I repeat, can*not*—be fully manipulated by anyone who is not a Planeswalker. My own Spark—my own connection to the Blind Eternities—enables me to do things with etherium that cannot be matched by any plane-bound mage, no matter how powerful."

"So I'd have to find a Planeswalker to turn this thing off."

"One particular Planeswalker," he said. "Me. Unless you know of another Planeswalker who is a mechanist of my ability. To the best of my knowledge, there has ever been only one other being with the requisite abilities, and he has been lost in the infinite reach of the Blind Eternities for decades. Nicol Bolas himself can't find this being. Nothing that can be done by you or anyone you can find will work, and any serious attempt will likely kill you. Your best course is to resign yourself to your situation, and console yourself that it is temporary."

"Is it?" I said. "Temporary?"

"Unless I am slain or incapacitated," he said. "Think of it as a vacation."

I wasn't worried. Not really. Not yet. Though I had a feeling that after a try or two demonstrated Tezzeret wasn't lying, I might start getting a little anxious.

Baltrice found the words that I didn't even really want to think, let alone say. "This 'fiendish task' of yours—just how dangerous is it?"

He turned to her with a decidedly pensive look. "I do not expect to succeed," he said evenly. "Nor do I expect to survive the attempt."

"Then why in the hells are you gonna try it in the first place?"

He sighed. "I have never been a notably original thinker," he said. "My gifts lie in the realms of attention to detail, and—I believe the phrase is—an infinite capacity for taking pains. The device I inflicted upon you, Jace, is a slight elaboration of one that has recently been inflicted on me."

"You?" I blinked at him while I tried to figure out how I felt about that. "I kind of think that should make me feel better."

"But it doesn't," he said, again frank and almost friendly. "I know."

"So when you don't *survive* the *experience*," Baltrice said heavily, "what happens to him?"

"Eventually? Insanity," he said with a half-apologetic shrug in my direction, "and a horrible death."

"If he's gonna go that way anyway—" She stood up, and flames gathered around her head and shoulders. "Give me one good reason why I shouldn't roast you right here."

"Because," he said seriously, still squatting, showing no slightest sign of worry, "that prediction was based on my working *alone*."

She looked at him, then she looked at me, and I looked back at her, and that flush on her cheeks got brighter. So did the flames. "Oh, come on, not really, no way . . ." she said. "You are *not* expecting me to—no *way*!"

Tezzeret shrugged. "I have never been a great fighter, even when I had my arm and all the resources of the Infinite Consortium to back me. You, though—Baltrice, you are more than a great fighter. You're a one-woman bloody damned army."

Her flush spread up around her eyes, replacing some of the white-hot anger she'd been carrying there a second before. "You took me easily enough."

"I took *him*. You?" He still had that open but serious look on his face. "If I'd had to fight you, I'd be dead already. You surrendered to save Jace's life."

"And you're asking me to do it all over again."

"His life isn't actually saved yet," he pointed out. "And if what you really want is a clear shot at me, where's better for you to stand than right at my back?"

She looked at me, and again I looked back at her, and I could see that somehow both our lives hung on what I said next.

"I . . . I can't ask you to do this for me," I told her, and if I had even a whisper of a chance to undo the spell, I wouldn't have to make the speech. "I sure as hell won't order you to. Do what you think is best. Not for me. For you."

She sighed and chuckled ruefully. "You little turd," she said to me, shaking her head. "Like I'm gonna say no after a speech like that."

Tezzeret's gaze flicked back and forth between her face and mine, and he had a distinctive steely glint in his eyes—a lot like he used to look when one of his inventions had performed exactly as designed.

Baltrice said, "So what's this fiendish task?"

Tezzeret stood. "I am to find a Planeswalker known as Crucius the Mad Sphinx, who was last seen here on Esper, some decades ago," he said. "By literally no coincidence at all, he is that other Planeswalker I spoke of just now—the one being in the Multiverse who is better at handling etherium than I am. At least, I believe him to be superior, and I think I am justified in my belief by the fact that it was Crucius who invented etherium in the first place, and that Crucius is to this day the only being who ever has had the ability to create it."

"Oh, I get it," Baltrice said. "A little extra incentive, right? So you want me to think that if you and I can find him, *he'll* be able to take care of Beleren . . . and I won't need you anymore."

"That is an accurate summary of the situation."

"You expect me to believe it? You can't smell the giant pile of Way Too Convenient heaped on top of that story?"

Tezzeret's lips compressed briefly, and after a moment he nodded. "There are a number of features of my new life that seem to be, well . . . overly contrived is, I think, the best description," he said slowly. "As though I had set about to create an entirely new machine, then found the parts already manufactured and laid out precisely in order on my workbench. Having been conscious for less than twenty-four hours, I have been too busy trying to survive to spare any time for deep analysis of my situation. I surmise that there is an underlying teleology here, but I have not yet been able to verify it."

"Sucks to be you, huh?"

"Sometimes," he said. "The pertinent detail is that I have been forced into a role very like the one I had originally intended for you, Jace. I discover that I don't like it any better than you did, and I have decided—not being a notably original thinker, after all—to employ the same solution you did."

"I don't follow."

"Nicol Bolas," he said. "You remember Nicol Bolas."

"Only in bad dreams."

"I'm going to kill him," he said as though he was commenting it looked like rain.

It was a good thing I was already sitting down. I could only stare. Baltrice spluttered like a balky skyrocket. "You . . . you *what*? Are you completely frappin' *cracked*?"

"Very likely. But cracked or not, the fact remains," he said. "I *am* going to kill Nicol Bolas."

"Oh, sure," I said when I found my voice. "And while you're off burning down three-quarters of the Multiverse, I'm supposed to sit here in Vectis with my thumb up my butt?"

"Not at all. You," said Tezzeret with that eerie calm that was starting to look more and more like crazy every time I saw it, "are going to look after my father."

THE METAL ISLAND
PRINCIPLES OF DESIGN

A curious feature of human memory," Bolas murmured as he disengaged his brilliant blue memory siphon from Jace Beleren's brain, and returned the mind-ripper's unconscious body to the plinth with oddly gentle care. "You remember being in pain, but you don't remember the pain itself."

Nearby, Tezzeret still hung in a Web of Restraint, though a less uncomfortable one. "I suspect," he said, "that it's an artifact of construction."

"I'm sorry?"

"The human brain is largely a signal-processing apparatus. As such, it is divided into specialized sectors. Pain is a product of specific neural activity in a specific sector of the brain. Memory arises of neural activity in a different sector. The pain sector is not activated in the process, except in pathological cases. If it hurt as much to remember pain as it had to experience it, there would be little disincentive to repeat the experience. Which would defeat the design function of pain in the first place."

"Of course—the lecture on mechanics. You're so predictable."

"I'll take that as a compliment," Tezzeret replied. "Reliability is the most useful objective measure of superior design."

The dragon's brows arched to a comically skeptical height. "Am I to believe that your personal design is supposedly superior? And if it weren't, am I to believe that you would actually admit it?"

"My design," Tezzeret replied imperturbably, "is a work in progress. I find myself more interested in what you're *not* talking about. And why."

"Tezzie, Tezzie, come *on*. Do you actually expect me to waste breath discussing your preposterous vanity? It's just you and me here, Tezzie. You don't have to pretend that you really *believe* you can kill me. How about we just stipulate the truth and move on, shall we?"

Tezzeret said, "No."

"Excuse me?"

"I'm not prepared to stipulate. It's not the truth."

The dragon belched a gust of incredulous laughter. "Are you prepared to stipulate that you're batshit insane?" he said.

"And which of us is the more predictable, after all?" Tezzeret said. "Whenever confronted with something you do not understand, you dismiss it as irrelevant, misconstructed, or damaged."

"Does being completely staggering *cracked* count as a design flaw?"

"Not necessarily," Tezzeret said. "What if I am insane, but also right? Perhaps being *completely staggering cracked* is not so much a design flaw as it is a fillip of stylistic excess—baroque filigree on a headsman's axe, if you see what I mean."

"Were you always this nuts? Did I just not notice?"

"I can't say," he replied. "However, you should bear in mind that whatever I am now—how well or poorly I function—is largely the result of your own talents, or lack thereof, as a designer; the result of your presumed gifts as an artificer of human flesh. It seems clear to me that you were less than wholly satisfied with who I was previously. When you restored my consciousness and functionality, I can only assume that you made certain alterations. You would not be the first artificer to discover that his device exhibits unexpected—perhaps unwelcome, even actively dangerous—features, as a result of insufficient foresight, skill, and preparation."

Bolas chuckled. "So whatever's wrong with you is all my fault, eh? Because you're just a machine."

"Hardly," Tezzeret said. "No competent artificer would design humans as we are: so limited an array of operating environments; so many useless parts; vital systems so inefficient and prone to breakdown that the vast bulk of the energy we expend is wasted in mere maintenance—maintenance which, even if performed *perfectly*, is still insufficient to materially lengthen productive life span. Not to mention that we are difficult to repair, and prohibitively expensive to replace."

Bolas exposed jagged teeth within a curl of a grin. "It was my understanding that, mm, *human replacements*, to use your term, are not only free, but that, ah, their *construction* is considered an enjoyable recreation."

"Think of it in machine terms," Tezzeret said. "Preliminary assembly puts the constructing unit—the mother—on reduced service for, on average, one third of the gestational period, while consuming even more resources than she had before. Once born, a human is not functional; primary assembly requires, on average, seven years, during which the child is literally nothing but an energy sink, consuming time, attention, and food without any return except dung. To achieve full physical function requires, on average, about sixteen years. And this leaves aside questions of training and education, emotional stability, and the disciplined intellect necessary for self-direction, all of which require even more time and energy to inculcate. If people had any idea just how expensive a human being actually is, they'd take better care of themselves."

"You're *awfully* chatty, all of a sudden."

"With less than one thousandth the energy expenditure that creating a fully functional human being requires," Tezzeret went on, "I could design and build a device capable of everything a human can do, including creative problem solving, singing, writing poetry, whatever you like—not to mention creating its own replacements—and do it for a thousand years."

"How is it," Nicol Bolas said distantly, once more frowning down the beach beyond the captive Planeswalkers, "that every time I talk to you, I end up getting a speech about how smart you are?"

"Our whole relationship is about how smart I am," Tezzeret said. "It goes back to your predictability."

"Good liar, too."

Tezzeret smiled. "When I have to be."

"If you're so smart and I'm so predictable, what have I been waiting for?"

"You're waiting for an interplanar gate to open down the beach."

The dragon jerked as though he'd been stung. His long sinuous neck practically put a kink in itself to bring his huge yellow eyes back around to stare down at the human. He made no effort to conceal his surprise; on the contrary, he fixed his gaze on Tezzeret with predatory focus. "And why do I expect it?"

"For the same reason you knew Baltrice and Jace were planeswalking in. You've learned some clockworking."

"I dabble, I dabble. As a hobby," the dragon admitted. "How did you know?"

"You're seeing the future—what, a few minutes out? Something like that. Silas Renn could to that trick—see the quantum smear of possible futures and watch events develop as they become more and more likely."

"And so it's possible," the dragon purred, "that I am what I eat, after all."

"It was probably the last thing he taught you."

"Oh, please. In twenty-five thousand years, you think I never learned clockworking?"

"I'm sure you did," Tezzeret said. "Funny that you needed to learn it again, isn't it?"

Nicol Bolas went very, very still.

"You're not the dragon you used to be, old worm," Tezzeret said with an odd note in his voice, one almost of sympathy. "You're not even the dragon you were twelve years ago, when I stole the Infinite Consortium out from under your tail. You put a good face on it, but the cracks in your mask have begun to show. Someone who knows how to look can see right into you."

"Oh?" The dragon's voice sounded like the early notes of a distant volcanic eruption. "Then what am I thinking right now?"

Tezzeret smiled again. "You're remembering how you had thought my declared intention to kill you had been merely a vain boast. Now you're reflecting that suddenly you're not so sure, and you're wondering if perhaps you should kill me before you find out."

The dragon's response was to turn fully to face Tezzeret, to spread his wings and draw mana from throughout the Multiverse until the air around him blazed with power.

Tezzeret said, "You're not going to like how this ends." 137

TEST OF METAL

Nicol Bolas lifted one enormous fist. "I'll regret it in the morning, right?"

"In the morning you'll be decomposing on this beach."

"I'll take my chances."

"You can see futures. In how many of them am I dead?"

The dragon's fleshy brow ridges drew together, and his fist lowered, just a bit.

"Look into the futures that arise from you assaulting me now," Tezzeret said. "In how many of them are you alive?"

Bolas's eyes widened, and his fist fell forgotten to his side. "It's not . . ." His voice was no more than a strangled whisper. "How can you . . . it . . . just isn't *possible*. . . ."

"You need to understand that our relationship has turned a corner," Tezzeret said, and walked out of the Web of Restraint as if it wasn't even there.

Bolas stared. "You can't *do* that!"

"Sorry," he said. "You might want to take a seat. We should talk."

"It's a *trick*," the dragon snarled. "It's some kind of illusion—once you're dead, it'll be—"

Tezzeret sighed and lifted his right hand above his head, then clenched his fist with a yank as if plucking unripe fruit from a tree. As though animated by the gesture, the leading edge of the right wing of the Metal Sphinx—a single vast girder of etherium, by itself larger and heavier than Nicol Bolas's whole body—shrieked through the air and slammed into the dragon just below his wing joint with crushing force.

Bolas folded around the impact, and went skidding helplessly back to sprawl in the sand. His roar of sudden rage sounded a bit thin and wheezy, but thoroughly sincere as he scrambled to rise and gathered power to strike back.

Tezzeret said, "Think about the future."

Bolas hesitated.

"Look around you," he went on. "Think about where you are, and what this place is made of. Think about who I am and what you have made of me."

The dragon cast his gaze toward the etherium trees, at the etherium sphinx and the etherium plinth, the etherium rocks and the etherium sand on which he rested. Then very slowly, very cautiously, he adjusted his posture to a feline seated position, wings folded and tail curled around himself, and he looked upon Tezzeret with a decidedly more guarded expression. "So."

"I know it's a shock," Tezzeret said. "But at your age, you should have learned that many truths we regard as immutable are, in fact, surprisingly context dependent. For example, when I acknowledged earlier that you are the most powerful being in the Multiverse, it would have been more precise to say: in the *rest* of the Multiverse."

"I see I have underestimated you."

"You always did."

"You could have killed me at any time. From the very first instant I arrived."

Tezzeret spread his hands. "Surprise."

"You can kill me right now. Why don't you?"

"You may as well ask why we haven't played Intimidate the Naked Prisoner. Or why I haven't insisted on calling you Nicky, or perpetrated any of the various indignities with which you have amused yourself at my expense," Tezzeret said. "The answer to all three is an aspect of character that I value; one which you, I might add, conspicuously lack."

"And that is?"

"Manners."

The dragon's response was a contemptuous snort.

Tezzeret shrugged. "Manners are commonly derided by those who have none, just as education is derided by the ignorant, refinement by the coarse, and intellect," he said with a tiny sigh of apology, "by the stupid."

The dragon's growl, low in his throat, had much the same brick-grinding quality as had his earlier chuckle. "Who in the hells cares about your *manners*?"

"My manners, for better or worse, are keeping you alive."

"This is a joke, right? Some kind of a put-on. You're just yanking my tail."

"I would never taunt someone in my power," he replied. "To mock those who have power *over* you is a valid occupation of anyone with the wit to do so; witness satirists, jesters, and court fools across every plane of creation. Rulers who mock their subjects, on the other hand, only advertise their unfitness for the position they hold. Taunting the helpless is the province of scumbags, assholes, and doltish thugs like you."

He lifted a hand before Bolas could respond. "No disrespect intended; I use *doltish thug* in its technical sense: a violently criminal blockhead."

"You're too kind."

"Now that I think of it," he mused, "I may owe you an apology for my earlier use of the word *stupid*; *blockhead* is a more apt term. It's not that you can't think; it's just that you don't like to."

"You're enjoying this."

"No more than is appropriate, I hope," Tezzeret said with a thin smile. "When I allow the gate to open, it is very important that you make no sudden move, and that you make no attempt to exert power of any kind. Either will be dangerous for you. Possibly fatal."

The dragon blinked. "When you *allow*—?"

"Yes."

"You *are* yanking my tail."

"Bolas," Tezzeret said patiently, "weren't you at all curious about why you kept seeing an interplanar gate in your immediate future, while none ever appeared? Every time you looked for it, I delayed its opening—which is to say, I moved the gate farther along our time line. I couldn't risk allowing our visitor to arrive before you and I had our little talk."

"Who is this visitor you're so worried about?"

"One of three. We're about to find out," Tezzeret said. "Before you arrived, I had determined that there were four candidates, but the fourth was Silas Renn, so unless he was a *great* deal more skilled a clockworker than I gave him credit for, we can rule him out. Another candidate is Crucius himself."

"Now I'm interested," Bolas said. "Is that what you were talking about when you said, 'There is no secret'?"

"No," he said simply. "Another possible candidate is me."

"Really? You? I mean, another you? Using a gate?"

"How do you think I got here in the first place?"

"Huh. Were *we* here when you got here in the first place?"

Tezzeret smiled. "I'm not telling."

"Wouldn't that be some kind of paradox—put you in two places at the same time, something like that?"

"Where we are is all one place," Tezzeret said, "and time, old worm, is a slippery concept. Especially here and now. Because here, it's *always* now."

The dragon snorted a gust of greasy smoke. "The next time I bring you back to life, it'll be without a mouth."

"Once our visitor—whoever it turns out to be—has come and gone, you will be free to leave."

"Sure I will."

"Whether you believe me or not is irrelevant," Tezzeret said. "I am inviting you, however, to stay yet awhile."

"Just to be friendly?"

The human shrugged. "We have known each other for well over a decade. An eyeblink to you, of course, but a substantial fraction of my life. In that time, we have never achieved a real understanding; our relationship has been a structure of your domination set against my resistance. I would prefer not to simply reverse that dynamic."

"Not to mention that any *reversing* of that *dynamic* is over as soon as I get the hell out of your fantasy playground here."

"Which is why you will be free to leave."

"You sound like you actually mean that."

"I am done with *taking* from you, Bolas. I have no more interest in your freedom than I have in your life. But I wish to share with you the progress of the journey you set me on. I have some hope that when you understand what I have experienced—what I have done, and not least, what you have made of me—you will realize that you have nothing to lose, and a great deal to gain, by simply letting me go my way."

"Live and let live."

"Exactly."

"Why not?" Bolas said. "It's not as though either of us has ever been known to hold a grudge."

Tezzeret displayed just enough thin smile to signal that he'd registered the sarcasm. "If our visitor proves to be the individual I regard as most probable, she will be elderly, and likely quite frail. I tell you this by way of warning. Do not make any movement that I might interpret as hostile. As she will be unable to defend herself, I will defend her. Aggressively."

The dragon's brow ridge arched again. "She must be something special."

"I'll introduce you," Tezzeret said, and gestured toward the sand directly in front of the plinth, where presently a shimmer in the air gathered itself into a broadly arching span of silvery plane. This plane was vertical and free-standing, and it showed the very faintest of ripples chasing one another across it, as if perhaps some current of the Blind Eternities stirred the surfaces of the two universes.

"There?" Bolas said in mild surprise. "When I was seeing it, the gate—"

"Was several hundred meters down the beach, yes," Tezzeret said. "I've shifted the gate so that she won't have quite so far to walk."

"You are a wealth of surprises today."

"The measure of character lies not in how powerful you are, but in how you use the power you have."

"And you're just full of half-nifty aphorisms, too. I bet you've been saving them up."

"I've been preparing this conversation for a long time," he admitted with a fractional widening of his thin smile. "I'd hate to leave anything out."

"Is that the Good Manners version of gloating?"

"Hush now. Here she comes."

Out from the far side of the shimmering plane hobbled the wreckage of an ancient sphinx.

Even at her obviously advanced age, she was huge, much larger than an ordinary sphinx, very little smaller than Bolas himself. Her wings hung in tatters, her feathers showing iridescent azure only in patches, as though most of them were dying or dead, little more than naked quills hanging from perished follicles. The joints of her enormous legs were swollen, and her toes were knobbed with arthritis. Her shield-shaped head swung uncertainly, as though seeking an angle that would allow her cataract-webbed eyes to focus, and her skin was everywhere crosshatched with striated scars that once had held etherium filigree of extraordinary complexity and grace.

Facing away from the Metal Sphinx, she spoke to the only figure her ancient eyes could discern. *"Dragon. I am no threat to you, and what remains of meat on these old bones will be stringy and tough."* Her voice was thin, a breathy rasp, as though her vocal cords had shredded from age. *"Let us be civil with each other, though our lands be at war. I do not come here for battle."*

"Don't worry about me," Bolas said. "I'm not from Jund—and even if I was, I wouldn't exactly go to war for them. And looking at you, no offense, I just lost my appetite."

"It is well, then. There is a human, a mage, called Tezzeret the Seeker. Do you know this man?"

"A little," Nicol Bolas said. "He's right behind you."

"Indeed?" The sphinx began the slow and apparently painful process of turning herself about. *"Tezzeret?"*

"I'm here, Your Wisdom." Tezzeret vaulted down from the plinth, landing catlike on the etherium sand. "I am honored by this meeting, and gratified that you have achieved the transit."

"As am I. When Kemuel revealed the stricture of the Riddle Gate, I very nearly despaired."

"But only nearly," Tezzeret said fondly, "for here you are: a living testament to your own greatness of spirit."

"You flatter like a vedalken, child."

"I only attempt to emulate their gift of conversation. Flattery it may be, but truth it is."

She tilted her face up toward the hundred-times-larger face of the Metal Sphinx. *"And so,"* she said, her rasp going even hoarser with awe, *"this is the place, and the hour, you prescribed?"*

"It is, Your Wisdom."

"And so this . . ." She shook her head helplessly, in the face of wealth enough to buy her whole planet dozens of times over. *"This . . . extravagance of etherium . . . I can feel him. I can feel him near."*

"He is, Your Wisdom."

"Yet I see nothing but blur." Her great face shone with tears. *"And so I have crossed entire universes to see him, this once and final time, stripped away every scrap of my power . . . only to have my eyes fail me at the last. The final bitter jest in my mockery of a life."*

Tezzeret bent down and took a handful of the etherium sand. "Your Wisdom, if you'll permit me—?"

She slowly, painfully, lowered herself to lie in the sand like a great winged cat. Tezzeret reached up and laid his free hand gently upon her face, and the etherium sand in his other hand spilled upward, as though the local gravity had somehow been reversed. It gathered into the filigree scars across her face, and then without heat, fused itself there.

She blinked, and blinked again, and when she looked up into the majestic face of the Metal Sphinx, she gasped.

Tezzeret said, "I did not invite you here to see you disappointed."

"Oh, Tezzeret . . ." she breathed. Tears like liquid diamonds caught the brilliant sun in points of fire. *"Oh, my child . . ."*

"Shall I give you privacy?"

"Please."

He backed solemnly away from her, then turned to walk over to Bolas. Behind him, an etherium-colored mist gathered in the air around the Metal Sphinx and the sphinx of flesh.

"I am, I think," the dragon said, shaking his head in wonder, "as close to speechless as I have ever come. The way the old beast carried on, you'd think that bloody statue was Crucius himself!"

"When I said there is no secret," Tezzeret said through another of his slim smiles, "*that's* what I was talking about."

"That—? *That*?" The dragon's great yellow eyes widened, and for a long second his huge lower jaw swung loose. "That's *him*?" he wheezed as though he couldn't quite get his breath. "That—that statue right there—that's *Crucius* . . . ?"

"Some of him. It's more accurate to say that the Metal Sphinx is an *expression* of him. Everything in this place is an expression of Crucius and of his not-so-mortal remains. He is what he made, and what he made is him."

"All this time—ever since—you were *standing* right there, when you said you know everywhere he isn't. You were *standing* between his *paws*!"

"Yes," Tezzeret said. "Interested in more of the story?"

TEZZERET
RIDDLE ME THIS

S o, Tezz," Doc said thoughtfully inside my head, "this
Silas Renn character—you know what I like about him?"

Watching in the scrying dish as Renn strode about as
though he were actually doing something useful in the
Academy's defense, shouting orders at the top of a voice
I had hoped to never hear again, I could say only, "No."

"Me neither. What a tool, huh?"

"I agree. And as a master mechanist, I am a recognized
authority on the subject."

"Tezz—wow. Was that a pun? Is it my birthday?"

"Hush now, Doc. He's moving."

"What, somebody's gonna hear me?"

"No, but I have to pay attention. The only reason he does
not know he is being observed is that our surveillance is not
focused on him personally, but generally, on the chamber.
If I lose him, he will be difficult to reacquire without giving
myself away."

"So? You're still afraid of him?"

"No. I despised him," I muttered as I adjusted the point-
of-view angle in the scrying dish to follow Renn out into
the corridor. "I was never afraid of him."

"Even when he was handing your ass to you with a
complimentary swirly on the side?"

"Like most weak men, he is dangerous only when
frightened," I said.

"If he's so weak, how come he kicked your butt up and down that courtyard all the time?"

"Weak in character, not in ability."

Renn paused at an intersection long enough to berate a couple of the Order's chairwomen. I left the vision silent—I have heard enough of Renn's self-righteous upsloper ranting to last me several lifetimes—but I took the opportunity to adjust the scry view to where it could cover the intersecting corridors in any direction.

"His natural magical ability outstrips mine by an order of magnitude. And his family is obscenely wealthy—they bought enough etherium for him to replace most of his body. In three years of trying, I never defeated him."

"You don't sound too worried about losing again."

Several nearby detonations rocked the building enough to shake not only dust from the ceiling but flakes of stone from the buttresses.

"I didn't come here to fight, Doc."

"Good thing, too," he said. "Save your fighting for sometime when screwing up won't get me killed along with you."

"If we have to fight, I've already screwed up," I muttered. The shrieking discharge of the city's anti-dragon artillery set my teeth on edge.

A string of detonations laddered rising thunder as though coming straight for me; the final blast seemed to be just next door. The room pitched and bucked like a maddened gargoyle. Dust and razor-edged stone chips filled the air. Statues that had stood for centuries tumbled from their pedestals and shattered on the floor.

"I *hate* that—that *explosion* thing!" Doc whined in my ear. "What in the hells *are* those?"

"I'm not sure." Renn was moving again. I turned the scry-view angle to follow. "Magical, mundane, whatever—I hope never to be close enough to one to find out. Don't worry too much; the Academy's defensive screens will deflect any that might hit us directly."

"Which isn't gonna do us a hell of a lot of good if the concussion knocks down the building and thirty bajillion tons of stone falls on our head," Doc said. "I still think we could have done this from a little bit farther away. Like, say, Bant."

Further blasts, however, sounded only in the distance, and shortly they too faded. No more than a few moments passed before the sirens outside wailed the all clear. The etherium chime on the desk by my left hand gave out a musical *ping*. "All right. Apport interdiction's suspended while they evacuate the wounded, which means that right about *now* . . ."

There came a deep, resonant thump, more like distant thunder than nearby explosives, which was, to my educated ear, exactly the sound I'd been expecting—the air displacement created by something very, very large teleporting into the Academy's courtyard. In the scrying dish, Renn jumped as if stung and ran for a window.

"Do you get tired of being right all the time?"

"If I were right *all* the time," I muttered, "you and I would have never met."

Reaching out with my mind, I found the tiny device Baltrice wore in her ear. *He's heading for the courtyard along the west colonnade. It would be best if you were there first.*

Her muttered response was conveyed through the same link. *Really? Boy, it's a good thing I've got you around to remind me about crap we already planned.*

The upside of this method of communication was that I didn't have to endure running commentary from Doc. I pulled the scry view to the colonnade and briefly angled it into the courtyard to confirm my expectation: the immense, elegant majesty of the Grand Hegemon of

Esper, flanked by two young adult male sphinxes near enough to her size to have been her sons, all three shimmering with a fortune in etherium filigree that shone even through the residual smoke of the raid. The balance of her retinue was more or less as expected, human and vedalken mages, homunculi, a pair of juvenile firedrakes, none of any concern or consequence to me.

Renn shortly entered view, striding briskly toward a small clot of maids and porters who stood gaping just short of the colonnade, as a personal visit by the Grand Hegemon was a once-in-a-generation event. He snarled at them with his characteristic flap of the hands, and I touched the control on the rim of the scrying dish to pick up audio, as this was about to become amusing.

The maids and porters scattered like a flock of startled geese, except for one huge and hulking porter who didn't seem to hear. The porter just stood there without reaction, leaning casually on the long handle of a push sweep. "Boy! Porter!" Renn snapped, stomping forward. "Are you *deaf*, boy? I said *get out of sight!*"

The porter still did not react. Renn's face was nearly as red as his crushed-velvet surplice by the time he got close enough to the porter's shoulder to yank a sleeve. "I will count to *three*, boy, and when—"

The porter responded with a casual backhanded pimp slap that smacked Renn off his feet and sent him skidding along the corridor, out of sight from the courtyard. "Who are you calling *boy*, bitch?"

"You know," Doc said as we watched the semiconscious Renn try to fumble out some kind of defensive magic, "you gotta give her points for style."

"She does make a vivid first impression."

Before Renn could remember what plane they were on, Baltrice pounced like a feral viashino, hooked an enormous

150

MATTHEW STOVER

hand around one of Renn's etherium ribs, then picked him up like a suitcase and gave him a good shaking. Once she had satisfied herself that she had shaken him well before using, she turned him rightway up and slammed him into the wall. "Shh, now, sweetcake. Don't make a fuss."

"You, ah, you, ah—" Renn still seemed to be having trouble understanding exactly what was happening to him. "This isn't—do you *know* who I *am*?"

"I'll tell you what I know." She lifted her free hand, which now sprouted flame hot enough to melt steel. "I know etherium won't burn," she said, "but I'm pretty sure your balls will."

"You can't *do* this!"

"You don't know what I can do," she said. "Screw with me and you'll find out."

"What—what do you want from me?"

"I want you to take me to the dance, sweetcake." She set him down and stripped off her porter's coveralls, revealing a very credible—if I do say so myself—surplice-and-cloak outfit such as those worn by the Anointed Fellows of the Arcane Council of the Order of the Seekers of Carmot. "I know you can't see it without a mirror, but that fancy glowy hunk of etherium you're using for a heart? Now it's a little *extra* glowy. What that means is that any time I start to worry you might be trying to get smooth with me, every part of your body that *isn't* etherium will burn to the kind of ash that blows away in a soft breeze. With me so far? Good."

She got rid of the coveralls, then paused a moment to raise her arms, admiring what was—again, if I say so myself—a spectacularly detailed illusion that they were both constructed of etherium.

"The other thing you should absorb here," she went on, "is that you're *not* on fire right now because I'm *stopping* the little extra glowy business from igniting, get me? You savvy what'll happen to you if anything happens to me? Here's a clue: it's the same as what'll happen if you so much as sneak up a hint of a shield to interfere with my control. Or if a sudden move breaks my concentration. *Fwhoosh.* Soft breeze. Got me? No? Give me a sign here, Renn. Wave a flag. Send up a flare."

"You can't—" Renn swallowed and started again. "It's *impossible*—no such spell *exists*!"

She smiled. "He told me you'd say that."

"He? There are others? How many?"

"Depends on how you count," she said through a predatory grin. "There's at least one of them who's gonna give you a pretty nasty shock."

I found myself with a bit of a predatory smile of my own as I pushed the scrying dish aside. "If only I could have been there to do it myself," I murmured.

Through the device in Baltrice's ear I could pick up their voices as Renn made introductions. *"Arcane Fellow Silas Renn, and—"*

"Baltrice," she said. *"Just Baltrice. It's a, y' know, an honor and all that."*

"You are called by a single name, then?" The voice of a sphinx is different from that of other creatures, for their vast hollow bones can function also as organ pipes, and so every phrase from a sphinx is a motif, and a speech can be a symphony. *"That is uncommon for a human, is it not?"*

"Yeah, well," she said through a crooked grin, *"a last name's just for people who want you to be impressed by their parents."*

I made a mental note to give her a bonus.

There followed a bit of hastily stammered conversation, as Renn haltingly attempted to explain why the rest of the Arcane Fellowship was not on hand to greet her.

He couldn't exactly admit the truth, which was that every Arcane Fellow and even many of the lesser masters were out desperately scavenging etherium. Etherium, as the basis of most weapons and an adjunct to every combat mage's power, was central to Esper's war effort . . . and the Seekers of Carmot, who had been pretending for many years to know how to make the stuff, now were faced with either providing for the whole land's needs, or publicly confessing their decades-long conspiracy to defraud the public.

Sangrite had been discovered in the mountains of Jund (with whom, inconveniently, we were currently at war), but carmot, the last essential ingredient—in an irony that warmed me every time I thought about it—remained so elusive that the masters couldn't even agree on what it was, much less where to find any. This meant that for the first time in the entire history of the Order, the Seekers of Carmot were out in the world, and—not to grind too fine an edge on it—they were actually, well . . .

Seeking carmot.

I doubt I'll ever stop finding that funny.

While it probably would have been even more amusing to leave Renn twisting in the wind of his own lies with his underclothes hanging out, Baltrice moved the plan in its intended direction with her customary bluntness. *"I believe Master Fellow Renn might be unaware that the Exalted Hieresiarch of the Order has unexpectedly returned, and awaits the Grand Hegemon in the Vault of the Codex."*

Renn was unquestionably unaware of this, as it was a bald-faced lie—but as I had anticipated, he was too concerned with protecting his own anatomy to do anything other than play along.

"He awaits me?" Sharuum fluted somberly. *"Then go we shall. There might we slake our thirst for knowledge at the original spring."*

They proceeded on through the Academy's innards without delay—due to protocols that were rigidly enforced at the Academy's construction, all public areas were easily accessible to sphinxes, most well-mannered dragons, and all but the very largest gargoyles—while Renn kept trying to summon some plausible excuse for preventing the Grand Hegemon from entering the Vault and discovering that the legendary mystical Codex Etherium to be wholly legendary and not mystical at all.

Sharuum shed members of her retinue at every juncture. By the time they reached the Tower of the Vault, only the two young male sphinxes remained, and she set them to guard the doors behind her.

Sharuum, Baltrice, and Renn wound their way up the great spiral stair to the spire-top Vault of the Codex. At the last, Renn was reduced to simple pleading. *"Please, Your Wisdom—the Vault is not intended for any but the Fellowship!"*

"I suppose that when one is made of glass," Sharuum replied solemnly, *"everything looks like a stone."*

At the door, he gave it one last shot. *"But—but—but—"*

"That's already two more than most folks have any use for," Baltrice put in, bless her snide little heart. *"How full of crap do you have to be to need three butts?"*

"Your Wisdom—Your Wisdom, please!" he stammered, pretending he hadn't heard. *"In the entire history of the Order of the Seekers of Carmot, no being who is not a Fellow of the Arcane Council has ever been inside the Vault!"*

This moment was, because I share with Nicol Bolas a regrettable fondness for the dramatic, when I reached out with my mind from where I stood—on the far side of the Vault, leaning on the lectern that held the Codex Etherium—and opened the door.

Carefully framed so that the swirling dust motes in the single shaft of sunlight from the roof portal above shimmered around me in a golden halo, making me shine in the gloom-shrouded chamber like a fugitive angel, I spread my hands with an apologetic shrug.

"I've never been a fellow of anything," I said, "and I've been here twice."

✷ ✷ ✷ ✷ ✷

There was very little commotion. Sharuum was even more inscrutable than is common for her opaque kind; Baltrice, of course, had known I would be there; and Renn was gob-smacked beyond speech.

"Your Wisdom." I stood up straight, of course, in the presence of my queen. "Please come in, and make yourself as comfortable as may be possible. Baltrice, if you could please see to Master Renn. He may need assistance in finding a seat."

Renn finally found his voice. "*You . . .*"

"Surprise."

"It's not *possible . . .*" He seemed to be having difficulty getting his breath. "I *saw you die!*"

"You share that honor with a surprising variety of others."

Sharuum lingered beyond the Vault door, eyeing me with wholly understandable caution. "*If this is your Hieresiarch,*" she piped to Renn, "*please convey my compliments to his doctor.*"

"Is she *hitting* on you?" Doc whispered in my left ear. "I think she's hitting on you. Wow, that makes her like a, whaddayasay, zoophiliac, right?"

I made as much of a *shh*-ing noise as I could manage without making Sharuum wonder if I might be impersonating a teapot.

"The *Hieresiarch*—? Him? He—he—" Renn sputtered. "He's the man who *murdered* the Hieresiarch!"

"The latest previous, Your Wisdom, a decade ago," I explained. "Nor was it murder."

"He was an *old man*!"

"He was attempting to rob me. I defended myself and my property."

"*Rob* you?" Renn said wildly. "Rob you in his own *study*?"

I sighed. "Baltrice?"

"Yeah." She put a hand to Renn's etherium breastbone and shoved him into a chair. "Sit."

"The current Hieresiarch is elsewhere," I said, "presumably mugging innocents for their etherium."

This comment turned Renn such an alarming shade of purple that I briefly wondered if his etherium heart might after all be vulnerable to spontaneous arrest.

"*Ah . . .*" Sharuum came slowly over the threshold, watching me as if I might be some exotic, unfamiliar, possibly dangerous bug. "*Tezzeret, isn't it? Tezzeret the Renegade—I've encountered your legend.*"

"Your Wisdom is very kind. Though I would resist the epithet *the Renegade*, as it implies that I broke faith with the Order, when the truth is precisely opposite."

Sharuum did not appear interested in the distinction. "*Is there an epithet you prefer?*"

This stopped me for a moment; I'd never actually thought about it. "I suppose," I said finally, "*the Seeker* suits me as well as any I can imagine. Unlike these fraudulent Seekers of Carmot, my search is real."

I watched closely to see how she would take this characterization of the Seekers, but again my powers of observation were insufficient to penetrate her seemingly infinite opacity. "*I have been given to understand that you are dead.*"

"He's *been* dead for more than *ten years*—" Renn forced out in a strangled gasp, and his hands went under his

MATTHEW STOVER

surplice, no doubt seeking some sort of anti-zombie spell or some such silliness.

Baltrice said, "*Fwhoosh.* Soft breeze."

Renn, with uncharacteristic insight, decided to shut the hell up.

"*Ten years?*" Fully within the Vault now, Sharuum brought her own light with her, in the softly twinkling radiance of her fantastically intricate etherium filigree, as well as the miniature solar system of etherium droplets the size of strige eggs that orbited around the majestic sun that was her humaniform mask. "*My information is younger than that—hardly dry, much less weaned.*"

I inclined my head. "Your Wisdom has excellent sources."

"Hey—hey, didn't Jace rip up your brain in, like, a whole different *universe?*" Doc hissed. "You think she knows about us? Well, not me, but about, y'know, Planeswalkers and such?"

"I have reason to believe she does," I murmured.

She inclined her head to take in a different view of my face. "*To whom do you speak?*"

Hmmm. Distressingly good ears. I took a breath. "As do many tinkerers, artists, and others who spend too much time alone, I have developed an unfortunate habit of talking to myself, Your Wisdom. I humbly beg your pardon."

"*For mumbling, or for lying?*"

I drew breath to protest, but the faintly sly smile that touched her humanlike lips was enough to stop me. "*You spoke truth, not honesty,*" she fluted, "*and thought I wouldn't know the difference.*"

Well.

I took a second or two to try out my response in my head before I let it pass my lips.

"I have spent entirely too much of my life around beings all too unfortunately resembling Master Renn, Your Wisdom," I said. "It has left me ill-prepared for thoughtful conversation."

"A pretty answer," she piped with a hint of amusement. *"A thorny union of truth and honesty, birthing graceful flattery."*

I inclined my head. Feeling myself flush, I did not trust my speech. It was unexpectedly gratifying to be appreciated by someone with real intellect.

She went on. *"Please assure your stealthy friend that he need not whisper, and then please introduce him."*

"Hey—hey, is she talking about me? She can hear me? How can she hear me?"

"The Grand Hegemon, Doc, was not born into her title, nor did she win it at dice," I said. "Your Wisdom, I call my friend Doc, short for Doctor Jest. My friend is stealthy from necessity, not discourtesy. His body is, for good or ill, coextensive with my own. He speaks to me by manipulating the nerves of my left ear. He and I have been . . . joined . . . only recently, and we are still unsure of our relations to each other, much less the rest of the world."

"And now we have an answer of more honesty than truth—but truth is, after all, merely fact," she piped.

"Whoa, crap, she talks like *you*!" he hissed.

"I have a more melodious voice."

"Um, yikes. Flinch. Cower."

"And Doc—if I may address you thus—would you care to share exactly where and how you learned the word zoophiliac?"

"Ah . . . not really. That is, hmmm, if it please Your, uh, Wisdom, I respectfully answer, well, no. I would not care to. My thanks." He tried once more to whisper. "How long do I have to keep this up?"

"Until you are satisfied you have sufficiently embarrassed us," I said.

"Yeah, okay. I'm done then."

"In the future, child," Sharuum piped, *"it may serve you well to remember that one never knows who might be listening."*

This was, I reflected, a useful admonition for me, too.

"In the interest of sparing your valuable time, Your Wisdom, may I speak at some length? I hope to briefly outline my understanding of the parameters of our situation, in hopes that you may be able to correct where I am mistaken, and enlighten where I am ignorant."

She graciously inclined her head.

"Wow, you *do* have nice manners."

"Shh." I moved out from the lectern of the Codex and stood before the great sphinx, close enough that should she choose, she could crush me with her forepaw.

"This is what I know," I said. "I know that Esper is lately engaged in a pair of brushfire wars—one of aggression against Jund, and one in defense against Grixis. I know that both of these brushfire wars are escalating to full military conflicts of a sort our land has never known; the significance of today's bombing raid against this city is not lost on me. I know that we of Esper are far, far fewer in number than our enemies, and that the survival of our land rests wholly upon our superior arcane weaponry and command of magic. I know that our superior weaponry is dependent upon etherium, as is the depth of power of our mages, and that numbered among our land's enemies are powerful beings who have come to understand the power of etherium, and who seek to deny that power to us by taking it for themselves. I know that even the limited war so far has exhausted, or nearly so, our land's etherium reserves, and I know that the publicly proffered rationale for Your Wisdom's travels has been to seek among the

159

vedalken, the Ethersworn, the Proctors of the Clean, the Architects of Will, and finally here, to the Vault of the Seekers of Carmot, for any surplus etherium, and to seek those who might create it anew. And I know that this publicly proffered rationale is an intentional deception."

This came out sounding a great deal more harsh in my ears than it had in my mind. For a moment I mentally stumbled, struggling for words to continue; for his part, Doc contributed a hoarse, "Tezz, buddy, listen—don't piss her off. Really. Oh, *crap*—I think she's really mad!" which was, as usual, the opposite of helpful.

But despite Doc's alarm, Sharuum showed no reaction. She made no move of any variety. I was unable to determine that she was breathing. I swallowed, and took a deep breath of my own.

"It is legendary among the Seekers that Your Wisdom was the closest confidant of Crucius the Mad himself. The Seekers of Carmot teach their adherents that it was Crucius who installed you as Grand Hegemon, and that you learned more of his secrets than any other being, living or dead. That all Esper's recent advances in the exploitation of etherium flow, ultimately, from you."

I discovered I was sweating, though the Vault was dank and chill.

"If all this you say is true," she said with slow and careful precision, *"what significance do you attach to it?"*

"That you know full well a truth known by only a few beings outside this very room: that the Seekers of Carmot have never had any secret of etherium's creation. That you know full well the supposed Codex Etherium is *blank*. That no one other than Crucius himself has ever created etherium, and that carmot itself, the 'missing ingredient' of etherium, is entirely *fictional*. That there is no such thing as carmot. It has never existed and it never will."

MATTHEW STOVER

ɸ

I found myself gasping a bit for breath. Apparently that's another thing I'm still angry about.

Sharuum stared at me without moving for what felt like a very long time, then finally showed a hint of emotion by taking a deep breath and releasing a melancholy sigh.

"*I am very sorry for your loss,*" she said, and turned as if to leave.

"And I am very sorry for *yours,*" I answered sharply, "though my loss is real, and yours may be as fictional as carmot."

She stopped in the doorway.

She stood very, very still.

"*I will ask that you explain yourself,*" she said softly, as though speaking only to the downward spiral of the Great Stair. "*Please do so with the clear understanding that I may decide I am angry enough to destroy all of you and raze this sickening mausoleum of fraud to the naked rock it stands on.*"

Baltrice gave me a look, brows raised over flames in her eyes, frankly asking my permission to commit regicide. I held up a hand, partly because I wished no harm to Sharuum . . . but mostly because Baltrice had no idea of the magnitude of power she faced. She'd be killed even sooner than I would, because—unlike me—she wouldn't be running away.

"At a certain point in my researches," I said carefully, "I could no longer avoid the question: Why is the Grand Hegemon of Esper *really* visiting the etherium cults? Any salvageable metal can as easily—*more* easily—be collected by any number of official mages and wizardly functionaries who have more power than they know what to do with; and why is she seeking an answer she *already knows* does not exist?"

"*And you are certain of this?*" she said, still facing away. "*That the answer I seek does not exist?*"

"On the contrary, I'm certain that it does. The answer is fictional only because the question is likewise. The real question has an answer fully as real."

"Yet I have no answer at all." Now she sounded only tired. "Sphinxes are creatures of questions. We leave answers to those naïve enough to seek them. I wish you joy of your answers, Tezzeret the Seeker; elsewise there will be none to be found."

She moved on out the door and very likely would have proceeded down the stairs and out of Vectis, back to her secluded island in the Sea of Unknowing, had I not said, "He's alive, you know."

I heard her stop. I heard her start again, and stop again. And then I heard her turn around. "I hear both truth and honesty," she said faintly, a bit breathlessly, as though not allowing herself to hope. "How are you certain?"

"When I find him, shall I remember you to him?"

"Little mage . . ." Slowly, slowly, she came back to the door, her face wholly blank but her stare as fiercely concentrated as that of a hungry dragon. "Little human mage, how do you hope to achieve this, where the great powers of our world have failed?"

"I am little, and human, and a mage. But that is not *all* I am. You and I both know that our world is not the only world."

Renn made a choking sound; I indulged in a passing fantasy that he'd swallowed his tongue. "Um, Tezzeret? Hey," Baltrice said uncertainly, "are you really sure you want to be having this conversation? Here? With *her*?"

I moved toward Sharuum, slowly, reverently, to place myself once again between her forepaws. Laying my life at the mercy of her whim. Looking up into her ageless, beautiful face, I discovered that her eyes were damp with unshed tears.

"This conversation," I said, "is why I have hazarded my life to meet you, Your Wisdom. To bring you this news, and to ask a single question."

"I fear your question has no answer," she said. "Crucius could not teach even me the creation of etherium. He said no Esperite could ever accomplish it, no matter how powerful. Nor did he share with me any slightest knowledge of carmot, of what it might be, or where it might be found."

"Then I suppose we're both fortunate that we're less interested in the creation of etherium than we are in finding its creator."

"I fear my beloved wanders beyond the walls of death," she said solemnly. "For decades, the greatest of my servitors—and I myself—have sought him in every corner of creation, yet no trace of his passage has ever been discovered. I have even set clockworkers to shift in time back to when I know he was here . . . only to find that he is gone even from the past."

Really? Now, that was interesting. . . .

"I have dreamed . . ." she went on. "Still I dream . . . that he is returned, that he has come again to set the world aright. This Conflux—this catastrophe that has crushed Esper together with Naya and Bant, with Jund and Grixis—this was to him a dream of peace. Of wholeness and sanity. He said that etherium itself was the key to restoring a sundered universe . . . but the wars, the Great Maelstrom, wild destruction unleashed upon every living thing . . . This is what I fear he foresaw. This is what I fear he fled, in hopes that his leaving might somehow stop, or even slow, this unimaginable cataclysm that has overtaken our world. I fear his flight was to escape this future. To end, in sorrow and despair, a life he had devoted to the hope of peace. Elsewise why would he not return to save what shreds of our land that remain?"

"I can't usefully speculate on why he hasn't returned," I said, "but you should know that he is alive indeed.

My source is . . . uncommonly reliable." An astonishing thing to find myself saying of Nicol Bolas, but I was done trying to lie to Sharuum. "Perhaps you simply don't know how to look."

"Uh—" Renn coughed, trying to clear his throat while he leaned as far away from Baltrice as he could without falling off his chair. "You mean *where* to look, don't you?"

"Yes," I said, my gaze never wavering from the great sphinx's. "Of course that's what I mean."

"Ah," she said. *"Ah, little human mage, shall I give you the answer to a question you do not know to ask?"*

"Any answer you might offer, Your Wisdom, will be gratefully accepted."

"He told me once, centuries ago, that if he were to vanish wholly from the world, there would come, some years along, a mage in search of him. He said I would know this mage because he or she would be a created thing, not of this world, bearing not the slightest scrap of etherium. He said this mage would be a creature all of flesh while being only metal."

"Were those his words? The slightest *scrap*?"

She nodded, and a wave of prickling climbed the back of my neck. "Go on."

She said, *"I had taken this to mean a mage of extraordinary strength of character, and of power so great he had no need of etherium enhancement. In truth, his very words crossed my mind when you, Baltrice, introduced yourself."*

"Me?" Baltrice managed to look flattered and profoundly skeptical at the same time. "Really?"

Sharuum smiled sadly. *"Should you again venture to impersonate a mage of Esper, you'd do well to get yourself an actual etherium arm, and better a leg or two, as part of your disguise. Illusion deceives only those who do not think to look for it."*

"Yeah, okay, sure," Baltrice said. "Uh, no thanks, okay?"

"Crucius said that on that day, I should say two things to this unlikely mage," Sharuum said. *"I'm afraid they may be of little or no use in your search. Crucius, like any sphinx, was fond of riddles, wordplay, and obscure aphorisms—and he perhaps more than most. The first was an epigram that I ventured just outside this door, to judge your reaction,"* she said to Baltrice. *"He asked me to say, 'When one is made of glass, everything looks like a stone.' "*

"Might even be true," Baltrice said with a shrug. "If you're enough of a coward."

"It's not a commentary on courage," I said. Something about it struck me strangely. More than strangely; the saying seemed to coil around my mind, slipping around knots and in through nooks and crannies as it searched for something solid to latch on to. Where it could grow. It was an unfamiliar sensation, and wholly unpleasant. I found myself dizzily holding on to my forehead as if doing so could brace me against toppling over.

Partly in hopes of driving this effect away with a new thought, I asked, "And the second?"

"A much more traditional riddle: simple questions that require a complex answer. Riddles welcome that sort of inversion; the more complex the riddle, the simpler the answer . . . and the reverse."

"All right," I said unsteadily. "All right. I'm ready."

"I suspect you aren't," she said. *"It's very simple, and those are the hardest of all. Crucius suggested I should ask you, where do you search for what can't be found, and what do you say without saying? What is your sky when you're tombed in the ground, and whom do you rescue by slaying?"*

Baltrice snorted. "Oh, *that's* deep. Be still my beating heart."

"It's not . . ." I had my hand on my forehead again. "It's . . . I don't know. I think it's deeper than it sounds. . . ."

"Crap, I *hope* so."

And then I realized what Sharuum had actually just said. I looked up at her, and my chest felt as though it were being crushed within an invisible fist. "You said . . . Did I hear you correctly? Did you just say that Crucius suggested you should ask *me*?"

She smiled faintly, and this motion of her cheeks was enough to spill tears down her face. *"He didn't mention you by name, child."*

"Wait . . . wait," I said. I squeezed shut my eyes and tried to massage ideas into my brain through the outside. Even thinking clearly about this riddle was impossible for me—it was too entirely alien. I understood the principle perfectly—surface paradox reveals a deeper answer—but it pointed to this answer in a language I simply could not decipher. Riddles? Metaphors? Epigrams and aphorisms? I am an artificer. A *mechanist*. I deal in *fact*. My business is force and reaction, torque and shear, mass and energy— what can be measured, calculated, and designed to work in the *real world*. I have entirely the wrong sort of mind for this kind of . . .

Oh.

"Wait," I repeated. "Wait—Crucius. He was a clock-worker as well as a mechanist, yes?"

Sharuum said, *"He had many gifts. Clockworking was among them."*

"Then it is . . . at least *conceivable* . . . that he could have looked forward through time and seen us standing here, right?"

Baltrice was starting to look worried. "What are you talking about?"

MATTHEW STOVER

"Analysis," I said breathlessly. "Wait.... It breaks down perfectly...."

"This is, ah, I mean, if I may . . . ?" Renn said. "Clockworking is, after all, my specialty."

"You want to help? Help *me*?" I said. "Who are you, and what have you done with Silas Renn?"

"I'm not a monster," he said in a tone that clearly implied the phrase *unlike you*. "The direction of time is actually irrelevant to the function of magic. It's equally probable that Crucius, as a clockworker, could have looked backward from the future and advised his previous self to confide his message to the Grand Hegemon."

"A nonpertinent distinction," I said to Sharuum. "In either case, he *could* have known I would be the one to whom you would tell these things. In fact, there is a specific flow of alternatives—I could draw a chart. . . ."

"Tezzeret," Baltrice said, "sooner or later somebody's gonna worry about how long we've been up here. Worries like that can lead to bloodshed."

I took her meaning. "All right. Specifically: either these messages were intended to be passed to me, or to someone else, right?"

"The latter is more likely," Renn muttered sourly, but he was absolutely right, and I said so.

"Yes. I am one man. The spectrum of alternatives, in terms of statistical probability, makes the likelihood of me being the One in Question infinitesimal—but that's irrelevant to the problem. If I am not the One, we have no useful solution; whatever we try can't be expected to succeed. But if I *am* the One in Question . . ."

"I get it," Baltrice said, her eyes wide. "If it's you, then he *knew* it would be you—and the questions would be ones he *knows you can answer.*"

"Exactly. Granted that, we arrive at another alternative: either Crucius wanted or expected me—us—to find him, or he didn't. If he didn't, then the questions are deceptions to lead us in the wrong direction . . . but if he did?"

"*Tezzeret,*" Sharuum said seriously, "*listen to me and heed my word now. If you find Crucius—if you can bring him to me, or me to him, if even for a heartbeat, all that I have is yours. Everything. My treasure, my power, my subjects, my realm. Yours, for one more heartbeat beside my beloved.*"

My brain whirling, I was barely paying attention. Where do you seek for what can't be found?

When one is made of glass, everything looks like a stone.

"*If* Crucius the Mad wants to be found, and *if* he hoped I might be the one to find him," I said, astonished at myself for this unexpected conviction, "I know exactly where to start looking."

TEZZERET
A LONG AND WINDING ROAD, WITH ZOMBIES

The only good news in my forescout mirror was that we had finally reached our destination. The rest of the news was that our destination was surrounded by zombies.

A *lot* of zombies.

Someone had gotten here first.

A simple exertion of will twisted the levitation fields of our gravity sleds and dropped them both to the white sand. The gravity sleds had proven to be almost ridiculously useful up till now. Having designed and constructed them myself, I could take a certain pride in how well they had performed. Both were virtually pure etherium, representing the entire contribution of the Grand Hegemon to this expedition—her personal reserve of etherium, almost seventy pounds. The variable levitation magics—to provide motive power in addition to keeping them aloft—were quite standard, even pedestrian; the particular elegance on which I prided myself lay in the shimmering blue variable energy screens that had not only protected us from wind and sun, but also shielded the sleds themselves from the incredibly abrasive winds of the Glass Dunes, not to mention that the sleds themselves had only two moving parts.

I had hoped to ride them right up to the entrance of the Labyrinth, but clearly that was not to be. It would be a shame to disassemble them, but there was no help for it. Given this new development, I knew I'd need the etherium.

We might have to fight.

"What's wrong?" Baltrice's voice came to my mind just slightly muffled by the anti-grit screen I had tweaked into her earpiece—a smaller and lower-powered version of the screens that protected the gravity sleds. Channeling the extra magics had forced me to almost quadruple the size of the earpiece and to build in a support band that Baltrice wore around her head. Not fashionable, perhaps, but it would keep her alive.

I would have preferred to reserve that etherium for other uses, but she was unwilling to use direct mind-to-mind communication, and considering for whom she worked, I couldn't blame her. "There a problem?"

Zombies ahead, I sent, to keep Doc out of it, but he'd already seen what I had in the mirror. "Zombies?" Doc said. "Are you kiddin' me? You're worried about *zombies*?"

"Can you count?"

"Sure—two, four, eighteen, carry the twelve—urk. Hot festering *crap*! There's like a *million*—uh, a million six, give or take a couple thousand."

"My estimate was a million two, but you have better eyes—eye—for this sort of thing, even though you're using mine. We both could be off by as much as a million, or even several," I said, "because there's no way to tell how many are already inside."

Baltrice dismounted her sled and walked over. She reached up to pull the earpiece. I said, "Leave it."

"What in the hells for?" she said with a skeptical squint. "I hear you fine."

"Feel that breeze? Remember what I told you about the sand?"

"Tezzeret, I fart harder than this breeze."

"Well, don't do it in my direction, then. If you remove the earpiece, it will deactivate your anti-grit screen. The glass powder on that breeze will instantly begin to abrade your corneas, which will not only progressively blind you, but it will hurt. A lot. And there is a very long vedalken word that I'm not going to inflict on you, which is the specific term for the permanently disabling lung damage caused by breathing the powdered glass in the desert. The powdered glass is why we *call* it the Glass Desert."

"Aw, hells, Tezzeret, I know. You already told me eight times. It's only—well, you know. Where I'm from, the stuff that'll kill you is big and scary and makes loud noises and crap. This dying-from-just-how-the-place-is gunk just seems all wrong."

"It may be. But there's nothing you or I can do to make it right. Are you with me?"

"If I weren't, I'd be blind and coughing, right?" She nodded toward the progressively higher rides of the dunes ahead. "What's the deal on your zombies out there?"

"They don't have to breathe, and they don't need eyes. And there're a lot of them."

She shrugged. "Zombies burn."

"Indeed they do, but that's not the real issue. What matters is—well, to talk about it is pointless. I can show you from the top of that dune."

"All right, juice up the sleds and—"

"No more sleds. We brought them too close to the Labyrinth as it is. We may have alerted those ahead."

"And so we rode them this far why?"

I shook my head. "In the Glass Desert, accurate navigation is impossible. There are no maps, and there is no reliable measure of distance. A two-mile hike may take you ten miles from your starting point, or one, or leave you farther from your destination than when you began."

"That's why your scout thingies, right?"

"Exactly. And that scout thingie," I said, nodding toward a metallic sunflash at the top of the farther dune, "is the last of them. We won't need more."

She frowned. "Don't much like the sound of that."

"Yeah, me too," Doc chimed in.

"You won't like the look of it, either."

✷ ✷ ✷ ✷ ✷

The Crystal Labyrinth stands at the center of a vast, deep bowl of sand known as the Netherglass, some 20 miles across. Today, that is; the dimensions of the Netherglass are as variable as any other distance in the Glass Desert. I am given to understand that the Netherglass never shrinks below a fixed minimum of four miles across—but only because to do so would make it impinge upon the Labyrinth itself.

Even from almost 13 miles away, the Crystal Labyrinth is of a wholly astonishing appearance. Its walls and roofs are white as milk quartz, with no stain or sully to be seen, perhaps because constant abrasion by the scouring winds of the desert erode and erase all substances that might otherwise darken it. The Labyrinth proper is a structure of twelve immense rectangular buildings, set precisely in a great ring about three miles across.

It is said the dimensions of the Crystal Labyrinth are the only constants in all the Glass Desert.

Each of the great structures is in fact a vast hall of twelve stories, each story containing one hundred rooms, with each room having from two to twelve doors. Six of the stories of each great hall are above ground, and six are subterranean, directly below the upper. The connections between the buildings are said to exist beyond normal space. There are thresholds within the Labyrinth that might connect the lowest corner of one hall with the uppermost of one at the opposite end—and if you turn back, often you will not return to the same chamber you left.

All I could uncover that described the interior of the Crystal Labyrinth was recorded by one Faltus Mack, the sole survivor of a quite large and well-funded expeditionary party some thirteen years before. His account speaks of walls, floors, and ceilings of glass, some transparent as air, some opaque as stone; of blazons and guide paths disappearing behind him as soon as he would quit a chamber; of walls that seemed to shift when he was not looking—though he never saw one move—leaving him unable to determine whether any room was in fact one his party had visited before, or a room of similar configuration wholly elsewhere. He also speaks of encountering other seekers, unfamiliar pilgrims, some of races unknown to Esper, speaking languages that cannot be transcribed in our alphabet. He speaks of meeting members of his own party, who were alive though he knew them to be dead, and on one occasion actually encountering himself, or some phantasmic doppelganger that claimed to be he, filthy, wild of hair, clothed in rotting rags, and speaking only disordered fragments of sentences. By the time Faltus Mack finally escaped, he was entirely mad, of course, but mere madness is not sufficient to impeach his account.

When I shared this information with Baltrice before our departure from Vectis, she became a bit dubious about our propects. "This is your idea of a vacation spot?"

"Think about the riddles," I said. " 'When one is made of glass, everything looks like a stone,' and 'Where do you seek what cannot be found?' The Labyrinth is literally the only place on all of Esper that Sharuum and her agents can *never* search; no one has ever reached the center and returned to the outside world. And, not to grind too fine an edge on it, it's made of glass."

"Oh, this just keeps getting better. You are one literal-minded sonofabitch, aren't you?"

"Yes," I said, "and we must operate under the assumption that Crucius knew this when he laid the trail."

"How do you know it's not just a practical joke? Or, like, demented rambling? I mean, come on, we're talking about a sphinx, right? A *crazy* sphinx. Did you ever hear the joke about the sphinx who was so crazy that other sphinxes *noticed*?"

"According to Sharuum herself," I said, "there is a sphinx of unimaginable power at the heart of the Labyrinth. She named him Kemuel the Hidden One, and she believes he is the oldest living creature on Esper. She is uncertain if this Kemuel reached the center by navigating the Labyrinth, or if it might have been originally built around him."

"How nutty does this crap have to get before you just give up?"

"I don't know," I said. "I'm not sure I have any idea what *nutty* is anymore."

"Got a mirror?"

I conceded the point. "You don't have to go."

"Yeah, sure. Then I'd have nothing to do but hang out and watch my boss's hideous doom and crap. Include me out on that one, huh?"

"You are unexpectedly tender of heart."

"Yeah, well, don't tell anybody."

"There is also this: the Crystal Labyrinth is by far the oldest structure on all of Esper. Descriptions of its exterior are among the earliest writings of the vedalken culture, which is vastly more ancient than the human. If Faltus Mack is to be believed, however, the Labyrinth behaves like a machine."

"A machine to do what?"

I shook my head. "I can't say. Kill people who get lost, certainly—but there's no way to know if that is a designed function or if it is merely ancillary, like a side effect. This, however, is certain: If one wishes to deter intruders, one does not hide at the center of a maze. One does not build a maze at all."

"What, now you're thinking *Crucius* built the Labyrinth?"

"I am reserving judgment on that; I can only say that it is not impossible. I am certain that whoever did build it is a mechanist whose boots I am not fit to wipe." I shook my head helplessly. "I don't even have the words for how far beyond me—beyond *anyone*—the Labyrinth is. Crucius is the only being I can think of who'd even come up with the concept."

"Woo. Crap. Damn, Tezzeret," she said, "all these years I've been dead-bang positive that the stars'd burn out before I ever caught *you* being *humble*."

"It's not an attitude I cultivate."

"You're scaring me."

"Myself as well. It's Crucius. He's like . . . staring into an infinite abyss. Anything you can imagine might be in there, and what's actually in there you probably can't imagine."

"How powerful *is* he?"

I shrugged. "How bright is the sun?"

"Oh, sure. Sure. One hour with a nice-lookin' sphinx and you're all up in their gnomic utterance crap. Do you even know how old he is?"

"I cannot venture a guess that would have meaning."

"Aw, come on, for crap's sake, Tezzeret, you know how old Nicol festering *Bolas* is!"

"Time and age are not the same for a clockworker as for others. Even Planeswalkers. It's at least conceivable that when Crucius decided he needed a Labyrinth, he clockworked his way back to pre-vedalken days. That way he could build it without fear of interruption."

"Wait," Baltrice said, massaging her forehead with one hand. "You're saying—wait, seriously? Okay. So twenty-thirty years ago, whatever, Crucius decides to disappear, so he figures to go back to like the beginning of *time* to build himself a place to *hide*? So that it'll already be there when he needs it in ten thousand years or whatever?"

"Possibly. It's also possible that he built it because he knew that he would one day disappear, and he wished to leave a trail to lead someone—we're assuming me, or someone like me—to wherever it is he has disappeared to."

"So, now wait again—*now* you're saying that the Labyrinth *isn't* intended to keep people out?"

"*Labyrinth* is not a fancy word for *maze*. They are two different things. A maze is a puzzle path, a set of cognitive traps intended, for entertainment or some darker purpose, to trick or baffle those who try to navigate it, and prevent their success. A labyrinth is *supposed* to be solved. Many classical labyrinths have only a single path, and many have no walls at all. Treading a labyrinth from entrance to center is intended to affect those who do so in specific ways—usually to produce some variety of meditative or contemplative state, but sometimes for other uses. There is a whole subspecialty of magic devoted to the effects of following esoteric pathways."

"Yeah, I've heard of them. Whackos. All whackos. You can only follow so many multidimensional loops before your brain goes loopy too."

"Becoming *loopy*, as you say, is actually the point," I said. "The key to understanding a labyrinth is to recognize that who you will be when you reach the center is not who you were when you set out. In other words, the Crystal Labyrinth is not intended to keep *anyone* out, but in order to reach the center, you must transform yourself into the person the designer wants you to be."

"What, like a giant self-help book? *Building a Better You in Only Fourteen Thousand Rooms*?"

"I prefer to think of it as an entry code, or an elaborate lock. To reach the center, instead of merely knowing a password, you must *be* the password. The Labyrinth itself machines you into a key to turn its own particular lock."

"You know, there's a point where piling on more education just makes you soft in the head."

"Yes," I said. "I am living proof of it."

⁑ ⁑ ⁑ ⁑ ⁑

Once we had labored up the long slope of soft powdered sand to the top of the dune, she could see what I meant—for perhaps a mile around the Crystal Labyrinth, the desert could not be seen through the solid press of zombies. She signified her understanding with a low whistle and a breathy, *"Damn . . ."*

"Yes."

"I guess somebody took down the Vacancy sign."

"In so many words."

"Wow."

Doc said, "Zombies give me the willies."

"You don't even have a willie."

Baltrice shot me a sidelong look. "Doc?"

"Yes. He doesn't like zombies."

She looked back down into the center of the Netherglass. "Well, somebody sure does."

"Yes," I said. "Here, look."

I turned my hand downward, and the tiny forescout device lifted from the sand. Spreading my fingers thinned and expanded the device into a hoop of etherium as wide in diameter as my arm was long. A simple adjustment of the refractive index of the air within the hoop made a section of the Crystal Labyrinth spring into focus as though we were only yards away, instead of miles.

The zombies all faced inward. They pressed against one another until they formed a solid writhing mass of flesh and bone, as though they were a crowd come to see some insanely huge undead entertainment, for which the Labyrinth was the ampitheater.

"It looks like they're trying to get inside."

"Yes."

"Well, okay. Sure, there's a lot of them," Baltrice said, "but we don't have to fight them all at once, right? Hells, we can fly right to the nearest door, clear them out and seal it behind us. Even if they're already inside, so what? They're just *zombies*. If we have to fight our way through shoulder-to-shoulder zombies in all fourteen thousand rooms, I don't figure it'll raise too much of a sweat. Take a long damn time, though."

"Yes. That's not our problem."

She squinted through the etherium hoop, then leaned to the side to take in the full scene. "Oh. Oh, sorry, I get it," she said with an apologetic shrug. "My first thing's always the tactical situation. You know."

"And that's why I'm glad you're here," I said. "Now for the strategic question."

"Yeah. Strategic. And the answer's no: I've never even heard a *story* about a necromancer who could summon a million zombies all at once."

"Likely several million," I said. "I am acquainted with several beings who are, or have been, worshiped as gods, and I've never seen any of them do anything that even approached this sort of scale. I don't think Nicol Bolas himself could do this. Not all at once."

"That's why I was wondering if they might have just marched here," she said. "Doesn't Esper share a border with Grixis these days?"

"Yes," I said with a sigh, "but that gets us nowhere—to march zombies all the way from Grixis through the winds of the Glass Desert? Keeping the flesh on their bones would take more power than summoning them directly."

"Oh, sure. Cheer me up."

"It only gets worse from here," I said, massaging my forehead. I'd never been the sort of person who gets a headache from thinking too hard—until, apparently, now. "I have an idea—almost a conviction—that I really, really hope is mistaken. You and Doc are two of the smartest people I know; I'd like you both to listen, and point out holes or blunders in my analysis. All right?"

Doc said, "Really for real? You want *my* opinion?"

"Yes. Baltrice?"

She shook her head, blinking as though I'd awakened her from a daydream. "Sorry, Tezzeret. Sorry—I guess I'm, like, hallucinating or something. Because I could have sworn I just heard you ask me to check your work."

"Ha," I said, "and ha."

She blinked some more. "You mean I *wasn't* hallucinating?"

This gave me brief pause. It underlined once again the seeming difference in who I am from who I once was. I remember being disdainful of Baltrice's intellect, just as I remember the starkly malicious hatred I'd nursed for Jace, and the erratic fits of temper from which I had suffered—I just can't remember why I felt that way.

Being me was proving to be unexpectedly interesting.

I returned my attention to the task at hand. "It is a truism of both artificing and mechanistics that entities are not to be multiplied without reason," I began.

Baltrice held up her hand to stop me. "Skip the lecture, huh? 'Multiplying entities' is the flavor of crap I dropped out of school to avoid."

I nodded. "Simply put, you don't design five parts to perform a function that can be performed by one, yes? The only time you design the five parts instead is if you want to build in extra features that require flexibility of function, or if one piece will be only adequate, while the five will become superb."

"Yeah, okay," Baltrice said. "It's the KISS thing, right?"

"I beg your pardon?"

She shrugged. "That's what they call it where I come from. KISS. It stands for 'Keep It Simple, Stupid.'"

"An elegant phrasing, and proper advice," I said. "However, *simple* comes in a variety of sizes and colors. We're assuming, for example, that all those zombies are the work of one necromancer."

"What, you think it's like an *army* of the bastards? Because those guys aren't exactly team players, if you know what I mean."

"Yes. Under ordinary circumstances, it's more probable to meet one spectacularly powerful necromancer than an organized band of several hundred ordinary ones. But where this framework breaks down is when you consider *why* this necromancer—no matter how insanely powerful—is spending so much of that power to solve the Crystal Labyrinth, and why it's happening *now*."

"Solve it?" Baltrice and Doc said together.

"Those zombies cannot be there for defense, nor to discourage intruders; anyone out here in the Glass Desert will have more than enough power to simply avoid them—fly over them, teleport or gate past them, or if we're talking about someone like you, burn hundreds of thousands of them to ash and walk in before the survivors can reach you. No: I am fairly certain that what we're looking at here is an attempt to reach the heart of the Labyrinth."

Baltrice frowned "How do you figure?"

Doc said, "BFI, right?"

"Exactly," I said under my breath, then spoke up for Baltrice's benefit. "We artificers and mechanists of Esper have a pet acronym of our own: BFI. It stands for Brute Force and Ignorance. Let's say, to Keep It Simple, that we're looking at one and a half million zombies. The Crystal Labyrinth is reputed to have fourteen thousand four hundred rooms, which means the necromancer has at his disposal more than one hundred and four zombies *per room*. Zombies don't need to eat, drink, or sleep; in fairly short order, even working at random, they will have explored every possible path. Once every path is known, the necromancer can just bloody well teleport in."

"Hey, *I* can probably do that!" Doc chirped. "I can teleport, remember? It's like the only actual thing I can actually do. Except hurt you. And there's only one place I can teleport you to. But still."

"There is nothing about you that I have forgotten," I reassured him.

"Put like that, it sounds easy," Baltrice said, grim. "Hells, the bastard could have done it already."

I shook my head. "If he has, why are all the zombies still here?"

"Holiday decorations," Baltrice said. "How in the hells should I know?"

"And we still haven't answered the main question: Why is our necromancer working so hard to reach the heart of the Crystal Labyrinth? And why *now*?"

"I don't get you."

"There's no treasure," I explained. "There has never been even a legend of treasure. All that lies at the heart of the Crystal Labyrinth is a single ancient sphinx—who may or may not be alive, if he ever existed."

"Well, that sphinx and—if you're right—some clue to lead you to Crucius."

"Exactly," I said. "Why tells us who."

"Yeah?" Her face cleared. "Oh, I get it. You're thinking about that snotty little clockworker from the Seekers, right?"

"Silas Renn," I said. "Beyond the three of us and Sharuum, who knows that the path to Crucius might be found through the Crystal Labyrinth? Who's rich enough to hire however many necromancers he might think he needs? Who would sacrifice his entire family's fortune and all of his remaining body parts to discover the key to creating etherium?"

"Huh. 'Why tells us who.' Huh." Baltrice shook her head. "And all those years, you kept telling everybody with ears that *why* means nothing at all."

"Did I?" I said. "I can't imagine what I must have been thinking."

"You should have let me kill him back in Vectis."

"Perhaps." At the time, I had been unwilling to upset Sharuum, nor did I wish to spark an all-out brawl with the Seekers of Carmot—especially not when the city's defenses included apport interdiction, so we couldn't teleport out if things went bad. And if I'd tried to planeswalk, Doc would have dumped me back in that sangrite cave on—in—Jund. And I had discovered myself unwilling to destroy Silas Renn. Despite the danger he represented, he was not trash.

He was something I had not yet found a use for.

"So, it's this Renn guy who's got you all worked up? He's not so much of all that."

"Renn is *tremendously* powerful. You caught him by surprise, distracted by the arrival of Sharuum and her retinue. Do you remember how powerful I was? Back when I had my arm?"

"Yeah."

"Renn and I studied together for three years. I fought him at least once every examination period—thirteen times, in fact. I never beat him."

Baltrice frowned. "Never?"

"And he wasn't even allowed to use clockworking," I said. "At the Academy, clockworking is forbidden in sanctioned duels unless both participants agree to it beforehand."

"For real? How come? I mean, sure, chronomancy is kind of weird, but it's hardly—"

"Chronomancy is not even on a nearby plane to clockworking. A clockworker can actually control time. You understand teleportation. To a clockworker adept, time is simply another spatial dimension. They can jump forward and backward in time as easily as you or I might teleport across a room."

Her frown turned into a scowl. "So if I hit him with something that rocks his world, he can just, like, jump back to right *before* I hit him and deliver a preemptive smackdown?"

"It's more complicated than that—clockworking is fiendishly difficult and, no pun intended, time consuming—but essentially, yes. He can also control your own personal temporal flow in ways no magic at our command can counter. No shield will stop you from getting old. And that's not all."

She winced. "It gets worse?"

"A good clockworker—which Renn is—can, with proper preparation, move *sideways* in time."

"What in the hells is that supposed to mean?"

"You'd have to ask a clockworker for the details," I said. "I've never looked deeply into the theory, and so I have only a layman's knowledge. The best I can understand is that time isn't a single straight line—it's more like a big rope, braided and rebraided out of an infinite number of different temporal strands. Every time you make a choice—turn right instead of left—you split off a new temporal strand. If the choice you make doesn't affect other nearby main lines—if you arrive at your destination at the same moment you would have if you'd turned the other way—your strand gets braided back into the main cable and everything proceeds as usual. But a clockworker adept can sense the nearest strands of other main lines and decide which one he wants to be in. In other words, he can pick and choose the outcome he wants, and move himself into the time line where that's what happens. And he can take you with him."

"Wow."

"Yes. The only limitations of clockworking are the power of the adept and the dictates of probability—the more improbable the outcome the adept is looking for, the more power it takes to get himself into that alternate line. Even though it's not something he can pull off on the spur of the moment, the only real defense against a good clockworker is another clockworker."

"And he got here first," Baltrice said, "and brought all his friends."

"Yes."

"And he knows we're coming, so he's had time to prepare."

"Yes."

"And he might be inclined to be a little stern with both of us."

"That's it. See any holes?"

"Other than the bleeding ones that are about to start opening up all over both our bodies?" She stood for a long moment, staring grimly at the stark reality clustered at the bottom of the Netherglass. When finally she spoke again, her voice was hoarse and harsh. "This was what you were talking about, when you said you won't survive."

"Not specifically."

"How about we walk away? Just pitch it. Because I'm looking down there, Tezzeret, and all I'm seeing is an assload of undead that you and I will probably be joining. I think we are *way* out of our league."

"I can't walk away."

"That you talking, or Doc?"

"Doc is silent on the subject," I said. "He doesn't want to die any more than I do—but he also can't let me back off. You, on the other hand, are under no obligation to perish at our side."

"I don't suppose you'd be interested in popping back to Vectis to pull your doohickey out of Beleren's brain first, would you?"

I only looked at her.

"Sure, what did I expect?" she said. "You're not the merciful type."

"More merciful than he was," I said. "He's alive. And he may yet be whole and hale."

"If we win."

"Yes. If we win."

She took a deep, deep breath as though about to take a plunge to black water, without knowing whether she'd ever breathe again. Finally she let it out in a gust, shook the kinks out of her shoulders, and said, "All right. Let's do it."

"Baltrice—"

"Shut up, Tezzeret. I mean it. Shut up because whatever you're about to say, I really don't want to hear."

I stood in silence.

Eventually, she turned to me. "You have a plan, right? Tell me you have a plan."

I said, "I have a plan."

THE METAL ISLAND
LIFE AND TIMES

S till reclining upon the etherium sand, the ancient
  dragon snorted another gust of greasy, meat-scented
smoke. "What a pathetic creature you are."

Tezzeret smiled. "Flatterer."

"You spew egomania like a sneeze sprays snot. Except
snot tastes better," Bolas said. "Maybe you should kill me
now. Put me out of your misery."

"If death is what you're looking for, you need only wait,"
Tezzeret said. "Or, I suppose, ask me nicely."

The dragon rolled his eyes and took a deep breath in an
apparent attempt to control exasperation. "Do you understand just how preposterously self-centered your whole
theory of reality is, you demented little gutter monkey?
'*Oooh*, Crucius did everything just for *meeeee* . . .' 'Oooh,
Rennnn's waiting there to *spank* me!' Revolting."

"Thank you."

"You did understand, even back there, that for your
theory to be accurate, Crucius would have had to anticipate
not only your brains getting scrambled by Beleren—all
right, to be fair, anyone who knows the two of you saw that
one coming—but he would have had to somehow make me
glue your pieces back together and strong-arm you into
looking for him in the first place."

"When you put it that way, it does seem unlikely,"
Tezzeret said mildly. "And yet, here I am."

"Not because Crucius planned it this way."

"As soon as the Grand Hegemon departs," Tezzeret said with a casual wave toward the cloud of etherium-colored mist that still enveloped Sharuum and the Metal Sphinx together, "you are welcome to ask him."

"Like I actually believe any of this."

"I can say with considerable certainty that at this moment, nothing in any universe depends upon whether you believe in it or not," Tezzeret replied. "I knew an Ethersworn monk once, who made it a practice to believe six impossible things before breakfast; if he could manage only five, he stayed in bed."

"Baltrice was right," Bolas muttered. "You've spent too much time around sphinxes."

"Disquieting, isn't it?" Tezzeret smiled thoughtfully toward the great statue. "I may be coming to understand how they think."

"Tezzeret." The musical harmonics of the Grand Hegemon's voice wafted from the cloud like audible incense. *"We are finished."*

Tezzeret raised a hand, and the cloud faded. Sharuum backed way from the Metal Sphinx as though unwilling to take her eyes from its etherium face. *"You have done all that was asked of you, and more. The word of a sphinx is not lightly given, nor can it be broken. As promised, all that I have is yours, to keep or to abandon, to build or to destroy."*

Tezzeret said gravely, "Thank you."

"Is this a joke?" The dragon's scaly jaw dropped toward the sand while the rest of him was in the process of rising. "Did she just give you the *plane*?"

"Part of one."

"It's a pretty nice thank-you gift."

"Yes." He looked up at Bolas, who now towered over him. "Sit."

The dragon glowered down at him, but sat.

"Stay." Tezzeret walked toward Sharuum. "I will return you now to our land."

"Must you? I had . . . hoped . . . I might abide here. For . . . company."

"You cannot," Tezzeret said. "You have given yourself to me, per our bargain, and this is my will: that you return to Esper and rule as you always have, that you place your great wisdom in service to our land and all who call it home, and that you treat all of my possessions as your own."

The great sphinx stared down at him, uncomprehending, silent with astonishment.

"If I should chance to change my mind," he said through his thin smile, "I'll let you know."

Her eyes drifted shut, and she lowered her head until Tezzeret might have touched her mask-shield with his hand. *"Your gracious nature confounds me, Tezzeret,"* she piped solemnly. *"I do not know how to address you with proper honor, as the master of my life and all I possess."*

"If you choose to address me by any word other than my name," he said, "I would be honored to be called your friend."

Behind him the dragon grunted disgustedly, "Since when do you have friends?"

"Bolas." Tezzeret did not turn around, and his voice was mild as the ocean around them: a gentle surface beneath which lurked unimaginable threat. "Manners."

The dragon growled low in his throat, but subsided.

"Then my friend you shall be," piped Sharuum, *"unto the end of my days, and beyond. It will be written upon my tomb, first among my titles: 'Friend to Tezzeret the Seeker.' "*

"Thank you," he said, and reached up to touch the edge of her mask-shield with one hand.

The etherium that had filled her scars turned once more to liquid, draining down her face like silvery tears. *"The etherium strands—the tears of my beloved—bring light to my eyes and strength to my limbs. They cannot remain?"*

"From this place, one can take only what is brought from beyond," Tezzeret said. "And memories."

"Then let it be so. Memories are more than I'd hoped to gain."

Tezzeret gestured, and the rippling plane of etherium-colored interplanar gate reappeared. "Give my regards to your son."

Sharuum, Grand Hegemon of Esper, looked back at him with a smile and, astonishingly, a wink. *"It will be done, my friend,"* she said, then entered the gate and passed beyond the universe.

Tezzeret turned toward where Nicol Bolas sat upon the etherium sand like an obedient puppy—a sixty-foot-long, fire-breathing, horned, scaled, and impressively fanged puppy, but obedient nonetheless.

"As I promised, you are free to depart as well, Bolas," Tezzeret said, "but my tale nears its end. I hope you might be interested enough to stay yet awhile."

"Your tale is closer to its end than you think." The dragon's eyes went sleepy, and a hint of sneer curled one corner of his upper lip. "You've gotten so good at riddles, try this one: What's at each end of a tale?"

"Our business doesn't have to take very long, but if you choose to be difficult," Tezzeret said, "it can take the rest of your life."

"Aw, Tezzie, come on! Play along."

"Don't call me Tezzie," he said. "Before you answer, recall that here and now, I *can* stop you. And I can promise you won't like it."

"Tezzeret, then. Humor me." The dragon's sneer spread toward a mocking grin. "What's at each end of a tale?"

With a tiny irritated shake of his head, Tezzeret said, "Fine. I give. What's at each end of a tale?"

"At one end, nothing at all," the dragon said. "At the other, an asshole."

Tezzeret made a face. "Up to your usual standard of wit."

"You just don't get why it's funny. It's a double pun," said Nicol Bolas. "Come on, Tezzie—*you* called me an asshole. . . ."

"I called you a doltish thug."

"You're missing the point." Bolas dropped the playful mockery in favor of a darkly infinite certainty. "I am the end of your tale."

Tezzeret frowned, and clouds gathered overhead, spitting jagged lightning.

He cleared his throat, and the Metal Island trembled with earthquake.

He lifted his hands, and the eldritch energies of the etherium around him supercharged his layered shields until he blazed with power, brighter than the sun itself. "Do we need to have this conversation all over again?"

The dragon bared his fangs. "Want to see a trick?"

"No."

"One little trick. You'll love it. I promise."

"Watch mine instead." Tezzeret made a fist, and from the sand shot upward girders of etherium thicker than a man's chest that in an instant had curled around the dragon and braided themselves into an impenetrable cage that flared with every color of power. "Don't try to draw mana, and don't touch the bars. I tell you this for your own protection."

The dragon shrugged carelessly. "You showed me yours. Let me show you mine."

"Save it."

"But it's a really good trick. Here, watch," Bolas said, and vanished.

Utterly and completely, as though he had never been there at all.

Instantly Tezzeret slapped his hands together in front of him, interlacing his fingers. The bars of the etherium cage became razor-sharp blades and crushed themselves into a jaggedly solid mass.

But among them he found no bloody chunks of dragon.

The dragon's footprints were gone from the etherium sand, and no trace of even his previous presence could be detected by any magic Tezzeret could command.

He looked over his shoulder at Baltrice and Jace. The Webs of Restraint that had bound them were gone, and both of them were stirring from their magically enforced unconsciousness. Rubbing her eyes, Baltrice pushed herself dizzily up to a sitting position. "What's going on?"

"Something bad."

"Where's the dragon?"

"I don't know. That's why it's bad," Tezzeret said. "Get ready to fight."

"I'd rather not," she said, even as she climbed to her feet and shook her shoulders loose. Flames kindled in her hair and licked down along her arms. "This is not exactly a big red-mana kind of place."

"You're welcome to go find one." Tezzeret extended his arms, and the sand beneath his feet poured upward along his legs, trunk, arms, and head until he was fully encased in shining etherium armor.

Baltrice made a face. "*That* stuff again. Think it's gonna work this time?"

"We'll find out. Meanwhile, you'll want to protect Jace."

"Jace?" Her eyes clouded over. "Yeah, I better. Hey, boss, you awake?"

Jace groaned and rolled onto his side. "What happened?" he said faintly. "Did we make it? I was having the weirdest dream. . . ."

Baltrice looked at Tezzeret. "This would be a *really* good time for you to take your doohickey out of his brain."

"I disagree," the mechanist replied, as Nicol Bolas flickered back into existence right in front of him.

The dragon reared, forelimbs and wings spreading wide, and brutally intense flame rained down upon the artificer. Baltrice barely managed to raise shields around her and Jace. From what she could see, Tezzeret's armor seemed to be working just fine. He didn't appear to notice the hellfire raging around him. He made a quick motion of his right fist, as though delivering a punch to an invisible opponent.

And the dragon exploded.

Even without flame or blast, the detonation was spectacular. Enormous chunks of dragon flesh trailing black blood sailed through the air. One great wing whirled out over the sea like a thrown dinner plate and splashed into the water. His hind legs gouged long divergent furrows through the etherium sand; his tail crashed into the trees far along the beach. His head got caught in a high juncture of the etherium spars that made up the Metal Sphinx and dangled there, his eyes still glaring balefully down upon the humans below.

"Hot festering *crap*!" A flash of fire burned away the thick gobbets of dragon blood that had smeared across Baltrice's shields. "Did you really just *do* that?"

"Yes."

"You just *killed* Nicol festering *Bolas*!"

"No."

Right atop the steaming pile of internal organs, Nicol Bolas flashed back into existence. He stretched forth his talon and annihilating energy poured forth, setting the air itself on fire. The power blasted Tezzeret backward and down, sliding into a deep, steep-sided pit of white-hot etherium sand. The fringes of the back blast alone chewed into Baltrice's shields so fast that she had to grab Jace and dodge back along the plinth to keep them both from being roasted alive.

The dragon kept pouring the blazing torrent of power into the pit as though he couldn't be bothered with trivial things such as conserving mana. He blasted Tezzeret with levels of energy that should have killed him along with the artificer, as power of this magnitude could be maintained only by pouring his life into the assault along with every scrap of mana he could gather. The intensity of the attack liquefied the sand, turning the pit into a cauldron filled with molten etherium, into which Tezzeret sank like a sounding stone.

And out from which he arose once more, lifting smoothly into the air as though borne aloft by the power that should have destroyed him.

His armor didn't even look hot.

He clasped his hands in front of his face, and the dragon's blast was instantly extinguished. He pushed his doubled fists straight downward like a man hoisting himself out of a pool, and the great dragon himself pitched helplessly headfirst into the molten etherium.

A volcanic eruption of flame and burning metal from below blasted upward around Tezzeret without noticeable effect. The effect on the dragon was more spectacular, as his entire head instantly flash-burned to ash, and his neck roared with flame and burned all the way down to his breastbone.

"Wait . . ." Baltrice said, scowling. "What in the hells?" How does plain old white-molten metal burn his whole head to ash when a few minutes ago her best shot couldn't even make the bastard *blink*?

Tezzeret again displayed no sign of jubilation. He drifted sideways over the huge smoking corpse of the dragon and took up a position on the left forepaw of the Metal Sphinx.

And waited.

Behind him on the plinth, Jace clutched at Baltrice's arm. "Something's wrong. . . ."

"Oh, you think? What was your first festering *clue*?"

"No . . ." His other hand went to his forehead. "No, it's the dragon. The dragons."

"Yeah, that's what gave it away to me too," she said, yanking Jace with her to take cover behind the Metal Sphinx's elbow.

This time two Nicol Bolases appeared simultaneously, on either side of Tezzeret. One simply lashed out and grabbed the artificer, while the other bent his neck to bite the mage in half.

"I'm *telling* you," Jace insisted fiercely. "These dragons—these Bolases—they aren't really Bolas."

"So what? They're nothing we want to tangle with."

"Baltrice, *listen*—I've touched his mind before. And these dragons—they look like him, they might even wield some of his power, but they don't even *have* minds. At all."

"You can read them? Or, y'know, *not* read them or whatever? What about Tezzeret's doohickey?"

Jace shook his head. "Maybe it doesn't work here or something, but that's not important—"

"Hells it isn't—that's what we came here for, which means it's time to go." She peered around the vast etherium elbow for a quick look at how Tezzeret was doing.

Both dragons who had restrained him had been reduced to redly glistening skeletal remains, their flesh having melted and dripped away, puddling beneath their bones in huge pools of meat syrup. But now *four* dragons came at him, two with magic and two with claws and teeth, and to Baltrice's experienced eye, it looked like Tezzeret was starting to feel the pressure. More and more he seemed to be focusing on defense, and his counterstrikes were no longer instantly lethal.

Not that it would have mattered if they were, as eight more Nicol Bolases came wading through the gore of their predecessors, waiting their turn to attack.

"Jace, we gotta get gone," she hissed. "Tezz can't hold 'em off forever, and after they get him chewed and swallowed, they're still gonna be hungry. Your magic's working and who in the hells cares why or why Tezzeret's getting killed by mindless whatevers or why any damn thing else because I think I hear my festering mother calling and she's been dead twenty years so come *on*, let's *go*!"

A blue haze of power crackled around Jace's head. "Wait—they're *not* fake," he said, his brow furrowed in concentration. "And they're not illusions. . . . It's like they're *dead*. Like . . . like—"

"Like *zombies*," Baltrice said through her teeth. "Son of a *bitch*. Now my day is festering complete. *Vess*."

"What?"

"I said Vess. As in that little zombie-sucking slut bag you used to like so much."

"Liliana? What would she be doing here?"

"If I were a little faster, she wouldn't be doing anything anywhere," Baltrice growled. "Find her."

"But she *wouldn't*—wait. Oh, hells," he said. He reached out with his right hand, and a flash of white shot from his fingertips and whipped around another of the Metal Sphinx's spars.

Out from where the white mana had vanished stepped Liliana Vess, her lustrous raven hair falling in curls around her flawless face. Her dancer's lithe grace was not in evidence, however; she moved jerkily, resisting every step, a broken marionette dragged forward by white fire that wreathed her arms and legs and chest.

"Jace . . ." she said softly, her eyes glistening with welling tears. "Jace, I didn't know it'd be you. You have to believe me. I'm sorry—I'm *so* sorry!"

"I'm not," Baltrice said, and blasted her with a flame bolt so powerful that the beautiful necromancer was instantly burned down to her bones. "Go zombie *that*, bitch."

"*Baltrice*!" Jace gasped. "Baltrice, what have you *done*?"

"No more screwing around, Jace," Baltrice growled. "Are we leaving, or am I going alone?"

Liliana's charred bones were still skidding across the plinth when Jace and Baltrice heard her voice again. "Well, *that* wasn't very nice."

They whirled. She stepped out from behind a different spar, alive and whole and not even singed, the air around her grayed with layered shields.

Baltrice's lips peeled back from her teeth, and another flame bolt gathered in her right hand—but before she could attack, she was blasted with glistening obsidian ooze from a third Vess, who was perched atop a curve of an overhead beam. The smothering goo knocked Baltrice sideways, and it clung to her shields, chewing down through them even as it caught fire from the shield and began to burn away.

"What in the hells?" As he sprang to Baltrice's side, Jace raised his own defenses and pushed them thicker and deeper until everything he saw was some shade of blue. The roaring and blasting from Tezzeret's battle against the conflagration of undead dragons rocked the world around him, and by the time he reached Baltrice, two more Lilianas had appeared, rising over the rim of the plinth, carried in the arms of spirits like black smoke with embers for eyes.

"You should give up, Jace," one of them said.

He could no longer tell which Liliana was speaking.

"There will be as many of me as we need, Jace. You can't win. Fighting will only get you hurt."

"Baltrice, what's going on?" he said, low, poised for combat. "How can she do this?"

"She *can't*," Baltrice snarled. "The only way she could pull *this* off is if she's with a sonofabitching—"

"Clockworker," Nicol Bolas supplied cheerfully from behind them, just as his huge talons closed around them both. "Right you are. Congratulations. Now don't struggle, and this doesn't have to hurt."

Jace went boneless in his grip; he knew better than to fight Bolas. Baltrice, who also knew better than to fight Bolas, fought anyway, unleashing the full fury of her power, which could not even singe his talons.

This'd be the real Nicol Bolas, she figured. She still couldn't make the bastard blink.

"Sad little girl," the dragon said. "Did you think I wouldn't be ready for you? Sleep now."

A curl of power coiled in front of her face, then stabbed in through her shields almost without resistance. She collapsed into unconsciousness.

Jace took advantage of this brief distraction to slide a tendril of thought into the great dragon's mind. Having become a great deal more proficient a mind ripper since their last encounter, he nursed a half-formed hope that he might be able to erase himself and Baltrice from Bolas's mind, at least for long enough that they might be able to slip away. But in the instant he had within the dragon's brain, he found something so astonishing that he gasped, "What in the hells is *that* doing there?"

Nicol Bolas turned his mind and gaze to Jace. "What in the hells is what doing where?"

Before Jace could reply, a flash of blue snaked under the dragon's wing and speared into Beleren's face—and Jace's mind vanished. Simply disappeared.

It was gone as though his body had never been more than a mannequin. His body still breathed and his heart still beat, but the young mentalist was mind-dead.

As dead as Tezzeret had been.

Bolas snarled and twisted around—but Tezzeret was still battling the corpse dragons. Someone *else* must have done this. Or was doing it. Or was going to do it shortly. Or something. Even when he could do it himself, clockworking didn't actually get easier to think logically about.

"Lilianas!" he said. Most of them were out in front of the Metal Sphinx, controlling the zombie Bolases that Tezzeret was so studiously dismantling, but a few were still lingering back here within the sound of his voice.

"Yes, Great and Mighty Bolas?" all eight of her replied in unison. She always called him that, and he didn't even mind the bitter edge of sarcasm in her voice; he liked the title well enough that he might make it official. It would be particularly amusing to make Tezzeret use it. "Get up there and help your other selves stomp Tezzeret." Bolas stopped for a moment, frowning. He was suddenly dizzy and decidedly queasy. A side effect of so much clockworking all at once? Or the effect of whatever it had been that Beleren saw? Whatever it was, he decided the time had come to bring this charade to a close.

He shook his head clear and said, "Don't kill him. Just beat him until he can't fight back. I need his mind intact."

"As you command, Great and—"

"Save it. Just do as you're told," Bolas growled around his clenched teeth. Suddenly it wasn't funny anymore.

He tucked away the pyromancer and the mind ripper's empty body into an alternate time line, one in which Tezzeret had never reached the Metal Island. With the aid of a minor binding to preserve them in suspended animation, he could be confident that they would be there whenever he wanted them.

"I really should have learned this stuff a long time ago," he said to himself. He decided not to think about Tezzeret's suggestion that he'd learned clockworking centuries or even millennia before, and had simply forgotten. He remembered well enough being a functionally omnipotent master of time and space, back before the Final Mending, but those powers were far beyond him now. Clockworking was a different approach to almost the same thing, and was gratifyingly easy, for a being of his intellect and power.

If he ever figured out how, he might just slide over to a temporal main line where the Final Mending never happened. If he could find one, anyway. When first he'd searched for a main line where his power was undiminished, he'd discovered there weren't any—which might indicate that the rabble of meddling Planeswalkers who'd forced the Final Mending down Dominia's throat had been right all along. Bolas was gracious enough to grant them the possibility. It was easy to be generous, considering their Final Mending had killed them all.

A resounding detonation and its attendant spray of putrefying dragon blood and meat jerked him back to the present. He snarled at himself. Woolgathering again—and this time in the middle of a *fight*. An ugly trend, underlining the urgency of his project. No more daydreaming, he told himself. No more. Focus.

Tezzeret had said Bolas wasn't the dragon he used to be, and Nicol Bolas had no intention of allowing the mechanist to discover how right he was. But even the tiniest sliver of a Bolas was worth a billion Tezzerets, and it was just about time to make that clear.

Just about time—Bolas chuckled to himself. Even after twenty-five thousand years, he was still his own best audience.

He moved out from the matrix of spars to give himself a little room to work; not that he actually needed *room* for what he was going to do. Clockworking as Bolas practiced it was primarily a mental activity, where all the interesting bits clustered around the intersection of perception and will, but nonetheless moving a little farther from the Metal Sphinx made everything roll along a bit more smoothly. Something about that vast mass of concentrated etherium fogged him up, somehow. He couldn't actually lay a talon on what it was, except that the more etherium was around, the more difficulty he seemed to have keeping his mind on the business in front of him.

He reflected that once his business with Tezzeret was complete, he might want to destroy this entire universe. Removing all this etherium from creation would be doing himself a favor—but it would also more or less defeat the purpose of this whole endeavor. If only the damned stuff weren't so bloody *useful*.

He sighed. Life would be better if he'd killed Crucius a thousand years ago . . . but on the other claw, he hadn't yet fully explored the limits of this clockworking power. Perhaps that thousand-year-ago moment wasn't entirely out of his reach—though some of the temporal stranding involved would be tricky. He might just be jumping himself into a different preexisting main line, or creating a new one, and he wasn't entirely sure how he would know the difference—or if there even was a difference. And he wasn't really sure whether or not jumping back to waste Crucius might be a good idea, or if he'd be correcting a mistake he already hadn't made . . . and then the specter of the Final Mending hung over his past, too.

Though he no longer could entirely recall, he had a sense that the catastrophic damage to Dominia had something to do with time and paradoxes and, well . . . something. He couldn't quite bring it to mind.

It was damnably difficult to navigate five dimensions with a four-dimensional mind. He supposed it would improve with practice; after all, he hadn't met any of his future selves showing up to warn him he was making mistakes. Of course, if his future selves were anything like him, they wouldn't give a hot squirt about anyone except themselves, including who they used to be, which was him. After all, he wasn't in any hurry to jump back to deliver warnings to his own previous selves. Self. Whatever.

His attention was again rudely yanked back to the present by the broken, smoking corpse of a Liliana, which had sailed through the air in a high enough trajectory that she smacked squarely into his face, very nearly going up his nose.

He snapped his head side to side, snarling. What in any flavor of damnation was happening to him? With fierce concentration, he cast his perceptions sideways through time, searching the improbability-frayed temporal strands nearby. There were only two or three more time lines where he lay dead on the beach. He reached out to summon those corpses to his own strand, where they might be put to good use by any among his multiplicity of Lilianas. . . . Wait.

His multiplicity of Lilianas had become surprisingly less multiple.

Unless one added to the count the dead Lilianas who lay scattered about the etherium beach in various states of catastrophic disrepair.

He nodded to himself; he should have expected this. Tezzeret had identified the root of his immediate problem and now was concentrating his counterstrikes on the Lilianas, who were considerably less durable than reanimated undead dragons—not to mention that those undead dragons wouldn't be reanimated for very long without her power to direct them. Bolas searched nearby temporal strands, but he'd already raided them for their incarnations of Liliana. If he went farther afield, he could find only temporal strands in which the treacherous little necromancer had never bound herself to obey him in the first place, which made yanking any more of her into the middle of this brawl definitely inadvisable.

Tezzeret always had been clever.

But it was exactly his cleverness—the primary feature of which was his ability to focus profoundly on whatever immediate problem he faced—that here would destroy him. No matter how smart Tezzeret might be, no matter how incalculable the power he could wield in this place, he was still only human, with a human brain inside his human skull. He could truly focus only on one thing at a time.

Dragons, however . . .

Due to their saurian ancestry, most dragons retained great knots of neural ganglia between their wings and at the base of their tails, so large and complex that they were essentially subsidiary brains; the evolutionary adaptation that allowed them to coordinate their subbrains gave many dragons a multitasking capability far beyond any human's imagination. And Nicol Bolas's capabilities were beyond the imaginations of dragons.

His mind was a vast and cluttered place, stuffed with twenty-five thousand years of memories, half-forgotten spells, and disordered remnants of dreams and aspirations. Millennia before, he had begun a process of compartmentalizing his mind, setting up an organized mental structure that allowed him to access information he wanted without having to sift through metaphorical mountains of irrelevancies. In the process, he'd split off functions of cognitive processing, virtual minds whose responsibility was the management of each of their particular sectors of knowledge, experience, and skill.

While it was true that this strategy wasn't currently working as well as it once had—a serious degradation of function that he was certain was wholly due to the destructive effect of the bloody Final Mending—it was more than sufficient for his current needs.

He assigned one submind to keeping track of Baltrice, and of Jace's body, while investigating the source of the blue mana spell that had killed his mind while leaving his body intact. Another submind was occupied with examining his recent interactions with Tezzeret, especially with regard to Sharuum and the Metal Sphinx who may or may not be Crucius in whole or in part. A third submind managed the fight on the Metal Island—mostly a function of feeding bits of mana to bolster the defenses of whichever of his dead selves was currently being dismantled, and of monitoring his remaining Lilianas. He wanted to finish the fight with at least one left, because she was both valuable and amusing, and while he valued her as an asset, he didn't want to go to the trouble that might be required to ensnare another version of her. This left his primary consciousness with nothing to worry about except subduing Tezzeret.

As he set about doing so, he found himself considerably amused by the occasional boasts that Tezzeret liked to make, about being the Multiverse's greatest master of etherium. Apparently Tezzeret's enormous intellect had managed to slide right past the fact that Bolas himself had *created* the Seekers of Carmot, and that there was nothing known by any of the Seekers that would not be known to the dragon as well. Not to mention that there were a number of features of etherium that Bolas was reasonably certain only he knew (and possibly Crucius, if the elusive sphinx ever turned up again). One of these was that due to etherium's peculiar nature—existing simultaneously in reality and in the Blind Eternities—there were certain vulnerabilities that someone with the right sort of power might exploit.

The right sort of power, in this case, was a combination of planeswalking and clockworking.

Nicol Bolas subdivided his primary consciousness into three parts. One part undertook the mystical focusing of will that was the beginning of planeswalking. The second undertook to summon a specific subset of the dragon's memories dealing with a certain type of magic. The third phased its attention into the near future, scanning the probability smears for hints of coalescence. When the first part completed its task, a hole in reality began to rip itself open . . . but instead of stepping into it, Bolas used the second part of his primary consciousness to reach into the Blind Eternities with an intention to doing one or more of a list of magics at his command, while the third kept focused on the future, seeking one that would end with Tezzeret in his hand.

The submind that had been processing his interactions with Tezzeret warned Bolas sternly not to kill him; there was still too much to be learned.

"I'm not going to kill him," Bolas muttered to himself. "But this is going to hurt."

He could judge the potential effect of each magic on his second part's list by scanning the probable futures that shifted and developed as the second part considered this or that spell, power, or combination of such. Neither the first nor third part of his mind was actually aware of what spell he ended up using, but they didn't have to be; the second part had that issue fully under control, as it was able to use the ætheric dimension of Tezzeret's armor to channel a combination of telekinesis and minor shaping that transformed, in the current reality, the inside of the mechanist's etherium breastplate into a blade that shattered his breastbone, slashed open his heart, and severed his spine just between the shoulder blades.

"How's *that* for power?" several of his subminds said in unison, as at least three of them saw—and one felt—the mechanist's heart spew most of his blood out through the joints in his armor.

The Tezzeret-tasked submind, though, reacted with enough alarm to give Nicol Bolas actual pain.

"I already said I'm *not* going to kill him!" Bolas snarled. "Shut the hell up."

As Tezzeret fell dying to the blood-caked sand, Bolas's fourth submind released the power that held all but one of the Lilianas in this temporal strand. The last Liliana simply blinked in astonishment at her inexplicable victory until that same submind reached into her brain and said, *Sleep*, whereupon she collapsed into unconsciousness.

This freed up that submind to rejoin his primary consciousness, and—as the assigned tasks of two of the three divisions of his primary mind were complete—he reassembled an uncharacteristically large fraction of his mental resources to attend to the dying mechanist.

He stretched forth a talon, and Tezzeret's limp body rose into the air and floated into his grasp, dripping liquid etherium as though the armor were ice instead of metal. When Tezzeret was once again naked, Bolas—who had a somewhat more detailed understanding of human anatomy than did nearly any human alive—worked a simple charm that placed the mechanist in a state of suspended animation similar to that of Baltrice and Jace. Bolas estimated that if he ever chose to reanimate Tezzeret, he'd be able to repair the physical damage with very little permanent loss of function.

He looked down with a contemptuous sneer upon the human lying broken and bloody in his grip. "As though I could ever be in any danger from *you*, you pathetic worm. I am *Nicol Bolas*! What have I to fear from any mortal mage?"

His second submind—that troublesome Tezzeret-tasked one again—inquired silently that if Bolas had never been in danger, why were all those nearby temporal strands loaded with his corpses? Which was a wholly disquieting question, and one he had no intention of pondering.

His primary consciousness reflected that his condition might be more grave than he'd allowed himself to believe. How far must you have deteriorated to have begun to heckle yourself?

He paused for a moment to assess his situation. His Tezzeret issue seemed to be well in hand—literally—and the lightly snoring form of Liliana could be easily enough shifted into suspended animation, and both of them could without much difficulty be stored next to Jace and Baltrice on the Metal Island in that nearby temporal strand . . . so this was exactly what he did.

"I suppose that means I win," he said. "*Whoopee*."

It was impossible to be much elated by victory over such pathetic opponents; celebrating this triumph would be like doing a victory dance after stepping on an anthill.

Still: not bad. And accomplished by very little cost or exertion on his part. He supposed he could give himself points for style—for what Tezzeret would call elegance. Poor little Tezzeret . . . just another of the ants.

He could not quite make himself believe it, though. It didn't seem real. Had he really snared not only Tezzeret, but Liliana, *and* Jace and Baltrice, after all this time?

Apparently so. He could not find a temporal strand anywhere in which they were not his prisoners. So that, in so many words, was that. Period.

He glanced up at the expressionless face of the Metal Sphinx. "And I'm pretty sure *you're* not going anywhere."

The sphinx—after the custom of his kind—did not reply.

Bolas stepped close to the sphinx's cleanly abstracted semblance of a forepaw, and he laid his own talons upon it, marveling in the thought that this, right here, might be all there was left of Crucius. All there would ever be.

"What were you thinking, though? What brought you here? Why is this place what it is?"

He supposed he would find these questions a great deal more compelling if he actually cared about their answers. He had not only five more Planeswalkers to add to the considerable assortment under his absolute control, but also now this unimaginably vast trove of etherium. He discounted Tezzeret's assertion that it could not be taken from this plane. The sets of What Tezzeret Can't Do and of What Bolas Can't Do did not intersect in any meaningful way. Discovering how he could take the etherium—*all* the etherium—with him was simply a question of evaluating powers that Tezzeret did not have, lore that Tezzeret did not know, and magics that Tezzeret could not work.

All this etherium, and all the many Planeswalkers in his hands, and now that he thought about it, he realized that what he had right now might actually, finally, unexpectedly, be enough.

"Maybe I really *have* won. Won it all. *Hmp. Whoopee* again." He sighed. "My Crowning Moment of Triumph should really have been more dramatic."

He passed some considerable interval wandering a bit aimlessly around the island, admiring the etherium trees and the etherium grass and the etherium outcroppings of bedrock that shouldered into the light. And speaking of light . . . He frowned down at the shadow he cast upon the etherium underbrush. Something about his shadow was troubling him, and for a long moment he couldn't seem to work out what it was.

Ah, that was it. His shadow hadn't moved.

Well, it did move when he did—it was after all his shadow—but its *angle* was exactly the same as it had been when he'd first arrived here. Hours ago. Did this planet not rotate? What in the hells was going on here?

Where we are is all one place. Here, it's always now.

He moved around to the front of the vast etherium plinth, kicking aside heedlessly the ragged remnants of both his own corpses and Liliana's. He was not sentimental, and pity was alien to his nature. Even self-pity. Something was going or had gone or will go terribly wrong, and his clockworking ability seemed to make it or had made it or will make it worse instead of better.

He had to know or he had to go. Probably both.

He spared the infantile doggerel on the plinth's east face only enough of a glance to register that it was written in a long-vanished dialect of Classical Draconic. . . . Wait, that was the language his *parents* had spoken . . . a language no living creature had heard or spoken in the twenty-four thousand years since his birthplace had been destroyed and all his close relatives slaughtered (to be precise, since his birthplace had been destroyed and all his close relatives slaughtered *by him*). He then indulged a passing wonderment at how Tezzeret could possibly have even recognized the glyphs for what they were, much less deciphered what they stood for.

He actually turned to ask before he remembered that he'd sequestered Tezzeret in a different temporal strand, and that awakening him to inquire would not only require a considerable expenditure of mana to heal his wounds, but it would also force Bolas to endure more of the artificer's unspeakably irritating conversation.

Bolas shook his head, disgusted with himself again. Really, this advancing senility or whatever it was had gotten entirely out of control. Good thing he had all this etherium, and all his captive Planeswalkers, because he really needed to get his whole personal recovery and reconstruction business fully under way before he forgot what it was he needed to ... what?

He couldn't remember why he had to remember anything, much less what it might be. How was he supposed to think around here? An unanswerable question, which led him inexorably toward an even less pleasant contemplation.

Wasn't he breaking down a great deal faster than he should?

Had to have something to do with the etherium. Or with this particular plane, as etherium had never had any noticeable effect on him anywhere else. Or with Crucius or the Metal Sphinx or whoever was supposed to be either one of them, whenever they might be each other, or not. Or something.

More damned *riddles*.

He shook his head again, but somehow instead of clearing, the shaking only thickened the fog inside his various minds. How *had* Tezzeret deciphered the glyphs? How could he know Classical Draconic at all, much less the dialect of Bolas's native mountains? Bolas decided that maybe it was worth both spending the mana and enduring the aggravation in exchange for some answers . . . if he could just recollect where he'd stashed the deanimated mechanist. . . .

Oh, yes. Of course. Over in that temporal strand with Jace and Baltrice and his last-remaining Liliana—the time line where Tezzeret had never made it to the Metal Island.

He stopped, scowling. "Wait . . . wait, there's something wrong. . . ."

Tezzeret *had* made it to the Metal Island in that time line. That's what was wrong. Bolas had just *put* him there. But that didn't make any difference. It couldn't. Could it?

Somehow, he couldn't escape the feeling that it had been a bad idea.

Either way, the whole business worried him. It was as though when he'd done it, he hadn't even been paying attention. . . .

Nicol Bolas discovered that for the first time in his life, he wasn't certain about *anything*. And he didn't like it. Not one little bit.

"Fine," he muttered. "This, at least, is something I can fix."

He cast his perception once more sideways in time; all he had to do was find a temporal strand where he had decided not to stick Tezzeret over there, but to keep him close, here on the beach. Simple.

In concept, anyway.

In execution, however, it was not only unexpectedly complicated but thoroughly disquieting. He discovered there was no time line, *anywhere*, in which he'd made the choice he was looking for. In fact, he could not find one where he'd made any other choice at all. Did that mean he'd never really *had* a choice? That it was some kind of preposterously predestinated fate or something?

He was beginning to favor the *or something*, as he found to his dismay that in fact no temporal strand—not a single one within the considerable range of his perception—showed any sign of Tezzeret *at all*, save only the strand where the artificer lay on the etherium beach, suspended animation holding him minutes from death. And now Bolas recalled that earlier, when at Tezzeret's invitation he had scanned their future—when he had found so many of his own corpses on so many versions of the beach—he had seen nothing of Tezzeret at all. *Nothing.* Alive or dead or anywhere in between.

How could there be only *one* of him?

Bolas had a feeling he'd be able to work it all out easily if he were only somewhere else, far away from the Metal Sphinx, the Metal Island, the world that was ocean itself—far from whatever it was that was pumping pea soup into his brain. He gathered mana as easily as he might take a deep breath, then ripped open the surface of the universe so that he might step through into the Blind Eternities.

But how *could* there be only one Tezzeret? And how could Tezzeret read Classical Draconic? And what was up with the whole sun-not-moving business? And if it *was* etherium messing with his brain, shouldn't he figure out how and why? Wouldn't leaving all these mysteries behind him be tantamount to driving stakes through his own hearts?

The rumblings and mumblings of his various subminds as they mulled over these and other troubling questions were so diverting that when he came back to himself, he found his rip in reality had closed without him ever having taken so much as a step toward it.

This, he realized, might be a problem.

With great determination and preternaturally focused

MATTHEW STOVER

intention, he again exerted mana and ripped open a portal to the Blind Eternities.

And some indeterminate interval later, he again found himself standing on the beach with unanswerable questions chasing one another's tails through the various and sundry compartments of his mind, the rip having closed while he was woolgathering.

"All right, I'm done. That is exactly as much as I am going to take," he muttered to himself. "Time to fix it, or to burn down this whole bloody universe. Or both. Extra bonus points for whoever guesses which."

His face contorted into an involuntary snarl as he fixed his intention upon the temporal strand where the four Planeswalkers lay side by side. With a needlessly violent wrench of will, he thrust himself into their time line.

He stood over Tezzeret's body, which might as well have been a statue. When he noted that his angle of shadow here was subtly different from that of the time line he'd just left, his snarl deepened to a rictus of rage. He snatched up Tezzeret's body in one hand and with the other gouged a ton or so of etherium from the plinth. Then he jammed Tezzeret's body fully into the now-viscous metal, let the metal reharden around him, and then simply hurled it with all the strength he could muster—physical and magical— out over the infinite ocean. He didn't even bother to mark where it would hit the water, some hundreds of miles from the island, but turned instead to the other three deanimated Planeswalkers.

He took just a moment to fasten each of them with his power so that he could summon them from anywhere across the Multiverse. Then, one at a time, he picked them up, ripped open reality, and shoved each at random into the Blind Eternities. There was no way to predict where any of them might end up, or if any would ever reappear into ordinary reality. While this might be disastrous for unprotected Planeswalkers, the power of Nicol Bolas would preserve them intact until the end of time, and a considerable while beyond it. All Bolas knew for sure—all he *needed* to know—was that he could bring them to his hand at will. The magic that held them in suspended animation and bound them to him could be broken only by a mage more powerful than its caster. Bolas felt justified in his confidence that the existence of said "more powerful mage" would remain safely hypothetical.

That being accomplished, he turned his attention once more to Tezzeret. Being in the same universe—especially this one, which seemed to be otherwise uninhabited—relieved Bolas of any need for physical proximity. Tezzeret's deanimated form was still sinking, far out in the ocean, plunging ever deeper into mile upon mile of crushing lightless depths, but for Bolas it was a simple matter to spear the mechanist's frozen brain with a tendril of power, and delve again into Tezzeret's memories.

He hesitated for one final moment, as one of his subminds—probably the same one that had been heckling him earlier—quietly observed that going back into the artificer's memories was *exactly what Tezzeret had invited him to do*, which really turned his stomach for a moment. The sensation resembled dread.

He couldn't remember the last time he'd been actually frightened.

And he couldn't imagine why he would be frightened now.

He bared his fangs, silently but sternly instructing that mouthy submind to shut the hell up before he permanently reassigned it to bowel-management duty, and pushed his mind for the last time—really the last time, he promised himself, really *really*—into Tezzeret's past.

TEZZERET
SOMETHING STUPID

This is a stupid plan," Baltrice said. "And that's coming from a girl who knows something about stupid plans. I've come up with some doozies. But never *this* stupid. Seriously, Tezzeret, you're begging him to kill you."

"Not quite," I said, a bit abstractedly because most of my attention was focused on fashioning greaves and sabatons out of my sled's remaining etherium, while reserving enough for rerebraces, vambraces, and gauntlets. "I'm allowing him to choose whether or not to do so, which is not the same thing."

"Might as well be," she said. "What in the hells are you gonna do when he makes you start to age like a year per second or something?"

"In that eventuality," I said, "I'll depend on you to rescue me."

"Yeah. And hope that I can get to you—or him—before he kills you."

I returned my full attention to my work; the obvious needed no validation.

"I'm just worried, that's all," she said. "Waiting gets to me. Doesn't it bother you?"

"You're waiting," I said. "I'm working."

The sabatons seemed to be coming together nicely. Creating my armor from the untempered etherium of my gravity sled obviated the need for tools or workshop.

The metal was more than malleable enough to shape with my will alone. It meant as well that the armor would not prove to be much of a defense against spear, sword, arrow, or javelin—but those were not the sorts of threat that concerned me.

I manipulated the several joints of the sabaton's instep, to ensure that its flexibility sufficed to allow me to walk normally without being so loose that it might expose my tender flesh to Silas Renn's untender attentions. Finding it suitable, I created its mate without difficulty, donned them both, and moved on to my greaves.

"You're betting a hell of a lot that he's a reasonable man," Baltrice said.

"I am gratified by your concern."

"I'm not worried for *you*," she said. "No offense."

"None taken."

"It's—well, you're tossing my boss's life in the pot, too. That's who I'm worried about."

"Of course you are." The greaves were actually quite simple, and fitting them to my calves was the work of a moment. I moved on to the gauntlets.

"What's *that* supposed to mean?"

I glanced up at her. "The nature of your working relationship is not a mystery to me."

She squinted at me suspiciously. I went back to work on my gauntlets.

"I still don't see how doing something stupid isn't actually stupid."

"I won't pretend it's not stupid," I said, "but I believe that of all the varieties of stupid at our disposal, this is the safest."

"The safest way to go in would be to find the bastard in one of your scrying bowls, then open this gate of yours right behind his neck and boil his brain till his skull explodes."

MATTHEW STOVER

Φ

"I have explained the issues with direct assault," I said, again a bit distantly, as the gauntlets proved a bit more complicated than I had anticipated. To make them glove-like, with individually jointed fingers, might consume enough etherium that I'd need to cannibalize some of Baltrice's sled to complete my bascinet. "Renn may have been here for weeks, subjectively—even months. He knows your abilities, and mine, and he has had more than sufficient time to prepare a defense against any attack we can devise. Which is why we're not going to attack."

"Yeah, I follow the logic. It's just not exactly my style, you know?"

"Yes." I looked up from the gauntlet, a frown curdling upon my brow. "Nor mine, in fact. The old me—the angry man with the etherium arm—would no doubt use this etherium to devise several Tezzeret doppelgangers of some sort, thinking to use them to confuse Renn's foresight, as cover for a lightning sally of overwhelming destructive force."

"Hey, I *like* that one!" Doc chirped.

Baltrice said, "Sounds un-stupid to me."

"Doc agrees with you," I said, "which is reason enough to abandon it."

"Aww, Tezz, that hurts."

"I wonder if you even know what it is to *hurt*," I muttered in reply. "Do you understand suffering at all?"

"Have to listen to you, don't I?"

That was, I reflected, a fair point. "Baltrice, there is no form of attack that Renn can't anticipate. Given enough subjective time, he can scan very nearly all his possible futures. The attack I just described is no doubt among them. And this is why I have no intention of attacking him—why I *can't* intend to attack him, or so much as plan a contingency assault. Any tactic I can devise, no matter how subtle or arcane, will be obvious to him in the very instant he first sees me."

She shook her head skeptically, watching me sidelong. "You *are* different," she said.

I shrugged and went back to work on the gauntlet. "So are you."

"Do you ever wonder who you really are?"

"I don't know what you mean." The solution for the gauntlet was clear—a succession of five overlapping bands to cover the backs of my hands and fingers, so that making a fist would protect my entire hand, though my palms would remain bare.

That being accomplished, I focused my will to once again draw from the plates threads of etherium finer than hairs. The hand being relatively more sensitive than the chest and back or the legs, worming those threads in through my skin for the direct connection to my motor neurons was exceptionally uncomfortable, rather like dipping my hand in boiling water. But the direct connection would allow me to use the armor much in the same way as I had used my erstwhile right arm: as an extension of myself.

"You know Bolas did something to you, right?" Baltrice was still giving me that sidelong squint. "That he made you different from who you used to be?"

"It seems the simplest explanation. Otherwise, the difference in my behavior would have to be ascribed to some conjectural experience in a hypothetical afterlife— an afterlife I can neither recall nor seriously imagine."

The only problem with the vambraces and rerebraces was how to properly joint the elbow. It would have been easier if plate armor had ever been the fashion on Esper, as opposed to our defensive magics. All I had to work from were some none-too-detailed memories of Bantian crusaders and my own ingenuity.

"Doesn't it bother you? I mean, it's like he turned you into one of those golems you used to make all the time, except you're self-aware. You're so calm all the time, it's festering *creepy*. Don't you ever feel like you should, you know, act like the *real* you? Do things how you know the real Tezzeret would?"

I set the vambrace on her gravity sled, and for a long moment I stared at the sand beneath my feet. I had no idea how to express an honest answer to her question.

At length, I could say only, "Baltrice, I *am* the real Tezzeret."

"Yeah?" She squinted at me. "How do you know?"

I spread my hands. "How do you know you're the real Baltrice?"

"Well, I—I mean, you know, what do you want me to say? I just *am*."

"Yes. I, too, just am."

"Except you're not," she said. "Look, I spent a lot of time with you back before—you know. And I've spent time with you here. You are *not* the same guy."

"Did you like my previous self better?"

"Oh, Hells no," she said. "You were a dead plumb rat bastard."

"Then what are you complaining about?"

"I'm not complaining. I'm wondering. I'm wondering what goes on inside your head. Because, you know, there were a lot of things the old Tezzeret could be called, but hard to read sure as hell isn't one of them."

"Perhaps you find me hard to read because you're looking for depth where there is none to be found. I am what you see. Neither more nor less."

"Depth, nothing. You're completely festering screwed in the head, and you act like you're *glad* about it."

"Baltrice, let me turn this around," I said slowly, and with great care, as this was a subject to broach with her gently. "I, too, remember you as being different from who you are now. The Baltrice I knew was . . . Well, let's just say you seemed unhappy. Viciously unhappy. And you seemed to be interested primarily in inflicting unhappiness upon as many other beings as possible, often in the form of burn scars."

"Yeah, I wasn't very nice." She shrugged. "Still not."

"But you are," I said. "You smile now. You laugh. You occasionally make a joke that doesn't involve harming or humiliating someone. You think about things other than how to hurt people."

"Yeah, well, I found a better job." She waved a hand. "Again no offense."

"Again none taken." I smiled at her, as openly and innocently as all my craft could conspire to display. "But suppose, for just a moment, that your happiness had a foundation more concrete than simply enjoying your work. Suppose someone had *made* you happy—say, for the sake of argument, with a secret wish like what you'd find in children's adventure stories. If some mysterious benefactor had cast a spell to transform you from the bitter, angry, aggressive woman you once were into the confident, cheerful woman you've become, wouldn't you be grateful?"

"Are you kidding?" She stared at me incredulously. "If some bastard put magic on me to screw with my life? You think I'd *thank* him?"

"I would."

"I'd jam both hands in his ass and rip him in half from the bottom up." She looked as though even considering the possibility had brought anger to a rolling boil. "People who screw with me get third-degree thank-yous."

I maintained my smile, to show her I'd not intended to make her angry. "I suppose you haven't changed so much after all."

"Festering *right* I haven't." She was still tilting her head, though, and giving me those sidelong looks. "You're really saying you're okay with it? Knowing that Nicol Bolas stuck his talons into your brain and stirred it like soup?"

"That was Jace," I reminded her.

She flushed. "He had reason."

"Granted," I said easily. Jace Beleren was a subject about which I could not expect her to be rational. "But Bolas was the one who, to extend your metaphor, *un*-stirred my brain. With his own real-life version of that spell from the adventure stories. Hypothetically. I'm confident it's within the range of his powers to alter my brain to make me less volatile, less avaricious, more focused, possibly even more intelligent. More capable in every way. If this is so, I owe him more thanks than I do hatred."

"Are you nuts?"

"Yes, I have lost my precious arm—but Beleren did that, not Bolas. What Bolas has done is restore me to life and health, and to set me forth upon exactly the fantastical quest I had painfully outgrown, and was forced to abandon decades ago—and because of who I've become, I may actually have a chance to achieve what has always been my heart's most cherished desire. How can I not be grateful? Should I hate Bolas for making me a better man?"

"He made you a better *tool*."

"I still fail to see why you think this should upset me."

"And I can't understand why it doesn't. Tezzeret, you're barely even human."

"Yes," I said, picking up the vambrace again. "That's exactly my point."

I stopped for a moment before triggering the gate, pausing with my fingers on the control surface of the intricate etherium archway, and looked back at Baltrice. She crouched on her sled, bobbing gently a few feet above the sand. "Controls functional?"

"Sure." She demonstrated by manipulating the twin control sticks to spin the gravity sled fully around, shoot it toward me, and bring it to an instant stop a hand span from my legs. "Same as when you asked two minutes ago."

"It'd be better if you'd let me set you up with a mindlink."

"Maybe in my next life."

"Those control sticks are the sled's only moving parts," I reminded her severely. "If too much sand accumulates—"

"I know, I know."

"How's the view?"

She flipped forward my most recent modification to her earpiece, a jointed arm that supported a small ring of etherium a couple of inches in front of her left eye. I blinked as I found the earpiece—ear-and-eyepiece—with my mind. "Focus all right?"

"Dunno." She squinted through the loop. "All I see from here is a giant festering pile of stupid."

"Hey, same as me!" Doc chimed in.

"Exactly," I said, which served as a sufficient response for them both; her view came from the perspective of my left eye. "Doc, I need your whole mind on the job, all right? Sometimes you see things I don't, which may very well make the difference between success and an ugly death."

"I'm with you, Tezz. In every conceivable sense. But you know if I had even a hint of a better idea—"

"I'd be thrilled to hear it," I finished for him. "Baltrice. Ready?"

"Close to it as this lifetime's gonna get."

I sent a pulse of mana through my hand into the control surface of the transit gate, and within its archway, the view of the dune beyond wavered and wiped itself away, showing now an up-close-and-personal view of several thousand zombie butts.

"Wow," Doc said hoarsely. "Wow, they're worse from close up, huh? Practically smell 'em. Shudder."

"Yes." One last glance over my pauldron to Baltrice. "A transit gate is not like a conventional teleport," I reminded her. "It's a reality warp, to bring the two points together."

"Yeah, yeah, yeah, like a magic door. I get it."

"Just bear in mind that it's *not* a magic door. Do not linger on the threshold," I said. "I'm holding it open with my own power. When you activate it, the gate will draw on the innate power of the etherium of the archway. It will stay active for only about five seconds, so don't delay. If it deactivates while you're passing through, there will be part of you there, and part of you here, and both parts will be messily dead. Right?"

"Right," she said, all business now.

"If the gate fails somehow with you on this side of it, remember that your sled is *very* fast. We're only fifteen miles out, which that sled can cover in less than two minutes from a standing start. Just don't—"

"Stand up or stick my arms out from the energy screen, or do anything stupid. Stupider. I got it."

"If all goes well, you'll never need to move at all. I will let you know via the earpiece when matters are settled. Then you can either return to Vectis or stick with me, at your discretion."

"Yeah, and how likely is all to go well?"

"It's not. At all. But the possibility must be prepared for."

"Yeah." She gazed pensively through the etherium archway at what I would face at the Labyrinth. At length, she took a deep breath and said softly, "Luck to you."

"And to you. To us both."

"It's a hell of a thing you're doing. A hell of a thing," she said. "But I guess you never were a coward. Maybe you're not so different after all."

"You'd be amazed." I turned for the gate.

"Tezzeret?"

I paused at the threshold.

"Have you thought about—I mean, what if he actually takes you up on it? What'll you do if he just, like, opens his arms and says, *Glad to see ya, come on in?*"

"Drop dead from the shock," I said, and stepped through.

TEZZERET
PAVANE FOR A DEATH PRINCESS

I arrived a few yards short of the outer fringe of the zombie mob. Checking back over my shoulder revealed no sign of the gate, which was as it should be. I triggered the eye-and-ear link built into my bascinet. "You there?"

"Everything's go," she whispered in my ear.

"All right, then." I activated my armor's primary defenses, took a deep breath—and was seized by a fit of uncontrollable retching.

"Duh-*ammn*," Doc said. "Gag. Choke. Guess I was wrong about smelling 'em before, huh? Gag some more. Retch, too, just to be sociable."

I was unable to reply, as the feculent miasma of decay gases unleashed by the rotting flesh of a million-plus zombies had exceeded by far the limits of my imagination, and thus also overwhelmed my countermeasures. I was wholly occupied with trying to avoid filling my bascinet with my own vomit.

Holding my breath did not help, as the air I inhaled might as well have been a chemical weapon. It scalded my nose and throat, and presumably my lungs as well, triggering an equally convulsive spasm of coughing. Eventually, I gathered enough of my mental resources to tweak the armor's anti-sand field, intensifying its blue crackle so that it would burn off noxious decay products as it did the desert's powdered glass—and so I was once more able to breathe.

"Tezzeret, what happened? Are you hit? What's going on?"

"Nothing. It's all right. Zombies stink."

"Well sure they do, but—"

"Imagine swimming in nyxathid vomit."

"Ooo. Damn, do I have to?"

"I have a fix. One moment." I was able to mentally retrace my armor's link to her ear-and-eyepiece, and adjust her anti-sand field as I had my own; she couldn't be much use to me if she was retching too hard to breathe. "That should cover you. Now it's your turn to cover me."

"I'm on it."

I activated another prepared spell, this one a very straightforward sonic illusion, which made the sky seem to crack with thunder, and followed with words that might be heard, like thunder, for tens of miles.

"MY NAME IS TEZZERET.

"I AM NOT HERE TO FIGHT. I WOULD SPEAK WITH THOSE WHO SEEK THE CENTER OF THE LABYRINTH.

"WITHOUT MY HELP, YOU WILL NOT SUCCEED.

"MY NAME IS TEZZERET . . ."

I damped the sound within my bascinet so that I might hear not only Baltrice, but also my own thoughts.

I allowed the illusion to cycle through three full times, while bending all my resources toward detecting any response, be it hostile, friendly, or neutral. It was a matter of some ironic amusement to me to have created an illusion intended to convey truth.

When I discovered no response beyond attracting some carnivorous interest from nearby zombies, I activated my primary defensive screens and began to walk toward the Laybrinth.

The zombies, of course, closed in upon me. I activated the outermost layer of my armor's defensive screens, which I had devised with Baltrice's help, as I find her solution to our zombie problem to be both elegant and efficient. Any zombies bold enough to actually attempt to touch me instantly burst into flame hot enough to set not only their whole bodies ablaze, but to spread to the others pressing in behind them. My progress was necessarily slow—being incinerated was no deterrent to their functionally mindless appetites—but it was steady, and served the additional purpose of making it absolutely clear to Renn and his presumptive army of necromancers that I was not attempting anything resembling stealth or swift assault.

Instead, I simply pushed on, the apex of a long wake of burning zombies, in the reasonable belief that the necromancers ahead wouldn't begrudge the loss of a few tens of thousands of their undead servants, and hoping that they would presently respond to the audible illusion, still thundering above me, by ordering their minions to stand aside.

However, I burned my way through the zombies all the way to the base of the nearest structure without any noticeable reaction from anyone or anything except the zombies, who continued to slog toward me and immolate themselves.

The external surface of the Labyrinth had the texture of glass etched to appear frosted. It was clearly not susceptible to burning or melting, no matter how much power I fed into my incendiary outer screen. There was no visible entrance, which was not distressing; quite the opposite, in fact—had I found a door on my very first approach, I would have assumed it was a trap and moved on. "Doc? Do you have any preference for which direction we should move?"

"Does *away* count?"

"Yes and no. It is a direction, but it's not one we'll take."

"Oh, sure. Y'know, I'm getting the feeling that you get us into these situations on purpose."

"It seems unlikely." I turned my back to the wall and edged to my right, the inferno of zombie fire following my path.

"That's a nonanswer," Doc said accusingly. "What it *seems* doesn't have much to do with what it *is*. And unlikely isn't the same as untrue."

"Correct on all three counts," I said. "You're learning." The column of greasy black meat smoke from the zombies was already a couple miles tall. If Renn and his necromancers for some reason couldn't hear my thunderous illusion, they should certainly be able to track my progress by the smoke.

"I think you put us in mortal danger to shut me up."

"If so, it doesn't seem to work."

"You know what I mean. You talk me into crazy stunts like *this* little adventure, and once we're in it and I really see how much danger you've put us in, it's too late for me to do anything about it. Unless I want to get us both killed."

"Your veto power does seem to be limited by circumstance."

"That's *another* nonanswer," he said. "Do you practice that crap, or does it just come naturally?"

I allowed myself a fractional smile. "Both."

"And that's *another* thing." His voice rose. "You think it's *funny*."

"Somebody has to."

"See, that's what I'm talking about! It's *not* funny—and you sure as hell shouldn't be *enjoying* yourself right now!"

Still no sign of activity from our presumed adversaries. "Doc, if I wanted to spend my life listening to complaints about my behavior, I'd have gotten married."

"Oh, like we're *not* married. How much more 'of one flesh' do you think we could get?"

MATTHEW STOVER

"First, I'm really not comfortable with that."

"Try if from *my* side."

"And forget the 'of one flesh' business. Worry about the 'till death do us part' angle."

"Um, yeah. Speaking of death—activity on our left."

I turned to look back the way we'd come. Other than burning zombies, there was nothing I could detect. "I don't see it."

"That's too far. Keep our back to the wall, then scan forty-five degrees off perpendicular."

"It's *my* back."

"Whatever. Relax. Got it?"

A few dozen yards away, a number of zombies appeared to be pulling back from the crush, as though avoiding the flames of their closer brethren. "That's activity?"

"You see it happening anywhere else?"

I didn't.

"They're not doing it on their own," Doc said. "It's being done to them."

"Threat assessment?"

"Shrug. Too early to tell."

A mental adjustment that thinned my greaves and sabatons by shifting some of their etherium into the equivalent of boot lifts gave me a slightly better view. The opening gap had become a ring, as several hundred zombies had turned aside from their mindless pressing in upon the Labyrinth to gather themselves into a roughly circular clot of undead. There was motion in the middle of that clot, and shortly I was able to make out what it was: the innermost zombies had either fallen or laid themselves down on the sand, and the zombies around them were walking on their bodies until they too reached the center and laid themselves down. The pile of recumbent zombies grew as tall as the creatures themselves, and the upright specimens were forced to clamber up the growing mound.

"You have any idea where this is going?"

"No," Doc said. "But this looks like a good time to fire up the rest of your shields."

Sharing his perspective, I did exactly that. "Baltrice," I said, "are you seeing this? I seem to be getting some sort of response."

Silence.

"Baltrice?" I said, more sharply. "Baltrice, *respond*."

Frowning, I sent my mind into the etherium circuitry of our linked ear-and-eyepieces. Mine, built into my bascinet, appeared to be perfectly functional, so I bypassed it and sought Baltrice's device with my mind . . . and found nothing. As though the device no longer existed. My heart began to pound like a living creature trying to bash its way out through my sternum.

Apparently I was not yet the emotionless golem she had described. "Doc. We're in trouble."

"Oh, you think? Are you watching this?"

The mound of zombies had grown nearly ten feet tall, and likely three times that in diameter. Now their rotting flesh had begun to melt as though they lay under a waterfall of aqua regia. But whatever power might be liquefying their flesh, it left their skeletons untouched, even as it dissolved tendon and ligament. In moments, the mound of zombies had become a pile of naked, disjointed bones. The bones themselves began to move, lifting and twisting and fusing themselves into a web-work archway that anchored itself upon a ring fused of the remaining bone. The archway stood ten feet tall, and the ring on which it stood was perhaps sixty feet in circumference. In the very instant it was complete, an eldritch reality whorl distorted the view through the arch.

A transit gate not unlike mine, differing mainly in materials.

When the view stabilized, I was looking into what appeared to be a lavishly appointed sitting room, and looking back at me was what appeared to be a young woman of exceptional beauty, her lustrous obsidian hair unbound and draped in ringlets to perfectly frame her flawless oval face. She wore a wrap of translucently sheer silk, artfully layered to leave exactly enough to the imagination. She said, "Tezzeret. It's been a while."

"Vess," I said slowly. "*Liliana* Vess. The necromancer. I remember you."

"That'd be more flattering if it hadn't been quite so much work. We need to talk."

"You're a Planeswalker. . . ." More and more about her was coming back to me, but in glacial drips and drops, slower than cold treacle—almost as though the information had been deliberately obscured. By Bolas, undoubtably. But why? "I don't recall you having *this* level of power."

"That's part of what we need to talk about," she said impatiently. "I work for Bolas, just like you. We don't have very much time."

Interesting. Almost interesting enough to divert me from my immediate necessities, which included reestablishing contact with Baltrice. "Are you alone?"

"For now. Briefly."

"Silas Renn."

She nodded, her gaze flickering from side to side as though he might unexpectedly appear.

"How long before he gets back?"

"Depends," she said. "How long do you think it'll take him to kill Baltrice?"

✳ ✳ ✳ ✳ ✳

The sitting room on the far side of the transit gate was every bit as well-appointed as it had appeared. I stood in the middle of a rug that undoubtedly cost more than my father had earned in his entire life. I was still in my armor with all my shields working, excepting only the outermost, as it is an ungracious guest who sets his hostess's house on fire.

The sunlight had a peculiar quality here, brighter and warmer than I'd ever experienced on—in—Esper, as well as displaying a distinctly more golden color. Bant, perhaps? I had not yet had the leisure to acquaint myself with the finer details of our newly conjoined planes.

I tolerated an extended account of why Liliana Vess had helped Jace escape from my presumably villainous clutches, and how she had managed to defeat some dark interrogations to which I had apparently subjected her, and why this and how that and who everything else, seemingly without end; her tale was larded with evasions, rationalizations, and excuses for various acts of which I had no memory at all.

There was no reason to reveal this to her; quite the opposite. Her account offered substantive insight into how she thought, and into what she took to be the truth of why, and the power and ruthlessness she was willing and able to wield in pursuit of her goals.

That I stood there at all was the result of a coldly rational assessment of Baltrice's chances against Renn—especially if he'd managed to take her by surprise—and my own chances of rescuing her against a forewarned and fore-armed clockworker.

If I survived the morning, I might have an opportunity to avenge her.

At length, I felt I had to cut Vess off, in the interest of expediting our negotiations, though there was one point of curiosity that I felt should be satisfied. "I am still unclear why you would have bound yourself to Bolas's service," I said. "I should think a woman, mage, and Planeswalker of your obvious intelligence and experience would know better than to sign *anything* in blood, much less a binding contract with Nicol Bolas."

She looked a bit nettled. "You work for him too."

"Against my will," I said. "Whereas the sort of contract you signed is willing by definition. No one sells their soul by accident, through deception, or under duress. It doesn't work like that."

She looked away, a shadow settling upon her face, dulling the sparkle from her eyes. "There's willing and there's willing, and not all duress is created equal," she said. "Let's just say that Bolas was the best choice I had left."

"Your other options must have been dire indeed."

"You can't begin to imagine." She shook her head to drive the shadow away. "We need to talk about Crucius and Bolas and Renn."

"Are you accepting my offer?"

"I'll take any help I can get. Even from you."

I shrugged away the insult. She did not know me anymore, if she ever had. "Your brute-force-and-ignorance approach has failed to solve the Labyrinth. Believe me when I tell you it never will."

"Bolas gated the zombies in from Grixis," she said grimly. "But it was my idea."

"He's not fond of wasting mana on futile operations," I said. "But neither am I. If you—or he—had bothered to ask me, I could have told you in advance that it wouldn't work. And, more usefully, I could have told you why."

"You can tell me now."

"I can."

After a second or two, she said, "Well?"

"*Can* is not synonymous with *will*."

Her face set as though carved in cold stone. "What do you want?"

"I want—I need—some assurance that I can trust any single word that comes out of your mouth."

She allowed herself a humorless laugh. "Trust? We're both grown-ups here, aren't we? If you don't want to work with me, you're welcome to go back to burning Bolas's zombies."

"He has you in a screw press, yes? And he's tightening it every day."

"Every hour," she said. "He has zero faith in your ability to find this Crucius character on your own."

"Was making a deal with me your idea?"

"I'm desperate, Tezzeret."

"An imperfect rhyme."

"Damn it, *listen* to me! Bolas knows *everything*—your little chat with that sphinx-queen of yours and the whole damned thing."

"I anticipated that he might know what transpired at the Seeker Academy," I said, "but that's far from everything. What's your offer?"

"You don't understand," she said. "You've got it all backward. He knows way too *much*—he can probably solve the Labyrinth by *himself*."

"I doubt it."

"We have to stop him. Somehow."

"A project even more dubious than locating Crucius."

"If only," she said. "The last thing in the Multiverse we want to do is give that bastard what he wants. We need to make sure he *never* finds this sphinx of his. Never."

Doc whispered in my left ear, "Don't even think about it. Unless you want to ruin our friendship."

"An interesting proposition," I said to Vess. "Assuming, for the sake of argument, that I am willing and able to conspire with you against the dragon, what do I get out of it?"

"Same as me," she said. "Your life and your freedom. If we win."

"Ah."

"Did you ever stop to think *why* Bolas wants to find Crucius?"

"I have several theories."

"Me too. Except I actually know something about what Bolas is up to."

I confined my response to, "Oh?"

She cast a nervous glance around the room, as though checking the corners for indiscreet spies. "I don't know how he plans to do it, and I don't even know why, but I've got a lead on what. You know how he gets playful sometimes, and how he likes to tease you with Mysteries of the Multiverse You Will Never Comprehend? Well, he's not as good at it as he used to be. It's almost as if he can't really remember what he's already said. Over the last few months, I've been able to piece some bits together, and what I'm seeing doesn't look good. Tezzeret, I think he's going to kill us."

"Us?"

"The Planeswalkers," she said. "All of us. All of us he . . . well, owns. It has something to do with these oaths of fealty he's collecting. And he's planning to . . . do something. To us. All at once. And from how he talks, he's not expecting any of us to be around afterward. I'm not sure how, or when, but he is absolutely certain that he can, and will, do whatever in the hells he's planning."

"He never suffered from self-doubt."

"It gets worse," she said bleakly. "I think he's going to destroy the universe."

"*Excuse* me?"

"That's what it sounds like. This whole plane and every-body on it. Grixis, Esper, Jund, Bant, and Naya. All the damned stars in the bloody sky. Everything. All at once."

"That would be . . ." I said, searching for the proper word and finding only, "unfortunate."

"And maybe not just here. Ravnica. Kamigawa. Lorwyn. Mirrodin. Who knows? I'm not sure Bolas himself knows—he's getting more erratic every day. Tezzeret, he could wipe out the whole Multiverse by *mistake*."

"A daunting prospect. But I'm not sure either of us can do much about it."

"Crucius," she said. "Crucius is on his mind a *lot*. All the time. You and I aren't the only agents he's set to looking."

"So what exactly are you proposing?"

"We have to find him first. I don't know if Bolas needs him as part of his scheme, or wants to kill him to keep him from interfering, or some combination of the two, and I'm not sure it matters. What matters is keeping Bolas's talons off Crucius. Permanently, if possible."

"It's an attractive proposition." For good reason—she had clearly designed it that way.

"It's like she read our minds," Doc said.

"She didn't have to," I muttered.

"I'm sorry?" she said. "You'll have to speak up, unless you want to take off that stupid helmet."

"I'm more comfortable like this." Her chain of reasoning had little effect on me. I don't need an excuse to oppose Nicol Bolas and everything he does with every resource at my command. She didn't need to spin an apocalyptically grandiose rationale to make me believe she'd do the same. I would have believed it if she'd offered no reason at all. To know him is to hate him.

None of it mattered. "How do we proceed from here?"

"First," she said, "we get rid of Renn."

"Kill him?"

She frowned at me. "Of course. What did you think?"

"I prefer plain language."

"Bolas and I thought Renn might be useful. Before he sent me out here, he took Renn off somewhere and mind probed him or something. Renn doesn't even know as much about Crucius as you do. Now that you're here, he's just extra baggage."

"That's not entirely accurate."

"How about if you add on top that he's going to kill you on sight? That he's probably already killed Baltrice—no loss to me, I hate that lumbering bitch, but you always seemed to care about your people. And—"

Again she looked away, and a very pretty flush climbed her exquisite neck. Her tone, however, was flat and as ugly as the grinding of ill-fitting gears.

"So?" Liliana said. "How about it, Tezzeret? Are we on?"

I sighed. "I sympathize with your situation, and I hope you believe I would help you if I could. However—"

"There's *always* a however," she said bitterly.

"Yes. When it comes to reaching the center of the Crystal Labyrinth, Silas Renn is more necessary than you are."

She stared at me in blank astonishment. "You think you can cut a deal with *him*? He's completely *insane*—he can talk like a normal person, but inside he's baying at the bloody moon."

"I've allowed for that," I said. "It's said you have to be crazy to study clockworking, and the more you learn, the crazier you get. The ability to choose between realities can disconnect you from all of them. Crucius was known as the Mad Sphinx for a reason."

"Is there no way I can change your mind?" She turned toward me, and I noticed her translucent silks had begun tending more toward transparent—but not as transparent as she was. "Are you *sure* . . . ?"

"Liliana Vess," I said gravely, "you are very likely the most beautiful woman I have ever seen. Looking at you, I can't so much as recall the face of another woman. If I were foolish enough to allow myself even a fantasy that you might actually be attracted to me, matters might be different. But it is my business to see things as they are. An unsentimental view of your offer makes the transaction all too plain."

She didn't seem abashed in the slightest. She found an even more fetching angle for her lovely eyes, and her silks continued to evaporate. "A girl does what she has to," she said. "Just like you."

"What I have to do doesn't include you," I said. "The sad truth is that I am interested only in finding Crucius—for that I need Renn, and he needs me. Neither of us needs you."

Her face darkened; she even glowered beautifully. "You always were a bastard."

"Possibly. My parents weren't forthcoming on the subject."

She turned and flounced to the door. "Well, *screw* you, then—"

"I've already declined."

"And you can find your own damned way back to the Labyrinth!"

She could not be allowed to simply leave. I turned, extending a fist, reaching for her with an invisible hand of power, and the sunlight had a peculiar quality here, brighter and warmer than I'd ever experienced on—in— Esper, as well as displaying a distinctly more golden color. Bant, perhaps? I had not yet had the leisure to acquaint myself with the finer details of our newly conjoined planes. . . .

I thought, *Wait a minute . . .*

Shortly the bones themselves began to move, lifting and twisting and fusing themselves into a web-work archway that anchored itself upon a ring fused of the remaining bone. In the very instant it was complete, an eldritch reality whorl distorted the view through the arch.

This isn't right, I thought—but I wasn't sure why. "Doc?" I said hoarsely. "Is there something wrong about this?"

"You mean other than the zombie gate and the fires and Baltrice not responding?"

"Baltrice . . ." I remembered something else about Baltrice, or thought I did, but I couldn't quite bring it into mental focus. "Baltrice."

"Tezzeret, what happened? Are you hit? What's going on?"

"Nothing. It's all right. Zombies stink."

"Well sure they do, but—"

"Imagine swimming in nyxathid vomit."

"Ooo. Damn, do I have to?"

"I have a fix. One moment." I was able to mentally retrace my armor's link to her ear-and-eyepiece, and adjust her anti-sand field as I had my own; she couldn't be much use to me if she's retching too hard to breathe. "That should cover you. Now it's your turn to cover me."

"I'm on it."

That feeling of *wrongness* only increased. "Baltrice, change of plan. I might be under attack, and it could be Renn, and—I don't know. I have a feeling that I can't explain. Be on your guard."

There was no response.

"Baltrice? *Baltrice!*"

When designing on the fly, it's generally best to start from the middle, and work one's way outward from there. Also, the cuirass and cuisses would be simplest to create, requiring no more than an approximate fit. All the jointing and lapped plating would come later. I held a hand above my etherium sled, and its dorsal surface began to ripple and bulge as I drew forth the metal for my first pieces of armor.

Doc said, "Eugh. What's that smell?"

I ignored him. The rim of the Netherglass was some three miles away and downwind. Though zombies are rightfully notorious for their odor, I strongly doubted we could smell them from here.

Roughly five pounds of etherium poured upward toward my hand, pulling free from the sled in an inverted teardrop. Using both of my hands to aid in the focusing of my will, I softened the metal and spun it like dough for flatbread to form it into a disk of uniform thickness . . . and I smelled the odor Doc had been talking about. It wasn't zombies.

It was blood.

The smell is unmistakable, but considerable blood must be spilled before the scent is obvious to an ordinary human nose, especially outdoors. And this odor was accompanied by a distinct undernote of sulfur, as well as a hint of the proteinaceous soot that arises from charred meat.

I had a thought that Baltrice might, conceivably, be cooking something on her sled behind me . . . but an animal she had freshly killed? In the middle of the Glass Desert? It was so improbable that I paused a moment, struck by an overpowering conviction that I had done this before. And that what came next would be bad.

"Just like déjà vu all over again, isn't it?"

I froze. If I live a thousand years, I will never mistake that voice, the blend of upsloper condescension and petulantly malignant mockery.

The etherium dropped into my hand, and I left it there.

240 "Renn."

"This is the part where you turn and attack, Tezzeret." He sounded like he was looking forward to it. "Come on, don't be shy."

"Or turn and run," Doc buzzed in my left ear.

I told both of them, "No."

"You will, you know," Renn said. "And soon. For all the good it'll do you."

"I didn't come here to fight."

"Oh, it won't be a *fight*, Tezzeret. You attack, then take a nap. Hardly qualifies as combat."

"Are you sure he's wrong?" Doc said nervously.

"Nobody needs to get hurt," I said.

Renn snorted a contemptuous chuckle. "That pyromancer of yours didn't agree," he said. "Kind of a hothead, isn't she?"

In his mind, that had probably sounded funny. "Where is she? Is she alive?"

"Guess."

"Renn—"

"You can try to beat it out of me."

"Some other time."

"He took out *Baltrice*?" Doc sounded appalled. "Just now? While we were standing here?"

"No," I murmured. "He's going to take her out after I leave. He won't even get here until we're in the middle of the zombies."

"Then how can—why is he—I mean, what?"

"It's complicated."

"Oh, really?"

"The armor was a great idea," Renn said conversationally. "I've always admired your ingenuity. You'll never know how many times you beat me. I should say, time lines where you beat me."

Doc said, "Something tells me this isn't one of those time lines."

"Shh."

"Finally, I just got aggravated enough with losing that I decided we should have our chat before you make any. This way, we skip the whole fight and get straight to the part where I torture you. A lot."

Finally I turned. Renn leaned casually on Baltrice's gravity sled, its etherium dulled by a thick coating of fresh-looking blood. The area around it was drenched until the powdered glass was wholly black. The scent of charred meat rose from his clothing—but it wasn't his flesh that had burned.

"You don't have to torture me, and you have no reason to harm Baltrice," I said.

Renn snorted. "I don't have to eat," he said, gesturing with his etherium arms to his etherium chest, in which the sole remaining organ was his etherium heart. "But I eat anyway."

"I'll tell you what you need," I said.

"Oh, don't do that."

"It's why I came here. Specifically. To share what I know."

"You always were tiresome," Renn said. He pushed himself off the gravity sled, to stand balanced on the sand. His personal shields crackled and spit as they disintegrated the powdered glass on the wind. "Listen to me, Tezzeret. You've *already* told me everything you know. I've been torturing you for several days—recreational torture, really. Just for fun. To pass the time. I'll get so bored after I torture Baltrice to death. You told me everything before I even *touched* her."

"Does he know he's not actually making sense?" Doc whispered.

"He is making sense," I muttered, "just not to us. Get ready."

"For what?"

"Then why are you here, Renn?" I spread my hands. "You know everything I know—why talk to me at all?"

"I don't know *everything*," he said, walking toward me. The golden haze of his shields intensified, and blazing white mana gathered itself around his fists. "I'm still trying to figure out how you escaped."

"Did I? Well, well."

"It's not even possible," he said. "I have you restrained by a mana siphon and shackles made out of these sleds, so you can't use any magic at all, and I have you in a hundred thousand-to-one hypertemporal field. So I can watch you age. And then I blink . . . and you're gone."

"Interesting."

"I thought so," he said, and lashed out with both hands. Blinding white energy erased the sun and the sky and the sand and everything in the universe except for Renn himself. It caught me and held me in its unbreakable grip, turning my own mana reserve against me, so that the harder I struggled, the stronger it became. "Tell me how you escape, and I'll let you live long enough to try it again."

"I have a better idea," I said through my teeth, clenched hard enough to chip by the power of Renn's binding. Focusing my will in a specific way—not unlike imagining a musical passage so vividly that I could change which mental instruments played it—did not require mana. "I'll tell you when I see you again . . . about, hmmm, let's say, twenty minutes from now."

Renn tightened his magical grip until I could no longer breathe. "Really? And where you will be in the meantime?"

I could not speak to reply. Instead, I winked at him.

His sneer of triumph coagulated into a frown of uncertain disbelief that warmed me to the centers of my bones. Then I uncoiled the focusing of my will, exactly as I would have if I'd had command of my own mana . . . exactly as I would have if I were trying to planeswalk.

There followed an exceptionally gratifying *blam*, which erased Renn and the desert and the gravity sleds, to dump me gasping on the floor of a large, dimly lit cavern lined with glowing red crystals, which smelled strongly of dragon.

"Y'know," Doc said peevishly, "you *could* have just asked. . . ."

TEZZERET
BLOODSTONE, STONE, AND BLOOD

I shoved myself up to my knees, but my heaving chest and trembling legs wouldn't let me rise the rest of the way.

"You think we could have cut that a little *closer*?" Doc said. "Not like we were in a *hurry* or anything."

"Doc, please." I squeezed my eyes shut and set my hands upon my temples, trying to squeeze the whirl in my mind down to a manageable torrent. "If we weren't in a hurry then, we certainly are now."

"In a hurry to do what? Take a nap while we wait for Bolas?"

"Screw Bolas."

"You first."

I'd brought no actual tools into the Glass Desert, but the fabric of my tunic and breeches could be cut and braided into a variety of useful types of rope, and the leather of my boots could be useful for strapping. But best of all were the steel of the toe caps and the strap that stiffened the sole, not to mention the grommets. As soon as I thought of this, however, I realized my feet were cold. Worse, I could feel the texture of the sangrite crystals with my toes.

Opening my eyes confirmed my analysis. "Naked? Really? You couldn't have even left me my boots?"

"Complain to management," Doc said. "I was designed as a fail-safe, not an ejector seat."

I let it go; we had no time to bicker. "Twenty minutes," I said grimly. Without tools.

"Twenty minutes till what?"

"Renn dialed us back along my subjective time line so he could get at me before I made the armor. He couldn't have attacked Baltrice while I was standing there; I had turned away from her only a few seconds before you smelled the blood and smoke."

"What happened to her, then? Why was she gone and Renn there?"

"It's possible Renn was talking to us from our future. Did you notice how black the blood was? And the smoke odor was too faint. On his time line, he might be hours ahead of us—maybe days."

"What, he was talking to us from *after* he takes out Baltrice? After he's *going* to take out Baltrice? Something like that."

"Yes. Me—us—too."

"So in *our* time line, he hasn't attacked her yet? Even though in *his*, he grabbed her days ago?"

"My best guess," I said, "based on how long it seemed to take from when I began the armor to the moment that our eye-and-ear link went dead, he will attack her in just about twenty minutes."

"Clockworkers give me a headache."

"Yes."

"So you think we can get there in time to warn her, or something?"

"Or something."

"Hey—hey now, you're not thinking about actually *being* there, are you? Tezz, come on, are you nuts? The guy just yanked us *backward in time*. You want to *fight* him?"

"No," I said. "I want to beat him."

"To save *Baltrice*?"

"And myself. And you."

"I don't get it. Seriously. We can just *sit* here. Bolas'll show up to kick us out again, and he can broker a deal with Vess, and we're in. Crap, Tezz, we might be able to get Bolas to step on Renn—that way we don't get the *snot* beat out of us. Or get *killed*."

"Baltrice doesn't have that much time."

"So?"

That brought me to a full stop. So indeed. "Don't you like her?"

"Do I need to remind you that she's tried to kill us at least once already this week?"

"To protect Jace," I said. "She can't help it. I don't hold it against her."

"Well, *I* do. Let the fat cow die. *Our* business is Crucius."

"We need Baltrice," I insisted. "We *need* her."

"Oh, I get it," he said. "Whether I like her doesn't matter. *You* like her."

I frowned. "Apparently I do," I said slowly. "But that's not the issue."

"I don't give a ten-pound bucket of *rat* poo what you think the issue is. Maybe I can't stop you once crap starts—but I *can* stop you from starting it yourself." He underlined his point with a vividly distinct sensation of having my testicles ripped away.

I took it with no more reaction than an involuntary tightening around my eyes. "You'll have to do better than that."

"Think I can't?"

"Doc, listen to me. I don't have time to explain. I need you on my side for this. It'll be worth it. I promise."

"This *what*? What's gonna be worth risking both our lives?"

"It's kind of a . . ." I took a deep breath. Might as well tell him the truth. "It's a practical joke."

"You're pulling our leg."

"On Bolas," I said. "It's a practical joke on Nicol Bolas. A good one."

"*How* good?"

"Let's put it this way: If rage doesn't make his head explode on the spot, he'll have to suck it up and pretend he *likes* it. He'll have to *thank* us."

"Wow."

"Are you in?"

"You should have told me this in the first place," he said. "Sorry about the nut sack thing."

"No harm done." Which was, after all, only the truth. "Can you keep time?"

"I'm supposed to be a clockworker?"

"No. *Count* time. Specifically: seconds."

"You mean like 'one Vectis, two Vectis'? Sure. How many seconds?"

Allowing for three minutes of recovering from the teleport and bickering with Doc, discovering I was naked and getting my thoughts organized, plus perhaps thirty seconds of sag time for final adjustments. . . .

"Nine hundred and ninety."

"Starting?"

"Now."

"One Vectis. Good thing I don't lithp. Three Vectis, four Vectis—"

"Silently."

"Check. Sorry." His voice evaporated into blessed silence.

An unsentimental appraisal of the odds against me was not encouraging. Last time, I couldn't even get out of this cavern without help. I had no way to know if Baltrice was

MATTHEW STOVER

still at her sled by the transit gate. I had no way to know if she was free or captured, fighting or already dead. I knew for sure only one thing.

I knew where Silas Renn would be in twenty minutes.

I have come to think of myself as a resourceful person; in fact, I have flattered myself into believing that given a specific problem, a specific time frame, and specific materials, I can deliver not only an effective solution, but an elegantly creative one.

I had about sixteen minutes to prove I haven't been kidding myself.

I arranged myself into a rough simulacrum of a comfortable position and applied my full attention to the problem. Unfortunately, this specific problem was a long-standing one, and one to which I had never achieved any working solution at all. Three years of trial and error. Mostly the latter. Three years of hypotheses and experiments, resulting only in bruises and humiliation. Disgrace. Expulsion, and murder . . . but I couldn't think about that now; dwelling on my failures was diversion. Distraction. Nothing more than an excuse to lose. I didn't need an excuse.

I needed to win.

Getting away unharmed had been a victory in itself, though I could take no credit for that. I had escaped because he didn't know about Doc. What else could I do that Renn didn't know I could?

It was imponderable. I shook my head and moved on. Everything in its turn. First: escape. If I couldn't get out of the cavern, any tactical plan was moot.

This cavern had already proven to be secure against my best efforts. I had been unable to reach the Blind Eternities after awakening here, and now I found that an attempt to teleport proved equally futile. Something about the sangrite not only blocked my mana channels, but seemed

TEST OF METAL

249

to absorb mana directly; opening more channels only brightened the blood-colored light in the cavern.

So: sangrite is a mana sink. Not just stored energy, but actually gathering energy every instant it remained untapped. A lot of energy, I reminded myself, in view of what had happened to the sculler in Tidehollow, not to mention the two mercenaries at my father's hovel. I needed that power. I needed to harness it somehow.

Without making myself explode.

Dragon's blood, Bolas had said. Spilled in mortal combat. Stress hormones and glucose. I pondered briefly whom Bolas had killed here, but only briefly. The blood's original owner was no concern of mine. He lost it. I found it. The end.

But I wished I could ask him a question or two.

A quick search of the cavern failed to locate any sangrite chunks broken loose from ceiling or wall. A brief but painful attempt to yank or kick some free ended with me limping away on a bleeding foot . . . but then a sputtering sizzle ignited behind me, and my naked back registered sharply painful heat. I looked over my shoulder.

The floor had erupted into blinding fountains of raw power as high as my chest, like the insides of blast furnaces fueled by mana. Several, in fact.

Every spot where I had set my bleeding foot.

Interesting. Soluble in blood. Soluble in other fluids as well? "Doc. What's the count?"

"Two hundred eighty-six Vectis, two hundred eight-seven Vectis."

"Good. Keep on it." I frowned, disturbed with myself, because without any logical reason I could imagine, I felt that he deserved at least a warning. "Doc, listen. You'll want to pull back from my sensory nerves, if you still can. Some of this may hurt. A lot."

"Two hundred ninety-five Vectis. Thanks, Tezz. You're a pal. Two hundred ninety-eight Vectis."

Apparently I am, I thought. What a strange person I had become. And getting stranger as I went.

The blood smears on the floor burned themselves out in seconds. I bit down on my tongue to fill my mouth with saliva, which I promptly spit on the floor. After wasting a few seconds waiting for an ignition that never came, I smeared the spittle with one hand and could detect no change in viscosity, coloration, or temperature, which led me to the conclusion that spit lacked some essential characteristic necessary to the reaction. Still, sangrite had dissolved and ignited in the bare smears of blood; it was possible that sangrite's structure might be similar to rock sugar, halite, or similarly soluble minerals.

So I tasted it.

I went over to a wall and gave it a cautious lick—it would be unfortunate if I discovered sharp edges in the deposit by setting my tongue on fire—and found that it had no flavor at all that I could detect. Not so soluble as I'd hoped; it seemed the reaction was blood to blood. Crystal to liquid, and liquid to crystal.

Eating the stuff seemed to be out of the question. Injection was problematic; if the sangrite dissolved only in blood, there seemed to be no way to liquefy it without causing catastrophic ignition. The closest thing I had to a working hypothesis involved direct injection of intact crystals. But how could I even try it without making myself explode?

My only hope was to find or make crystals that were very, very small.

But without any sort of useful tool, how was I to *make* crystals small? I didn't even have a chunk that I could knock against other chunks to flake off chips, nor did I have the ability to free such a chunk. If only I had a tool, any tool—or better yet, a couple of pounds of etherium—hells, with no more than an ounce or two of etherium, I could ...

Wait.

I stood very, very still. Thinking.

I discovered I was smiling. One answer that solves three problems.

That's elegance.

"Doc—the count."

"Three hundred seventy Vectis."

Less than nine minutes. Not enough time. Not nearly enough time.

It didn't matter.

Standing nude in the center of the cavern, I closed my eyes and focused my will, and shortly there appeared in my perception a chaotic array of very, very faint points of energy, glowing faintly like stars on a misty night: a halo around my scalp, clustered around my groin, and scattered among my hands and feet. I fixed my attention to them each individually, and to them all generally, and pulled them out from under my skin.

It was a point of curiosity to me that now, here, where I struggled to intercept a catastrophe of monstrous proportion—one so dire and immediate that all the resources of the Infinite Consortium might not have sufficed—the tools I had to work with were those I'd acquired a lifetime ago, in my father's Tidehollow hovel: my intellect, my clarity of purpose, and my talent for rhabdomancy.

Not to mention the tiny slivers and shards of etherium lodged under the skin of my scalp and groin, hands and feet, that were half-forgotten remnants of what I had stolen from my father.

Stolen is a stark word. Someone less devoted to precision than I would likely try to justify such a theft as some sort of moral necessity; I myself have been guilty of such. For many years I had thought of myself as a victim who had transformed himself into a clever rogue-hero like those of childhood fables, using ingenuity and patience to win freedom against impossible odds—and though that was exactly what I had done, at the same time, the unsentimental truth of the matter is that I had been only a clever thief. Worse than a thief: a bandit. A ripper.

I had used my mind instead of a weapon, but that was a distinction of style, not substance. Irrelevant to the truth.

Yes: my father was a bad man. Is a bad man. A drunkard, a wastrel, an addict, a violent abuser of my mother and myself—a figure of terror before he became one of contempt. And yet—

And yet there had been two things left in his life that he'd called his own: his tiny trade in etherium scraps, and his son the rhabdomant, who had kept him in business. And I had ripped them both forever beyond his grasp.

As he had taught me, all those years ago: whatever can be taken, will be taken.

I took from a man who'd had nothing else.

While I was contemplating this unflattering concept, I was also bringing forth all those residual shreds of etherium that had lingered under my skin all these years. Tiny spheres crawled across my skin like silvery mites, gathering themselves in the palm of my left hand, until finally they all joined into a single smooth ball, a half inch in diameter and weighing less than an ounce.

It would have to be enough.

A particularly bright fist-size sangrite protrusion from the nearby wall seemed a likely spot to test my idea. A brief inspection revealed several faults and fissures, one of which extended all the way to its surface near to its joining with the rest of the wall. I formed the etherium into a tiny needle, which I used to scratch open a vein in the back of my hand. Clenching my fist produced a satisfactory droplet of blood, small enough that I did not need to worry about it dripping on the floor and blowing one of my feet off. I stuck the end of the needle into the blood droplet, and with my mind thinned the needle while gradually hollowing an internal channel up its length. This produced a slight vacuum, enough to draw a little of my blood up within it, converting my needle to an etherium pipette.

I sealed the end of my pipette, and *very* carefully wiped the exterior. Inserting it as far as was practicable into the surface fissure of the protrusion, I caused the etherium to open and retract very briskly, so that I could step away before that portion of my blood inside the protrusion could react with the sangrite and detonate. Which it did.

With a stunningly intense *crack!* the sangrite protuberance exploded from the wall as though shot from a ballista. It hit the far wall, and the impact produced a shattering blast of raw power that lifted me from my feet and slammed me into the wall—fortunately without drawing blood.

Detonation on impact. Interesting. But inconvenient.

"YOW!" Doc exclaimed in my ear, louder even than the explosion. "*Warn* me when you're gonna do something like that!"

"Doc," I said, checking my bones as best I could for fractures, "I'm gonna do something like that."

"Oh, very funny."

"It's not a joke." I climbed back to my feet and stepped carefully over some fragments to locate a few tiny chips. I wet my finger and touched the smallest of the chips—a sliver less than half an inch long, and so thin that it looked clear. Folding my pipette into tweezers, I took the splinter and jammed it into the lateral side of my left butt cheek.

For what seemed like a terribly long time but was probably no more than a second or two, nothing happened—but then I felt a definite surge of energy from the splinter, for a bare instant before my ass caught fire.

Nothing actually exploded, which was a relief, but a patch of flesh almost an inch in diameter spit fire and poured black smoke and felt, for about five seconds, as if it was burning all the way into to my hip joint.

"Ow wow *wow WOW*!" Doc wailed. "You had to do it on the *left* side, didn't you?"

"It's good manners to share. What's the count?"

"Are you kidding? After you set our *butt* on *fire*?"

Meat-scented smoke trailed up from a charred divot about the size of the end of my thumb. He wasn't kidding: it hurt. It felt like someone was excavating my butt cheek with a red-hot spoon. And that was the good news. "Where were you when you lost track?"

"The late seven hundreds."

"Not the answer I was hoping for." Three minutes. I'd been right all along—not enough time. Not as much as I needed. No more tests. No more theories. This would either work, or it would kill me. Us.

I hate improvising. *Hate* it. Improvisation is for people too lazy or stupid to plan.

A group of stupid, lazy people that now included me.

I dropped to my knees at the edge of the scattered chips and splinters of sangrite. The cleavage appeared to be largely orthorhombic, which was fortunate—most fragments tended to be long and thin, like a crystal stylus. The problem was that the tiniest flakes seemed to be fading away—shrinking like sublimating dry ice. Which explained why I had found no existing fragments on my initial search. The damned stuff *evaporates*.

Why is it that nothing ever turns out to be easy?

I gathered as many of the medium-to-large crystals as I could fit into both hands and began to stick them into the only place where, first, I wouldn't lose them, and second, I wouldn't run the risk of having my colon explode; that is, I stuck them into the long tangles of my hair. Time pressure made my hands tremble, ever so slightly. I carefully kept the crystals away from my scalp, especially those with sharp edges, as having my head blast open would be only slightly less traumatic than full rectal detonation, and that only because I would be too dead to suffer.

And that was the easy part.

I found one crystal that had shrunk to two and a half inches long and about a tenth of an inch in diameter. I held it in the palm of my right hand, along with my tiny bead of etherium.

"What's that for?"

"Shh. We're not going to get a second try at this."

I stared at the etherium bead. It rolled across my palm to the crystal of sangrite, then flowed over and around it, encasing the sangrite in metal. I then refined one end of the etherium to shape it into the sharpest, stiffest point that raw etherium could hold. That accomplished, I used the fingertips of my left hand to locate an intercostal space to the right of my sternum just above my heart, then brought my sangrite-filled needle there and put its point to my skin, the needle angling to aim behind my sternum.

"Um, Tezz? You mind telling me what you're doing?"

"In a moment."

"Seriously. What are you doing?"

"This." With a sharp movement of my right thumb, I stabbed myself in the chest, driving the whole needle in as far as I could push.

"*Ow*! Damn it!"

"My thoughts exactly," I gasped. The pain crushed my breath away—like being stabbed with a rusty gate latch. Must have inadvertently nicked a rib. "But . . . so far so good . . ."

"You say that like it's going to get worse."

"We met only days ago, yet it seems you've known me all your life." I closed my eyes and wasted some few seconds settling my mind and summoning my concentration; a mistake in this part of the operation might kill us both.

Even if I did it *right*, it might kill us both.

I hate improvising.

I found the needle with my mind, and I induced tiny projections of etherium to stick out from its front end, then slowly creep along it to the rear, while at the same time causing smooth etherium to flow forward from the rear to become new projections—like a conveyor belt in reverse, or the linked-chain treads of a heavily armored vehicle. In sum, the effect was not unlike the scales of a snake. The threads gave the needle purchase on my surrounding tissue, so that it could pull itself slowly—*agonizingly* slowly—toward my aortal arch.

"Oh, crap," Doc moaned. "Oh, you bastard. You do this to me on *purpose*—I apologized for your balls, didn't I?"

"This is not . . ." Speech was difficult through the clench of my jaw. The needle felt bigger than my thumb and as though it was using fishhooks to claw its way through my chest. ". . . *punishment*. If even a tiny gap opens in the casing . . . and blood touches the sangrite . . ."

"I get it. *Ka-boom. Splat.* How in the hells did you talk me into *this*?"

"By not . . . telling you about it . . ."

"Y'know, *real* friends don't keep secrets."

"How would . . . you know?"

"Awww . . ."

"Here's a plan . . ." I gritted. The needle had reached the wall of my aortal arch. "Before we take our swing at Bolas . . . you tell me your secrets, and I'll tell you mine."

"What secrets do *I* have?"

"You'll be surprised." I closed my eyes, and with one spasm of will, I stabbed the needle through the wall of the aorta so that its tip entered the largest flow point in my entire bloodstream.

Doc said, "*Golghhg . . .*"

I agreed. The needle seemed to be impinging on a nerve cluster. I felt the stab again with every beat of my heart.

"All right," I said. Pain, yes. But: no shortness of breath, no faintness, no tachycardia—probably hadn't torn the aortal wall, or not badly, at any rate. "All right. So far so good."

"I *hate* when you say that."

"Now comes the tricky part."

"*Now*?" Doc sounded appalled. "What was that *last* part, then?"

"That was the 'difficult but probably won't kill us' part."

"Oog. That means this part—"

"Is really damned tricky. Yes."

I took a deep breath. "This is how it's going to work. This sangrite seems to be the next best thing to solid mana. And concentrated. Activated by contact with blood. Instead of jamming a crystal straight through my skin and setting another part of me on fire, I believe that a very, very fine powder fed directly into my bloodstream might distribute the reaction throughout my body in a controlled fashion— so I can use its power without blowing myself apart."

"Come again? You want to *mainline* powdered *dragon blood*?"

"More than mainline. I am equipping the etherium needle with very, very tiny grinding gears, that very, very

MATTHEW STOVER

slowly crush the sangrite as it's fed into my aorta. If it works the way I'm hoping, the dust particles will spread through my whole body in a few seconds."

"This sounds like a *really* bad idea."

"It is."

"I am *not* okay with this."

"You don't get a vote."

"Like *hells*—"

"It's already done," I said. "I did it while I was describing it to you. Stop me now and you'll burn us to death."

"Damn it, Tezz!" he shouted furiously, loud enough to make my ear buzz. "We just *talked* about this kind of crap!"

"No. We were *going* to talk about it," I said, extending my arms as each and every hair on my body stood on end, crackling with spits of energy discharge. "That conversation will take place in a future that'll never happen."

"What's that? Is it working, or are we dying?"

"Both." The hissing in my ears swelled to a full-on hurricane. Arcs of blinding white lightning writhed and sizzled from my hands to the floor, to the walls, to my head. More power than I'd ever felt. Far more than I knew what to do with—but to do nothing was not an option. If I tried to restrain this power, I'd detonate like that sculler.

I felt my blood go fizzy. I felt my heart begin to boil. My brain would be next.

I let the power lift me up from the cavern's floor. I let it clothe me in searing light. Seeking the Glass Dune, where a transit gate would be standing near two etherium gravity sleds, I sent forth my mind . . .

And I could say only, "Ohhh . . ."

"What is it?" Doc said, shouting to make himself heard over the hurricane in my head. "What do you see?"

Hanging in the air, bound to the cavern with chains of lightning, I breathed, "*Everything . . .*" because that is exactly what I saw.

Everything.

I saw the mountains of Jund, the jungles of Naya, the golden plains of Bant, the endless oceans of Esper, and the smoking hellscape that was Grixis. I saw leotau-mounted lancers crashing through a formation of scourge devils while the skies above them were filled with shrieking death struggles between angels and kathari. I saw a hundred stormcallers on the Cliffs of Ot, chanting as they diverted the winds of the Eternal Storm to buffet back flight after flight of swooping dragons. I saw whole armies of elves and humans hurling storms of griffins, hydrae, and chimeras against massed formations of infantry whose armor blazed like the sun itself, while leonin shook flashing weaponry and roared their challenge to the champions of their enemies. I saw Sharuum in her chambers, Nicol Bolas brooding in Grixis, my father collapsed in his hovel. . . .

And I saw the transit gate beside the gravity sleds in the Glass Dunes, where Silas Renn stretched out a hand, and the artifact he held blasted power at the back of an unsuspecting Baltrice.

"Hang on, Doc," I said, my voice sounding very far away, half buried in the howling hurricane inside me. "It looks like we're going to be a little late."

" 'Better late than never,' " Doc shrieked into the wind, "is just a bloody figure of speech!"

The power blasting outward through my skin allowed no time for a conventional teleport, but I didn't need to use one. Power was its own answer: with power such as this, I could reach out like Nicol Bolas himself and simply yank and rip and squeeze reality into the shape of my desire. I seized that part of Esper's existence in the grip of my mind, then dragged it close so that I could pass from the cavern to the desert with a single step.

My arrival cracked the sky.

Through the rip I came, blazing in the air dozens of yards above them. The light from my body whited out the colors of the desert, Baltrice and the sleds, and the hand Renn had raised to shield his eyes.

I spoke in thunderclaps.

"I BELIEVE YOU'VE BEEN EXPECTING ME."

TEZZERET
EVEN A BROKEN CLOCKWORKER

The fight was short, by comparison to the hours of mock dueling Renn and I had inflicted upon each other at the Seeker Academy. This confrontation was over in less than a minute. However, when fighting a clockworker, less than a minute is not as brief as it sounds.

He stood perhaps a dozen meters behind where Baltrice was still in the process of being blown off her sled. He had abandoned his usual melodramatically flouncing cape-and-tunic outfit in favor of a simple pair of breeches and heavy boots, leaving exposed his torso and arms, which were constructed of baroquely latticed cobalt-etherium alloy, and his etherium heart shone through his chest like a fist-size golden sun. Only his head, his hands, his groin, and his feet were still flesh. On any other day, his overwhelming etherium advantage would have rendered him functionally immune to the most potent attacks at my command.

This was not, however, any other day.

Her head thrown back and arms wide, her balance tipped far forward beyond the nose of the sled, Baltrice looked as if she might be posing for an action illustration. A motionless cloud of what I assumed to be droplets of her blood sprayed backward from a ragged hole in the back of her tunic, just between her shoulder blades. She hung in the air, frozen, in the middle of pitching onto her face.

My best guess was that Renn had stream-shifted behind her and hit her with some kind of hypersonic ballistic projectile. Or a group of such. Hypersonic because she must have been hit before she heard it coming, ballistic because her automatic defenses would have layered her in impenetrable shields in the instant any magic had been directed against her.

He'd shot her in the back.

"Tezzeret?" Renn said, loud but casual, squinting against the blinding glare that crackled from my skin. "Is that you, old friend?"

"*Friend*?" Doc sputtered in my ear.

"I've got him. Check out Baltrice as best you can," I muttered. "I need to know what *exactly* has her frozen there."

"This is not how I imagined us to meet again," Renn called. "I was sure you'd have clothes on."

"*WE DON'T HAVE TO FIGHT,*" I thundered down at him.

"Oh, I think we do."

"*WE CAN COOPERATE. FIND CRUCIUS TOGETHER.*"

"Cooperate? Absolutely." Renn raised his right hand and summoned a grayish, unwieldy artifact. If he was still as unimaginative as he used to be, this would be the same artifact he had used on Baltrice. "Cooperate by holding still."

He pointed the device at me, and in that instant I understood. He was not simply a psychopath, a bloodthirsty maniac attacking for sport. He was attacking because he thought he had no choice. He was fighting the man I *used to be*. In self-defense.

When one is made of glass, everything looks like a stone.

He narrowed his eyes, and from the end of the device came a flash like fire.

His personal shields had to be down to permit physical projectiles' passage, and so I thrust my hands forward, twisting them sideways to again open rips in reality between us, two of them, as this was an opportunity to experimentally verify a hypothesis I'd formulated some years ago. I'd proposed that there is no interdimensional conservation of vector. In plain language, when allowing a moving body to pass through a reality warp, its vector on re entry will be, effectively, any direction I feel like.

One of my rips in reality gaped in the path of the hypersonic projectiles and swallowed them whole, while the other rip opened in front of Renn, but below his line of sight. Specifically, it opened less than two feet in front of his knees at a shallow angle. Even as the artifact's sharp report reached my ears, the projectiles the device had fired blasted up through the second rip and hit Silas Renn square in the crotch.

As Nicol Bolas would say: Now, *that's* comedy!

The impact lifted him up on his toes and tore a sizable hole in his breeches in exactly the most embarrassing possible place—which was not, however, actually embarrassing for Renn, because all that was displayed through the hole was a mess of raggedly bloody meat. This was not a serious wound for him; lacking anything resembling a working circulatory system, he was in no danger of bleeding out, and those etherium legs would go right on keeping him upright and mobile even if his pelvic bone was shattered.

Still: it must have stung.

His face went white, and an instant later it was red enough that even the glare of energy I cast upon the dunes could not bleach it away. And he wasn't blushing. He made

MATTHEW STOVER

a fist with his free hand, and sheets of gauzy blue layered themselves around him as he cast the artifact aside.

"That *might* have hurt," Renn said scornfully, "if I were nothing but a meatbag like you—but the power to regenerate my flesh is built into my enhancements, scrapper boy. I barely even felt it. Now watch how a *real* mage fights."

Taunts. Just like the old days. Did he think we were in the Academy's arena, showing off for the Masters? After all these years, he thought he could still get into my head with smack talk. Pathetic.

Being pathetic, however, was no guarantee he wouldn't kill me.

He finished the gesture of casting the artifact aside by pointing toward it and shouting some sort of trigger word, while with a swift twist of his opposite hand—another school yard trick—he now unleashed a swelling torrent of blue fire that roiled up at me. I had no idea what it might be.

I assumed it was some sort of temporal manipulation. I employed my best hypothetical defense against clockworking, which was to force another rip in the fabric of reality, and place this rip where it would intercept his spell and suck away his blue torrent as swiftly as he could pour it forth.

It worked well enough—except he didn't show any sign of canceling the spell, and I didn't know how much energy that opening could channel before closing—or if adding energy might instead *swell* the rip until it swallowed us all. Or the whole desert, or Esper, even all of Alara. Possibly even the Multiverse itself.

This is why I hate improvising.

I was using a power I didn't understand to fight other powers I also didn't understand—which is decidedly *not* my game. On the other hand, I reflected, at least I wasn't losing.

Yet.

"Doc. What do you have on Baltrice?"

"Uh, you do remember that I can't see her unless *you* can, right?"

"Sorry." I swooped around to another spot, where the frozen form of Baltrice was in my field of vision, a dozen meters beyond Renn. "A little busy here."

"I still hate that guy."

"I still agree."

Renn shot from his other hand rectangular sheets of azure fire, one after another, like playing cards or baffle curtains. They expanded as they came at me, and went from transparent to translucent, heading for opaque. My best guess: some kind of at-range shield, possibly an exotic flavor of telekinesis.

I used my left hand to intercept the rectangles with a twisting chain of lightning. The lightning seemed to stop their approach, chewing through their middles, again one after another, on its way toward Renn—though each rectangle held longer than the one before it had, which wasn't promising. I had no way to know how long my sangrite-supercharged power would last, and Renn wasn't even breathing hard. "Doc. Baltrice?"

"Got it," he said. "Nothing fancy—time's running about a tenth of a percent of normal for a couple of yards on all sides of her. Each second for her is about seventeen minutes for us. Cold storage."

"This could be a problem," I said through clenched teeth, opening every mana channel I had to pour power into my continuous writhe of lightning.

Renn canceled his blue torrent—whatever in the hells it had been—and gestured with his right hand, drawing blue sigils that danced in the air like fey-charmed runes. My lightning hung transfixed on one of those blue rectangles—which didn't look inclined to fail—and there were still at least two more of them between Renn and grievous bodily harm. "What are those damned shields, then?"

"Same kind of thing," Doc told me grimly. "Hypotemporal boundaries. Each one marks a downshift of about half. Between those last two . . . let's see, a quarter, an eighth . . . yeah. One two-hundred-and-fifty-sixth of normal."

Damn. "How long can he keep them up?"

"How should I know? You're the one who said he could have spent subjective weeks or even months getting ready; best to assume he can do whatever he's doing as long as he feels like doing it."

"Yes." I tried to loop my lightning and hook it around the outside of the rectangles, but they moved instantly to intercept, seemingly without requiring any attention from Renn. Worse news. "What about those glowing runes in the air?"

"Shrug. More clockworking?"

The runes were still dancing, but as Renn added to them, they began to organize themselves into a curving band . . . bent into a broad half-circle arch. "A gate?"

"Hey, that's it! A *temporal* gate!" Doc chirped. "He's going for another time line—we got him on the run!"

"I don't think so." Flee? From me? Not Silas Renn.

He stepped into the gate and vanished.

"The gate's still open—go get him!"

"I don't think so," I repeated. The only plausible reason for the gate to still be there is that he wanted me to go after him. I'm just not that gullible.

Those time shields were still between me and the gate—but I had a work-around. I did my new reality-rip trick in front of my chest, and opened another one at the mouth of the gate—sighting through the warp showed me Renn crouching on the far side, so he wouldn't get caught in the kill zone of the five (!) etherium drakes he had waiting for me, who would have made very short work of me indeed, supercharged or not.

I extended my power through the reality warp—into the one in front of me and out of the one fronting the gate—like a hand of lightning, and just grabbed the smug prick and hauled him back here where I could uncork another swing or two. Or five. Or eight.

However many it took until the bastard stopped moving.

My lightning hand couldn't breach his personal shields, and I couldn't seem to drag him into the warp itself—but that was no reason to just let him go. I'd never get a better chance to test his personal shields against the altered physics of an area where time was passing, say for example, at roughly one tenth of one percent of normal. It was worth the experiment.

I threw him at Baltrice.

He flailed wildly in the air, magic flashing and blasting out of him in all directions, seemingly at random, but some of them must have accomplished something, because suddenly everything was happening very . . . very . . . slowly . . . the crackles and blasts of battle deepening to a grinding, almost subsonic rumble.

Renn inched through the air toward Baltrice, and I got it: he'd thrown some sort of temporal distortion to give himself time to figure out what to do—but in his panic he'd accidentally caught me in the spell's fringe, for which I was grateful, because I was about to be in a great deal of trouble. Those damned etherium drakes were heading into Renn's gate.

Coming for me.

Four of them unfurled their wings with the majestic grace of schooners raising sail. The fifth, showing either better reflexes or more initiative than his comrades, had turned his wide-gaped mouth toward the reality warp and now belched forth a roiling burst of flame. I canceled the warp instantly, but my reflexes, no matter how enhanced by Renn's spell, couldn't force the warp to close all at once. As the ragged edges of reality gradually sewed themselves back together, I was treated to the unusual view of dragon-fire boiling slowly toward me, creeping through the warp, and unfolding like a thunderhead until it pillowed into me and blasted me backward and up into the sky.

Slowly.

The lightning from my skin protected me from anything worse than sunburn, but matters would be different when they all ganged up on me. And I was in no mood to waste my limited powers fighting e-drakes. I had a better idea.

Renn, meanwhile, stretched a hand toward Baltrice, and he must have canceled the hypotemporal field that restrained her to avoid catching himself in it like a fly in magical amber. She lurched into motion, though still (subjectively) very slowly, pitching forward over the nose of her sled, heading for the dunes face-first. Renn came tumbling glacially after her.

This looked to me like a chance to get up close and personal.

I grabbed reality between them and yanked it to within one step, arriving directly in the path of Renn's cold-molasses tumble, which I intercepted by leaping forward to grab the back of his neck, yank his head toward me, and smash his face into my knee.

The slow-motion squash of Silas Renn's nose was possibly the most exquisitely satisfying sensation I will ever experience.

Suddenly—though not unexpectedly—time around us regained its normal flow when my knee broke Renn's concentration along with his nose. Back in full speed with no time to react, he and I crashed together with stunning force. His greater momentum carried us backward, and we hit the sand in a heap. Renn somehow had gotten his head into the pit of my stomach, and the impact drove all hope of breath from my lungs and made ragged patches of black skate across the cloudless sky above.

I rolled over on top of him and hooked his etherium collarbone with my left hand, which was all I could manage before I had to simply lie across him and try to force air back down my throat. Fortunately, Renn was in no better shape; he lay with only whites showing through his slitted eyelids, and his open mouth bubbled with blood from his nose.

"Tezzeret . . . ?" Baltrice rolled over with a grunt and sat up. I was passingly pleased to note that her face, unlike the rest of her body, had no powdered glass on it—because her ear-and-eye device was still working. "What happened to me? What's wrong with my back? What the hell's going on?"

I tried to tell her, but could manage only a strangled croak. I gestured weakly at Renn with my free hand.

She stood up. "Well, all right, then. Get off him and I'll take it from here."

I shook my head emphatically and waved her gaze toward the blossoming formation of e-drakes converging on us. "Bigger . . . problem . . ."

Her brows drew together. "Yeah. I think they're playing my song."

Fire licked along her arms and legs and whooshed skyward from the top of her brush cut. "My back feels funny—weak. Numb," she said, eyes on the e-drakes to gauge their approach. "And wet. How bad am I hurt?"

"Not . . . badly," I managed to gasp. "I've got . . . Renn. Stop . . . the drakes . . ."

"Don't mind if I do." She clenched both fists, and a flaming dome of shield flared to life, sheltering Renn and me, but not her. She stepped between us and the diving drakes, and she didn't bother with a personal shield.

All five of them went straight for her, and the blast of fire from five e-throats was so intense the dunes around us looked like the inside of a blast furnace. Embers spit into my hair and across my back even through Baltrice's shield, and the flames slagged the dune to smoking slabs of glass for meters around. When the fire died away, Baltrice hadn't moved. She just stood there, squinting up at them, fists on her hips as though she'd decided, in the spirit of fair play, she'd given them one free shot.

Now she tilted her head to crack her neck, and rotated her shoulders to loosen the cramping around the wound in her back. "Well, all right, then." She sounded cheerfully businesslike. "Damn me if you sad-ass bastards aren't right in the middle of the last stupid thing you're ever gonna do."

Watching Baltrice unleash her inferno of destruction, I decided she was living proof of the adage, "If you love your job, you never have to work for a living."

The etherium drake is one of the last surviving remnants of what is very possibly the worst idea in the history of Esper. Centuries ago, the earliest rudiments of what would become the Ethersworn decided that since etherium was supposed to "sanctify and morally elevate" whatever is joined with it, they should start enhancing even the beasts, to speed the world's transformation into a paradise. Which was appallingly ignorant in itself, but they didn't stop there.

When these self-appointed saviors got together to figure out what species should be the first on which they'd try their Noble Work, they chose the Esper firedrake.

The firedrake was, before these chucklebrains began to meddle with it, the single most dangerous predator on

Esper. Smaller than true dragons, not significantly smarter than sewer rats, and lacking the broad-based magical prowess of their draconic relations, the firedrakes made up for their genetic deficits in sheer mindless ferocity.

Sluice serpents can be avoided by staying away from the cesspits; kraken keep to the deep ocean; striges are more of a nuisance than a threat. Flocks of firedrakes, however, who have, on their *good* days, the temperament of rabid viashinos, might at any time take it upon themselves to flock together and wing off to some randomly unlucky spot, then attack and immolate everything for miles around. Everything. Ships. Caravans. Villages. Rocks. Each other. No one knows exactly why.

Maybe they just like to watch things burn.

The proto-Ethersworn spent a generation or two stalking firedrakes, tranquilizing them, and replacing various parts of their bodies with refined etherium. To the astonishment of no one other than themselves, the Noble Metal seemed to have no beneficial effect on the behavior of firedrakes. At all. So, in their typically clot-headed fashion, they concluded that this must be simply because the firedrakes hadn't been enhanced *enough*, and they undertook to remedy this delusional problem by making a very real problem several orders of magnitude worse.

Just as it does for any other living thing, etherium made firedrakes stronger.

This was long before the days of the shortage, and so by the time any *sane* people realized what these moonbats were up to, there were several hundred firedrakes whose *entire bodies* had been replaced. They even replaced the creatures' *brains*, which had no noticeable effect on their physiology beyond making them a great deal more difficult to kill, and making their moral character, if they could be said to have one, even worse.

Where before they had been ridiculously dangerous, savagely unpredictable horrors, full-body replacement transformed them into mindless, near-indestructible engines of destruction.

Sharuum, in her wisdom, commanded the moonbats to clean up their own mess, which made no appreciable dent in the numbers of e-drakes but in short order did an admirable job of thinning the moonbat population. Eventually the Grand Hegemon was forced to take a personal hand. She gathered the bulk of the land's sphinxes and led them on a sequence of hunts over the course of a decade or two, until there were no more e-drakes to be found. Somehow, however, the creatures persist in reappearing at inconvenient moments.

Informed opinions on the reason for this are split. Optimists tend to believe new e-drakes are being created by a radical splinter sect of the Ethersworn, still carrying on their Noble Nut Job in secret. Realists are of the opinion that the creatures have found a way to breed.

Dangerous as they are, their most destructive power is the annihilating fire they can vomit at will—and to assault Baltrice with flame was worse than useless. The more flame they poured onto her, the stronger she got, and when a couple of them stooped like falcons to try their luck with fang and talon, she just opened her arms and invited them in with a truly happy grin.

The closest e-drake was clearly astonished to discover that Baltrice could herself claw and bite with the best of them. She slipped the beast's viperish fang strike, got one arm around the thing's long, snaky neck, and grabbed its wing joint with her free hand. In a second or two, the joint ran from red to yellow to white as radioactive milk, and dripped down through the e-drake's ribs while the wing flopped off, twitching into the dunes.

I could happily have whiled away the whole afternoon watching Baltrice dismantle her new toys, except that this was the moment Silas Renn chose to hook his thumb into my left eye.

"Uh, by the way," Doc said, "did I mention he's awake?"

That was also the moment I discovered that the boiling had subsided from my blood, that the lightning crackle was gone from my skin, and that I was suddenly tired.

Very, very tired.

Not yet *dead* tired, though that state loomed in my immediate future.

Exhaustion, however, was not enough to stop me from twisting my head, latching my teeth into the ball of his thumb, and biting down until he squealed like a tea kettle. He got his other hand up under my chin and dug his thumb into my parotid gland until I had to let go so I could turn my head away, after which he undertook to deliver a very efficient, thorough, and professional beating, focusing on my face, my lower abdominal wall, and my groin.

This was a particularly inconvenient moment to discover that the education of scions of the House of Renn included comprehensive training in personal combat.

This was particularly inconvenient because I hadn't been in a fistfight since I was (approximately) eleven years old, and because my lack of expertise was compounded by having only one hand I could use to defend myself. If I let go of his collarbone, he'd throw me off and roast me in roughly a heartbeat and a half.

Worse, it seemed that his etherium enhancements, in addition to being impervious to anything I could do with hands, feet, or head, also made him stronger than a rhox berserker. Each blow of his fists opened a cut on my face and shot stars across my vision, or ripped muscles and battered internal organs, or crushed my testicles until I had to vomit bile from my empty stomach, or inventive combinations thereof. "How's it feel, scrapper boy?" he sneered in my face. "Bet you never thought I could beat you at this *too*, did you?"

I could not have answered him if I'd wanted to. Soon he got bored with thrashing me, and decided to break my grip on his collarbone by pinching the muscle between my thumb and forefinger with *his* thumb and forefinger, which was so unexpectedly and unbelievably painful that I yelped and jerked as if I'd been stabbed. But despite his enhancements, his hands were still only flesh and bone. With my free hand, I grabbed his thumb and pried it off me.

"Where I come from, this is *foreplay*," I mumbled through smashed and bloody lips. "In a fight, we're more like—" and I completed the sentence by yanking his thumb in a direction thumbs are not designed to be yanked.

The joint snapped with a satisfyingly wet crunch.

"Cesspit scum," he snarled, his face white with killing rage. "After I beat you unconscious, I'm going to drown you in your own sewage."

"You don't have the balls. Remember?" I let go of his thumb, reached behind his head, and grabbed a fistful of powdered glass that I pounded into the ruin of his nose. "*This* is how we do it in *Tidehollow*, you snotty upslope bitch."

The powdered glass spread across his face. I encouraged the spreading by pounding him with the outside of my fist as if it were a hammer. I may not know much about fist-fighting, but I do know how to swing a hammer, and there are few humans who can truthfully say they do it better.

Renn gasped from the impact, and when his mouth opened I hit him again, this time downward on his lower incisors, hyperextending his jaw with another wet crunch.

He howled. In Tidehollow, that would be the moment to pound sand into his open mouth, so I did.

A cave brat from my part of the slum would also twist his hand on Renn's face, to grind the sand harder into his mouth and into the ruin of his nose, to force it into his eye sockets, thumb it under his eyelids, and pack it into his tear ducts.

I did that, too.

Then I hit him again. And once more for good measure. And one to grow on.

He gagged, and choked, and tried to howl some more, acting generally helpless and beaten, which I didn't believe for a second; I knew how tough he used to be, and I assumed that now he was likely tougher. The fight would be over when one of us was unconscious. Or dead.

My suspicious nature paid off when I glimpsed a flash of blue sparks at the corners of his eyes, and so managed to avert my eyes before his Immaculate Form—a very minor magic, barely a cantrip, used for instantly cleansing oneself and one's clothing—blew all that sand away from his face and straight at mine. Before I could get back to business, one of his arms snaked around the back of my neck and he caught his opposite forearm to lever his other arm across my face.

I had been expecting him to throw me off. By the time I realized what he was doing, he had locked my head into the crook of his arm. His hold tightened with the mechanical progression of a bench vise. "Tidehollow's *nothing*," he whispered in my ear. "This is how *men* fight."

That built-in body regeneration of his seemed to be working entirely too well.

"Uh, Tezz . . . ?" Doc said worriedly. "It seems like we're in trouble here. Are we in trouble? Tezz?"

I couldn't answer because my mouth was jammed full of etherium forearm. I managed to find his hands and clawed at them, trying for another fingerhold or a grip on his broken thumb, but of course he wouldn't let me catch him that way again. "Oh, no no no," he hummed. "You don't want to do that, and here's why."

His grip tightened. I heard an alarming crunching sound that seemed to be coming from inside the back of my skull. "Do you know how I practice this hold?" he murmured. "On granite boulders. Until they shatter."

Apparently my rhox-berserker metaphor had been something of an understatement.

"Tezz? *Tezz*! Do something!" Doc was starting to panic—and he sounded calmer than I was. Sangrite exhaustion seemed to have drained every drop of my mana reserve as well. I tried to organize my mind into planeswalking configuration, thinking that maybe Doc could 'port us back to the cavern—but all I got was a moan of dismay that indicated "It'll be *hours* before I can do *that* again!"

This, I thought, is a stupid way to die.

"How should I kill you? Let me count the ways," Renn mused happily. "Squashing your head like a rotten melon has a certain visceral appeal . . . but no, no, that will never do—it would be over all too quickly. How might I do it *leisurely* . . . as if I have all the time in the world. Because, after all, I do."

What could I have been *thinking*? Had I been thinking at all? I had *never beaten him*. Not once. But I had let my supercharged blood boil drag me into exactly what he was best at—single combat. Idiot.

Stupid, stupid, *stupid*.

Dying—again—would be bad enough. Dying because I was too stupid to live was more than I could take. If only

I had stopped to think—because, after all, the only trait in which I had a real advantage over Renn was intellect, though one couldn't prove it by anything that happened today. I had blindly thrown myself against him, my puny, all-too-mortal flesh against his unlimited power of etherium—

Wait.

The unlimited power of etherium . . .

Manipulating etherium didn't require mana. Not for me. The metal itself would furnish the power. Renn was half lost in his fantasies of torturing me to death. I was half lost in my blinding epiphany that there was one more thing I could do that Renn didn't know I could do.

Rhabdomancy.

With only the slightest twist of will, I could perceive the etherium in the area. All of it. Renn's body. The transit gate. The gravity sleds.

The needle in my aorta.

I chose the needle in my aorta for my first move. It withdrew from the blood vessel, leaving only a bead in place to seal the puncture. With no need for caution, I wrenched the needle back out through my ribs, my pectoral tendon, and my skin. I decided against a bravura line; why warn him? With my mind, I shaped the needle into a thin blade, then stabbed it through the iris of Renn's right eye.

He screamed, throwing me aside, clawing at his face, ripping bloody stripes with his fingernails. I counted myself lucky that the shock hadn't made him reflexively rip my head off, but his incredible strength nearly killed me anyway: throwing me aside involved sending me spinning through the air, twisting helplessly until my spine crashed into the arch of the transit gate hard enough that it very nearly broke me in half. Gasping, I fell to the sand, my arms and legs twitching and flopping in partial seizure.

MATTHEW STOVER

278

If Renn pulled himself together before I could do the same, he was going to kill me anyway. I couldn't even get up. Couldn't stand and take it like a man. Maybe I could crawl. Maybe.

Power had made me stupid. I had been strong, so I didn't bother to be smart. A mistake I swore never to make again.

Though the lesson would be wasted if learning it killed me.

I had a chance. One chance, because all that power was gone now, and my intellect was again on the job. One chance.

I reached out with my mind and activated the transit gate. A view of the zombie mob in the Netherglass opened above me, for I lay only a few feet from the gate's threshold.

Renn stopped screaming. Perhaps the twist of power had been enough to remind him that he hadn't killed me yet. His left eye fixed upon me, and his bloody mouth stretched like a nightmare ogre. "*Running?*" he shrieked, hurling himself toward me. "*Run* then! Run! I'll start by severing your *legs*! *One festering joint* at a *time*!"

But when he got close to me, he skidded to a stop, staring down at me in open puzzlement, because I wasn't trying to crawl through the gate. That was the moment he realized it was a trap. I saw it in his eyes.

He knew he was about to die.

His mouth opened like he was going to ask what in the hells I thought I was up to; he managed to say, "Tezzer—" before my gravity sled at full shrieking speed smashed into the small of his etherium back hard enough to cut an ordinary man in two. Renn was no ordinary man, and the gravity sled weighed less than thirty pounds, so the impact only knocked him forward, stumbling, trying to regain his balance.

It was enough.

Arms flailing, he actually would have made it—stopped himself short—had I not managed to make one twitching foot move at the last second, to hook his ankle and send him headlong into the transit gate.

Not through the gate. Into the gate.

Into the gate because I canceled the spell just as his head and shoulders broke the plane of transmission. About half his torso, his pelvis, both his legs, and one arm fell on me. Which hurt. But I really didn't mind.

The rest of him—head, shoulders, heart, and one arm— was lying on the sand of the Netherglass, fifteen miles away.

Perhaps my prejudice against improvisation was unfair. My own, just now, had produced satisfactory results.

Less than elegant, far from painless, and passingly humiliating, but satisfactory.

I lay there for a second or two, trying to regain enough breath to tell myself I was still alive. When I found my insistence sufficiently convincing, I got up and triggered the transit gate again.

On the far side, Renn's remaining arm was scrabbling for purchase in the soft powder, trying to drag itself, his shoulders, and his head off toward some imaginary safety. He seemed to be in some kind of shock. When I stepped through the gate and moved around to head him off—so to speak—he didn't seem capable of speech, producing only a thick gargle, a few lip smacks, and a pop or two.

"Stop it, Renn. It's over."

His eyes rolled, and his hand reversed course, and I sighed. Once the shock wore off, he'd be dangerous again; magic is a function of the mind, and his would, given the chance, come through this largely unharmed. His heart was still glowing in what was left of his chest, and the enchantments that served him in place of blood and lungs and other organs could keep his head alive indefinitely.

The last thing I wanted to do was give him a chance to reassemble himself.

I stepped over him and caught his wrist, lifting him from the ground. His eyes rolled, and his mouth worked, and now he was able to form intelligible words. *". . . kill me . . . Tezzeret . . . kill me. . . ."*

"You're too valuable to waste simply because I hate you," I said. "I gave you a chance to cooperate by choice. I will not repeat that mistake."

". . . Tidehollow scrapper bitch . . ."

"Hush now. Try not to heckle me while I save your life."

The severed ends of his enhancements were leaking mana like blood. It was the work of a moment or two for me to make contact with his etherium and manipulate its function sufficiently to seal the severed strands of lattice-work. That accomplished, I mentally took hold of the tiny blade in his eye and stretched it into an ultrafine thread, about a third the diameter of a human hair. I sent that back through his retina and along his optic nerve, which must have been a bit uncomfortable, because it made him shudder and moan.

Using the thread, I probed his brain matter until I found his sleep center. Hooking one end of the thread there, I sent the other directly into his pineal gland and worked the thread to feed its small mana current as a trickle charge. In about five seconds his eyes closed, and he relaxed into slumber.

A gust of breeze came from behind me toward the transit gate, bringing with it enough odor of zombie that I borrowed a bit of Renn's shoulder joint to put up an anti-glass-and-stink field. Looking through the gate, I understood why the breeze seemed to blow from here to there, as the Glass Dunes for a mile or two on the far side were no longer so much dunes as they were glass—molten glass, at the base of a firestorm bigger than most thunder-heads. In the heart of the firestorm, Baltrice still battled three of the e-drakes, all of them appearing to be having a fine old time.

I looked from the firestorm to the million-strong zombie army in the Netherglass, and back again to the fire. It struck me that as long as I had a pyromancer in mortal combat with etherium-enhanced firedrakes, there was a more useful location for their battle.

Reaching out with my mind, I found Baltrice's ear-and-eye piece. *Renn's down,* I sent. *Still having fun?*

Would it be too corny for me to say I'm just getting warmed up?

Over here in the Netherglass, I have a, ah . . . pest control issue. One that's begging for personal attention from you and your playmates. Can you lead them through the transit gate?

Incendiary sanitation? My specialty. Hold the door, we're on our way.

Making sure I did so required nearly all the strength I had left. I sagged to the ground, and set the sleeping Renn down beside me. I hugged my knees and tucked my battered face against them. For what felt like a very a long time, I could do nothing except sit there and shiver.

So this was what winning felt like. Finally.

Triumph. Victory.

Whatever.

"We won, right?" Doc said. "I mean, we did win, didn't we? This has to count as an old-fashioned ass-whuppin', huh? An authoritative spanking. A whack and smack that cracked his rack. We beat him like a red-headed stepchild. Thumped him like a rented drum. . . ."

"Doc. Enough."

"Yeah, yeah, sure. Whatever. Must feel good, though. Right? After all these years?"

I took a deep breath, then sighed it out. I didn't reply. I didn't have anything to say, because victory didn't feel like anything at all.

I felt nothing but tired.

One more thing, I told myself. I lifted my head and gazed off toward the incomprehensibly huge monolithic halls of the Crystal Labyrinth.

One more thing.

TEZZERET
THE REAL ME

I sat on the sand, tinkering with Renn's perceptual powers while Baltrice incinerated the last few thousand zombies. To the limits of my vision around us, the desert was stained with black soot and dusted with white ash. A vast pall of smoke filled the sky above the Netherglass, casting a permanent twilight upon the Crystal Labyrinth. Given that the peculiarities of the area included a huge stationary vortex in the prevailing winds, it was possible that the smoke would be there forever. Or at least until some powerful stormcaller could be persuaded to blow it away.

I had to pause in my tinkering every so often; the clothing I had magicked for myself was not quite sand-proof. I had been more comfortable naked.

The telemin halo I'd fashioned out of Renn's etherium-alloy body had turned out unexpectedly well. The external screening and impact cage was almost three feet in diameter; the bowed centering struts screwed into Renn's skull had enough flex to provide effective shock absorption. I daresay within this halo, Renn was in no danger of impact damage; I could have bounced him like a rubber ball without doing more than making him dizzy. The six carry handles I had built onto the impact cage's exterior projected far enough to prevent the halo from rolling on any surface less than a thirty-degree incline, and I certainly wouldn't be placing Renn's head on any slope steeper than that. He was too valuable.

A few more threads of pure etherium, similar to the one that kept him asleep, inserted into other parts of his brain allowed me to directly access his entire perceptual system—which was, I discovered, unexpectedly impressive. In addition to being able to see, smell, hear, taste, and feel what was in front of him, he could do the same with objects that were only *potentially* present, as well as objects that were long gone. Though as the interval increased, perception dimmed, it was still a useful talent.

Most interesting of all was his ability to see sideways in time. With the expenditure of considerable mana—easily done, given my current plenitude of etherium—he (and I, through him) could directly perceive the consequence of any given choice or string of choices, as the temporal streams bifurcated outward from each decision point. The more probable any given potential time line was, the easier it was to see.

It did not take much power at all to see time lines where Renn had won the fight.

I had decided not to tell Baltrice what would have happened to her if we'd lost. If she had so much as a hint, I could never have stopped her from killing Renn, and I was going to need him to navigate the Labyrinth.

Having left intact the magics that sustained his life and healed his injuries, I anticipated a virtually unlimited potential use-life for my Rennoscope (Rennscanner? Rennometer?). All his physical needs provided by the magics, he might well survive a century or more, which was far longer than I would need him.

Someday, perhaps, if I found myself in a sentimental mood, I might decide to rebuild him into a man. It was possible.

But not likely.

Once she had finished up, Baltrice rode her gravity sled over to where I sat with Renn's head. She slid off and mopped sooty sweat from her face with a grimy sleeve. "Well, that's it. Probably more inside, but no trouble. I got to tell you, I *still* don't understand why our army of necromancers didn't whip out a few thousand nasty beasties to piss on my bonfire."

"You will. Patience."

"Is that all you have to say about it? *Patience*?"

"It's an underrated virtue."

"Tell you what, then: you keep all of yours and take mine too. What there is of it." She propped her hands on her hips and stared back at the featureless, opalescent enormity of the Labyrinth. "What now? Straight in?"

"No."

"You have a better idea?"

"Usually."

"I'll tell you, I don't think anything I can do will affect the structure itself. The walls don't even pick up soot."

"It's not ordinary crystal. I'm not sure it's physical."

"Huh?"

I let one shoulder twitch in half a shrug. "It has occurred to me that if Renn's hypotemporal shield trick were to be made a great deal more powerful—if time never passed at all at its surface, or nearly so—it could, theoretically, look like that."

She shook her head. "Glad I'm not the one who has to figure stuff out around here."

"You do very well at it, though. How's your back?" I had adapted the autohealing magic Renn had built into his body to treat our various wounds—an imperfect solution, but the best we had.

MATTHEW STOVER

She worked her shoulders back and forth a few times, then shrugged. "It hurts. But it's not gonna kill me. How's your face?"

"Likewise." I gave her a lopsided smile, which was the best I could do around the swollen bruises and barely closed cuts that covered most of my head. Two of my teeth were loose enough that they might fall out before I had time to repair my jaw, but the long-term effects of the rest of my injuries would be only scars. "It hurts."

As did my hands, my legs, my guts, and virtually every other part of my body to which I could put a name.

"Bruises and a couple new scars? Small enough price to pay for living through a scrape like that," she said. "I won't forget what you did today, Tezzeret. You didn't have to come back for me. You went in *knowing* what he could do. Put yourself between him and me. I'm not sure I would have done the same for you."

"If I'd left you there, I'd be dead now. Or soon." It seemed wisest to avoid elaborating further.

"Well, I'm grateful anyway, huh?" She looked down at Renn's head, and nudged the telemin halo with her drake-skin boot. "He dead yet?"

"No. I need him alive."

"Isn't he kind of excitable, though? Loses his head in a crisis, right? He like, y' know, flies off the—"

"Don't."

"Don't what?"

"Don't mock him," I said. "Please."

"Why in the hells not? You think he wouldn't be gloating over *us* if this had gone the other way?"

"His behavior isn't my concern. Mine is."

"You seem pretty concerned about *my* behavior."

"I'm not. But allowing you to taunt him would be rude."

She flexed her shoulders and thrust her chin out toward me pugnaciously. "And if I decide I feel like doing a victory fandango up and down that back-shooting bastard's face, just exactly how do you figure to stop me?"

"By asking you not to," I said. "Politely."

She glared at me for about a second, which was as long as she could hold the glare before she cracked a smile. "You are some piece of work," she said, shaking her head and chuckling. "You really are."

"Compliments on my design and construction should be addressed to Nicol Bolas."

"I wonder if he knows exactly what he's got here. Something tells me that behind that deadpan of yours, you've got a surprise or two for him, too."

This didn't seem to call for a reply. Out from a pocket in my magicked clothing I brought the etherium thumb ring I had made for her. "Here."

She took it from my hand. "Jewelry? Are you sure it's time to take our relationship to that level?"

"You can wear that on your thumb—or, I suppose, given the size of your hands, on your fourth finger."

"What's it do?"

"It's a locator, that's all. When I'm done, I'll signal. You'll know it's me because the ring will light up and tingle. It will direct you to wherever I am. It's etherium; it'll never run out of power."

"When you're *done*?" She flushed, and tiny flames began to flicker in her eyes. "What, is this the brush-off? The Take a Festering Hike, Fat Bitch?"

"It's a promise," I said. "You have done everything I've asked of you, and more. You have earned Jace Beleren's freedom. Even if I fail. Even if I die."

I lifted my own hand to show her the matching ring I wore on my left thumb. "Your ring will lead you to this one, wherever it might be. If necessary, your ring is encoded with a summoning that will draw mine to you if I am dead or it is lost. Even if I am not available to do so myself, bringing the two rings together will impart the secret of safely removing the device from his brain."

"Yeah?" She looked at me sidelong, measuring. "Maybe I should, y'know, bring them together right now. Save myself the trip."

"Despite having done a stupid thing or two in the past few days, I'm not an idiot. I'll prepare my ring when you are far, far away. As I've mentioned before, I don't want us to fight. I would be sorry if I killed you, and sorrier if you killed me."

She stared in open disbelief. "You want me to just *trust* you on this?"

"Yes," I said. "Is that a problem?"

"Well . . . damn. I don't know. It sure as hell ought to be." She sighed and lowered herself to the sand beside me. "You are without a doubt the damnedest sonofabitch it's ever been my dubious pleasure to meet. Probably should've roasted you back in Tidehollow."

I nodded. "I've enjoyed working with you again."

"You say that like you mean it."

"Because I do."

"Crazy thing is, I actually kind of believe you." She slipped the ring onto her finger and held out her hand to admire it. "Goes with my hair, huh?"

"That hadn't occurred to me," I said, "but I suppose it does. Baltrice, I have something to tell you. We may not meet again, and there is one thing I truly do hope that you will believe about me."

She gave me that sidelong look again. "Is this where you profess undying love? Save it. You're not exactly the guy of my dreams."

"Baltrice." I laid my hand on hers. She let me. "I like to imagine that Jace Beleren knows how fine a friend he has in you. I hope he does; I certainly do. And I want you to know that I hope I might, someday, deserve a friend who cares as much for me."

She flushed and looked away. "Tezzeret . . . come on. What do you want me to say?"

"Nothing. I just want you to know. And I want you to believe that I mean you no harm."

"*That* sounds like trouble."

"It's not impossible."

She heaved herself to her feet and turned to face me. "I guess this is so long, then. Shame I can't take the sled. Handy little gadget."

"I need the etherium."

"Yeah, I know. Look, Tezzeret, I'm not so good with the whole farewell thing. It'll just take me a minute or two to shift off-plane—"

"I have two more gifts for you." I pulled the navigator out of the same pocket. "It has a concealed catch—just here, do you see? Press it like this and the device opens."

"It's a locket."

"It's a navigator. Very much like your ring, actually. Single use, I'm afraid, but I think you'll appreciate having it. If there is someone you need to find, for any reason, all you have to do is take something of them and secure it inside. Any sort of tissue sample will do—a drop of blood, a hair, even a fingernail paring. The navigator will show you where that person is and help you chart a path to him. Or her. It's very effective, as long as your target is not using some rather advanced types of magical conceal- ment. It works best on someone who doesn't know you're after them."

"Target?" she said warily. "What's this about?"

"It's about my third gift, part of which will be a transit gate to what I believe is an apartment in Bant. I think you might be interested in going there because, as recently as this morning, our necromancer was there."

"Necromancer? One?" She looked suspicious and appalled at the same time. She threw her arms wide, to encompass the soot and smoke and ash throughout the Netherglass. "This was all from *one guy*?"

"Not a guy," I said. "If you had the chance to scour the entire Multiverse for one particular necromancer's ass to slow roast in the deepest furnace in Grixis, who would that necromancer be?"

Her eyes widened. "Are you kidding?" Her teeth came out, and in her eyes was only flame. "*Are you festering kidding me?*"

"Not about this," I said. "I'm no fan of hers myself."

"Your gift is a shot at her?"

"Yes. Do you like it?"

"Oh, man, if I had any way to tell you . . ." She shrugged herself into full blaze. I had to raise a hand to shield my face from her heat. "Get to work on that gate, bud. I need to pick up my ride."

She stuck two fingers in her mouth and unleashed an ear-stabbing shriek of a whistle that would have done credit to a Vectis dragon-raid siren. Up over the white monolith of a Labyrinth hall soared the wickedly gleaming sinuous body of an etherium drake. A few powerful wing beats sent it toward us in a steep dive.

The choking noise I made was the sound of my trying not to swallow my tongue.

Baltrice grinned at me. "They're not *all* bad. Some of 'em are just, y'know, misunderstood."

Realizing my mouth was hanging open, I shut it with

a clack that sent a white jolt of pain through my loosened teeth.

The e-drake landed a few meters away. Baltrice ambled over to it, spreading her arms, and I found myself in the preposterous position of witnessing something I could never even *hint* about without being named a liar or a madman. The etherium drake settled down onto the sand, folded its wings, and laid its head on Baltrice's shoulder.

"Good boy." She patted the back of its skull, and I heard a low, metallic grinding sound that might actually have been the creature *purring*.

"I call him Mr. Shinypants," she said, happy and fierce at once. "That gate, huh?"

※ ※ ※ ※ ※

Night falls suddenly in most deserts, but the Netherglass now had twilight of a sort: the light of the setting sun reflecting downward by the dark cloud of zombie smoke, casting a dully bloody glow upon the Crystal Labyrinth.

And upon me.

The color was essentially identical to the sangrite glow in the cavern; a simple fact, noted without consideration of coincidence or teleology. If it turned out to be relevant, I'd think about it then. I had no interest in noon or midnight, day, night, or anything in between. I did not feel the weather, and my vision had nothing to do with light.

I sat on the sand of powdered glass in the center of the Labyrinth, my legs folded beneath me, and on my knees the head of Silas Renn.

I cannot say how long I sat there. Days, at least. Months? Years? There is no way to know. At some point, my injuries healed. I didn't notice. The power I drew from the vast wealth of etherium at my command relieved me of any need to eat, drink, or eliminate, and it did so without requiring the intervention of my attention or any fraction of my consciousness at all. I needed all my consciousness for something else.

I was watching myself solve the Labyrinth.

By tapping into Renn's temporal perception, I could trace the probability-ghosts of myself entering the Labyrinth, and once inside, my own knack for rhabdomancy enabled me to track them by the etherium they—I—carried. Will carry. Potentially. Every twist, every turn, every ascent, descent, or jump.

While I did so, I used a knack from my days at the Mechanists' Guild to make my hands automatically pull from the etherium around me a series of thin wires, bending, twisting, and occasionally breaking each as I worked them into precise three-dimensional representations—models—of every path I saw myselves take. My long, long experience with precision ensured that these models would depict each path exactly. I had no need to model the Labyrinth itself; the paths were all that mattered.

I had built around myself a pair of rings, constructed so that the lower served as a base in the sand, while the upper could rotate freely along it. At twelve precise intervals around the movable ring, I had affixed a tall cross of etherium wire. The crux of each one marked the entryway of one of the great halls of the Labyrinth. The cross piece marked ground level. Each pin became the anchor for a worked-wire chart of all possible pathways branching from that entrance. By rotating the ring, I could bring any given hall before me without having to shift my own position.

For a maze, that would have sufficed; a three-dimensional solution for a three-dimensional problem. This, however, was a four-dimensional problem.

At least.

Because, after all, it only *looked* like a maze. It was a Labyrinth. It became a maze—a deadly one—for any who entered unprepared. I would not be one of these.

Preparation is my specialty.

As I worked, I discovered paths that could join two or more others that had seemed to lead to dead ends. Using a slightly thinner, shinier wire to connect magical transit points—where a path might leap from the top of one hall to the bottom of another—I began to join every hall to every other in multiply iterated pathways, nearly identical . . . but each and every one unique. . . .

The space around me was almost half full of the etherium web work when I discovered the pattern.

I could *see* it: a mathematical purity that words cannot describe, an elegance that transcended language. . . . I could predict, now, the shape and length of the next wire, and what points it would join. More than predict. See.

Know.

Soon I could see two wires ahead, then five, then a dozen. . . .

Then all of it.

I saw what my model would become. This wasn't Renn's power. It had nothing to do with time; this was form and function, stripped to the deep structure of matter itself. I saw the future not with prescience, but with experience. I *knew* where each strand must be placed and what each wire must connect, for the model to make sense.

"To make sense" is actually an expression for how I experience natural law.

That is: truth.

This experience—this knowing—flowed out from me, directing my hands to assemble the half-dreamed vision in my heart. The impossibly perfect structure of the etherium

MATTHEW STOVER

matrix enfolded me, enwrapped me, joined around and above me like the vault of a cathedral.

I had trained my entire life simply to see this. To do this. To make this.

To be this.

My hands stopped. My eyes froze open. I could not dream of moving. Could not dream of breathing. Could not imagine being anywhere but here.

Ever.

I saw without sight, heard without sound, smelled without scent, felt without touch. Kneeling within this heartbreakingly perfect sanctum that was the only possible answer to the question of my existence, I thought: *What do you say without saying?* And discovered the answer was obvious.

The joining of mechanics and time . . . is a clock.

Crucius . . .

The interpenetrating structure I had built around myself—the etherium model of the relational matrix of the twelve Halls around me—was perfect. Was inevitable. Was impossible.

Was *context*.

What makes a clock work is the engineering of its mechanics. What makes it beautiful is the elegance of its construction. What makes it perfect is the precision of its heart.

There is no heart more precise than mine. I had no need to find the center of the Crystal Labyrinth. I was the center.

I had become the hands of the clock.

What I said without saying was *I am here.*

And I was.

Forever.

TEZZERET
MIDPOINT, FULL STOP

(M)y first clue that forever might not be actually permanent came in the mournful contrabasso chords of a very, very old sphinx. *"Greetings, Tezzeret. Welcome back, my old friend."*

I found myself naked (predictably; I had come to take the loss of my clothing as a routine feature of my postdeath journey) and entirely lacking the rest of my equipment, not to mention resources. There was no sign of my etherium model, nor of the Labyrinth, nor of the telemin halo and Renn's head. I was, in fact, kneeling on a strangely colorless grassy sward among a stand of similarly colorless tropical trees, and was staring up into the melancholy, etherium-crusted face of Kemuel the Ancient. The Hidden One.

Though I had never seen even a depiction of him, I knew he was Kemuel. *Knew* it. As if I'd known him since the day I was born.

Since the day *he* was born.

I'd made it.

I really had.

The sensation was remarkably similar to how I'd felt after beating Renn.

Eventually, I registered what Kemuel had said. I got up, trying to swallow a bolus of apprehension that had suddenly decided to claw its way up my throat. "What in the hells do you mean, welcome *back*?"

Creases appeared on his immense face like erosion scars on a granite cliff. *"The Seeker's Path has brought you here several times, my friend. The question is: What will take you the rest of the way?"*

"The rest of *what* way?" An incalculable weight of exhaustion gathered upon my shoulders, threatening to crush me altogether. I *still* wasn't done? "Several times?" I said weakly. "Please tell me you're not saying what I'm afraid you're saying."

The creases continued to deepen around his mouth and at the corners of his eyes, and I realized he was slowly—incrementally, glacially—working himself toward a smile. The old sphinx wore so much etherium, he was practically made of metal. *"I can answer any question that won't help you, Tezzeret. 'The rest of the way' means beyond where we are. The several times . . . well, you reach the Riddle Gate two or three times out of each ten thousand lives. On average."*

I rubbed my face. Ten thousand lives? Reincarnation? The thought of having to live out my *current* life was nearly more than I could bear. Ten *thousand*? And then I registered he'd told me that was an average. . . .

Two or three times out of *each* ten thousand lives.

I was so tired that I wanted to die. But something in my brain heedlessly refuses to stop working, no matter the circumstance, and at that moment it offered a tiny spark of hope. "Wait," I said. "Not sequential lives. *Parallel* lives. Different time lines."

"Yes."

I stared at him. He was utterly alien but at the same time as familiar as my father's hovel. "You're a clockworker."

"I have the gift, on my father's side. I don't use it."

"Why not?"

Those creases got even deeper, and some looked as if they might start to curve a little, too. *"Why would I?"*

I looked at him. He looked at me. After a long time looking at each other, I realized I had no answer. I couldn't even imagine that there might exist an answer that would make sense to him.

Sphinxes and riddles. I was heartily sick of both. "What is this place?"

"*You stand in the Riddle Gate, my friend. The end of your journey, or its midpoint; the distinction is yours to make.*"

The midpoint. The *Riddle* Gate. If I'd believed in any gods, I would have been calling upon them to curse him. And me. And themselves, too, while they were at it. "What's next? Where do I go now?"

"*I don't know.*"

"Excuse me?"

"*This is as far as you've ever come.*"

For some reason, I found this encouraging. "So what happens?"

"*The way back is closed, Tezzeret. If you do not pass the Riddle Gate, here you will live. Here you will die.*"

I looked around. No graves. No bones. No loitering Tezzerets. "What do I usually do?"

"*Your reaction to failure varies. Often you take your own life. Sometimes you attack me with such fury that I must kill you. On occasion, you have spent days or weeks—sometimes months—in conversation with me . . . and then you take your own life, or spend it in futile violence. This is how we have become friends.*"

"Would you be offended if I say I don't want to know you that well?"

"*Reality is not what we want, Tezzeret. It's what is.*"

I winced. When that truism had come up before, it had usually been me saying it to someone else; to be on the receiving end was unexpectedly bitter.

"It is not my task to lecture you, Tezzeret. I am not here to puzzle you, nor to impede your Search. I am on your side—even if only to avoid the unpleasantness of disposing of your body."

"What about my possessions? If you want to help me succeed—"

"I will not help you succeed. I cannot help you succeed. I hope that success will find you, and that you will find it. To aid you is beyond my power."

"Can you give me my etherium back?"

"It is not your etherium."

"Yes. Yes, of course," I said. "The Grand Hegemon's etherium, loaned to me."

"It is not hers to loan. All etherium is my father's. By his grace, some are allowed to borrow its use."

"Your father's . . ." I repeated numbly. That answered one question—but if Crucius was even older than the Hidden One, finding him alive seemed unlikely. "All right. It's his. But being allowed to, ah, *borrow* it for a while longer would be—"

"Etherium cannot enter the Riddle Gate."

"Really? Again, without meaning to give offense," I said, gesturing at his baroquely layered encrustations, "one must wonder—"

"I did not enter. My father built it around me, when he constructed the Labyrinth."

"Built it around you," I repeated, more numb than before. "And you've been here, all these centuries? Millennia?"

"It is the task he has given me."

That crusted mass of etherium must be all that was keeping him alive. On the other hand, if he were to unexpectedly expire . . .

As if he could read my mind, he piped, "Etherium cannot leave, either. It is as my father has made it: the stricture of the Riddle Gate."

"So you're trapped too."

"No: I linger until the Seeker passes the Gate. It is my task."

Two or three out of every ten thousand lives. On average. "I hope you'll forgive me for saying it sounds like a boring job."

"Boredom is an affliction from which sphinxes do not suffer."

"Of course." I would have thought of this before I opened my stupid mouth, if I hadn't been too tired to worry about playing smart. "Still, you must spend a lot of time alone."

"I pass my days in learning. I am a sphinx; a creature of questions. The Riddle Gate is a device of answers." The ancient sphinx lifted a paw, and we were no longer on the grassy sward but instead upon the Cliffs of Ot, looking down upon a sea crowded with refugee ships fleeing Vectis. *"Or Cloudheath? Would you enjoy watching Tiln construct the Rampart of Thunder? Perhaps Bant, if you have a particular favorite among their perpetual wars. Or Jund's Dragonstorm Aeon: dramatic and spectacular together. All of time and space are before us here. The Riddle Gate can show us every answer except the one you'll need to pass through it."*

I had no interest in sightseeing, nor in history. All of time and space, though ... "Can you show me where I can find Crucius?"

Kemuel the Ancient fixed me with a remarkably sharp gimlet stare. *"You can find my father anywhere you can find yourself."*

"How about this: show me where I *will* find Crucius," I said. "Where, as you say, I can find myself."

The smile stretched until his cracked leather face became an alarmingly hideous leer. *"Of course, my friend. But know that every Seeker sees this—yet the vision will become truth for only one. Which is not likely to be you. Any of you."*

I frowned. "There are other Seekers? Beyond multiples of me?"

"There is only one Seeker. But the Seeker is not always you. Nor is their Search identical to yours."

I rubbed my eyes. Discovering that I mostly understood what he was talking about was profoundly disturbing. The implications were worse. "We're not looking for the same thing?"

"I don't know," Kemuel said impassively. *"What are you looking for?"*

I stared at him. I didn't answer.

Because I didn't know. Not really.

I hadn't even *thought* about it. There was the job Bolas had inflicted on me, and I had Doc to crack the dragon's whip . . . didn't I? He hadn't said a word.

This was a subject on which he would have an opinion.

It occurred to me that he'd been silent for some while. Since I'd said good-bye to Baltrice, perhaps. I wasn't sure exactly what this signified, but I found myself gripped by a sudden and astonishingly bleak apprehension. The idea that he *might* not be there congealed in my throat like frozen snot. "Doc?"

There came no reply.

"Quit kidding around. You're not exactly the strong silent type," I said, but I knew the truth already. I could feel it.

The truth felt like a knife. Lodged somewhere between my stomach and my heart, where it stabbed me with every breath.

The Hidden One regarded me impassively. *"Talking to the voice in your head?"*

Anger ignited within me as if my bones had caught fire. "He's not a *voice*!" I snapped. "He's not some damned *delusion*, he's a—"

I choked on the word. This was ridiculous. More than implausible. It was impossible.

Should have been impossible.

But I had to say it. I owed him that much.

"He was a friend," I said. My eyes felt hot, and my vision blurred; I shook my head and looked away. I didn't know why I felt what I felt, but I have never been a man to deny the truth. "The only friend I had."

Reality is not what we want. It's what is.

"I did not mean that you are mad, Tezzeret. A few of you have spoken of a voice that drives you onward—usually bitterly. Sometimes with open hatred. You are the first to name the voice a friend."

"It's not that I like him," I said. "But . . . he's not *bad*. He wasn't the rotten bastard he could have been. He actually helped me. More than once; I wouldn't have made it here without him. And he was always there. I got used to him. It's . . . hard to describe. Of everyone who has ever had power over me, he's the only one who treated me better than he had to."

"Mercy is the greatest virtue."

"If you say so."

"You agree more than you think you do."

To me, that meant nothing at all. I shook my head. "I didn't even say good-bye."

"Why would you? You and he did not part. Precisely the opposite."

I looked up at the ancient sphinx. He looked down at me.

"None of you hears voices in this place other than mine and your own. The Seeker faces the Riddle Gate alone."

I barely heard him. I was still thinking about *Precisely the opposite*.

Was is possible?

He certainly did seem to understand me better than anyone I've ever known. Including my family. He had my sense of humor—at least, down in the guilty-pleasure slush that I usually make a point of not saying aloud. He reminded me of the sort of individual I sometimes thought I might have grown up to be, had I been born into a life less dire than that of scrappers in Tidehollow.

Yes: I had hated Doc instinctively. At first. He'd tormented me with the merciless malice of a demon child. At first. But even at the very start we had, for example, shared a profound hatred of Nicol Bolas. In fact, the only times we'd really disagreed were when he got angry because I was risking our lives.

My life.

Some long-lived creatures have the ability to establish subsidiary selves—subordinate personalities, more or less—to help keep their ever-increasing store of memory organized; dragons are one of these creatures. Anything Bolas could do to himself, I was certain he could do to me. Not to mention it would tickle Bolas right down to the toe-jam between his talons to have set me against myself.

And if it were true, what did that say about what I want? Had Doc been driving me toward Bolas's goal, or toward my own? What if they were the same?

And if they weren't, what was the difference?

At some point, I sat down. After an unknown interval, I realized I had been staring past Kemuel, silently thinking about nothing at all. It felt as though I had been doing so for a very, very long time. The sort of interval that is usually measured in decades.

The Hidden One hadn't moved.

Patience is not a virtue to a sphinx. Patience is his nature.

"I know what I'm looking for," I said eventually. "For now, anyway. I'm looking for the way through the Riddle Gate. If I don't have that, nothing else matters."

"Very good, my friend! And how do you propose to find a path where every Seeker fails?"

"That's the easy part," I said. "I'll ask you to show me."

Kemuel's eyes widened, then closed to slanted slits. The ancient sphinx drew himself up, the size of a dragon and twice as dire. His voice boomed like thunder among high mountains. *"And what do you expect me to do when you ask, you tiny clot of impudence?"*

"That's what I want to find out," I said. "You've mentioned the task your father gave you. I'll be surprised if it's to warm the ground with your butt while you wait for a Seeker to show up and keep you company. And I am rarely surprised."

The Hidden One glared down upon me as though lightning from his eyes might strike me dead.

Having been trapped in a cavern at the mercy of Nicol Bolas, however, had surgically excised any tendency I might have had to be intimidated by a stern look. "Kemuel the Ancient, called the Hidden One, I conjure you in the name of your father Crucius, in the name of the Search, and in the name of every friendship we have ever shared: Describe your task," I said, and added, "Please."

The stark threat in his glare might as well have been chiseled into a mask of stone. Until one eyelid drooped and reopened, and those erosion scars began etching themselves into his face all over again.

Blinking, I said, "Was that actually, just now—I mean, did you just *wink* at me?"

"Your manners have improved," he said with an indulgent chuckle that sounded a bit like wind chimes the size of a boat. *"Come, my friend. Stand at my side, and we will speak of my task."*

I went to the indicated spot. So close to his shoulder, the warmth of his body was like an iron stove on a winter's night . . . and all I wanted to do was lie down, let that warmth enfold me, and sleep. Forever.

But there'd be plenty of forever to sleep through if I didn't pass the Gate.

"I am permitted to show you one thing you have never seen, and remind you of two things you already know."

"All right," I said. "Show me."

"This is what awaits you beyond the Riddle Gate," he said, and with no gesture nor slightest flicker of expression, where we stood transformed into paradise.

A land of etherium.

Of nothing *but* etherium. Trees. Stones. Grass. Sand.

"Ah," I said.

It was all I could say.

I found myself on my knees, for I had no strength to stand. Gasping. This was what waited for me beyond the Gate?

This?

"This . . . ?" I whispered. "This is where I'll find him? This?"

I had never *dreamed* . . .

It was all *right here.* In front of me. Around me. I was already *there* . . .

One step away.

I knelt, gazing upon the answer to every question I had ever had, and then I could wait no longer. I wrenched myself to my feet and lurched forward. Nothing stopped me. I recovered my balance and began to walk. Then I began to run.

I ran until I had no breath. Until my feet bled. Until exhaustion slammed me to the ground as if I'd been hit with a thunderbolt.

When at length I regained my senses, the ground on which I lay was not etherium.

I rolled over. Kemuel was three paces behind me. He hadn't moved.

I hadn't moved.

"If it were that easy," he said, *"no Seeker would fail."*

Yes. Of course. Painfully I sat up and nodded in resignation. "I was . . . overcome."

"You always are."

"But I'm not giving up. I'm hardly beaten."

"Yet."

Wait—I had it. Obvious. So obvious it might not have occurred to any other me. The Riddle Gate must be interplanar—I was looking at a *different plane*. Seeing it, I could walk there.

Just not with my feet.

I gathered power and ignited my Spark . . . but found no Spark to ignite, and no power to gather.

"In the Riddle Gate, there is no power save etherium."

And there is no etherium save . . .

When I looked at him, he wore a sad smile that was also somehow fond. *"Often, you die in the act of attacking me."*

Again: of course.

I sank back to my knees, scrubbing at my face with both hands as if I could erase exhaustion, and hope, and despair, and every other feeling and thought in the screaming whirl inside my head. Not for the first time, I was reminded what a burden it is to be human.

"All right," I said. I held my eyes closed, my only hope of lessening the inexorable gravitation of the unimaginable etherium beyond the Gate. "So. This is . . . this could have been designed specifically for *me*. To torment me. Torture me. One step from more etherium than I have ever imagined could exist in the Multiverse. One step from Crucius. One step from the secret of creation itself. One step that I cannot take, for lack of etherium."

I shook my head, helpless. "This is my personal hell."

"Etherium only gets in your way," Kemuel said gently.

"All right. The other things—the ones you say I already know. The reminders you are permitted to give. Please, tell me."

"The first is one that I believe you are in the midst of experiencing," he said. *"When one is made of glass—"*

"Everything looks like a stone. Yes." I took a deep breath, nodded, and took another. Somehow, the aphorism helped me calm myself. I seemed to be regaining some of my ability to think.

"I understand. The situation does not have to be designed to torture me. It may be this way because there is no other way it can be; the bitter irony I face here may be an effect of who I am, rather than how it was made. Yes."

I took another deep breath, and the rest of the whirl within my head slowed, and seemed to settle itself into a manageable progression. When one is made of glass, everything looks like a stone—*but . . .*

I turned to meet the unfathomable gaze of the Hidden One. "On the other hand," I said slowly, "sometimes what looks like a stone *is* a stone. And sometimes a stone has my name on it."

Kemuel's smile broadened. *"You make me very proud."*

"I can't imagine why. All right, I get it. I think. What's the other reminder?"

"I am permitted to remind you of the one way you solved the first two lines of my father's riddle."

"How I—?" I put a hand to my head. The whirl seemed to be spinning up again. "The *one* way?"

It hadn't been one way at all; the solutions were barely even *related*. The first two lines . . .

The first solution was the product of analysis. Logic. Intellect.

The second was the product of diligence. Thoroughness. The infinite capacity for taking pains.

The only thing the two had in common was me.

Fierce light inside my head burst to blinding life.

Me?

The fierce light burned my whirl of confusion away. "Me . . ." I heard myself saying. "It was *me*."

The solutions had been mine. Mine personally. I hadn't solved "Where do you look for what can't be found?" and "What do you say without saying?"

My answers had been where *I* would look for what can't be found, and what *I* could say without saying.

Analysis and diligence are two of the four defining traits of greatness in an artificer. The third was exactly what I was experiencing right now.

Inspiration.

The next line had been, "What is your sky when you're tombed in the ground?"

Well, I was tombed enough, metaphorically. The Riddle Gate was an open grave, just waiting for me to lie down. Tombed . . . buried alive, or dead, and it didn't matter. It couldn't matter. Not in the tomb.

What was my sky? The answer to my prayer, and forever beyond my grasp? What tortured me every time I so much as thought about it? What did I long for more than life itself?

I opened my eyes and looked at my answer.

"Oh . . . *god* . . ." Tears gathered in my eyes. Why

did I *not* have a god to whom I could appeal? Even a delusional dream of divine mercy would be better than this.

To die staring at the only thing I really want.

But . . . the sky, *any* sky, is a metaphor, too. It's a mental construct, a boundary we imagine, to imaginatively divide infinite space. It's not real—it's not air, or clouds, moons, planets, or stars. It's . . . what?

It's always out of reach from wherever you are.

You can't grab it. You can't buy it or sell it. It can't be broken, or stolen, chained, or freed. Because it can't be owned, it belongs to everyone.

To everything.

My eyes drifted shut. I said softly, "You're kidding, right? Please say you're not serious."

"But I'm not, and I am."

"Etherium gets in my way."

"Yes."

"Because it's as much an idea as it is a substance."

"Yes."

"And etherium can't pass through the Riddle Gate."

"Yes."

"Even the dream of it. Even the hope for it. As long as etherium is *something* to me, I'm trapped here."

"Yes."

"The only way I can get to where I most want to be . . . is to not care if I ever make it."

"Yes."

"So." I sighed, opened my eyes, and stared out from the Riddle Gate at my dream of paradise, forever out of my reach. In order for me to get there, it has to not be paradise anymore. Not for me. "I imagine this is when I usually take my own life."

"I am sorry to say that it is."

"At least now I understand why." I shook my head. "How am I supposed to do this?"

"I don't know. None of you ever has," he piped sadly. *"This is why the Riddle Gate will be your end: succeed or fail, the man you are will die here. But the Riddle Gate will be the midpoint for the Seeker who finally passes through; for the rest of your days, your existence will be defined by that passage. Not by your birth, your death, nor your rebirth—no matter how many times you experience each of them. You will mark your days by what came before the Riddle Gate, and what came after."*

Swell.

"So let's sum up. It looks to me kind of like this: I have spent my entire life turning myself into a man who can get here, because I have been, consciously or not, trying to get *there*," I said, jabbing a finger out at the etherium land. "If I wasn't trying to get there, I would never have gotten here. But in order to *actually* get there, I have to become somebody who never would have bothered to come *here* in the first place."

"Yes, Tezzeret my friend. This next will be what we sphinxes sometimes call," he said gravely, *"the tricky part."*

✳ ✳ ✳ ✳ ✳

In the fullness of time, I became that man.

I rose, gave my farewells to Kemuel—along with instructions for Sharuum, should she choose to follow me—and he said, *"Meeting her will be interesting. Instructive. I will be born several hundred years from now, when she is younger and my father is king."*

The man I had been would be irritated with that; the man I had become only nodded and stepped forth from the Riddle Gate onto the Metal Island.

For an infinite span, I kneeled on the etherium sand,

meditating upon the riddle of the Metal Sphinx. By the time eternity had passed, I had found my answer.

But if you want to know what that answer *was*, old worm, you'll have to give up this silly mind-siphon trick of yours and ask me yourself.

Politely.

Don't trouble to open my tomb; I let myself out. Oh, and by the way?

I'm right behind you.

THE METAL ISLAND
THE LAST RIDDLE

Nicol Bolas jerked as if he'd been hit by lightning.

That insufferable little clot of ghoul turd!

He should have killed Tezzeret years ago. The inarguable fact that he, himself, not only had *not* done anything so prudent as kill the artificer, compounded with the other inarguable fact that he, himself, had actually *healed* that festering pile of scrapings from a dung beetle's butt, made at least one of his subminds wonder openly if perhaps Tezzeret had been right about him.

Maybe he *was* stupid.

But having been stupid in the past didn't mean he had to be stupid now. The great dragon spun, a snarl on his face and a panoply of insanely lethal magics packed into each talon, his mouth, both eyes, both wings, and his tail.

Tezzeret sat calmly on the etherium plinth between the forepaws of the Metal Sphinx. He was smiling. This smile was not friendly, or reassuring, or even smug; it looked more like *pity* than anything else, and the sight of it spiked the dragon's rage pressure until it superheated his blood and he cared not the slightest if he was killed right here on this stupid beach in front of this stupid sphinx while doing something stupid, if only he could die with Tezzeret's blood on his fangs.

He spread wide his arms and wider still his great wings, and unleashed upon his enemy fell magics that could consume this entire universe.

Except he didn't.

He hesitated, confusion knotting his scaly brow. Again, he summoned the power of entire stars and rained flaming destruction upon his—

Except he didn't. Again.

"Do you know why not?" Tezzeret said.

Bolas flinched. Was that pestilent artificer reading his mind? Controlling his actions? Could the ramparts of his identity have been breached? His consciousness flashed through the countless chambers of his near-infinite mind, but he could find no sign of tampering.

"Predictable," Tezzeret said. "To save my time and your effort, it's not in your mind, Bolas. It's in your head."

"What?"

"You brought it on yourself, you know. We never had to be enemies."

"Enemies? Don't flatter yourself," the dragon sneered. "I am a god. You are a cockroach."

The artificer nodded amiably. "A reasonable metaphor, in a limited way. The cockroach is tiny, and weak, and can be crushed by a finger—yet still it can carry disease, befoul your food, and make your home generally disagreeable. And cockroaches are, as a group, very hard to kill."

"What are you nattering about?" Bolas snapped. "What does this have to do with me?"

Tezzeret shrugged. "It's *your* image, old worm. In those terms, what I've done to you is fairly simple. I've taken away your pesticide."

"You are such a preposterous—"

"Kill me," Tezzeret offered. "However you like. I have no shields and have summoned no magic. You can just step

Φ

313

on me, if nothing else; it's how one customarily destroys cockroaches."

Bolas growled deep in his throat and lunged for him, talons poised to rip the artificer into bloody shreds.

But he didn't.

"Because you can't. Well, you *can* . . . but you won't. Not for a while, at least."

Tezzeret's smile reminded Bolas of something unpleasant. With a lurch, Nicol Bolas realized that the smile looked like one he himself liked to show from time to time. Usually when someone he was about eat broke down and began to beg for their life.

But in Tezzeret's smile there was no sadism. Not even malice.

That, somehow, made it worse.

Bolas began to wonder, for the first time he could remember in all twenty-five thousand long years of his life, if he might be out of his depth.

"I should think you know me as well as any creature in the Multiverse, excepting only Kemuel and Crucius," Tezzeret said. "What's my talent? Not superficial, magic and rhabdomancy and artificing. What am I best at? What is my *specialty*?"

Bolas opened his mouth for a sarcastic reply, but shut it again without speaking. Shut it with a snap like a dry branch breaking, because he realized he *did* know Tezzeret's specialty.

Preparation.

"I want you to understand why I'm revealing what I've done to you in this particular way," Tezzeret said. "There is a lesson I hope you will take from this, and the only way I can be sure you've learned it is if you see it yourself."

"Games," said Nicol Bolas sourly. "Aren't I too stupid to understand the rules?"

"That's what I'm trying to find out. I hope you do, at least, understand the stakes," said the artificer. "We're playing for your life."

Bolas sat, folding his wings about himself in what he hoped might look like nonchalance. He'd suddenly become very cold, and he didn't want to start shivering.

"Do you remember what I said to Jace Beleren, right after my device settled into his brain?"

Bolas had no need to search his memories for that particular tidbit. "You said you were going to kill me."

"Yes. And I did."

"Are you mad?"

"I killed you dozens of times," Tezzeret said. "Remember?"

Bolas thought of the corpse dragons he had pulled from parallel time lines, and he discovered he was getting colder rather than warmer.

"I kept on killing you," Tezzeret said, "until finally I found a Nicol Bolas I didn't *have* to kill. Does this make sense to you? Do you understand who you are and why you are this way?"

Bolas swallowed.

"You don't have to answer. Only think. The device I put in Jace's brain was there not because I feared he'd interfere with me. I put that device in there because *I knew you would read his mind*. Someday. Somewhere. And when you did, that device would flow into you right along with Jace's memories. Once that was done, I could kill you . . ." He shrugged. "Whenever. Any time I happened to feel like it. Because that device is in *your* brain now."

Tezzeret sighed apologetically. "The tricky part was programming it to reach the proper neural nexus in your brain. A bit of trial and error there, thus a few extra dead dragons on parallel beaches. I'm sorry for that, by the way."

Bolas snorted. He'd felt not the faintest sting, let alone the shattering agony that Tezzeret's device had inflicted upon Beleren. He opened his mouth to express just how pathetically contemptible Tezzeret's little charade had become, but the artificer held up a hand.

"It's not there to hurt you. It's more of a short circuit than a punishment—and besides, I suspect your pain tolerance is beyond the capacity of any device to surpass."

Bolas blinked. That had sounded almost like a compliment....

"Basically, it shuts down your motivation to kill me. Or any Planeswalker. I decided I could spare that much mercy for Jace ... at least partially because I could so vividly imagine the look on your face when you discovered you couldn't hurt him."

Bolas could think already of a dozen ways to get that device out of his brain, and once he did—

Again, Tezzeret seemed to be reading his mind. "It's not permanent," he said. "I'd be very surprised if it took you more than ten minutes to remove it. But it gives us the opportunity to have this chat."

Bolas had a different chat in mind. With a very subtle, impenetrably camouflaged exertion of mana, he reached out for a time line where he had never used his mind siphon on Beleren. A quick temporal shift, and matters between him and Tezzeret would be different.

Lethally different.

But he couldn't. The time lines simply weren't there ... or, worse, he couldn't see them. The cold seemed to have penetrated his bones. He sent his perceptions forward and back along the time line he was already in ... except he didn't. He couldn't.

He remembered being *able* to clockwork. He didn't remember *how*.

Tezzeret nodded sympathetically. "You have to keep in mind that I had a *long* time to prepare for our meeting on this beach."

"Apparently so."

"I have come to believe that clockworking in general is a very bad idea. Even in the hands of a well-intentioned mage, it has the intrinsic potential to rend the fabric of the Multiverse—which makes it a particularly bad idea to let *you*, for example, use it. So you can't. Possibly forever."

Bolas could no longer contain his disbelief. "That's *impossible*—you *can't* just take a *power* away from me!"

"Yes. The only person who can do that to you is, well . . . you."

"What?"

"Jace Beleren wasn't the only one with a trap in his mind," Tezzeret said. "This one was a little subtler. I've given your clockworking powers into the care of a superpersonality of yours. I based my design on your work. This subpersonality actually understands how dangerous clockworking is, and so he'll make sure you never do it again. I have given you something more valuable than all the etherium that has ever existed."

He smiled, and now Bolas did see a trace of that malice that had been formerly absent. Tezzeret said, "I've given you a friend."

"What?" Bolas thought for a moment that his eyes might bulge right out of his skull. "You *didn't*—you couldn't *possibly*—"

"Doc," said Tezzeret, "say hello."

And Nicol Bolas heard a thinly wiseass human voice buzzing in his left ear. "Hiya! Hey, it's *nice* in here! Damn, Nicky, we shoulda got together *years* ago!"

Tezzeret looked unconscionably pleased with himself.

For one horrible second, Bolas was afraid that for the first time in twenty-five millennia, he might actually burst into tears.

"Aww, come *on*, Nicky. It won't be that bad. Well, not *that* bad. Okay, it'll be pretty bad. But look on the bright side: as long as you don't try to pull your clockworking crap, I won't have any reason to talk to you."

Bolas could understand already how that would become a substantial inducement. "What have you *done*?" He was almost moaning. "How have you—you could not *possibly*—"

"I know you haven't spent much time in Esper, and certainly not in the slums," the artificer said casually, "and so there is no reason you would know our word for a small, improvised weapon, kept concealed on one's body until its stroke can kill."

Incomprehension piled upon humiliation on top of dread, Bolas could only stare.

The artificer leaned toward him and lowered his voice as though imparting a secret. "In Tidehollow," he said, "we call it a *tezzeret*."

❋ ❋ ❋ ❋ ❋

Sometime later, after giving him an opportunity to recover his composure, Tezzeret approached the dragon in a gentle, almost companionable way. "I know you're angry. Embarrassed. Even humiliated. Please understand that it is not my intention to make you feel that way. Please believe that all this has not been arranged to do you any harm at all."

"Oh, and I would believe this why?"

"If it had been my goal to humiliate you," Tezzeret said, "we would have had this conversation in front of an audience."

And before Nicol Bolas's astonished eyes, Tezzeret the Seeker reached outside the universe, and when his hand returned, it held the wrist of Jace Beleren.

"That's *impossible!*"

"Not here."

"But *how*—?"

"I can think of no reason why I should tell you."

"His mind's dead," Bolas said. "As dead as yours used to be."

"Yes." Tezzeret smiled. "I'm sure you're familiar with the concept of *poetic justice.*"

"That spell, during the fight—it *was* you!"

"Of course it was me. He might have spoiled my surprise." The artificer shrugged. "A properly partitioned consciousness can, as you know all too well, do several things at once."

"But killing him that way, all at once, painlessly—" Bolas cocked his head, squinting sidelong. "Uncharacteristically merciful."

"My friend Kemuel would say that mercy is the greatest of the virtues."

"Yeah? And what do *you* say?"

Tezzeret's smile spread, but his eyes went cold and hard as chips of obsidian. "Virtue," he said, "is for good guys. You and I have other priorities."

"Ah. He's not actually dead."

A blue haze seemed to leak from the pores of Tezzeret's right arm. He opened his hand toward Beleren, and the haze became a crackling gap spark that spit itself into the mind ripper's face. "Not anymore."

Bolas arched an eyebrow. "He doesn't seem too lively."

"He's still suspended. I will leave him like that while I retrieve Baltrice and Liliana Vess. I have a bit of business with them that must be taken care of, and it might interest you to watch, if you wouldn't mind. I can ensure that they will not be aware of your presence. Please?"

"You're *asking* me? You're asking for *permission* to preserve whatever is left of my *dignity*?"

"Yes," Tezzeret said. "It's only polite."

✷ ✷ ✷ ✷ ✷

Nicol Bolas sat on the etherium beach and watched Tezzeret revive the other three planewalkers. With a curiously private smile, he had kneeled beside each of them, placed his hand on each of their heads, and murmured, "Awaken. You are free. Arise and walk."

And they did.

Bolas couldn't even tell how Tezzeret had done it.

There was a predictable amount of commotion—especially between Baltrice and Vess, where Beleren had to get between them to prevent bloodshed—but Tezzeret got them settled down in an impressively swift fashion. He answered their most pressing question—"Where's that damned dragon?"—in a way that Bolas found obscurely tickling.

"It is always safest to assume," Tezzeret told them gravely, his deadpan unbreakable, "that Nicol Bolas is closer than you think."

"And what in the hells is up with *you*?" Beleren demanded. "What *is* this place? How did you get us away from Bolas? What's going on?"

Tezzeret favored him with the same smile Bolas had found so infuriating. Beleren didn't seem to like it any better. "Each of you has been of exceptional assistance to me in recent days. I hope to thank you, and to give each of you a gift. This place is . . . me. Or I am it. Or I will be, eventually. I did not take you from Bolas. He cast all three of you into the Blind Eternities. I have retrieved you; that's all. You are, I suppose, salvage. What's going on is our taking leave of one another. Is that clear enough?"

"Not even *close*," Jace said, starting toward him, only to be stopped by Baltrice's hand on his shoulder.

"Boss. Don't do it."

"I'm just saying hello to an old friend," he growled through his teeth.

"Well, don't," she said. "He's not who you think he is."

"Looks familiar enough to me." Beleren shook off her hand and raised his arms to begin a casting, and Baltrice gave his shoulder a hard shove that sent him stumbling sideways into the plinth.

"I'm telling you," she said. "He's not who you think he is. He can do things you can't even imagine."

Nicol Bolas reflected that he wouldn't have minded getting that particular warning himself.

"Are we done?" Tezzeret said evenly. "This is a bad time to fight among ourselves. There is still a *very* angry dragon nearby, who might wish to vent that anger on whatever people he can catch. You don't want to be those people."

He looked from one to another until they each subsided.

"Liliana Vess," he said, stepping to her side and taking her hand. "Your help was inadvertent, but valuable nonetheless. The gift I have for you is freedom."

She frowned at him. "Freedom?"

"Many of you—alternate Liliana Vesses from parallel time lines—had bound themselves to Bolas's service by blood pact. Are you one of them?"

"Well . . ." She flushed and looked ashamed of herself, providing what appeared to be answer enough.

"Listen to me now, Liliana Vess," he said, placing his hand on her head, "there are also many of you who have never bound yourselves wholly to the dragon. Close your eyes."

"I don't care what you think you can do, but there's no breaking that compact. I've tried. You wouldn't believe what I've tried."

"Please. Indulge me."

She sighed and closed her eyes.

"You, Liliana Vess, are one of the unbound. In your life, you have learned too well the perils of contracts."

"Of *course* I am," she said, shaking Tezzeret's hand off her head. "What? That's it? You tell me something I already know? Thanks for nothing. Literally."

"And you are welcome for something. Also literally."

"You think Bolas needs a signed contract to keep his hold on me?"

"Apparently not."

"I'm out of this place," she said. "Jace, it's been real. Baltrice, kiss my ass."

She stalked off along the beach, gathering the power to shift out.

Tezzeret turned to the pyromancer. "Baltrice."

She waved him off. "No presents. All I want is for you to take your doohickey out of Jace's head."

"That's already done."

"It is?"

Jace said, "It is?"

"Before you woke up."

Bolas noted that Tezzeret did not bother to specify which time.

Baltrice spread her hands. "That's all I need."

"It's all you want," Tezzeret said. "Not the same thing."

"Seriously. Looks like things are working out okay for you, and I'm glad for that. Really. Even though you served me up to Nicol Bolas like a snack tray; I figure there's no way you could have known."

"And I thank you for that generous estimation." Tezzeret stepped around her and reached for something on the plinth—a necklace. Its chain was pure etherium and its pendant a carefully shaped red gemstone that glowed with a light of its own.

Sangrite, Bolas realized. Why would the artificer give sangrite to his pet pyromancer?

"More jewelry?" she said with a lopsided smile. "Come on, Tezzeret—people are starting to talk."

"Baltrice, do you remember the conversation we had in the Glass Dunes, when I was working on my armor? About who I've become, and who you've become, and why?"

"Not really. Something's screwy with my memory about all that stuff. Probably something to do with Renn. Hey, did you ever settle that bastard?"

"Not personally." Tezzeret wasn't smiling anymore. "This necklace is, like the locator ring and the navigator, more about what it does than what it is, and again it's a simple device. Slip it on over your head, and you become invulnerable to all forms of mental domination."

"Yeah?"

Jace Beleren said, "What?"

She hefted it appreciatively, then shrugged her thanks. "Nice. Much appreciated."

Jace said, an undertone of urgency in his voice, "Baltrice, don't put it on."

"Why not?"

Nicol Bolas had occasionally produced, in his alchemical research laboratories, temperatures extreme enough to liquefy helium. He had never seen anything remotely as cold as the look Tezzeret then turned upon Jace Beleren. "Yes, Jace. Tell her why not."

"It's a trick," Beleren said. He was starting to sweat. "Baltrice, you trust me, right?"

"Sure, Jace." She looked puzzled. "Of course."

"Do you want to tell her why?" Tezzeret said. "Or shall I?"

"I don't get it." Baltrice seemed to be having difficulty processing what was happening, and her confusion was shading toward anger. "Why what? What are you two talking about?"

"Baltrice, you have to *believe* me—!"

Flames kindled in her hair. "Why *what*?" she barked.

"Why you trust him," Tezzeret replied, flat and cold as an etherium knife. "Put on the necklace, and you'll find out."

"Jace . . . ? Did you . . . *do* something to me?" She turned slowly, her eyes wide, and even though her voice was small and girlish, Beleren took a step back. "What did you do?"

Bolas didn't know what Beleren saw in her eyes. To the dragon, it looked like death by hellfire.

"Baltrice, come on! You know me better than that—you can't . . . don't let him *do* this to you!" Beleren pleaded, lifting his hands as though to shield himself.

"Cast that spell," Tezzeret said, "and die where you stand."

Beleren froze.

Shortly he must have decided Tezzeret wasn't bluffing, because he let his hands fall. "Baltrice, please—"

"Shut up! *Shut your festering mouth*!" She wheeled on Tezzeret. "What *is* this? Why are you doing this to us?"

"Because I like you," he said. "And I don't like him."

"But . . . but . . ." She looked as if something was breaking inside her.

"When he was my prisoner, he was tortured. For months. Tortured almost exclusively by *you*," Tezzeret said. "Have you forgotten that? Do you think *he* has?"

She looked stunned.

MATTHEW STOVER

"Yes: find out why you trust him," Tezzeret said. "At the same time you'll find out why he trusts you."

She clutched the necklace to her chest as though it were the only solid thing left in her world. "I don't . . . I don't want to know. . . ."

"My gift to you is truth," Tezzeret said. "I never expected you to thank me for it."

Tears began to well in her eyes. "Jace . . . ? What did you do to me?"

Beleren lowered his head. "I saved your life."

"That's not what I'm talking about—"

"Yes, it is. You just don't remember." Jace looked at her, and his eyes brimmed like hers. "Liliana—what she did to you—how she beat you . . . "

He shook his head. "She hit you with ghosts, Baltrice. Shades. She infected you with the shades of every living thing that had ever died at Tezzeret's tower. Even after we healed your body, the memory alone was killing you. Driving you insane."

"That's not—" Her fists clenched, and flames sprouted across her shoulders. "You had no *right*—it's not your call, Jace!"

"It wasn't," he said softly. "It was yours. Baltrice, I didn't want to. You *begged* me. I'm sorry. I'm so sorry. I . . . just couldn't think of any other way to save your life."

"How can I *believe* you?"

Tezzeret said, "There's one way to find out."

"Baltrice, *don't*—!" Jace said desperately. "The shades, the memories, all that stuff—it's not *gone*, Baltrice. I buried it, that's all. Putting on that necklace could *kill* you."

"Of course he would say that."

Baltrice looked wildly from one of them to the other, and then back again, baring her teeth like a cornered animal. "How can I . . . How am I supposed to *know*?"

Tezzeret stood impassive as stone. "The truth is in your hand."

Tears spilled over and rolled down her cheeks, and with a strangled sob she turned and stumbled away in the direction opposite the necromancer's.

Jace watched her go. His face was empty. Without even loss. "You bastard . . ." he said hoarsely. Quietly. Without inflection. "You evil, murdering son of a bitch. She was happy. Happy. Do you even know what happy feels like?"

"I suspect it very much resembles how I feel right now."

Beleren turned his empty face toward the artificer. "And what's for me? Do you kill me now?"

"I can be persuaded."

He looked down. "Then can I go?"

"I strongly recommend that you do."

His head came up warily. Frowning, he began slowly to back away.

"I don't want to kill you, Jace. You're too useful; I may need your talents someday. On the other hand, I don't see any reason I should let a vicious little gutter monkey like you walk off without a scratch."

"What are you going to do?" Jace was slowly lowering himself toward a crouch. To Bolas, he looked like a herd animal trying to be inconspicuous to a predator.

"Right now? I'm going to let you go."

"That's it?"

"For now. Your gift," Tezzeret said, "is fear."

He stopped. "I don't get it."

"You will. You never were a brave man. I have decided to remove from you the burden of courage. Take Baltrice, for example. Once she tries on that necklace, I would not want to be you. Not to grind too fine an edge on it, I would rather not be on the same plane as you. Because I would not be at all surprised to learn that Baltrice had incinerated an entire planet just because you were on it."

"Yeah, okay, whatever. I can handle Baltrice. She's a better person than you think."

"She was. Circumstances may change. And you have others to fear—me, for instance. Should I ever look in on you and decide you are insufficiently frightened, I will hurt you. I will hurt your family, if you have such. I will hurt your friends. Every person you have ever met will die screaming curses upon your name."

Beleren's jaw clenched. "Then maybe I should take you out right now."

"Too late," Tezzeret said. "You also have a little bit of a Nicol Bolas problem."

The mentalist went still.

"Do you remember that device in your brain? I should hardly think you've forgotten already. Would you be interested in what happened to that device?"

Beleren's only reply was a guarded stare.

"You gave it to Nicol Bolas. Against his will."

Jace went pale. "You—you *couldn't* have! It's not *possible*!"

"That's exactly what Bolas said. Another thing you two have in common."

"But—but I didn't have anything to *do* with it!" Beleren said, going even whiter. "*You* did it to me—and you did it to *him*—"

"And you helped."

"But I *didn't*!" he whined. "There was nothing I could have done about it!"

"Tragic, isn't it?" He sighed. "I suspect Bolas is not interested in subtle distinctions."

"But—what about *you*? *You're* the one who actually *did* it!"

"I'm touched by your concern," Tezzeret said. "You'll be comforted to learn that Nicol Bolas and I have reached an understanding. A truce. You might even call it a partnership."

"That's—that's not—I mean, you and *Bolas*? You're just making that up!"

"You think so?" Tezzeret said, opening his hand in a gesture of invitation. "You can ask him."

From the goggle-eyed whiter-than-foam countenance Jace Beleren turned up in his direction, Nicol Bolas assumed he was now visible. And since there was nothing, at the moment, he could do to harm either one of them, he settled for a fang-filled grin.

"Jace. Lovely to see you again. Lovely to . . ." He sniffed the air, broadened his grin, and sniffed again. "Is that fear? Delicious. If I were to, say, lunge at you suddenly, do you think you might wet your pants?"

Why not? It was funny. To Bolas, anyway. Beleren didn't seem amused, but there was no way to know for sure, as the mentalist's response was a gurgle like a dragon choking on a griffin bone, followed hard upon by a magically enhanced sprint for the tree line.

Bolas watched him go, and then he sighed. Diverting as this tiny episode had been, nothing had changed in his intolerable situation. He sighed again and looked down upon his tormentor. He said, "Partnership?"

Tezzeret said, "Yes."

"Are you insane?"

"It's possible," the artificer allowed. "A wasted question."

"Then a pertinent one. Why would I make a deal with you, much less keep it?"

"Because you need me."

"Do I?"

"No more games, Bolas. That's over for us. I know you're failing. Your faculties are degrading. You've aged more in the last ten years than in the last ten thousand. That's the only reason I was able to do what I've done to you."

The dragon frowned down at the artificer. He had to admit the scrawny little scut worm had a point.

"Listen to me: I don't know what you've planned, but I know it's big, and I suspect it is intended to repair your mind and rebuild your power. I also believe that your plan is going to involve a great deal of destruction, not to mention the deaths of many planeswalkers, including myself. This is where you and I have a problem. I'm not certain that you even *know* how destructive whatever you're doing will be. As far as I can see, you might have passed your mental tipping point, and millions or billions may die for nothing at all. So I'm going to help you."

Bolas stared. "You may need to say that again."

"Think about what you've seen here, since you came. Think about what happened on the beach, and what you took from my mind. Bolas, I know it's hard. Especially now. But *think*. What do you *know*?"

The dragon lowered his head. "I know that you beat me."

"Yes."

"You could have killed me at any time since I arrived here. I have been completely at your mercy the entire time."

"Mercy," he said, "is the greatest virtue."

"But you *haven't* killed me. You expect to get some use out of me."

"*Expect* is too strong a word. But I am allowing for the possibility."

"Because . . . there is no such thing as trash—only materials you haven't yet found a use for. Including me."

"Yes."

"This whole thing hasn't been about *you* at all. It's—you did all this—everything you have shown me, everything you have done to me, and everything you *haven't* done to me . . . you . . ."

Bolas felt the dawn of a sensation he could not identify. He wondered if it might be awe. "It was about *me* all along. . . ."

"Yes," Tezzeret said. "Also all about me. At the same time. Curious, isn't it?"

"To prove that I can *trust* you . . . and find out if you can trust me . . ."

Tezzeret shrugged. "Trust is too much to hope for between beings like us, Bolas. But you can believe I will not harm you unless you leave me no other choice. You can believe that I do not want you to kill billions, for good reason or otherwise, and I certainly don't want you to kill me. I believe that you want so badly to be restored to your former glory that you will accept help. Even from me."

"So this . . ." Bolas began to understand the feeling of the metal whirl that had plagued Tezzeret in the Riddle Gate. "So this is about the *fourth line*."

"The last riddle," Tezzeret said seriously. "The most important one; the one that requires the fourth trait of greatness in an artificer."

Bolas looked at him in silent query.

"Insight," Tezzeret said.

"Whom do you rescue by slaying . . ."

"Exactly. Whom do *I* rescue by slaying." The artificer offered his hand. "I don't want the answer to be you."

Bolas stared.

He had never, in all his vast life, felt so wholly at a loss.

"I suppose . . ." Bolas murmured. "I suppose . . . I don't, either." And to his own astonishment, he lowered one great talon and shook Tezzeret's hand. "Though I'll probably kill you anyway."

"But not today."

"Yes," Bolas said. "Not today."

A moment later, he discovered something still troubled him. "But Crucius," he said, waving a talon up at the Metal Sphinx. "That's really him? The Mad Sphinx?"

"Not really."

"Where is he, then?"

Tezzeret said gravely, "Speaking."

Nicol Bolas felt as though all the air had turned to stone and all the stone was piled upon his chest. "*You . . . ?*" he gasped. "*You . . . ?*"

"Of course not," Tezzeret said, grinning at him. "But the look on your face? I will treasure that for the rest of my life. It will keep me warm through the long winter nights."

After a moment, Bolas discovered himself smiling as well. "All right, all right. Very well. But still—tell me."

"Say please."

"Are you *serious*?"

"Manners cost nothing, though their value is beyond gold. Or even etherium," Tezzeret said. "If you like, Doc can teach you."

Bolas shook his head, and some fist in his chest, so old and tight and layered with scars that he had forgotten it had ever been there, now loosed and let him laugh outright.

"Please, then," he said, still chuckling, "tell me of finding Crucius."

"You're standing on him. More or less."

"Really? This isn't another joke?"

"It's not a joke, but it's not really him, either. It used to be him, and if the Multiverse is lucky, it might be him again. Remember how I said that here, it's always now? He was a clockworker. Will be a clockworker. Potentially. Probably the only clockworker I would actually trust to do clockworking."

"Was? Will be? Potentially what?"

"It's complicated. Things become other things. Seeds become plants. Drops become rivers. Eggs become dragons. But those transformations are a great deal more certain than anything that happens to, around, or concerning a clockworker. The same for me."

"I'm sorry?"

"That *Speaking* bit was a joke before—but it's also true. Sort of. Potentially true. Someday I may be him, or he may have been me. Formerly. Or both of us might be you. And vice versa. Or I'm what he turned into. And so forth. Like I said before . . ." Tezzeret shrugged. "It's complicated."

"Apparently so."

"It's true that there is no secret. It's just that language is insufficient to express truth clearly. That's why I decided it would be better to show you."

"But—" The dragon waved up toward the Metal Sphinx, and at the riddle engraved into the plinth. "What is all that, then? What's with the statue?"

"Beautiful, isn't it?"

"I, ah, well . . ."

"The dynamic balance of intersecting arcs that makes it seem as though at any instant it might wake up, yawn, stretch, and take wing for any place—any *time*—in the Multiverse. The simple purity of it—he has taken the ugly necessities of blood and bone, of eating, shitting, screwing and decay, and transformed them into clean, spare lines of perfect elegance."

"Hmp," the dragon said. To Bolas, the only thing more boring than art was listening to someone talk about art. "You sound as though you envy him."

"To become as he has become," Tezzeret said seriously, "is my heart's fondest dream."

"Why don't you, then?" The great dragon gave a shrug that encompassed the whole world that was ocean. "In this place, you are master of all you survey. Literally. There is nothing in this entire *universe* that does not answer to your will. Not even me. If that's what you want to be, you can just . . . be."

Tezzeret nodded. "I can."

"So why don't you?"

"To be master of this place," the artificer said precisely, "is not what I'm for."

"What, some kind of higher-calling crap? Really? You expect me to believe that?"

"You can believe that I believe it." Tezzeret scooped up a handful of the etherium sand and let it trickle through his fingers. "You've heard of finding God in a grain of sand? Here, it's the literal truth. This place is its own master. There is nothing here that is not part of its own creator. Including me."

"But *I* made you."

Tezzeret shrugged. "Who made you?"

"Let's not go there, can we?"

"I don't expect you to really understand this. I'm not sure *I* really understand it. Crucius thought he had an answer to existence—he thought he understood himself, the Multiverse, and his place in it. This place is what he became after he found out he was wrong."

Tezzeret looked up into the face of the Metal Sphinx as though it were looking back at him. "I don't know if he decided there was no answer, or if he simply realized that whatever answer there was, he wasn't the one who could find it. So he set out to design and build someone who was."

Bolas snorted. "You?"

"Not me *personally*. Someone who can do what I have done. Who can become what I've become. Someone who can reach this place, understand what it is, and realize that the real Search is only now beginning."

The dragon sighed and let his heavy lids droop across his vast yellow eyes. The only thing duller than talking about art was mystical claptrap and gnostic flummery. "What about that riddle, though? Where did Crucius learn Classical Draconic—and how in any flavor of hell did you learn to *read* it?"

"Oh, it's not. It's whatever language you know best. As for the riddle, I wrote it." He shrugged and gave a tired sigh. "That is, I'm *going* to write it. The Seeker will. Someday. Currently, I presume that Seeker will be me. Of course, I didn't *know* I wrote it—will write it, whatever—until after I solved it. Inconvenient. But probably better that way."

"So? What's the answer?"

Tezzeret smiled. "I am the carmot."

"Really? That's it? That's the thunderbolt of enlightenment that turned you into . . . whatever in the hells you are? 'I am the carmot'?"

"Not at all. *I* am the carmot; *you* are an ill-mannered dragon with an unfortunate impulse control problem."

"I don't get it."

Tezzeret shrugged. "Watch."

He reached into the tangles of his hair and brought out a needle of sangrite about one-fourth the size of his little finger. "Don't be alarmed," he said, and stabbed the sangrite into his left eye.

His face burst into flame. The fire swiftly spread to the rest of his body, and his head . . . vanished.

Bolas scowled. The stump of Tezzeret's neck showed a clean, smooth surface, exactly the color of etherium. A moment later, Tezzeret's head wiped itself back into existence.

His left eye, along with its lid, its socket, and a diagonal band that extended across his face from his hairline above his right eye to his jaw at the left corner of his mouth, was now metal, metal the color of burnished pewter. . . .

He batted away what was left of the smoke. "Sorry about the odor."

"Not at all," Bolas said. "You forget whom you're talking to."

"Of course. Well, here," Tezzeret said, then stuck his thumb into the corner of his etherium eye socket and gouged out his etherium eye. He flinched, just a bit, as it came free. "Damn, that smarts. Here. This is my gift to you."

He tossed his eyeball to an astonished Nicol Bolas, who bobbled it for a second or two before getting a solid grip. He held it up to inspect it.

Solid etherium. Pure. And indescribably precious, not in money, but in power. "Impressive."

By the time he looked back at Tezzeret, the artificer had an eye of flesh in his etherium socket to match the one on the opposite side of his nose. He winked his brand-new eye at the dragon. "This is my body, broken for you. More or less."

"So it's *you*," Nicol Bolas said, a bit breathlessly. "You *are* the carmot. . . ."

"As I just told you."

"You'll forgive me for being surprised." A Planeswalker who can create etherium? Exactly why he'd been after Crucius in the first place. Power. Unlimited power. It was only a question of stuffing Tezzeret someplace he couldn't get out of, and his problems would be more than half solved. "I have underestimated you, indeed," he murmured appreciatively. Now it was only a matter of finding a work-around for this blasted device in his head, and—

"That will be all for now," Tezzeret said. "I'll be back in a day or two. Just to check on you. Make sure everything's all right."

"As if I'll still *be* here? I'm leaving *now*."

"No. You're not." He sounded disturbingly certain.

"How do you mean?"

"This place is, in one crucial respect, very like the Riddle Gate. You can't take etherium out of here."

"Very well." Bolas cast the eye aside without hesitation—after all, he had a line on an unlimited supply—and he reached out to rip his way into the Blind Eternities.

But reality did not rip.

He tried again, disbelieving, and once more in desperation, and then he wheeled, staring in horror at the artificer, who spread his hands and shrugged apologetically.

"You must not have been paying very close attention to my problem in the Riddle Gate," he said. "For beings such as yourself—such as I once was—leaving here is . . . difficult. But I'll give you this hint for free: the metal is easy to discard. Discarding your desire for it is a much more difficult operation."

"You're making this up!" Bolas breathed, hating the edge of desperation he heard in his own voice.

"Funny how people keep saying that to me."

"This is another of your stupid jokes! It *has* to be!"

"Compliments on the humor of the situation should be directed to Crucius—but under the circumstances, I am happy to accept them in his place." He turned and began to walk away along the beach.

"Wait! You can't just *leave* me here!"

"Of course I can." Tezzeret stopped, and now looked over his shoulder at the dragon. "In fact, I have to. Away from this place, my powers are as limited as they have ever been. It wouldn't be a heartbeat before you'd have me shackled and stuffed in your deepest dungeon. Which I would prefer to avoid. And as I said, I'll be back in a day or two. Then we can start work on your problem. Together."

"Where could you *possibly* be going that is *remotely* as important as *getting me out of here*?"

"I'm going to spend some time with my father," he said, and with a single step passed beyond the bounds of the universe.

THE METAL ISLAND
ENTER LEVIATHAN

Nicol Bolas settled himself onto the etherium sand. At last he could begin to excise the artificer's annoying little gimmicks and get himself out of here. "Damn, I thought he'd *never* leave."

"You and me both, brother."

Bolas lurched upright. The voice had been impossibly deep, impossibly dark, and most of all, impossibly *close*.

Behind him was a rip in the fabric of the universe, held open by some impressively sizable talons. Bolas gathered himself into a crouch—talons like those usually belonged to dragons, and from their dimensions, it wasn't impossible that this *new* planeswalking dragon, whoever it was, might be even larger than Bolas himself. "Take it easy, pal," the new dragon said. "I'm not here to fight."

"It's a good thing you're not," Bolas growled, "because you have no *idea* who you're about to—"

"It's more the other way around," the new dragon said as he shouldered his way into the world. He stopped, stretched, and gaped his great fanged mouth wide in a jaw-cracking yawn.

Nicol Bolas stared in uncomprehending astonishment. "You—you look just like *me*!"

"That's more the other way around, too." The dragon grinned down at him, and Bolas realized that despite the resemblance, this dragon was vastly larger than he was,

MATTHEW STOVER

ꟼ

and younger, and possessed of a staggering magnitude of power that Bolas could only faintly glimpse. All his senses, magical as well as physical, told him that this dragon was so powerful he shouldn't be able to even exist....

Nothing in his twenty-five thousand years of life had prepared him to face a being like this. "You—are you—who—I mean, what? What's going *on*? It's as if you're *me*."

"I am you," the new dragon said with a vast and gleaming fang-filled grin. "You're the one who's not you."

"What?"

"Nice job with Tezzeret, by the way. You learn a lot about someone by how he treats you when he's got nothing to fear. And now we've got him working for us willingly. Enthusiastically. Hells, he thinks he's doing us a *favor*."

Bolas still couldn't quite get his mind around what was happening, though a terrible dread had begun to curdle in his gut. "Us? What do you mean, *us*?"

"Oh, well, there's that, I suppose." The dragon waved a talon in languid dismissal. "By *us*, you should understand that I mean *me*. There is no *you*. Not really."

"What?"

"Yeah, I know, you're having a hard time with this," the other dragon said sympathetically. "There's a couple of reasons for that. One is that constructs like you have a pretty limited useful life span. You start to break down only a day or two after you're created. You must have noticed how it's gotten harder and harder to think."

"Constructs? Like *me*?" Bolas shook his head wildly, as though he could jerk himself awake from this terrible nightmare. "You're saying I'm...that I've always been..."

"Don't take it too hard," the other dragon said. "It's a fail-safe, really. Otherwise, every time I put one like you together, I'd have to chase you down and kill you myself, just to keep you from screwing around in my business."

"*Your* business? I still don't *understand*...."

"Of course you don't. In addition to that construct thing I told you about, I also had to make you pretty stupid."

"What?"

"If you were a tenth as smart as I am, you would have been ten times too smart to fall into Tezzeret's trap. As it is, you'll be dead a few hours from now, and your corpse will evaporate. If I want Tezzeret to find a Nicol Bolas here when he gets back, I'll have to make another of you. Maybe even several more."

"You're saying—you're saying that *you*—?"

"Damn, you really are stupid," the larger dragon said. "Well, I guess Tezzeret can't be wrong about everything, can he?"

The vast, unimaginably powerful dragon looked down upon the pale, dying simulacrum he had created, and sighed.

"Yes, idiot. I am the real Nicol Bolas," he said. "And I did not reach my exceedingly advanced age by being stupid enough to do my dirty work in person."

"No?" The simulacrum coughed weakly, and after a moment the real Nicol Bolas realized his creation was laughing. At him. "Doing it right now, aren't you?"

The real Nicol Bolas scowled and made no reply.

"Maybe that's the real lesson," the simulacrum said. "You should make a note of it, so you don't forget.

"Because when you come right down to it, none of us is as smart as we think we are."

THE BLIND ETERNITIES
WHO LAUGHS LAST

In the raging hurricane of chaos that was the Blind Eternities, Tezzeret severed the link of consciousness he had maintained with the etherium device in the head of the fake Bolas and allowed himself a small tight smile.

None of us is as smart as we think we are? he thought. *If you only knew.*

It would be difficult to seriously imagine a more successful operation. Yes, if he could have somehow effectively neutered the *real* Bolas, that would have been wonderful—but Tezzeret had never been so vain as to think the great dragon would be so easily taken. Or taken at all.

Still, the next best thing to controlling an enemy is controlling what they believe, and in that, Tezzeret reflected with what he considered to be justifiable pride, he had been exceptionally successful.

The *real* Nicol Bolas thought the artificer to be not only too dim to penetrate the deception of the simulacrum, but that he sincerely would exert himself to aid the dragon's plans. This would buy Tezzeret several days' head start at the very least. He briefly considered returning to the Metal Island exactly as he'd promised. After all, if Bolas actually went to the trouble of creating a new simulacrum, it would be an instructive measure of just how thoroughly duped the dragon was. . . .

He decided against it. There was such a thing as outsmarting yourself. Showing up somewhere the dragon expected him to be would be even more foolish than doing so with Renn had been. Better to just run. Take his head start and bury himself somewhere beyond the dragon's reach, and begin preparations for their next encounter.

Because there would be a next encounter, and he intended to survive it.

Whether the dragon did or not.

"Ravnica," he muttered to himself. To really lose oneself, there was no better plane than Ravnica. While he was there, he could look in on Baltrice. And make sure Jace Beleren was still adequately terrorized. "Ravnica it is, then."

"Sure, Ravnica's nice." A familiar wiseass voice buzzed in his left ear. "Let's just make one stop along the way, huh?"

Tezzeret froze. "*Doc?*"

"No, Giant Brain, I'm the Voice of festering *God.*"

"How—? I mean, I thought you were—"

"I was. But I'm all better now. Bolas has this errand for us. On Mirrodin. It'll be fun. Like a vacation."

"This isn't *possible—*"

"You're not exactly makin' me feel welcome, buddy. We don't need to have another little chat about who's actually in charge here, do we?"

"You were *gone,*" Tezzeret growled. "*Completely* gone—how did you get back *inside my head*?"

"Come on, Giant Brain. Now you're just embarrassing yourself. Really." Doc's voice carried a note of sarcastic pity that made the artificer want to stab himself in the ear. "All the places Bolas has been, all the stuff he's done—I mean, seriously. You just had a mindlink going to that etherium doohickey. Did you honestly think he just wouldn't notice?"

He put a palm to his face. "Kill me. Please, just kill me now."

"Aww, don't take it hard, Tezz! The team's back together, and we're hittin' the road. It'll be just like old times!"

"Now what's the *good* news?"

"Aww..."

"Tell me one thing, Doc," Tezzeret said. "Do you think Nicol Bolas knows the old saying about 'he who laughs last'?"

"How should *I* know?"

"I hope he doesn't. I hope he doesn't because one day soon," the artificer said through his teeth, "I'm going to teach him."

THE END

Tales of strange and deadly creatures emerging from the Mephidross are spreading faster than its corroded borders. They are the harbinger of a great corruption— the reawakening of Phyrexia.

THE QUEST FOR KARN

ROBERT B. WINTERMUTE

Venser—former apprentice and friend of Karn, Mirrodin's creator—and his Planeswalker allies Elspeth Tirel and the geomancer Koth know of the Phyrexian contagion and search for a way to contain it.

The potential savior and destroyer of the plane, Karn fights the corruption building inside him. As the new Father of Machines, what could stop Karn from spreading Phyrexia throughout the Multiverse? Even Tezzeret, armed with the secret of etherium, recognizes the consequences of such an outcome. If he can't master Phyrexia, he will look to those who can.

The corrosion begins . . .

MARCH 2011

For more information
visit www.wizards.com/magicnovels